EVALEEN

FROM RAGS TO RICHES

SANDRA RECTOR

ISBN-13: 978-1-0813-9286-4

Cover Design by vikncharlie

For anyone who has ever tried to start their own business; for my mother, Agnes Johnson; and for P M F Johnson, who never stopped believing.

Chapter One

Outside the front windows of the tenement building where Eva Doyle lived with her parents, the snow came down in windy gusts. It was another cold day in Emerson, Massachusetts in the winter of 1935. The Super had turned down the heat again to save money. Did he think they didn't notice, Eva wondered as she slipped on yet another sweater.

But she didn't blame him either. Half the people in the building, including her own family, were behind on the rent. Times were tough for everybody. Pa had lost his job as a mechanic three months ago and hadn't been able to find another one, although he had tried mightily, often getting up in the middle of the night to be the first in line.

Without a job to occupy him, a silent man to begin with, he became bitter and depressed and had taken to drinking cheap whiskey. When he was drunk, he often took his anger out on Ma and Eva, mostly Eva.

Everything Eva did seemed to irritate him. Mostly he seemed to resent the fact that he still had to feed and clothe her. She had tried hard to get a job and would have taken anything, but there were no jobs to be had for a teenager with no experience at anything. If it weren't for her uncle who still had a job and was able to help them out, they would have been out on the street months ago. That's where her parents were right now, asking her uncle for another loan.

She tried not to think about the cold or how broke they all were, or what Pa would do when he found out that she had stolen the emergency money for the ingredients to make her grandmother's skin cream recipe, money to be used only if someone were sick or dying.

Being extra careful now, she opened the fragile notebook containing her grandmother's skin care recipes and began searching for the skin lubricating cream her grandmother swore by. Her grandmother had given Eva the notebook right before she died. She remembered that moment well.

Eva and her grandmother, her mother's mother, shared a bedroom after her grandmother broke her hip in a fall and moved in with Eva's family. Eva loved having her grandmother close by. Often before going to sleep they would have long talks. Sharing secrets with the elegant old woman who understood everything and loved her just for herself was wonderful and comforting. One night Eva was helping her grandmother get ready for bed when her grandmother stopped what she was doing, and with great ceremony handed Eva an old notebook.

"This contains everything I know about skin care," she said. "Having beautiful skin has been my legacy and it can be yours too."

People were always telling her grandmother how beautiful her skin was, even when she was very old. She had shrugged it off like it was nothing at all. Eva knew better. Skin care was her grandmother's obsession. Eva's grandmother was not a raving beauty, but she had beautiful skin. Even in her eighties, bent over almost double with rheumatism, people were forever pleading for her secret. She would just smile and shrug as though having lovely skin in old age was the most natural thing in the world. Eva's own mother had never shown any interest in beauty, other than buying cosmetics from time to time, which she rarely used.

Together, they had sat up in bed and looked through the tablet with its yellowed pages and spidery handwriting while her grandmother explained the benefits of each recipe. Eva knew how important this was to her grandmother, and so for her sake she forced herself to pay close attention.

But afterwards, out of her grandmother's sight, Eva stuffed the notebook into her dresser drawer where she soon forgot about it, because what she wanted most in the world then was not to have beautiful skin but to be someone special, the kind of person Hero

Lyon would notice and take an interest in. At eighteen, Hero Lyon was over six feet tall with thick, blue-black hair that glowed like raven feathers in the sun. His almost-black eyes had a way of looking right through you, too. Every girl in high school wanted Hero Lyon. And every boy wanted to be just like him, cool and elegant and rich and not seeming to have a care in the world.

Unfortunately, as far as Eva could tell, Hero only liked tall, slim, blond girls with pale skin, none of whom she remotely resembled. Eva's freckle-filled face was more ruddy than pale. She wore her red hair in a pony-tail, which she cut herself with a scissors when it needed to be trimmed. Her hazel eyes were her best feature. They had a tendency to change to a pale olive green depending on the light and time of day. On the bad side, she was barely five foot three and big boned, the kind of girl who wouldn't look skinny no matter how much weight she lost. Her only real asset was her perfectly oval face, a face that looked beautiful in photographs but was in reality quite plain. Unlike Hero who lived in a large mansion on Trenton Hill with his family, Eva lived in a two bedroom apartment on the third floor of a tenement building on Hansen Street, one of a long row of tenement buildings all in various states of disrepair. The only redeeming feature on her street was a small park directly across from her building where Eva's grandmother used to like to sit in the sun and watch the people pass by. It was mostly occupied these days by hobos who always left a terrible mess.

Josh Goldman, her school chum, said redheads were already special since there were so few of them. Eva didn't believe him, though he was not the type to lie. Josh always thought the best of everyone, so his opinion didn't count. Everyone liked Josh. He was easy-going, trustworthy and a good friend. He was tall too, over six feet, and thin to the point of scrawniness. His blond hair had cowlicks that no amount of Vaseline Hair Tonic would keep down. He was nice looking, but not special like Hero. Nobody was.

It wasn't until her father lost his job that Eva, now in her last year of high school, remembered her grandmother's notebook. She was putting the laundry away one day when the drawer jammed and she saw why – the notebook was sticking up at the back of her drawer, which she found rather strange. But seeing it there, it occurred to her that it was a reminder from her grandmother to think about using her skin care creams as a way to make money. A lot of people were going door-to-door these days selling everything from used clothing to wood. Why not her?

The more she thought about it, the more excited she became. She knew her father wouldn't approve, but this was something she could do to make a little money and she decided to go ahead anyway. So she had taken the emergency money hidden in a bowl in the cupboard, money not to be used except for dire emergencies, and bought the lanolin and sweet almond oil she needed from the local drugstore. She reasoned that if she actually made some money, Pa would forgive her and be glad. If it didn't work, well, she didn't want to think about that right now.

So now she had decided to put her plan into action. She took a deep breath, and let it out slowly. Forcing herself to concentrate, she carefully opened up the dry and crackling pages of her grandmother's old notebook and set to work. Her heart was beating hard with a mix of fear that she was wasting time and precious cash on something that might not pay off and excitement that she was actually doing something to change her family's destiny. If everything went right, today would be a new beginning for them all. And if it didn't work out there was a good possibility they would soon have to go on relief, or even worse end up on the street, living in one of those tent cities on the edge of Emerson. The thought made her shiver but did not deter her.

She read the instructions for the lubricating cream slowly and deliberately twice, then began by running water into the bottom half of a large frying pan and lighting the stove. As she did so, she imagined the surprised look on Hero Lyon's face when he discovered his former classmate Eva Doyle, someone he barely noticed, was now a successful businesswoman, just as good as he was, maybe even a little better. She grinned at that impossible thought.

She said a quick little prayer, asking her grandmother for help, as she waited for the water to heat. She worried whether or not the cream would turn out right or, even if it did, would she have the nerve to sell it. Would anyone actually buy it from someone who was not a beauty herself, but rather on the plain side? She shivered at that thought, then forced it out of her head as she concentrated on measuring out the proper amount of lanolin and pouring it in the pan. She was just about to measure the sweet almond oil to add to it when she heard a knock on the door.

She froze, sure it was one of the neighbors who would discover what she was up to and tell Pa. She was flooded with relief when she heard the sound of footsteps climbing the stairs to the apartment above theirs. Hobos going from door-to-door to ask for food or money! There were so many these days. She felt sorry for them, but she felt even sorrier for the wives and families so many had abandoned.

Eva went back to work, stirring the mixture as it heated. She decided not to think about the half million women who'd been left to support their children alone and who she could do nothing about. As she stirred, she enjoyed the delicious aroma of the almond oil wafting up to her nostrils. From time to time, she dipped a finger into the cream and rubbed it on her arm. It felt silky and good and smelled wonderful.

When the cream was done and cooled enough to be handled, she poured it into the five small baby food jars she had found in the garbage and managed to collect, clean and label in secret. She wiped off the mouth of the jars with a dish towel and set them aside to finish cooling before screwing on the tops. As she waited, she admired the jars that proudly proclaimed, "Fresh-As-A-Daisy Lubricating Cream," with her name, address and phone number inscribed in tiny letters at the bottom, next to an equally tiny drawing of a daisy.

When she heard the familiar crunch of tires on the snowy street out front, she went to the window and looked out. She was just in time to see her father begin to maneuver his car between two other parked cars.

In a panic, working as fast as she possibly could, she scraped the melted beeswax from the counter and shoved the pan beneath the sink. She heard the front door open and her parents' footsteps on the stairs as she quickly snatched a tray from the cupboard and began to load up the jars. She was racing down the hallway towards her room with the tray when the door burst open and Pa entered the room. He was a big man, red in the face, with a mop of faded red hair that stood up like a wire brush.

"What's that I smell?" he said. "What the hell's going on here?"

Eva, stopped, frozen with fear, holding the tray in front of her.

"The roads are slippery and the snow is coming down so bad we could barely see out the windshield..." her mother said. She spoke hesitantly, her voice dying away uncertainly as she followed her husband inside.

"What you got in those jars?" Pa demanded.

"I made Grandma's skin lubricating cream," Eva said speaking quickly. "I'm planning to sell it door-to-door for twenty-five cents each and—"

"Nobody's got any money for shit like that," Pa said. "And look at yourself. Who'd buy beauty creams from a lump like you?"

He snatched the tray out of her hands and tossed everything in the wastebasket with so much force the glass shattered.

Eva's pride in her work collapsed instantly and she was filled with shame. A suspicious look crossed Pa's furious face. He hurried to the cupboard, yanked out the empty sugar bowl and held it out for her mother to see.

"It's empty," he said, spitting out the words. "Your daughter's a no-good thief."

Ma shook her head no and backed away, her face as pale as the white handkerchief she always carried inside the cuff of her sleeve.

Eva felt a familiar shiver of fear as Pa took off his coat, threw it angrily on the kitchen chair and began to unbuckle his belt with vicious pleasure. Eva had felt the sting of Pa's belt before, especially after he'd had a few drinks to spur him on. The last time he hit her was for leaving her coat on a chair instead of hanging it up. She had red welts for a week. Worse than the beating were his words.

"You're never gonna be nothin', and you're never gonna amount to nothin'."

She was furious at him for saying that and even angrier at herself for believing it. After that last beating, she had made a vow that no matter what happened she would never, ever let him hit her again.

Determined to keep that promise, she bolted for the door. As she fled down the steps, she could hear Pa's footsteps on the stairs behind her. She was just about to take off running down the sidewalk when she heard a terrible noise like a seagull screeching in pain. She turned around and saw Pa appear to dance in the air, then drop to a crumpled heap at the bottom of the stairs.

He lay there, motionless.

"Oh Pa, I'm sorry," she cried as she raced back to his side. "Are you all right, Pa? Please tell me you're all right. I'm so sorry. I won't do it again. I promise. Please, Pa. Tell me you're okay. Please..."

He did not answer. He just lay there, unmoving, staring wide-eyed at the snow-filled sky.

Frightened for his life, Eva raced back up the steps to call for help. When she reached their apartment, Ma was still in her winter coat, unmoving, staring out the window, a blank look in her eyes.

"Pa's hurt," Eva cried as she raced for the telephone. "He's on the steps out front."

Ma snapped out of her daze, and with a fearful cry rushed for the door.

Eva snatched up the phone and dialed the operator with icy fingers. The operator connected her to an emergency number. After giving the information, she raced back downstairs to her father.

She arrived just in time to hear him make a hollow, coughing sound and see a puddle of urine begin to form beneath his prone body.

"It's no use," Ma said, speaking almost in a whisper. "He's gone."

She began to cry, a low, tortured sound.

Snow continued to fall on his open, staring eyes and upturned angry face.

Eva sat down next to her, too stunned to cry. Death wasn't supposed to happen this way. It was supposed to come at night when you were surrounded by your loved ones, not like this and not in such a terrible way. And not when it was all your fault.

Two hobos chose that moment to shuffle across the slushy street from the park. They stared as if Eva and her mother were alien beings. Death was fascinating but apparently no real concern of theirs. Eva noticed the lack of emotion in their faces and the strange lack of it in herself.

A crowd soon gathered. Mrs. Smythe, a kindly widow who lived in the basement apartment with her crippled son George, came out and took charge.

"Go home," she said, shooing the people away. "This is none of your business. Go away now. Leave these poor folks be."

The hobos, seeing nothing to be gained here, shambled back to the park. The people who remained also began to drift away. An ambulance arrived shortly and double-parked as Eva and her crying mother sat next to the dead man. Two men dressed in coveralls leaped out of the ambulance and went to work on Pa. As Eva and her mother huddled together, miserable, not knowing what to do, a late model Ford arrived and parked behind the ambulance. A small man got out. He wore a blue overcoat much too large for him, as though he'd bought the coat in the size he wanted to be rather than the size he actually was. He talked in a low voice to the two men, who were now gathering up their equipment, then approached Eva and her mother. He introduced himself to them as the police chaplain.

"I'm sorry for your loss," he said, a look of kindly concern on his face. "Where do you wish to hold the funeral?"

At the word funeral, Ma broke down in a fresh wave of sobs.

"Wagenstein and Murphy," Eva said automatically. It was a funeral home she passed every day on her way to school.

The man quickly relayed the news to the men, who had begun to gather up their things, then he herded Eva and Ma up the steps to their apartment.

Only afterwards did Eva realize that he did this so that she and her mother wouldn't see the two men taking Pa away. Instead of consoling them or telling them what to do, as Eva had assumed, the chaplain asked her mother to sign some papers, then left as quickly as he had arrived.

By this time the daylight had begun to fade. Ma collapsed into Pa's old easy chair next to the radio and sobbed uncontrollably. Eva, dry eyed and numb, did the only thing she could think of to do. She picked up the phone and gave the operator Gussie's number.

Gussie was Eva's friend since first grade. She would know what to do. Gussie could always be counted on in any emergency. Both her grandparents had passed away in an old people's home during the last year and Gussie had taken care of all the arrangements. Her parents were not capable people. They had depended on Gussie ever since Gussie was ten and took it upon herself to call the insurance company to come and fix a hole in their roof caused by a hail storm.

"Pa just died and I don't know what to do," Eva blurted out when Gussie answered the phone on the second ring.

"Oh dear, I'm so sorry," Gussie said, all sympathy. "I'm coming over right now. Don't do a thing until I get there."

She arrived minutes later.

"Call the funeral home and set up a time to meet with them tomorrow," she announced, even before she had taken off her coat. "They'll tell you what you need to do next. Then call the folks who'll need to know. And for heaven's sake, Eva, put on something warm. You're turning blue."

Gussie helped Ma take off her coat.

"I know this is hard for you," Gussie said, "but right now, you need to make a pot of coffee and straighten up the apartment, because as soon as the word's out, folks will be dropping by to give you their condolences."

Ma and Eva did as they were told. Eva was surprised at how little she felt about it all.

"Something's wrong with me, Gussie," she said. "My father just died and I feel so numb."

"You're in shock," Gussie said kindly. "It'll hit you later, when you can begin to deal with it. Nature's good to us that way."

Chapter Two

"Herodotus Lyon the Second," the sheriff announced sharply, "your home is in foreclosure. You have been duly warned and must now leave. We're here to make sure that you do."

Hero Lyon the Third happened to be in the reception hall, where he'd gone to check the mail, and heard it all. He rushed to the door to see for himself what was happening.

Hero realized it was real when he saw the confusion in his father's eyes. The sheriff was right – they had been warned several months ago. Hero had been positive his father had taken care of it as he had always taken care of everything. Apparently not.

Seeing his father squint down at the papers the sheriff handed him as though his eyes hurt, Hero felt a surge of sympathy. Ever since Hero could remember, his father had moved in the world with great authority, respected by one and all. Until right now. Hero was desperate to help him. But what was there to do?

The Lyon's family's good fortune had begun to change the day bank examiners appeared at the bank where Hero's father was the president. The position that made Hero's father one of Emerson's leading citizens now caused the Lyon family to become one of its poorest.

Hero knew nothing about this until the day he showed up at his father's bank to ask for an advance on his allowance to go to the movies. He walked in his father's office unannounced just like he always did and was surprised to see two big men sitting in front of his father's big desk, their briefcases held stiffly in their laps. His father looked pale and sick.

"Illiquidity is rampant here," one of the men said, ignoring Hero's presence. "New deposits are non-existent. You must know that the position of this bank cannot be maintained."

Hero's expected his father to frighten the man with just a look, but it was his father who appeared to be frightened. People had stopped paying their loans. On one harrowing day alone, checks amounting to over twenty thousand dollars were returned for non-payment. His father had struggled mightily to find some solution, working with the debtors, burning the lights late each night. He worried so much that at one point he said he thought he was losing his mind. Month after month he fretted, but there was no solution. No amount of agonizing or staying awake nights or trying to coerce the bank's debtors to pay up made any difference at all.

He was not alone.

In the first years of the Depression, wages declined sixty percent and over four thousand banks failed, ten of them in Emerson, Massachusetts, a usually thriving city of two hundred thousand factory and retail workers. So many businesses had closed that Emerson was beginning to resemble a ghost town lately.

On the day the bank closed, Hero's father was allowed just enough time to get his hat and coat before being herded out the door along with his employees. His position as bank president was finished that day and their life savings were gone.

Hero had always taken it for granted that his family's good fortune would go on forever. He had been named for his father and grandfather. The name came from the Greek historian Herodotus, said to be the first historian. Hero's great-grandfather, who made a fortune loaning immigrants money at high interest rates, was a passionate student of history and a lover of all things Greek, thus the name. The family name, Lyon, was originally Leander in Greek, which meant lion man. The immigration official changed it to be more American.

Hero had been given everything his wealthy parents could lavish on him, with one exception: both parents insisted that he attend public schools through elementary and high school. His father believed it was necessary in life to have what he called the "common touch" in order to do business with both the high and the low. It was assumed that Hero would finish high school and matriculate at

Harvard, where his father had also gone. Hero felt that he belonged at Phillips Exeter or Choate or even Milton and resented attending a public high school, but sure of his exalted position in life anyway, he always walked the halls of Emerson High with a confident swagger.

That life was now gone forever.

"The keys," the sheriff said, as he escorted the family to the curb. He held out his beefy hand.

Hero still expected his father to come up with a bundle of unexpected cash or at least say something to put the sheriff in his place. Instead, his father meekly handed over the keys. The sheriff's sneering deputy stood by, one eyebrow raised suspiciously, as though they might try to sneak back into their own home. Hero was tempted to slug the sheriff and his ridiculous deputy, wipe the smug look from their pasty faces forever. He was younger and stronger and could probably take them both, but it would do no good and surely get them all in worse trouble, so he jammed his fists into his coat pocket and stared at the ground.

He was absorbing this lesson, absorbing it well: a man needed money. Cash in hand. If his own father wasn't able to supply everything, it would be up to Hero. At eighteen, he was a man now. He vowed to himself that money would never be a problem again. He would show them all.

"I'll be coming back in two hours to make sure you're gone," the sheriff threatened, before heading back to his car.

"Don't forget," the scrawny deputy added with a sneer. "Loitering is a crime."

The Lyons' family might have driven away in one of two cars they owned, except their cars had been repossessed weeks ago, along with most of their furniture. The family stood together in cold, miserable silence as lace curtains fluttered up and down their street. No one came out to sympathize or help. Hero, his face hot with shame, stood in his camel-colored cashmere overcoat, shivering with cold and waiting for his father to offer a sensible solution. Hero was ready to help, to do anything his father asked.

But his father, wearing his own cashmere overcoat, sat on a suitcase in the snow, his head in his hands, not speaking. Hero's mother stood next to him, her pale, frightened face partially hidden in a fox tail scarf worn over a mink coat. Her hands, in their kidskin leather gloves, clutched a brown paper bag filled with kitchen utensils. On the sidewalk lay a thin mattress that used to belong to one of the maids who had been let go a month ago, along with the cook and laundress. Hero had grabbed the mattress on his way out the door, thinking to find a use for it later.

Hero stared at his father hard, willing him to do something. His father had always been his guide: the wise one who knew what must be done, knew the next step to take. But what was the next step here? Hero felt a stirring panic as he waited for his father to do something, anything.

Suddenly a coughing rumble sounded in the distance and a baby blue Packard Runabout came driving up the hill. Some careless stranger coming to enjoy their humiliation? To Hero's surprise, the Packard halted on the street before them. The driver, a man with a bald head that stuck out of his navy blue overcoat like a turtle out of a shell, rolled down the window. Hero recognized him as George Carson, one of the wealthy men with whom his father used to do business. George had been to their home numerous times for dinners and charitable events over the years. He was the kind of man who blustered his way through life, shaking every hand like a politician.

Hero's mother buried her face deeper into her coat. His father stared straight ahead, refusing to acknowledge the man. Hero stood by, silently willing the man to get lost.

"Got that warehouse over on Washington," the man called out from his car. His eyes wandered over their things, but did not rest on any of them. "Can't do anything else with it since they closed the factory. You might as well use it as a place to live. Can't offer a job. Barely hanging on myself. Warehouse'd be rent free, until you get on your feet. 'Sides, it'll keep the bums from takin' up residence." He looked uncomfortable. "That's what's in it for me, so you see, it isn't really a handout. You'd be actin' as security."

Hero was astounded. Mr. Carson was trying to help them, something no one else was doing. At the same time, Hero felt ashamed that they had sunk so low that they needed rescuing.

"I don't want my wife or my son living in such a place," his father said sharply.

"What will people think?" his mother wailed, clutching at the pearls she had snatched from her dresser on the way out the door. "I'm willing to put up with a great deal, Mr. Herodotus Lyon," she whirled on her husband, "but you just better be careful, now."

"Have to live somewhere, ma'am," the man said impatiently. "Least this way you'll have a roof over your heads. Twenty-four families living in that Hooverville over by the tracks. Last week, cops rounded 'em all up and put 'em in jail, or they'd have frozen to death."

Hero glared at his father so fiercely that his father quailed. Would he just stand by and do nothing? What was wrong with him?

"Sir, yes," Hero said, stepping forward. "Yes, Mr. Carson. Thank you, sir. We'll take it. Absolutely. Thank you so much."

It was a shift in power between his father and himself so complete that Hero knew it would never shift back. For better or worse, Hero was now in charge of the family.

Hero made a tiny gesture and amazingly his father obeyed, stepping forward.

"I guess we don't have a choice," his father said, his voice flat. Then, almost shyly to Mr. Carson, "Thank you for your kind offer."

He took the key from the man's hand, but the look on his face was one of shame rather than gratitude.

Mr. Carson looked uncertainly from father to son, then nodded to himself. "Be seein' you, then. I'd give you a ride myself, but I don't have the time right now."

He put his car in gear and without once looking back, rattled away.

All three stood, watching him go.

When he was out of sight, Hero's mother took in a deep breath, wiped her eyes with the back of her gloved hand with a defiant gesture, picked up her small bundle and like a zombie began to walk in the direction of the warehouse district, five miles away. Hero's father sighed heavily, picked up his own bundle and followed her. Hero, feeling sick, like he'd just watched a bad accident, grabbed the mattress, balanced it on his head with both hands and joined his parents as they paraded down the street.

How dare Hero command his father in that way? How could his own father have obeyed? Hero wondered that as, heavy with his new responsibilities, he and his family walked down his former street filled with all the mansions of the rich, through the middle class neighborhoods and across the railroad tracks to the poor side of town.

A parade to poverty. Luckily, the day was unusually cold and the streets of Emerson, which normally teemed with people, were deserted, so only a few folks witnessed the family's shame. With each step, Hero grew more determined never to be put in this situation again; never to be vulnerable to such ridicule and harsh dealings.

And change he did. Although outwardly he remained ever charming and polite, ready for fun, behind this front he was always paying attention, learning from everything – how to take advantage of those weak enough to drink to excess when gambling, whose palm to grease to keep everyone happy. But there was one other vulnerability he took away from that day. Forever after, he hated confrontation. Hated especially the naked threat in the eyes of the deputy. Hero was not a coward – he fought when forced to do so – but he would always try to look ahead, to anticipate trouble, knowing there was never any profit in fighting. And he would always work hard to find some way around any threat. That was not entirely a bad thing, for he avoided those who dealt in violence, and he exercised an instinct for being absent at the times when violence came sweeping through some drinking or gambling establishment, for there were many angry, displaced young people looking to take their frustration out on someone.

#

When Hero and his parents arrived at the warehouse, they were exhausted, emotionally drained and chilled to their very bones. His father slipped the key in the door and the family numbly trooped inside. They were greeted by the smell – musty, oily, closed up, and something Hero couldn't quite identity that made him feel slightly ill.

The warehouse consisted of two rooms – in the store front was a big picture window so dirty that light could barely get through, and in the back, a large, dank, windowless room where a kind of oily sand covered the floor. Off to one side in the back room was a tiny, closet-sized room with a toilet and a wash basin. A cold draft blew through the many cracks in the walls.

His mother gave a great mournful sob and sank down onto the mattress that Hero set down on the floor in one corner. She came from a prominent family and had taken their prosperity completely for granted. The common touch was all very well and good and those who possessed it were spoken of reverently among her set, but always over tea in bone-china cups. Her people had little sympathy for those who allowed their fortunes to be frittered away through what they were sure was their own carelessness or dissipation.

She was still sitting on the mattress crying, Hero's father trying to console her, when Hero put aside his own despair and exhaustion and went back out to see what he could scrounge up for their new home. In an empty lot next to a closed restaurant he found a bent two-burner kerosene stove that could be used for cooking and for heat, some beat up pots and pans, a urine-stained double mattress and the back seat of an old car from a family who must have removed it so they could fill up the car with their belongings when they left town.

The car seat became their davenport. Two stained and ripped easy chairs, which he found the next day, completed their living room set. For food, his father had just enough cash left to purchase several cases of pork and beans at a special low price. From that day forward, they ate pork and beans with rice, pork and beans with catsup, pork and beans with garlic, pork and beans with onions. Pork and beans every single day. At night Hero and his father killed rats with an old pistol his father grabbed at the last minute. Hero's father never mentioned why he had chosen to take that pistol above their more valuable possessions, and Hero, not wanting to know, didn't ask. His mother moved about in a ghost-like daze, not seeming to notice anything.

Hero surprised himself with his ingenuity and resilience. Every day, he went out hunting for anything to improve their lot. He picked up coal blown off the box cars at the train tracks to sell, scavenged food from dumpsters, combed the Emerson dump for scrap metal to sell to dealers and for newspapers to fill the cracks in their walls – always with his ears open for news of a job or something that could be turned to his advantage. Surprisingly, he was not desperate, nor angry, nor even bitter: he was too busy thinking of some angle he could pursue to improve their situation.

The weight of their new life dragged on Hero and his earlier pride fought to reassert itself. Hero despised everything about their living situation, hated being cold all the time, hated living in such close quarters with his parents, hated the noise of the constant trucks that assaulted his ears day and night, hated the fact that the kerosene leaked out from the pump, making them all worry about fires and being asphyxiated in their sleep, loathed everything about their living situation. He intended to win in this life and he resented everything that resisted his efforts.

When he thought they couldn't sink any lower, the pork and beans ran out and there was no money to buy more. Hero stared at the emptied last can of pork and beans. Not even a trace of juice remained. Almost in a rage, he walked the four blocks to a building that looked like a grocery store with a big plate glass window. A long line of people stood in front of the building. Hero, feeling heavy and old before his time, took his place at the back of the line. As he waited, men, women, even children emerged from the building with cardboard boxes and bulging bags. When it was his turn, Hero gathered three cans of grapefruit juice, a bag of cornmeal, some rice, prunes and canned beans, then he left the building, his eyes downcast, careful not to look anybody in the eye. Accepting a government handout was a shameful thing. He had often heard his parents speak disparagingly of such people. But it was either pride or starvation – an easy choice. Back at the warehouse, he put the food away in their makeshift cupboard. Neither parent seemed to notice or care.

In the days that followed, Hero was careful not to lose his swagger and did what he could to keep up appearances. He washed his white shirt in the bathroom sink and put his dress slacks on some newspapers beneath the mattress at night to keep their press. When he couldn't stand the close quarters another minute, he went to O'Dooles, a three-two beer joint nearby. It was there he picked up a pool cue for the first time, since he could play for free. He had no idea what he was doing and was amazed when he actually hit a ball and it went into the pocket. But he soon fell in love with the game and played it at every opportunity. When business was slow O'Doole showed him a few tips, like how to develop a good stance or how to change his finger position to get a good bridge. Sometimes O'Doole would stake him to a few games. When Hero won, they split his winnings.

One Tuesday night in the middle of a game of pool, Tom Sullivan mentioned the Pinkerton Detective Agency in Chicago was hiring, looking for men who were bigger and stronger than most.

Hero signed up first thing the following day. To his delight he was hired. He didn't stop to wonder why they wanted big, strong lunks; he only knew it was a chance to make some money. High school was a moment in the unimportant past; just as college was a meaningless word to him now.

Chapter Three

On the last day of March Eva headed downtown, determined to overcome her nerves and give asking for a loan a try. The day was colder than usual but the sun was shining, a hopeful sign. To quell her anxiety, she concentrated on the spiel she planned to give to the bankers. If she succeeded in convincing them to give her the money she needed to begin, then maybe she could convince women to buy her grandmother's cream, and then by osmosis somehow gain the confidence she needed to make her own way in the world, and maybe even marry the best boy in town. She wasn't sure of anything right now, much less her ability to convince a banker to give her something as big as actual money. But Josh helped her write a business plan, saying all they could do was say no and that wouldn't kill her. Although she wasn't positive of that either, right now.

But her friends Josh, Gussie and Shu, all thought her idea was grand and sure to be a big moneymaker, so today was the day she had promised herself and them that no matter what happened or how nervous and scared she felt, she would give it a try.

It was Josh's idea to try the banks, who were slowly beginning to lend money again.

She had made up five jars, purchasing the ingredients with Ma's permission this time, using the little bit of money left over from Pa's tiny life insurance policy after paying the funeral expenses. She was dressed for the weather in a grey felt cloche, worn black coat, wool gloves and her mother's high heels, which were a half-size too small and pinched her feet.

Over her shoulder hung Ma's big old leather purse, filled with samples. She felt about her samples like a loving mother might feel about her children: pride, protectiveness, hopefulness and more than a little anxiety. Nestled next to the baby food jars filled with cream was the precious business plan.

The day was cold and the sidewalks even icier than usual as she hurried along.

"Success comes to those who try," she said out loud several times to give herself courage.

Napoleon Hill had said those very same words in a talk he gave on the radio about his study of millionaires and how achievement occurs. The line stuck in Eva's brain and it had been playing in her mind ever since. She chose to walk downtown today rather than to drive because she would need Pa's car and the quarter tank of gas it contained when and if she received some money from the bank to buy her supplies.

On her way, she passed an empty store front, one of several in a row of empty stores. Seeing her reflection in the window, she worried that she looked too ordinary and low class to convince anybody of anything. To fight her errant thoughts, she began to mumble the sales pitch she had written and rewritten so many times.

"How do you do," she said out loud to herself. "My name is Eva Doyle. I have in my possession a secret recipe for an amazing skin lubricating cream. It was handed down to me by my grandmother, who had beautiful skin, even in old age."

Eva mimicked taking the picture of her grandmother from her purse and handing it to the banker to look over. "Isn't her skin lovely? It is my intention to make and sell her amazing skin care cream door-to-door, so that other women might benefit from her expertise."

She pantomimed handing the banker a sample jar. "For the missus."

She smiled a practiced smile and it was then, according to her best fantasies, that the banker would smile a grateful smile back at her. Then would come the closer.

"In order to produce my grandmother's miracle skin cream in quantity, I will need a loan of one hundred dollars."

With a little flourish, she pretended to hand over her business plan, then fantasized sitting calmly, her hands resting nicely in her lap, while the banker read her plan over and made his decision.

In her best fantasy of all, the banker would look up with a big smile, say he could see for himself what huge possibilities her product had in today's market place, and immediately write her a check. She would smile, thank him and reassure him he would never have a reason to regret his decision. They would then shake hands and she would leave, all smiles.

"How do you do, my name is Eva Doyle," she said, again, and was so preoccupied with getting her speech perfect that she didn't see Josh approaching, and almost bumped into him.

"Hey, Eva," he said, stepping neatly to one side. "Today's the big day, huh?"

"Yup. I'm hoping they'll give me the money right away, so I can get started."

"They'd be fools to say no," Josh said.

"You think so? I'm so nervous, I'll probably pee my pants before I get out a word."

"And if you do," he told her, laughing, "just dry yourself off and go on to the next bank. There are plenty of bankers who never even met you. Besides it's been a while since the run on the banks. There should be a little extra money to loan out. Have a little faith, sweetheart."

For emphasis, he waggled his eyebrows like Groucho Marx and tapped the end of a pretend cigar.

"Oh Lord, I hope you're right," Eva said weakly.

"You can do this," he said, serious now. "I know you can."

He blushed bright red, for no reason that Eva could see.

"Thanks," she said and smiled. "I needed that."

"Hey, my timing always was impeccable," he joked. They both laughed.

#

Josh was already late for school, but nevertheless stopped to admire Eva as she hurried away. He had a look of such tenderness and longing in his eyes that, had she noticed, she would have realized with a shock how deeply he cared for her. Mingled with that tenderness was also a kind of heat. Quiet he might have been, shy he certainly was, but there was no weakness in Josh Goldman. He, too, was determined to succeed. When he did, he intended to win her heart, but he had a flaw that could be fatal for a young man courting a woman – too much patience. He honestly believed that he needed to build up his own worth before he could become worthy of her and make his intentions known.

#

Energized after seeing Josh, Eva hurried the rest of the way downtown and approached the first bank on her list, The First National Bank of Emerson, an imposing building with huge marble pillars. She took in several deep breaths to calm her fears, reminded herself again that success comes to those who try. She entered the bank, moving briskly across the marble floor to the reception desk, trying to act as if she belonged there, yet feeling terribly self-conscious in her mended coat and cheap high heels.

She could talk to herself in a positive manner all day, but she looked poor because she was poor. Knowing this hurt and shamed her. Worst of all, she had spent the little bit of money from Pa's life insurance after paying for his funeral, so if this didn't work, she and Ma would be in even bigger trouble than they already were. But she was here in the bank and there was no going back now.

She steeled her shaky nerves and approached the woman at the reception desk.

"May I help you, Miss?" the woman asked.

Eva was suddenly overcome by a wave of nausea.

Instead of asking to see a banker, she hurried off to the ladies room and barely made it to a stall before vomiting up her entire breakfast of weak tea and oatmeal. Crouched over the toilet with her eyes clenched shut and the stench of her own vomit in her nostrils, hopelessness overwhelmed her.

What were you thinking? she asked herself as she wiped her mouth with toilet paper. You don't belong here. How could you possibly think you do? And after what you did to your father, you don't deserve anything, much less to succeed.

A wave of shame and grief hit her and she felt sick all over again.

Go home, she told herself. Save yourself the humiliation. You're more suited to scrubbing floors than asking a big deal banker for money.

Instead, she stood back up.

"Success comes to those who try," she whispered to herself in the mirror at the sink. She finished cleaning herself off. She wanted to reassure herself, but the words sounded hollow and ridiculous.

Still, as she stood there, the anxiety faded somewhat. She reminded herself what she had promised herself she would do today. She could accept no excuses either, because for sure she would never get up the courage to do it tomorrow or ever again. This was it.

With that, she splashed some water over her face, rearranged her expression into what she hoped was a confident look, then returned to the information desk.

"How can I help you this time?" the woman asked, obviously annoyed.

"I would like to speak to a banker," Eva said. It came out more like a squeak than anything else, but it did come out.

"What is it that you wish to speak to a banker about?" the woman said, her voice changing to a more businesslike tone.

"I wish to apply for a business loan," Eva said. She felt her heart pounding in her ears and sweat dripping from her arm pits.

"It might be a while before anyone can see you," the woman said, her voice softening somewhat.

"I'll wait," Eva said, forcing herself to look the woman directly in the eye.

But the woman seemed to take that as a challenge.

"If you insist," the woman said, sounding even more annoyed. "You can wait over there."

She pointed to a row of wooden chairs in the middle of the lobby, then turned to answer a ringing telephone.

Eva sank down on one of the chairs, glad to have some time to sit down and compose herself. Her feet hurt, and they were icy cold from the walk downtown. She was actually shaking from nerves.

She was soon joined by an elegant elderly couple, who looked as though they had not aged so much as simply grown dry. She realized how poor and pathetic she must look next to them.

Suddenly she felt queasy again, but she didn't want the woman at the information desk to think she'd fled, so she stayed put. Thankfully the queasiness went away.

After sitting a while, she began to notice things, like the patches on the elderly man's trousers and the woman's shoes, which were worn down at the heels. Even the customers in the bank weren't as well dressed as she initially thought.

She began to relax a little.

An hour came and went.

Had the receptionist forgotten?

She probably hopes I'll just give up and go away, Eva thought, but she refused to relinquish her place. The rest of the chairs began to fill up with waiting customers. She kept her bottom defiantly glued to the chair, determined to sit there forever if necessary.

She was beginning to think the receptionist had every intention of never calling on her, when to her surprise, the receptionist stood up and headed her way.

"Mr. Jones will see you now," the receptionist said. She pointed to the door of one of three identical offices along one wall, before clicking away in her high heels.

Eva, her heart racing, stood up. Feeling shaky and strangely light-headed, she walked over to the office indicated. Inside, she sat down on one of two chairs in front of a pine desk, her hands held rigidly together in her lap. A man with droopy eyes, which made him look exhausted, entered the room shortly afterwards. He reminded her of Doofus, a neighbor's beagle. Aghast at the thought, she immediately put the thought out of her mind.

"What can I do for you?" He sounded impatient as he plopped himself down into the chair behind the desk.

"How do you do," Eva said, going into her spiel in a barely audible voice. "My name is Eva Doyle and…"

Her panic flared and she forgot her entire speech. She started again and mumbled out the parts she could remember. Finished, she timidly handed over her business plan along with a jar of her skin lubricating cream.

"For your missus," she said, too scared to look him in the eye.

He took both items like someone accepting dirty laundry, shoved the jar to one side on his desk without looking at it and began to skim her business plan. Eva sat on the edge of her chair, every nerve in her body tense. He began to smile as he read.

He liked it? He must! Please God. Let him like it. Please. Please.

But when he finally spoke, it was with a sneer in his voice.

"You gotta be funning me, lady," he said. "You want money for beauty creams at a time like this?"

"I'm not funning you," she said, biting her lip so as not to break down and cry. "I'm going to make a lot of money someday, and you'd be smart to invest in me at the beginning."

The actual words came out sounding like the cry of a wounded animal.

"Don't make me laugh," he said. His smile grew even more sarcastic as he rose from his chair and flicked his hand dismissively.

"I won't waste any more of your time," she said meekly. She gathered up her business plan from the desk, tucked it away carefully, and stood. She moved away slowly, precisely, in the way a person does when they're confused and have no idea which way to turn.

"Go home, lady," he said, noticing her confusion. "Find yourself a husband and have a couple of kids. Forget about trying to start a business. Let the men do that."

In a last insult, he let his eyes slide over her body in a lascivious way.

She felt a sudden burst of rage. How dare he?

She yanked the jar of cream from his desk and shoved it back in her bag. Let him keep his evil money and his greasy fingers off her precious bottle of skin cream. She gave him an angry look, then stormed out of the bank, not stopping to put on her coat until she was outside in the cold.

She could almost hear the sneer in her father's voice, asking, "Well, what did you expect?"

On the sidewalk, an emaciated black cat stopped to stare at her, before running away. Obviously even the cat thought she was worthless. Thinking about her father, she was sure he knew she would never succeed at anything. He was probably right.

The urge to simply return home almost overwhelmed her but she had promised herself she would try and so she headed in the direction of another bank.

A short distance later, she passed Ozzie's Café. The scent of the roasting chicken drenched her in rich aroma. Ozzie's was famous for its chicken, mashed potatoes and apple pie. How long had it been since they had eaten meat of any sort? The fierce hunger she felt for that chicken drained away her fear. Oatmeal, bread, weak tea and boiled potatoes. That was all they ate anymore and she hated it. This wasn't a game, it wasn't a joke.

If she were ever to succeed at anything, she had to go forward.

One block farther, at Northeast Savings and Trust, she forced herself to hold her head high and stand up straight as she marched through the swinging doors. The bank was not quite as impressive as the previous bank, but she didn't have to wait so long for the banker, an older man with a kind face.

On his narrow wooden desk were pictures of his family. Seeing those pictures made her feel a little better, and this time her voice didn't falter and sound so squeaky when she gave her spiel.

"Sounds like a good idea, but I can't help you," he said, when she finished. "We're barely holding on here ourselves. I'm so sorry."

After trying two more banks, where she wasn't given a chance to talk to anyone, much less an actual banker, bankers' hours were over.

Pa was right. Thinking about him now, a wave of sadness, regret and something she couldn't explain swept over her. She felt even worse. She trudged through the icy sidewalks towards home.

Chapter Four

The evening shadows slanted across the sidewalk, making it hard to see the slippery spots. Her feet hurt in the too-small high heels and were numb from the cold. What she wanted more than anything was to take off her shoes, have a hot bath and forget everything. She was so lost in her misery she didn't notice Josh, Gussie and Shu coming up behind her in a rush.

"Hey Eva," Shu shouted. "Wait up."

Shu had been Eva's friend since first grade. She was beautiful, with wide set green eyes and long, naturally curly dark hair. In Shu's family, nothing was made of her beauty, which was as taken for granted as having brown eyes.

Eva felt so defeated that the last thing she wanted was to run into someone she knew, much less her closest friends, but unable to avoid them, she sighed heavily and waited for them to catch up.

"How'd it go?" Josh chimed in. "Were they wowed?"

"Come on," Gussie demanded. "Tell us everything and don't leave anything out."

"They weren't wowed at all," Eva said, feeling a quiver of humiliation. "I couldn't convince anybody to give me a dime. Either they didn't have any money, they weren't interested, or they couldn't be bothered to see me at all."

"At least you tried," Gussie said, patting her on the back.

"Don't take it personally," Shu said, sympathetically. "The banks have gotten tight lately about giving up their precious greenbacks. It has nothing to do with you."

"I'd loan you the money myself," Josh said, "but I haven't worked but one evening this whole week at the brokerage, and I need to give the money to my folks."

"One of the bankers liked my idea but they didn't have any money to loan," Eva said with hollow enthusiasm. "Mostly I felt like I was wasting their time."

"Hey, I've got an idea," Shu blurted out. "We could throw a party. Everyone's desperate to have a laugh these days. We could charge people a quarter to get in and ten cents for a glass of beer. We should be able to get at least two glasses from every bottle. People have rent parties all the time to help pay the rent, why not a party to help you get started in business?"

"I have two bucks saved from my last paycheck," Gussie piped up, joining the excitement. "That ought to buy a few bottles of beer to start."

Gussie had a part-time job as a hired girl taking care of a railroad executive's crippled wife.

"And when that money runs out," Josh said, running the numbers in his head, as everyone knew he loved to do, "we can use the money we've collected to buy more beer. I'm eighteen, legal age as of last month. At the end of the night, we can pay Gussie back her money and the rest will all go to Eva's new business."

"Do you really think this could work?" Eva asked, not sure at all but not wishing to discourage her friends, either.

"Sure," Shu said excitedly. "We could pop popcorn. My Ma grows the stuff in a patch in the community garden. We got more than we need from last year's crop."

"Didn't you say something about your folks going out of town?" Gussie asked, turning to Josh.

"Yes, but that doesn't mean…" Josh started to object. His voice trailed off as he looked at Eva.

Everyone knew what Josh was thinking. His parents lived on Chandler Street in a three-story row house. The family owned several fine antiques that had been handed down over the generations. Lately, with Josh's father's hours cut in half at the brokerage, they'd been forced to sell some of their lesser pieces to get by, making the remaining pieces more precious than ever.

Eva didn't blame Josh for being hesitant. But there was barely enough money left for food after Ma paid the undertaker from Pa's life insurance policy. At the rate they were going, there was a good possibility they would lose their apartment soon.

"Please, Josh?" Eva said.

Josh caved in immediately, as everyone except Eva knew he would.

They set the party for the following Saturday, and made plans to get together on Wednesday to make flyers and post them around town. With the possibility that this could work spinning around her head and feeling gratitude for having such good friends, Eva went home, undressed, and took a hot bath. When she was warm once more, she and Ma ate the rest of the watery potato soup Ma had made the previous day. Ma didn't ask how Eva's day went, for which Eva was relieved, because she didn't want to worry her mother any more than absolutely necessary.

#

The day of the party loomed large and frightening. It didn't help that the sun refused to come out or that there was a foot of snow on the ground after snowing all night. To keep her mind busy, Eva cleaned the entire apartment, then spent the rest of the day worrying and waiting for Josh to call, giving the all-clear signal that his folks were gone and they could begin preparing for the party. The longer she waited, the more she was sure nobody would show up. The day was cold, too cold to go out, and besides nobody had any money. Even if they did, spending it on a party for someone they didn't know seemed frivolous. And what about Josh? He was taking an awful chance having the party at his parent's house. They would be furious if they found out, and who could blame them? And how would they ever pay Gussie back if nobody came? As the afternoon stretched into early evening, Eva, dressed and ready to go hours early, paced the floor until Ma, who normally wouldn't have noticed, grew exasperated.

"For heaven's sake, sit down. I can't hear a word they're saying on the radio with all that clomping back and forth."

To appease her mother, Eva sat down and began to thumb through the Sears Catalogue, but she was too anxious to concentrate. When Josh finally called at five o'clock, she was so giddy with relief that she grabbed her coat and ran the whole way to his house.

Shu and Gussie must have been anxious too, because they were already there when she arrived. After a brief discussion as to who would do what, they all set to work. Shu busied herself popping popcorn, Gussie hung crepe paper, Eva swept and dusted, while Josh went out to buy beer. Eva continued to worry that nobody would show up, but kept it to herself. Her friends were doing something wonderful for her and she didn't want to make them feel bad by sharing her fears.

"Gee, I hope Hero shows up," Shu said, after Josh returned with the beer. They gathered in the kitchen to place it in a washtub Josh had filled with snow to keep it cold. "Just having him show up could make our party a big success."

"I wouldn't count on it," Gussie said. "I ran into his dad the other day. I asked how Hero was doing, since I hadn't seen him around for a while. He said that Hero joined Pinkerton Detectives in Chicago. He didn't say what he would be doing, but knowing Hero I'll bet it's something exciting."

Chicago? Eva was stunned and strangely deflated. In one way, she was glad he wasn't coming to the party. She didn't want him to see her until she had succeeded. But Chicago?

"Wow, imagine that," Josh said, his voice heavy with sarcasm. "The great Hero Lyon having to work like the rest of us poor slobs."

He clicked his teeth and shook his head. "Things must be tougher than I thought."

"I bet he looks real cute in his detective outfit," Shu said, ignoring Josh's remark.

"Do they even wear a detective outfit?" Gussie wondered out loud. "I thought they worked undercover and wore the same clothes as everybody else."

Before Eva could add her two cents, Gussie switched the conversation to her favorite subject.

"You'd never know my boss was such a big deal," she gushed. "He acts just like everybody else. And oh, he's got this thick, wavy gray hair, and the bluest eyes you've ever seen. It's like they've got their own special light."

As Gussie rhapsodized, Eva's thoughts wandered to her own favorite subject, Hero Lyon. What if he decided to stay in Chicago forever? Would he ever return? Or see her become successful, if she ever did?

The friends continued to work and talk until eight o'clock sharp, when a knock sounded on the front door. Josh answered. Three burly young men wearing clean overalls, their hair slicked back and their scrubbed faces shiny with anticipation, appeared.

"Thank you for coming," Josh said, as he collected their entrance fee and ushered them inside.

"Hello there," Shu said with a welcoming, seductive smile as she placed a big bowl of popcorn on the coffee table in front of them. Her fashionable black slacks and fuzzy pink sweater showed off her every luscious curve.

Eva, relieved that somebody, anybody had showed up, hurried over to the Victrola and cranked the handle. The sounds of "It's Only a Paper Moon" soon filled the room as Josh poured them each a glass of beer, making sure to place coasters under each glass, and took their money.

Eva, Shu and Gussie sat on the antique fainting sofa opposite the boys and acted fascinated as the boys expounded on their favorite subject.

"For speed and power, the Ford has everybody skinned," said a boy whose face was covered with acne.

"Oh my gosh, do you really think so?" Shu said, her eyes open wide as though the boy had made a pronouncement of world import.

The boy beamed at the beautiful Shu, who beamed right back at him.

"My old man traded his 1931 Ford in on a 1930 President Eight Studebaker," one of the other boys said, his eyes on Shu. "It's got a straight eight motor and a spare tire mounted on each front fender. Gets eight miles to the gallon."

"Gee," Eva said, playing along, "you must feel rich, driving a car like that."

"Yeah," the boy beamed proudly, "I do."

When three other party goers arrived, Eva felt a little better. At least they would be able to pay Gussie back the money they'd borrowed. Then a group of five young women appeared, and three boys behind them, and Eva began to feel even more hopeful. As more party-goers arrived, she tried to count them, but soon there were so many that she lost track. She went to see if she could help Shu, who was doing popcorn duty. But instead of being at the stove popping popcorn, Shu was standing in the corner of the dining room talking to Sam Stryker. Sam was tall, square-jawed and handsome in a rough-hewn way. He was a star football player at Emerson High, much admired for his strength on and off the football field. The two of them huddled together, effectively shutting out anybody who might come close. Eva was annoyed at Shu but let it go and popped the popcorn herself.

As the party roared on, Josh moved around the crowded living room, removing several small porcelain items. He spotted a drunken boy purposely shoving a small bronze sculpture slowly towards the edge of an end table. Josh dashed over and grabbed it before it hit the floor.

"Hey, what'd you do that for?" the boy said. "I wanted to see if it would bounce."

"I wouldn't do that again, if I were you," Josh said, giving the boy a menacing stare. He rushed the statue off to the kitchen, stuck it at the back of a side cupboard out of sight, then hurried off to purchase more beer. He wasn't so sure it was a good idea to buy more beer for a crowd growing more boisterous by the minute, but for Eva's sake and the money they could make, he did it anyway.

When he returned, cigarette smoke filled the house like a fog. More than anything Josh wanted Eva to succeed, but things were getting a little out of hand. He felt a little better when a girl with a halo of frizzy bleached blond hair and wearing a red low cut dress sat at the piano and began to play. A crowd quickly gathered around her.

"Tutti frutti, be a rooty-tooty, find yourself a cutie," they all began to sing in loud drunken voices.

With a moment to think, Josh returned to the kitchen to move the statue to an upstairs closet, where it would be safer. He opened the side cupboard and reached inside. It wasn't there.

Oh no.

He was sure he had put it there. Hadn't he? Anxious, he searched the entire cupboard, then the rest of the kitchen, but it wasn't there either. He searched the living room and dining room, wending his way through the noisy crowd. Did someone steal it? What happened?

After looking for it on the first floor, he hurried upstairs to see if it had somehow made it up there. Peering into his folk's bedroom, he saw a boy and girl rolling on top of his grandmother's hand-crocheted ecru pineapple bedspread. His grandmother had spent a whole year crocheting that spread for his parent's wedding anniversary. How dare they? But before he could roust the rutting couple, the entire house shook like it had been hit by something hard.

Josh raced downstairs in a panic and discovered a circle of people yelling and screaming, and a fight going on in the dining room. He pushed his way to the center to find Tom, a tall, muscular boy from his high school standing over Jimmy, a somewhat shorter, thinner boy laid out on the parquet floor, blood gushing from his nose.

Tom yelled, "Don't you ever talk to my girl like that again."

Josh knelt down beside Jimmy, who opened his eyes.

"Are you all right?" Josh asked.

Tom circled, shaking his fist and screaming insults.

Josh looked up at Tom. "You need to stop this nonsense right now."

In response, Jimmy pushed Josh out of the way. Bright red blood gushed from his nose, down his shirt and onto the parquet floor.

"You better stay down where you belong, if you know what's good for you," Tom shouted.

Instead, Jimmy got unsteadily up on his feet, spit out some blood, put up his dukes and said, "Come on."

The crowd exploded in cheers and jeers.

Irritated, Josh, who was a foot taller than both boys, shoved his way between them. He clamped his hands on their shirts and lifted both of them off the ground.

"I understand you boys are irritated with each other," he said in a reasonable tone. "But you cannot fight in my house. Take it outside."

He marched the two boys out the door and set them, none too gently, on the front walk. They each staggered, and looked up at him, their eyes wide. Josh had never shown his temper before. It may have been shock more than anything that kept them from protesting.

The crowd, which included Shu's new boyfriend, poured out the door behind them to see the fun. Disgusted with them all, Josh returned to the house and went to the kitchen to pour the rest of the beer down the sink. The party was over, as far as he was concerned. He then went to the dining room to help Gussie, Shu and Eva clean up the mess.

Outside the dining room window the boys continued their battle as the crowd gathered around, egging them on. Jimmy landed a blow to Tom's jaw, knocking him down, then Jimmy himself tripped and landed face down in the snow. Finally, two burly friends of the boys picked them up like they were sacks of potatoes, threw them in the back of their jalopy, and they all drove away.

"Whew, what a relief," Gussie said, as she watched from the dining room window.

She grabbed a mop and began to wipe up the blood on the parquet floor.

The rest of the freezing partygoers returned to the house, but didn't stay long when they discovered the booze was gone.

By midnight, everyone was gone, including the couple from the bedroom and Shu's boyfriend, Sam. Josh shut the door on the last revelers and the four friends gathered in the kitchen.

Gussie opened the silverware drawer where the cash box was hidden, then let out a shriek.

"The money's gone," she cried, pawing through the drawer. Tears streamed down her broad face. "Someone stole our money. I put it right here."

Eva felt sick. "We're ruined."

Filled with despair and trying not to show it, she went to the broom closet and got a broom and some rags to clean up the kitchen.

"Not yet," Josh said with a smile, as he took the broom and rags away from her.

"What are you smiling about?" Gussie asked, crabbily.

"I don't see anything to smile about, either," Shu said sourly.

Eva was too crushed to speak.

"You'll see," Josh said. He opened the door to the basement.

Eva, Gussie and Shu, not knowing what to think, followed him downstairs to the furnace room. Josh circled around the furnace, disappearing from view. When he reappeared, he had the lock box in his hand.

"For you, Madame," he said, handing the box to Eva with a victorious smile.

Eva, so weak in the knees she felt faint, took it from him and shakily climbed the steps back to the kitchen. She sat down at the kitchen table. In spite of her trembling hands she managed to open the box, which was filled to the brim with bills and change. She stared at the pile. Tears of relief, hope, and gratitude sprang to her eyes.

"Don't cry," Josh said tenderly. "You're gonna be so rich someday, kiddo, and this is your start."

The ever-practical Gussie reached into her pocket and handed Eva a handkerchief, then wiped her own eyes with her sleeve. Eva tried to count the pennies, nickels, dimes, quarters and dollar bills, but gave it up because she was too confused to think straight. So Josh counted the money for her.

"Twenty-seven big ones," he said when finished, "minus the money we owe Gussie, so twenty-five bucks even. It isn't the hundred bucks you were asking the bank for, but it's enough to get you started."

"Yes, it is," Eva said happily, dabbing at her face with the now-soggy handkerchief. "Oh, I owe you all so much. If I ever become successful it'll be because you gave me my start. I'll never, ever forget what you did."

"Neither will we," Shu said, her eyes moist. Josh looked away so they wouldn't see the tears in his own eyes.

"You're going to be a huge success," Shu said. "I just know it."

"Gee, I hope you don't get so big you forget who your friends are," Gussie said.

"As if I ever could," Eva said, smiling through her tears.

That broke the tension and they all giggled at how miraculous life could be. They set to work cleaning up the house. Josh opened up all the doors and windows to air the house out, even though it was freezing outside. He didn't shut them again until they were all shivering from the cold.

#

With everyone gone and the house back to normal, Josh was thinking things through. If his folks found out about the party from the neighbors, he could at least show them that the house was not hurt, but what about the bronze statue? His mother loved that statue and was sure to notice immediately that it was gone.

Anxious, he searched the house twice over, but found nothing. He was about to give up, sure it was gone forever and wondering how he could ever face his parents, when he decided to look in the cupboard one more time.

To his great surprise, there it stood, in the very same spot he had placed it during the party.

He would never find out why the statue disappeared and then so strangely reappeared, though he would always wonder.

Chapter Five

Sunday morning, Eva arose right as the sun was coming up. She was anxious and ready to begin. She had spent most of the night wide awake, her thoughts reeling back and forth from terrible fear that this would never work and they would end up homeless, to sheer, crazy excitement that it might work so well it would make her rich.

Still in her nightgown, she sat at the kitchen table and began to make a list of the supplies she would need. She felt a deep gratitude for Shu, Gussie and Josh and what they had done to help her. She was determined to prove to them that it was worth their trouble. After she'd been working for a few minutes, Ma appeared in her own nightgown, poured herself some cold tea made the day before, and sat down opposite her.

"We made twenty-five bucks from the party," Eva said. "Can you believe it?"

For the briefest second, Ma's gaze went slightly out of focus, then she seemed to catch herself.

"That's nice dear." She smiled an absent smile and took a sip of her tea.

"But I'm worried, Ma," Eva said. "We're still behind in the rent."

"Mrs. Stapleton is a nice lady," Ma said. "I'm sure she'll wait a little longer."

"We can't be sure of that, Ma. Four apartments are vacant. She needs money, too."

Ma reached over and patted Eva's hand. "There, there dear. Don't worry so much. Everything's going to be just fine. Your father will take care of us."

Eva was confused. "Pa?"

She was going to say, Pa died, but Ma knew that. "Oh, you mean Pa will help us from heaven?"

"He's always been a hard worker," Ma said.

Eva hoped Ma was right about Pa. She also hoped he had forgiven her by now, but was sure that was about as possible as her forgiving herself. Just the mention of his name brought that horrible day back in vivid, awful detail. It was accompanied by a wave of sadness and guilt.

"Maybe if I sell enough jars, we can buy something to eat besides oatmeal," Eva said, to change the subject. "Course, I'll have to use some of the money I make to buy more supplies. But if I make enough, maybe I could even pay a few dollars on the rent."

As she spoke, the desperation and insanity of their situation hit her. "How can I talk about shorting our landlady? Am I a fool? I mean, we'll pay her back. Our family has always paid their debts. But we've got to give this a chance, Ma. We've got to gamble, right?"

"I guess so," Ma said, although she didn't look quite sure. She stood up, went over and plopped down on Pa's old easy chair in front of the radio.

"We'll be fine, Ma," Eva said, going over to the radio and switching it on for her. "I'll make sure of that. Don't you worry about a thing."

The tubes glowed inside the radio and a soft squeal emerged as the radio heated up. Soon the sounds of yet another soap opera echoed throughout the apartment.

#

Monday morning, Eva set off in Pa's car to purchase her ingredients. Her mood continued to waver between wild optimism and terrible anxiety. She noticed that despite so many businesses being closed and so many people out of work, the streets of Emerson were alive with cars and people. Maybe in spite of all the negative reports, the economy in Emerson was looking up.

She stopped at Kneeland Bottle and parked in their lot. Inside, shelves were bare in some places and only half-filled in others. She managed to find a case of small jars and was given a ten percent professional discount when she explained to the cashier that she was going into business and would doubtless be back for more.

At the drug store, she purchased lanolin. At the stationery store, she bought labels, paints, black ink and a decent pen with a nice sharp tip. On her way back to the car, she spotted Emily's Sweet Shoppe. Feeling a wave of confidence at the success of her new venture, she spent the change she had left on a bag of caramels for Ma.

Back at home, Ma was in the exact same spot she had been when Eva left, the radio still blatting away.

"I got you something, Ma," Eva said, handing over the bag of caramels to her mother.

Ma looked inside the bag, her eyes wide. "Oh, my gosh. Caramels."

She took one, tore off the waxed paper and popped it into her mouth. "Yum, oh boy, oh that's so good."

She handed the bag back to Eva. "Here, you have one, too."

Eva popped it into her mouth and took a long moment to savor the creamy, buttery, sweet taste.

"You keep the rest, Ma," she said. "I'm going to get right to work so I can make enough money to buy us another bag."

"You do that," Ma said.

She smiled as she popped another caramel into her mouth and returned to her radio program.

Excited to begin, Eva busied herself unpacking her bags, then set to work. As she ran water into Ma's big soup kettle to sterilize the jars, she chose to ignore the frightened voice in her head that kept saying she was wasting her time and this would never work. Instead she reminded herself she wouldn't know for sure if it worked or not unless she gave it a try. Sometimes it helped.

When she finished sterilizing the jars and set them out on a clean towel to dry, she realized with a start that it was already past their normal lunch time. Ma hadn't said anything, but ever since Pa died, she seemed to be more forgetful than usual. Eva quickly heated a can of chicken noodle soup, poured it into a bowl and brought it to her mother on a tray. Ma didn't even look up, but ate the steaming soup like someone stoking a furnace. Eva ate her soup at the kitchen table between pasting labels on the newly sterilized jars.

When she finished with that task and cleaning up the kitchen, she made up a batch of skin lubricating cream and after that a batch of hand cream, figuring she'd need at least two products to offer. When she finished, she took a long moment to admire her handiwork, then filled the jars and screwed on the caps, leaving them stacked up on the kitchen sink.

After a quick supper of fried egg sandwiches and tea, she went to bed and fell immediately asleep, only to be awakened an hour later by a nightmare of Pa sitting up in his casket, an angry, accusatory look on his face. But because she was so exhausted from her long day, she soon fell back asleep and this time slept without dreaming.

The next morning, after a quick breakfast she bathed quickly, dressed in her best outfit, a navy blue skirt and white blouse, fixed her hair in a French twist, creamed her face and hands with her own cream twice, then slipped on her coat, said a quick goodbye to Ma and left.

Her stomach was clenched tight with fear at the idea of knocking on a complete stranger's door, but if she could get up the nerve to do it once, hopefully the next time would be easier. At least she hoped that was true. Right now she wasn't sure of anything except she had to give this a try.

She worried that so many people were going door-to-door these days, selling everything from homemade cleaning products to old rags. What chance did she have to sell something no one really needed? Then she reminded herself sharply that President Roosevelt said there was nothing to fear but fear itself. Of course, that was easy for him to say, he was rich and powerful.

But nothing could be scarier than the bankers, and she had survived them. And if she failed, well, at least Hero wasn't around to see her make a fool of herself, and she could tell her friends she had tried.

A brisk wind pushed at her back as she hurried past a church, which had been converted into a soup kitchen. Lined up outside were men, women, and children. Some were young enough to cling to their mother's skirts, others were old people, but all shivered with the cold as they waited for someone to unlock the front door and begin serving bread and hot coffee.

Seeing them, Evaleen felt a shiver of panic at the fate that awaited her and her mother if she didn't succeed today.

At the corner of Holmes and Columbus, she paused before the first house, and took a shaky breath. Slowly, feeling like a condemned woman, she climbed the front steps. On the front door hung a wreath filled with pink silk tulips. Maybe the kind of woman who would put tulips on her door on such a cold day would listen to her spiel out of pity.

With that tiny ray of hope, Eva timidly knocked on the front door. A thin, harried looking woman appeared, carrying a baby with dripping wet diapers.

Eva took a quick breath, cleared her throat and began. "Ma'am, I wonder if you'd care to try a sample of my grandmother's famous Fresh-as-a Daisy skin lubricating cream."

Her voice was soft and quivery with fear.

The woman took one look at Eva and slammed the door in her face.

So much for tulips being a hopeful sign, Eva thought as she trudged back down the steps. To get up the nerve to do it again, she reminded herself that the woman didn't know her, had never met her before, and that it wasn't personal.

It didn't help. By the fifth house when she saw someone appear at the window but refuse to come to the door, she wanted to quit so badly, it was like an ache.

As Eva walked to the next house, she made a deal with herself that she could quit only after she knocked on one hundred doors. At the seventh house, a woman with gray hair up in pin curls opened the door a crack. She had an angry and suspicious look on her pale face.

"Ma'am, I'm the United States representative for Fresh-As-A-Daisy Lubricating Skin Cream," Eva said, speaking quickly, "and I would just love to give you a free sample…"

"Go away. I don't want any," the woman said sharply, and slammed the door.

Well, there it was. Someone else slamming the door in her face. But it did not kill her, although death might have been a relief right now as she still had to do several more before she could quit. Bracing herself for the next rejection, she continued on to the next house, positive if she stopped, she would never have the nerve to start again.

But if they didn't slam the door in her face or not answer the door at all, they said they were broke or not interested. After the thirty-fifth house, a kind of perverse, crazy feeling took over. It was as though she became someone else, someone numb, someone who, no matter what happened to her or how awful people were, would continue to bounce back like one of those balloons that shot back up every time you knocked it down.

At the fiftieth house, the woman didn't slam the door in her face but said she couldn't afford to buy anything right now. At number eighty-three, a blowsy-looking bleached blond reeking from a mixture of smoke, perfume, sweat and alcohol answered the door.

"Ma'am, I'm the U.S. representative for Fresh-As-A-Daisy Lubricating Cream," Evaleen said, trying to sound a lot more enthusiastic than she felt, "and I was wondering if I could give you a free demonstration to show you what an amazing difference my lubricating skin cream can make..."

"Have you looked at yourself in the mirror, lady?" the woman interrupted in a husky voice, filled with contempt. "If it ain't working for you, honey, what in hell makes you think it'll work for me?"

Before Eva could protest, the woman slammed the door.

For one long moment Eva stood at the door, unable to breathe. She felt like someone had slugged her in the stomach.

It was now obvious to her that she could never succeed at anything, much less convince someone to buy a beauty product. Pa was right.

To make matters worse, the wind suddenly came up and it began to snow, a flurry of huge, fluffy drops. Eva gave up, breaking her promise to herself. She headed for home.

"You look like a drowned rat," Ma said, when Eva walked in the door. "I heard from Alma upstairs that they're hiring at Gimbel's. Ten dollars a week. We might even be able to afford a little coffee if you made that kind of money."

"I heard that too," Eva said, slipping off her coat and hanging it up, "two months ago."

After taking a long hot bath for comfort and to warm up, Eva dressed in her flannel pajamas and joined Ma in the living room. She was surprised to see tears in Ma's eyes. Was Ma worried about her? Did she sense what a horrible day it had been?

"You okay, Ma?" she said.

"Josanna Thriepleton died in a terrible automobile accident," Ma said and wiped her eyes with her sleeve.

Eva's throat tightened, before she realized that Ma's tears were for a soap opera character.

But Ma was depending on Eva. If they were turned out of their home, Ma would become even more dazed than she already was. At least she had a roof over her head, oatmeal and canned soup, and her soap operas, if nothing else. On the street, there would be no respite for either of them.

Success comes to those who try, Eva repeated to herself again as she placed the jars of cream in the ice box, but the words sounded hollow. They were mere words and meant nothing. Worse, she would have to admit to her friends that they had wasted their time and that Josh had jeopardized his family's home for nothing.

In despair, she went to the full length pier glass at the end of the narrow hallway, turned on the hall light and studied her image closely, to see if she could find out what was so awful about her appearance that the blond woman felt she could say such horrible things to her.

Her mouth was as pale as her plain freckled face. Her red hair, combed so carefully into a French twist, was now falling apart in strings and looked like a damp, greasy mess. And nothing could hide the fact that she had thick legs, no hips and a flat chest. The woman was right. No wonder Hero Lyon never noticed her. Why would anybody?

Tomorrow she would go to the unemployment office and see if anyone was hiring someone with no experience at anything. Maybe she could get a job as a cleaning woman, although she was pretty sure she wouldn't be any good at that, either.

She returned to the living room and looked out the window. Snow mixed with ice beat against the windows. It sounded like someone throwing seeds. To distract herself from her misery, Eva sat down across from Ma and listlessly picked up an old movie magazine she'd gotten from Shu.

She began to look for something to read that would take her mind off her own troubles. She stopped at a page with photographs of Joan Crawford and her adopted children. In one of the photographs Joan Crawford was wearing a starched white apron and a red and white checked dress, her children lovingly gathered around her.

In her misery, she saw that Joan Crawford wasn't a beauty either, with her thick dark eyebrows and long nose.

But she sure looks like she thinks an awful lot of herself, Eva thought.

Eva studied the pictures for a few minutes more, then turned the page to a story featuring Katharine Hepburn.

"Slim and Chic and Oh So Highbrow," said the caption under her picture.

The rest of the article was not so kind. "People have difficulty understanding her, as she elongates every vowel," the article stated. "She never looks you in the eye either, but always around you."

She was also good-looking enough, Eva decided, but kind of bony and gaunt. Neither Joan Crawford nor Katherine Hepburn were what you'd call raving beauties. It must be something else.

Curious, Eva studied the photos of both women. It certainly wasn't their looks that made them so special. Maybe it was their makeup, the way they dressed, and the confident way they held themselves that made all the difference.

Seeing the two movies stars, Eva wondered if she could maybe fake it, too.

Her mother used to buy cosmetics when there was little money for anything else. Eva never knew why, since Ma rarely used anything other than a dab of lipstick and a little rouge now and then, and only when it was something special like a wedding. As a little girl, Eva had loved to play with her mother's makeup, until Pa said she looked like a tramp and made her stop. But Ma continued to purchase cosmetics until Pa lost his job.

It was to her mother's stash in the bathroom that Eva now turned.

To guide her, Eva ripped out the pictures of Joan Crawford and Kate Hepburn and propped them up on the back of the toilet tank. She studied their eyes, then tried to copy their makeup by drawing a line along the upper and lower lashes of her own eyes with Ma's eyebrow pencil. But instead of looking like Kate Hepburn or Joan Crawford, she looked like a raccoon, or someone in a horror movie.

Discouraged but undaunted, she washed it off and began again, using a lighter touch. Then she plucked her eyebrows with Ma's old tweezers, wincing with pain, until they had a decent shape, before darkening them carefully with Ma's eyebrow pencil. Next, she dipped her fingers into Ma's rouge, which had become dry, mixed it with a little of her grandmother's lubricating cream to moisten, and rubbed a little into the apples of both cheeks for a nice rosy glow. She examined the results critically, and felt a stir of hope.

She went on by putting a little of the same cream on her lips, then painted them with Ma's bright red lipstick. For the finishing touch, she brushed her red, shoulder-length hair down and loose, and added a bit of her father's old Vaseline Hair Tonic to give it a shine and keep it from blowing every which way.

Not quite sure if she had pulled it off, she went out to show Ma.

"What do you think, Ma? Do I look like a movie star?"

Ma looked up from her radio program. A serious expression crossed her pale face, as though she had spent her life making such judgments.

"Well, you don't look nothin' like one, but you don't look half bad, either. Might help if you wasn't so round-shouldered. You always look like you're carrying the weight of the world on those shoulders of yours."

Energized by her mother's comment, Eva fetched her mother's big health book from the cedar chest, placed it on her head and walked slowly towards Ma, her stomach sucked in and shoulders held back.

"Is this better?"

Ma gave her an appraising look. "Maybe if you held your chin up."

Eva walked slowly back and forth, trying to stand straight, chin up, pretending to be someone important. Ma stretched out her swollen, blue veined legs on the ottoman in front of her chair and watched. Suddenly Eva wobbled, and the big book fell to the ground.

"I can't do it," she said. Her misery felt like a dead weight inside. "People will think I'm a phony, like I'm trying to put one over on them."

The light faded from her mother's eyes.

"I can't help you there," Ma said, snapping off the radio. "Anyway, it's late. Think I'll go to bed."

In her bedroom, Eva sat on the edge of her bed and stared at herself in the mirror on her dresser for a long time. She could paint herself up and pretend to be somebody else, but the truth was the truth. Worse, she wasn't even smart enough to know what Josh was talking about half the time. And for sure Hero Lyon would never notice her, even if he ever did come back to Emerson. As always when she felt bad about herself, she then thought about her father and what he would say if he knew what she was up to.

Chapter Six

Still feeling depressed and discouraged the next morning, Eva paged listlessly through the movie magazine again, while having her breakfast of weak tea and oatmeal. She was desperate to think about something, anything else. Glancing at the photographs of Katharine Hepburn and Joan Crawford, she happened to notice that Joan Crawford wore a fashionable V-necked cream silk blouse with a necklace made of coins, and Katharine Hepburn wore wide-legged black pants and a white blouse with wide shoulders, along with a colorful scarf around her neck. Both looked understated and expensive.

Seeing them anew suddenly gave Eva an idea. There was no way she would ever be able to afford clothes like that, nor did she have anything that even slightly resembled their outfits, but she remembering seeing Shu in a pair of black wide-legged slacks at school. Shu's mother was a wonderful seamstress and made most of Shu's clothes, including her slacks. Would Shu loan them to her? She hated to ask, especially after everything that her friend had already done for her, but this was important.

Before she lost her nerve, Eva picked up the phone. Luckily, Shu answered on the first ring.

"Shu, it's Eva," she blurted out, a little too brightly. "I need a huge favor."

"Just ask," Shu said, cheerfully.

"Can I borrow your black slacks?" Eva said quickly, before she lost her nerve.

"My slacks?" Shu sounded surprised.

"You know, the ones with the wide legs," Eva said. She held her breath.

"Oh, those." Shu's voice turned thoughtful. "Sure, but I'm taller than you and a little bigger in the hips. I don't know if they'll fit you. What do you want them for?"

"To wear when I go door-to-door. I need some extra oomph."

Shu laughed. "You got plenty of oomph on your own, Toots, but if you think they'll help, I'll bring them over on my way to school."

Eva hung up the phone and breathed a huge sigh of relief. Asking someone for something went against her nature. At the same time, she was proud of herself for being able to ask at all.

Her attempt was especially wonderful since it worked and Shu said yes.

True to her word, Shu arrived an hour later, with the slacks slung over one arm.

"I'd love to chat," she said, thrusting the pants at Eva, "but Sam's waiting for me and he hates like hell to wait."

In turn, Eva handed Shu a jar of her skin lubricating cream to thank her. Shu stuck the jar in her book bag, then fled down the steps before anything else was said.

As Eva went to her room to try on the slacks, she wished that Shu would have stayed a bit, because she almost never saw her anymore and she missed her. Ever since Shu hooked up with Sam, she didn't seem to have time for anything or anyone.

Trying on the slacks, she was immediately discouraged. They were too long, too big in the hips and too small at the waist. She sat on the edge of her bed and despaired. She needed those slacks to give her the look she wanted, but she was no seamstress. Even if she were, she couldn't alter them without ruining them.

Her determination faltered until, looking over the slacks, it occurred to her she could maybe sew a temporary hem in the cuffs to shorten them, and tie a string between the button and the button hole to make the waist bigger like she'd heard pregnant women did. Then she could wear her long green sweater to cover the opening, and the fact that they were too big in the hips.

Hope returned, bit by bit. She could wear her simple white cotton blouse under the sweater, then she could maybe tie Ma's yellow and green scarf around her neck the way Katherine Hepburn did, for a little additional panache. As for her shoes, she would rub a new coat of black ink over the scuffed heels, and pray they didn't get wet.

It was probably ridiculous to think an outfit could change who she was. Pa would have made fun of her for even daring to think so.

An almost primitive sense of defeat swept over her. Then, strangely, came a hurt kind of anger. Just because Pa was a failure, did that mean she had to be a failure, too? Instantly, guilt poured in.

She had been so busy with her friends and trying to get Hero to notice her that she wasn't aware how worried and anxious her father had become. She should have tried harder to get a job. Maybe if she would have succeeded, Pa would still be alive.

She made a silent vow to her dead father that, for his sake, she would take care of her mother no matter what. And to do that, she had to make some money.

And to make money, she needed to stand out somehow. She remembered reading in that same magazine a short article about movie star's original names. Lana Turner's real name was Julia Jean Mildred Frances Turner, and Bette Davis's real name was Ruth Elizabeth Davis, both unimposing names, even on the plain side. But as Lana and Bette they were both perceived as glamorous. Obviously a person's name could make a big difference, too.

Just for fun, she tried out several versions of her own name. Eve, Evan, Elva, Evangeline, Evelyn, Evaleen. She stopped at Evaleen. She'd never known anyone named Evaleen. Evaleen was unusual enough that people could remember it easily. And the fact that it happened to rhyme with Queen was a good sign, too.

"Hello, my name is Evaleen," she said, trying it out.

Something deep resonated within her, and gave her goose bumps. She could be Evaleen, elegant, confident; Evaleen – a successful businesswoman.

Maybe Eva Doyle couldn't succeed, but Evaleen could. Evaleen would be braver, more self-confident, more queen-like than Eva Doyle could ever hope to be. Clothes, makeup, changing their name – it worked for movie stars, why not for ordinary people like herself? She laughed out loud at such a completely outlandish, impossible and outrageously wonderful thought.

#

"Hello, my name is Evaleen and I have developed a beauty product that I think you might be interested in," she practiced saying out loud as she drove to her first house that same afternoon. She was wearing makeup on her face, Shu's made-over slacks and her coat with new buttons from a coat she'd outgrown.

"And I am a queen." She added the last part to herself. The queen part would be her little secret, otherwise people would think she was insane for sure. But she liked the sound of it and it made her feel happy and proud.

She parked on Summit Hill, one of the nicer parts of Emerson. She told herself she was now Evaleen, proud, queen-like Evaleen.

Back straight, head held high, she walked briskly to the three-story colonial on the corner, took a deep breath, climbed the steps, then knocked boldly on the front door. Dried flowers in a basket were attached to the front door, giving the house a warm, welcoming look in spite of the cold weather.

A girl who looked barely out of high school appeared at the door soon afterwards.

"May I speak to the lady of the house?" Evaleen said, sounding more confident than she felt.

"I am the lady of the house," the woman said, "although my mother in law would probably disagree."

She cocked one eyebrow in mock despair.

Eva laughed. "May I please come in?" she asked, not bothering with her prepared speech. "My name is Evaleen. I've got something that I think will give your skin a nice, dewy look. I would like to give you a free demonstration to prove it to you. Are you interested?"

The woman's hands flew self-consciously up to her face. "Sure, why not?"

Elated, Evaleen followed the young woman inside. Soon they were sitting at the kitchen table. With the woman's permission,

Evaleen rubbed cream into her face, exclaiming over what a big difference it made.

"Only once in the morning and once at night does wonders," she said.

She held up a hand mirror to show the woman how much fresher and brighter her skin looked.

"You know what?" the woman said, turning this way and that to admire her glowing face. "I do look better. I'll take a jar. And a jar of your hand cream, too. My husband will probably kill me for spending our grocery money, but I don't care. I love the way my skin feels and so will he."

She laughed a wicked laugh, and winked.

Back out on the street, the sun chose that moment to shine down on her like a blessing. Maybe Eva couldn't do it, but Evaleen obviously could.

So it was Evaleen who hurried to the next house, a white two-story colonial with a turret. But before Eva could get a word out, the woman slammed the door in her face.

Eva reminded herself that the woman didn't know her, had never met her, so it wasn't about her or what she had to sell. And besides, Evaleen was a lot tougher than Eva and rejection didn't bother her nearly as much. Nor did she take it as personally, since she wasn't her real self after all.

Women continued to slam the door in her face, but at the fifth house, a young woman let her in and bought a jar of skin lubricating cream. At the eleventh house, the woman bought two jars of hand cream, one for herself and one for her married daughter as a birthday present.

Although a lot of people were too broke to buy anything, some women still had money to spend. Her new goal was to find them. The only way to do that was to keep knocking on one door after another.

By the end of the day, her back and shoulders ached from carrying her heavy bag and standing so straight, but she barely noticed. Her dream was working.

As brave, strong, confident Evaleen, she could do this.

That night, at home, she proudly poured the money she had collected onto the kitchen table. The coins clinked and clanked on the wooden table top, making a satisfying sound. Drawn by the noise, Ma left the radio and joined her at the table. An amazed, happy look crossed her pale face as Eva began to count the money.

"Fifteen dollars," Eva said, when she finished. "That's what I sold today, Ma. Can you believe it?"

"Why, you've got enough there to buy a little coffee," Ma noted, her face lighting up with joy. "It seems like forever since I had a good cup of coffee."

"I made enough money today to buy us something to eat that doesn't come from a can or box," Eva said excitedly, "and maybe even pay a little on the rent. By the way, Ma, call me Evaleen. That's my name now."

"Evaleen? I'm not sure I like that. Your father and I gave you the name Eva Marie after your father's aunt. It's a perfectly nice name."

"Ma, you were never that crazy about her. Besides, I need a new name, one that suits the beauty business better than just plain Eva. I have to get used to the idea of being Evaleen, and so do you."

Her mother looked at her silently for the longest time before she said, "To me, you will always be Eva, but if you think it will help your sales, I guess it's okay."

Eva felt a shot of relief. "The name made a real difference today in my sales, and I intend to keep it permanently. Besides, I like it. Now I'm going to call my friends and tell them how I did today so they'll know their faith in me was justified. Then I'm going to run down to Kroger's and buy us something else to eat for a change. While I'm there, I'll buy us a little coffee, too."

"Oh, boy," Ma said. Her eyes lit up. "That would be something."

Seeing her mother's happiness, Eva's joy expanded until it could have filled the whole world. Bursting with her good news, Eva picked up the phone and called Shu.

Her mother answered the phone.

"She's out with Sam. She's always with him lately. I don't know what to think."

Eva didn't know what to think, either. There'd been rumors around school about Sam. They said he had beat up a girl, once. She tried telling Shu what she heard, but Shu had laughed as though Eva told a good joke, and changed the subject. Eva let it go, figuring it was just a rumor and there was nothing to it.

Now she wondered again.

Eva called Gussie next.

"Congratulations," Gussie crowed. "You did it. I'm so proud of you."

"I was so scared, Gussie," Eva bubbled.

"But it didn't stop you," Gussie said. "I would have given up the moment the first time anybody said no."

"No, you wouldn't. Not if you needed to do it bad enough. Now if I can just get up the nerve to do it again tomorrow, and the day after that."

"Oh, you will," Gussie said. "I know you."

"By the way, call me Evaleen from now on."

"Evaleen? Why would you change your name?"

"Because I made more money when I began to think and act like an Evaleen than I ever possibly could as plain old Eva."

"Wow," Gussie said. "Change your name, change your life. I never thought of that. Maybe I could come up with a new name too. Hmm, I'll have to think about that. Evaleen, huh? Okay, Evaleen, if you say so."

Gussie changed the subject to talk about her boss, how amazing, how kind, how handsome, how smart, on and on.

When they finally hung up the phone, Eva immediately dialed the operator and gave Josh's number. As always, she was a little uncomfortable calling him, because girls weren't supposed to ever call boys, but today was special.

To her relief, Josh himself picked up the phone.

"Of course you were successful," he said, when she told him.

"Too bad you don't use beauty creams," Eva said. "You would be such a pushover."

"You're right. I always was a sucker for a good-looking woman."

Eva went on to tell him about her name change and to begin referring to her as Evaleen.

"Eva's a beautiful name," he protested. "Why change it?"

"Because when I acted like an Evaleen, sales picked up."

"Okay," he said, caving in immediately, as he always did where she was concerned. "If you say so. It'll take me a while to get used to it, but I'll adjust."

"Thanks Josh," she said. "I knew I could count on you."

The two friends said goodbye and she hung up the phone. Josh always made her feel good. Too bad he wasn't Hero.

As she drove to Krogers, she went over everything that happened that day, and lingered lovingly on her successes.

Back at home, Ma and she savored the hamburgers and the real coffee Ma made from Eva's purchases.

Eva ended the day by writing a list of everything she had to do tomorrow, something she would do every working day for the rest of her life.

Shu never did call back.

Chapter Seven

One year later, in June, Hero returned home on the train just about the time that Joe Louis became heavyweight champion of the world and Amelia Earhart was gearing up for her round-the-world flight. Hero loved the wild, open, anything-goes attitude of Chicago. He might have stayed forever except for his employer's discovery of his little scheme of loaning money two-for-one to his fellow employees. They were always running short of money right before payday. His scheme worked nicely until someone ratted him out to the boss, who fired him on the spot and threatened jail time.

Hero took it as a sign to return home.

Although unemployment was still high all over the country, things were beginning to look up a little. There was a good possibility that he could get a union job making five dollars a day driving a truck, although the idea didn't appeal to him much. Hero felt he was above that sort of thing and that something better awaited him, although he had no idea what that could be.

Back in Emerson, he hailed a cab at the train station and had the cabbie take him to the warehouse where his parents still lived. As he stepped out of the cab, he noticed the look of pity on the cabbie's face and it stung.

To show the man how wrong he was, Hero added a huge tip to the bill, then with a swagger headed for the warehouse. He saw a squirrel hanging upside down like a trapeze artist in the scraggly maple tree in the trash-filled empty lot next door. He paused to light a cigarette, took a couple of deep puffs and watched the squirrel's antics for a bit, then put the cigarette out, placed his Derby at the proper jaunty angle, opened the front door and stepped inside.

The dank, oily smell hit his nostrils and made him wince.

God, what a dump, he thought.

He'd been sending his parents a money order every month. Couldn't they have at least cleaned up the place? Through a crack in the door to the back room he saw a dim light. The only other light filtered through the lone dirt-crusted window.

"Mom, Dad, I'm home!" he shouted as he entered the back room. "Where the hell are ya? The prodigal son has returned."

"Hero, is that you?" His mother's voice sounded so weak and quavering that he didn't recognize it at first.

She rose from her chair at the kitchen table to greet him. His father stood next to her, wordless and stiff.

"It's disgusting in here and it smells," Hero roared. "How can you stand it? Hey Dad," he said, grabbing his father in a massive bear hug.

But his father did not reciprocate.

Surprised and hurt by his father's lack of reaction, Hero awkwardly let him go.

"Dad, God I missed you and Mom too." He spoke hurriedly to cover up his feelings. "Hey, I've got something for you."

He dug into the pocket of his jacket and pulled out a wad of cash he'd been saving to give to them at this very moment. He slapped it into his father's outstretched palm.

His father pocketed the money without a change of expression. It was as though his son had handed him a cheap souvenir, or money that was owed to him.

Hero, shocked at his father's lack of response, stepped back and took a good look at his parents.

His mother was thinner and even less substantial than before he left. Her eyes had an anxious look. She wore her pearls around her neck as always, but they looked out of place on her plain black dress, which had a large spot on the lace collar.

His father appeared shrunken and dry and old. His eyes had a shiny, wet quality they never had before.

As the three stood together, his father kept glancing down at a newspaper on the kitchen table as though he were desperate to finish some article he'd been reading. Hero's mother stood before Hero, wringing her hands like a frightened baby bird.

Seeing them acting so pitiful and weak irritated Hero, but that was immediately replaced by concern.

"Didn't you get any of the money orders I sent you? What's wrong? Are you sick? Mom, is Dad sick?"

His mother's mouth opened and closed like a fish drowning in air.

"He's fine, dear," she said, finally. "We're both fine. You're just so, so very loud now."

"It's because I'm glad to be home, Mom. There's a lot to be loud about. Jeeze."

He marched over to the cubbyhole where his father always hid his booze and pulled out a half-filled bottle. He noticed the label.

"You shouldn't be drinking this rotgut," he said. "I sent you enough money to buy better hooch than that. In fact I sent you enough money to live in a better place, too. Why in the hell are you still here?"

His father raised an arm aimlessly. "I… It's been…"

He sat down suddenly, looking at his hands as though wishing to do something with them, but not knowing quite what. He picked up the newspaper and began to read it, effectively shutting out his son.

Hero shivered. Why was his father acting so weird? It was like…like they were both loony, he thought.

"Dad, you're only fifty-three, for Chrissakes. It's too soon to give up."

His father nodded but continued to hunch over the newspaper like it was a lifeline. His mother stared anxiously at the floor, refusing to look at him.

Hero was horrified. His parents were worse off than when he'd left them. With all the money he sent, they should have been fine.

"What happened?" he asked. "I don't understand."

Slowly, painfully with many starts and stops, the truth emerged.

His father had given the money to a man he used to do business with. The man owned Gordon Investments and promised high returns. Other than buying the bare necessities, they invested all the money that Hero sent. At first the money they invested doubled, and then tripled.

"Things were going great. We were getting really high returns. We were about to put money down on a house, when..." his father said, not quite looking him in the eye.

"Gordon was indicted for running a Ponzi scheme," his mother said, finishing her husband's sentence.

"We got caught up in it," his father said. "I'm sorry, son. I'm so sorry."

Hero felt sick. He had sent half of every dollar he had been able to get his hands on, and they had literally tossed it away. While Hero was scamming others to give his parents money, someone was scamming them.

Hero might have laughed, were it not so painful.

"I still have enough money left to get you out of this Godforsaken hole," he said, stifling his anger. "I won't have you living like this."

"Don't swear, dear," his mother said.

She abruptly changed the subject. "Mrs. Gaithner came by the other day. You remember her, dear? She used to be your father's secretary. She brought us some bread she made. It was delicious. She said her son Jake still hasn't found a job and had to move back home. He's a welder, now. Do you remember him?"

"Jake Gaithner, a welder?" Hero said, going along with her. "He was selling Packards when I knew him. Making buckets of money selling cars to rich people."

"He has a wife and a family. He had to do something..." Her voice drifted off, as though it took a lot of effort to speak.

It was occurring to Hero that his parents had been completely defined by their titles – banker and wife of a banker, pillars of the community, to be looked up to and admired. Without those titles, they seemed like needy baby animals, unable to fend for themselves.

Clearly, his childhood was over. It was absurd to think that his relationship to his parents might stay the same now that he was grown up.

Grief took him, for them, for himself, and for all that had changed and would never be the same. He looked away so they wouldn't see the tears in his eyes.

"You still volunteering?" he asked his mother when he could control his emotions again.

"Oh no, dear," she said, in a tone as though speaking to a young child. "I haven't done anything like that for a long time. There's no money, you know."

"Volunteering is about helping people," Hero said, more sharply than he intended. "That's what you always said. You don't need money to help people. We've always helped others."

She shook her head, a tiny, pitying smile on her lips. "We're not in a position these days, I'm afraid…"

Hero was astonished to hear her speak so. She had the same cultured voice he remembered, but her face was so gaunt, and her eyes darted around the room. She had aged ten years in the time he was gone.

He asked a few more questions. She attempted to answer, but her replies became vaguer and vaguer, as though conversation exhausted her. Neither asked him about Pinkerton or Chicago or why he had come home or even where he got the money he sent them. In fact, they seemed to barely have any interest in him at all.

"I had toast for breakfast," his mother said weakly, as though her voice were about to give out. "And coffee. We had coffee…"

"We had vegetable soup for lunch," his father chimed in. "It was good."

"We're going to have a tuna casserole for dinner," his mother said. "You'll like that, won't you?"

#

That night, Hero slept on the old mattress on the floor. It felt even lumpier and thinner than before. He spent the night thinking. He had enough money to rent a place for his parents, rent a place for himself and buy a car, but not much more than that. There were no jobs that he would consider doing and although it was tempting, he decided not to run the risk of running his two-for-one scam in Emerson. He would have to find some other way of making money. What that was, he wasn't sure right now.

He spent the next day searching for a place for his parents to live. He returned that afternoon to announce he had found a furnished row house on Dorchester Avenue. The owner, a recent widow, was planning to move in with her daughter. She had tried to sell the house and lowered the price twice, but still no takers. Desperate, she decided to rent it at a reduced rate. As an incentive, she left her furniture for the new tenants. Although his parents were not enthusiastic, they agreed, and Hero had them moved in by the weekend.

Hero then found himself a two-room apartment on Branson Street near downtown Emerson. One room held a bed and the other room a sink, stove, kitchen table and chairs. He shared a hall bathroom with two other tenants. To get around he bought a used Ford Coupe.

His parents didn't bother to see where he lived, nor did they ask him about it. He wondered if they even noticed when he left. He worried a bit that he might be too much like them, himself.

In truth, had Hero not been supporting them, he would not have been affected by them at all. When anything became remotely painful for him, he merely shifted his attention to something more pleasant, a habit he had developed since the day their home was foreclosed upon. And more pleasant meant hanging out at O'Dooles, which was within walking distance of his apartment.

To pick up extra money, he began to bet on pool. Once a big farm kid accused him of getting him drunk and losing the first two games on purpose so as to increase the stakes. Hero denied it vehemently. The farm kid took a wild swing at him. Old man O'Doole, a former wrestling champ, picked up the kid by the seat of his trousers before the swing could land and tossed him out the door.

Later that same day, O'Doole met with Hero in private. Hero had heard the rumors about O'Doole, but had chosen to ignore them until now. Still O'Doole had always treated him well, and he hoped that would continue, although being close up and personal with the man always made him a little nervous because of his big size.

In his dusty office, from behind his beat-up old desk, piled high with papers, O'Doole got right to the point.

"I seen you play pool," he said. "You're good, and you never get rattled. And you're easy with the gents. Even that kid, you kept your cool. I like that. It's good for business, 'sides you win a hell of a lot more than you lose. So I have a proposition for you. I'll stake you at pool and when you win, I take a percentage, say fifty percent. Lose, you owe me nothin'. How does that sound, kid?"

Was he serious? But Hero could see by the look on O'Doole's face that he was dead serious. Hero couldn't believe his good luck.

"Play pool. Make money. Sounds good to me," he said, smiling.

The two men shook on it.

"Always remember you are doing business with people," his father used to say. "It's no good if there's only one guy making money, because if that's the case no one will want to do business with you."

Hero remembered those words and ever after was careful to make sure that O'Doole always profited from his being there.

#

A month later, Hero woke up around noon, his usual time. Once up and moving around, he thought about giving his old school chums a call to see how everyone was doing, but could not quite bring himself to face them. They all probably still felt sorry for him, a thought he couldn't abide.

Instead, he focused his thoughts on Lark Olson, who he promised to meet at O'Dooles around five. He had met her on the train coming home. She had gone to Chicago hoping to become an actress, but quickly ran out of money. Hero was smitten, but she made it abundantly clear that she had no intention of marrying someone as poor as he was. Still, there was a deep attraction between them and they continued to see each other.

It was a lovely spring day and Hero decided to walk the short distance to O'Dooles. The sky was filled with fluffy clouds and flowers bloomed everywhere.

He knew he looked sharp in his grey slacks, pale green shirt and white fedora tilted at the proper jaunty angle. When two young girls came towards him from the opposite direction, he tipped his hat and smiled a flirty, rakish smile. They smiled back, obviously flattered by his attention. He continued on his way, looking forward to spending some time with Lark.

Suddenly, it wasn't Lark he was thinking about anymore. It was the vision coming towards him, a woman with shiny red hair and skin that glowed like porcelain in the afternoon light. She was dressed simply in wide-legged pants and a white blouse, and walked with a confident, almost regal air. The one surprise was the big canvas bag she carried. It looked almost as big as she was. He realized with a start that he knew her from somewhere, but where?

He tried desperately to remember so he would have an excuse to approach her, but could come up with nothing. Maybe he could offer her some assistance with the bag. He sped up.

Seeing him approach, her face lit up with a big smile.

"Hero. What a surprise. Long time, no see."

Seeing the confused look on his face, she said, "It's me, Eva Doyle. From high school. Don't you remember?"

"Oh my God, Eva Doyle? That is you. I wasn't sure. You look so," he stumbled for the right word, "different."

She laughed at his discomfort. "Of course it's me, silly. Only I'm known as Evaleen now."

"Evaleen, huh? Nice. So why the big bag?"

"I sell skin lubricating creams that I manufacture myself from a recipe my grandmother used to make. You should buy your mother a jar. My cream works great on older skin."

She spoke quickly in a warm, professional sounding voice, the words tumbling out. Then she appeared to catch herself.

She slowed down and spoke in a more normal, conversational voice. "How about you? I heard you went to Chicago. How was it?"

Hero could not stop staring at her or breathing in her lilac scent. He could feel the sparks fly. Had she looked this good in high school, and he just hadn't paid attention? What an idiot he was not to have tried harder to get to know her back then.

"Chicago was okay," he said, pretending a nonchalance he didn't feel, "but if I had known you were going to grow up and look like this," he said, unable to stop himself, "I certainly would have come home sooner."

Then, because he didn't want her to know how attracted he was, he changed the subject. "How's your old gang doing?"

"Well, let's see," Evaleen said. "Shu married Sam Stryker."

As she spoke, she gazed deeply into his eyes, then seemed embarrassed at her interest and looked quickly away. Hero noticed and was delighted.

"You remember Sam, captain of the football team," she continued. "Sam keeps her pretty well occupied. I hardly see her anymore. Josh Goldman is going to college. He's getting a degree in finance – the company his father works for, the same place he worked part-time, sponsored him. Gussie hooked up with her boss. She was hired to take care of his sick wife and ended up falling for him." She stopped to take a breath. "Oh dear, I probably shouldn't have told you that. Gussie will kill me for spilling the beans."

"That's okay," he said. "I have a short memory. What about you?"

He was desperate to know every detail, including did she have a boyfriend.

"I'm living at home with my mother. My father passed away. He died of a heart attack."

Hero noticed the look of pain in her eyes. "Um, I didn't hear about that. I'm sorry."

An uncomfortable silence followed. He was about to ask if she'd like to join him for a beer sometime, when Lark appeared. She was dressed in a white skirt and a tight red sweater that showed her large, round breasts to best advantage. Her bleached, almost white hair was worn in deep finger waves. Her lips were a bright red, her blue eyes were lined with kohl, her overly-tweezed eyebrows had been drawn in a perfect thin arch.

"Uh, I'd like you to meet Lark uh, Lark, um..." He floundered about, embarrassed. Why couldn't he remember her last name?

"Zimmerman," she said finishing his sentence.

"Nice to meet ya," she said with dramatic flair. She gave Evaleen a scornful stare, letting her gaze go disdainfully from Evaleen's face down to her feet, then back again. "And you are?"

"Evaleen," Evaleen said, speaking in a smooth, confident tone. "Have you heard of Fresh-As-A-Daisy skin care creams? I own the company. I hope you don't mind my saying so, but your skin looks a little dry to me." She pressed her lips together as though concerned. "I have a product that could help you with that."

"Oh. My hands could probably use some work, too," Lark said, holding her two broad mitts up for Evaleen to see. A gold ring with a small stone gleamed on the wedding finger of her left hand. "Can your cream help these?"

"Isn't it beautiful?" she asked, noticing Evaleen's interest in the ring. "Hero gave it to me."

"Yes, it's lovely," Evaleen said not quite looking her in the eye. "I also make a good hand cream, and I happen to have a sample or two of both my skin lubricating cream and my hand cream. Would you like to try some?"

To Hero's dismay, Evaleen seemed preoccupied with Lark and not him.

"Sure, why not?" Lark said.

Evaleen handed Lark two small samples wrapped in waxed paper with Fresh-As-A-Daisy labels on top. "Try this for a few days. Your skin will look so much better, you'll be amazed. My number's on the packet. If you wish to place an order, you can give me a call. Now, if you'll both excuse me, I really must get back to work."

Evaleen gave them both a tight little smile and left.

Hero could still smell her lilac perfume as he watched her walk away. Seeing him stare after Evaleen, mouth agape, Lark gave him a withering look, which he chose to ignore.

"Let's go, Babe," he said to her. "All this talk is making me thirsty."

#

At five o clock, Evaleen headed for home, her long day finally over. She tried not to think about Hero, but the more she tried not to, the more she did.

He belongs to someone else, she reminded herself several timcs, then her thoughts would circle right back to how good he looked, how little he had changed, how wonderful it was to see him, and how he had looked right into her eyes.

As she opened the front door and climbed the steps to their apartment, she wondered if he was thinking about her right now. She hoped so.

"I lost my house keys," Ma said, breaking into Evaleen's thoughts as she stepped in the door. "I can't find them anywhere."

"Let me look," Evaleen said, putting her bag down on a chair.

She searched for Ma's keys beneath a chair cushion and wherever else she thought they might be. After searching the entire apartment, she gave up and went to get a glass of milk, and to her surprise found the keys on top of the butter dish in the refrigerator. This was the second time she found Ma's keys in the refrigerator, and she was beginning to worry about it. Ma was becoming increasingly forgetful.

As Eva started another batch of cream, she tried not to think about Ma or Hero, but to concentrate on getting everything just right, because a mistake could cost her money and time, neither of which she had to spare. She barely made enough to pay their bills, pay the rent, buy a few groceries and eke out a few nickels for The Salvation Army Home for Unwed Mothers, which she gave in Pa's name to assuage the guilt which haunted her nights.

Chapter Eight

Evaleen did not see Hero again, although she looked for him everywhere. One Friday night, two weeks before Christmas, Evaleen was writing down her expenses and sales for the week in the account book that Josh set up for her when the phone rang. Exhausted from her long day and not really in the mood to talk to anyone, she nevertheless picked up the phone, thinking it might be a customer.

"How the hell are ya?" Shu asked, not bothering with the preliminaries.

Evaleen felt a burst of pleasure at hearing her friend's voice again. "I'm fine. It's been a while."

Evaleen tried to keep the reproof out of her voice. "I was beginning to wonder if you were mad at me."

"Don't be ridiculous. I could never be mad at you. Why would you think such a thing?"

"I called three times, and Sam said you were either gone or napping. You never called back, so I didn't know what to think."

"Oh, that's just Sam," Shu said. "He's so forgetful. And now that I'm pregnant, he's worse than ever that way."

"You're pregnant?" Evaleen said, surprised and thrilled. "Congratulations."

"Right now I feel like a bloated pig and I've been having false labor pains lately, too. But that's not why I'm calling. Sam got a job working for the W.P.A. as a welder. We decided to throw a New Year's bash to celebrate. I figure one big blast before I pop. I told Sam if I couldn't have this party I would divorce him for sure, and for once he gave in. I don't give a damn what people say about hiding yourself behind closed doors when you're pregnant or spending money you haven't got. I need to have a little fun and to hell with whether the rent gets paid. If I don't get a few laughs, I'll die before this kid ever arrives. By the way, I ran into Hero the other day. Of course, I invited him to my party. I can't wait to see him again. He said he's coming for sure. Please say you're coming too. I miss you."

Evaleen caught a strangely anxious undertone to Shu's voice. What was going on here?

Evaleen knew that if she asked her outright, Shu would deny anything was wrong. Shu always did have too much pride. She was the kind of person who could be at death's door and insist everything was fine.

"I'd love to see you and Gussie and Josh too, but I've got a lot on my plate right now," Evaleen said, stalling for time.

"Oh, don't give me that. You need a break and I won't take no for an answer. New Year's Eve, eight o'clock. Be there."

Evaleen had to smile at Shu's mock serious tone. "Okay, okay, count me in."

"Don't you dare fink out on me, either."

"I won't," Evaleen said, laughing.

Shu's right, Evaleen thought as she hung up the phone. I do need a break and it would be great to see my old pals. As for seeing Hero and his fiancé, she wasn't so sure.

When she saw him last and their eyes met, the feeling of attraction was like a physical thing. But he was engaged to that Lark woman and Evaleen was being ridiculous for imagining something that didn't exist. Still, for her own peace of mind, she decided to avoid him if at all possible.

#

On Christmas Eve, Ma helped Eva decorate a small tree she'd purchased for a quarter. The next morning, over cups of steaming hot chocolate, they exchanged presents. Evaleen gave Ma a flannel nightgown, slippers and the console radio she saw the day she tried to get a loan from the banks. In turn, Ma gave Evaleen an opal necklace that her own mother had given her and a pair of mittens she had been knitting in secret. For dinner, Evaleen splurged and they had roast chicken, gravy, canned green beans and biscuits. And for once the radio was tuned to music instead of soap operas.

That night, as they sat together on the davenport listening to the radio, Evaleen looked over at her mother, so tiny and meek. She was worried about her. There were days when her mother could barely remember her own name, and kept asking the same question over and over, and other days like this when she was more like her old self. Thankfully, she was having one of her good days.

#

New Year's Eve, a little after eight, Evaleen, after spending the last two hours getting dressed and putting on her makeup, slipped on her camel wrap coat purchased from a second-hand store on sale and prepared to leave for Shu's party. She was proud of the coat. It fit perfectly and had a yellow lining that to Evaleen's mind was the same color as liquid gold. Underneath she wore a green velvet dress purchased from the secondhand store for a dollar. She purchased it specifically for the party because, even though Hero was with someone else, she still wanted to impress him. She justified the expense by reasoning that the dress could be worn for both special and business occasions. On her feet were black suede high heels, also used, but new to her.

The evening was cold and the air was sharp as she drove. At the duplex where Shu and Sam lived, tall evergreens, tipped nearly over by the heavy snow, appeared to guard the front door. Music and people talking in loud, excited voices greeted her as she carefully navigated the icy sidewalk and climbed the steps to the second floor. Feeling somewhat unsure of herself, she hesitated for a moment. Then, putting on a bright smile, she stepped into the sparsely furnished living room, already packed with people.

Shu rushed up to greet her. Her red-silk kimono did not hide the fact that she was very close to giving birth. Her face was flushed and her eyes were bright with excitement, which made her even more beautiful than usual.

At the sight of her very pregnant friend, tears popped into Evaleen's eyes.

"I missed you so much," she whispered.

"I missed you, too," Shu bubbled, oblivious to Evaleen's tears. "I'm so glad you could make it. I would love to talk, but I have to do my hostess stuff right now. I'll have to catch you later."

She rushed off before Evaleen could reply.

That was it? Evaleen felt oddly hurt. What was so wrong, that Shu couldn't stop for a moment to talk? Or was it something else? Almost against her will, Evaleen's eyes went to Sam, who stood alone in a patch of shadow in one corner of the living room. Devil-like.

Astonished at the unbidden thought, she was unprepared when Hero and Lark appeared and swept up to her. He wore navy slacks and a white shirt under a navy and white V-neck sweater. Evaleen thought he looked like an ad in Vanity Fair. Lark wore a tight red jersey dress that showcased every curve. A tide of panic rose within her at the sight of them both.

"Hello, stranger," he said.

"Hello," Evaleen said, acting a calmness she did not feel. Before she could say anything more, Josh showed up, almost clumsy in his rush to join them.

Josh, in his own clean-cut way, was just as handsome as Hero. Girls were always circling around him, although Evaleen wasn't sure he noticed. But the fire she felt for Hero was a thousand times brighter than what she had ever felt for Josh. Too bad too, because Josh was such a good man.

But Hero was the kind of man who could make you feel restless, hungry, hopeful, and despairing with just one look from those hot, dark eyes. Josh was simply a good and dear friend. Nothing like Hero, who was obviously in love with someone else, someone much prettier and sexier than Evaleen could ever hope to be.

"Excuse us, please," she said, desperate to salvage her pride and get away from Hero and his woman. "I'm starving and I need to talk to Josh about something."

She grabbed Josh by the hand and rushed him away towards the dining room.

"What was that about?" Josh asked as they stood together at the dining room table, noshing on potato chips and cheese dip.

"Nothing. I just wanted to spend some time with you," she lied. The words sounded fake, even to her. She hoped Josh wouldn't notice. "How the heck are you?"

"It has been a while," Josh said and smiled tenderly down at her. "I assume you've been busy becoming hugely successful. By the way you look fabulous."

"Why, thank you," Evaleen said, trying to give him her full attention, although her mind was racing after seeing Hero. "You look pretty good yourself."

She asked about his work at the brokerage and how his studies were going. He asked about her business.

After a few minutes, Tom Gordon joined them. Tom, short and rotund, was a writer who always had a slightly preoccupied air, as though he were secretly taking notes. He had a job working for the WPA writing government pamphlets.

When she happened to look up again, she saw Hero standing alone. Lark was off to one side, in deep conversation with a well-dressed older man. Evaleen caught Hero's eye, then quickly looked away.

Shortly afterward, unable to help herself, she looked over again to see if he was still there. He smiled back at her and headed in her direction.

Not wishing another encounter like the last one, she excused herself quickly, left the group and ducked into the kitchen to calm down. She was leaning up against a kitchen counter when Hero appeared through the kitchen door.

Thinking to avoid him, she slipped into the pantry and shut the door. She stood in the dark, barely breathing. Suddenly, the door opened and there he stood.

"Are you avoiding me?" he asked.

Her face heated up. "No, um, yes, um…shouldn't you be with your fiancé?"

"We're not engaged," Hero said. "Where did you get that idea?"

"She was wearing your ring. She said you gave it to her."

"Oh, that," Hero said dismissively. "I bought a ring off a guy selling a tray full of rings on the street and gave it to her. Is that what this is all about? Last I saw, she was slow dancing with some guy. Didn't look like she missed me at all. What about you? I can't imagine a beautiful girl like you doesn't have a guy stashed away somewhere."

Before becoming Evaleen, she would have gushed her gratitude at being told she was beautiful, then disparaged herself in some way. But she had learned the hard way that gushing, or running herself down, could lose a sale by making her appear weak and ineffectual.

She forced herself to sound calm and confident, something she had learned to do automatically, especially on days when sales were non-existent and she was positive it was her own fault and she would never sell anything again.

"Not at the moment. I really don't have time for anyone right now."

She couldn't help noticing that same fascinated look in his eyes as before. Just the thought that he was interested left her reeling with pleasure.

"How was Chicago?" she asked, anxious to change the subject.

"It's safer here," he said, as though standing in the door to a pantry, talking to a woman huddling next to some canned corn, was the most natural thing on earth.

"Chicago's a dangerous place right now. Even with Al Capone out of the way, his gang has pretty much taken over the unions. Strikes are going on all the time, and they can get pretty ugly."

She was about to ask about his job with Pinkerton when voices approached the kitchen. Hero quickly stepped inside the pantry and shut the door behind himself.

They stood together in front of shelves of dishes, pots and pans and canned goods in the pitch black. She felt her heartbeat speed up.

"I don't know about you, but I've been dying to spend an evening with some canned goods," Hero quipped.

"It's always been my dream," Evaleen shot back.

Before she could say more, Hero leaned over, put his arms around her, and kissed her full on the mouth.

"I've been wanting to do that since I saw you coming down the street looking like a movie star," he said, when he came up for air.

Instead of being thrilled as she had expected, Evaleen felt strangely bewildered. So many times she'd imagined this moment. So many times, in her fantasies, he took her in his arms and kissed her deeply, told her that he loved her, had always loved her and couldn't live without her. But it was somewhere elegant, like a fine restaurant with classical music playing in the background, or at the ocean as the waves pounded romantically. Not hiding out in somebody's pantry. In the dark. Strangely, the thought made her angry.

"What took you so long?" she asked, pulling away from him.

"I don't know what you're talking about," he said, reaching for her once more.

"I've known you most of my life, and you've never noticed me before," she said, ducking her head to avoid his next attempt to kiss her.

"I noticed you," he said. "In fact, I thought about asking you out before, but Josh was always hanging around you. What is it with you and him, anyway?"

"Josh is just a very good friend," she said.

"Whew," he said. "That's a relief. So, come to papa," he said, putting his arms around her and pulling her close. "Time's a-wastin'."

Evaleen didn't protest. She didn't have much experience with boys, much less someone like Hero Lyon. Other than a few stolen kisses behind the school when they were playing Truth or Consequences and a few group dates with Gussie and Shu, she really hadn't had much to do with boys at all. Josh had kissed her once, but that was more like a quick peck than an actual kiss, and didn't count because they were just friends.

"Come on," he said, when he noticed her hesitation. "One little kiss won't kill you."

Evaleen felt strangely reluctant and virginal now that it was actually happening. But before she could protest more, he kissed her again, crushing her to him. Maybe it was the liquor or the small dark place in which they hid or the sheer relief of knowing he wasn't engaged after all. Whatever it was, his kiss caused the most delicious sensations throughout her whole body. She kissed him back with complete abandon, drinking in the sweetness and passion and wonderful smell of his Old Spice. It was the best, most dangerous feeling she'd ever had. Better than any of her fantasies. When they finally came up for air, her heart was racing and her whole body felt hot and wet.

"I love you," he said in a surprised tone, as though he had just figured it out. "I love everything about you. The way you look, the way you move, the way you smell, everything. I'm crazy about you. I've never known anybody like you in my whole life."

Evaleen felt giddy and light headed. Had she heard right? Miracles never happened to someone like her. But whatever it was, this was too fierce, too wicked, and just plain too wonderful not to enjoy. She was in a dark pantry with the most handsome, exciting man in the world, and he was touching her in ways she could never have dared imagine.

"Honest, Eva," he said. "I swear to you I'm telling the truth."

"Evaleen," she said automatically. "I'm Evaleen now."

"Yes, Evaleen," he said softly. "I love you, Evaleen."

He sounded so sincere that joy flooded through her. Suddenly it was as if the world opened up before her, as though after a long hike through a dark and narrow mountain pass, she had come unexpectedly to a sunny green meadow.

"So why not give in?" he said, pressing himself against her, his hand creeping up to her breast.

"Because I don't want it to be like this," she said, shoving his hand away.

"Then you have to marry me," he said. His voice was full of awe, as though he'd just discovered this himself.

The shock of hearing the actual words that she'd fantasized about for so long coming out of his mouth, caused her to snap out of her blissful state. It was the booze, it had to be. He would never say words like this to her if he were sober.

The cold truth was that they were standing together in a pantry with the door shut, making out while a party was going on nearby. What if they were caught? She felt a stab of shame.

"You don't really mean that," she said, more sharply than she intended.

"Yes, I do," he said.

A kind of crazy, hopeful feeling swept over her. Imagine the two of them together, sleeping side by side every night, together every single day. She almost believed him.

But Evaleen was practical, and had just enough sense left to realize that if she said yes, he would probably wake up tomorrow and be horrified, then avoid her forever, rather than admit he had too much to drink and hadn't meant a thing he said.

"Ask me again when you're sober," she said.

"I'm not going to change my mind," he said firmly, almost belligerently. "I love you."

"I think we should get out of here," she said, taking a big breath before smoothing her dress with her hands and running her fingers through her hair. Her voice was calm, although she was trembling inside. "This has become a very dangerous place for both of us."

"Please don't go," he said in a pleading voice.

"We should at least make an appearance, for Shu's sake," Evaleen said, determined now to leave the pantry and return to the party.

"I meant what I said," he said, sounding irritated that she didn't believe him. "You'll see."

"I'm going to leave now," she said firmly. "This is not the right place for me or you."

Before he could kiss her again, she left the pantry and rejoined the party, which was now in full swing.

Trying to get her bearings by looking around, she spotted Shu in an intent conversation with three other people. Sam stood nearby, scowling as usual. She wondered why Shu, so easy-going and happy, was ever attracted to such a brooding, angry man.

Not wishing to interrupt them, she went in search of Gussie, but couldn't find her. She finally decided Gussie must not have showed up. Her boss probably called. The world could be falling apart and if her boss called, Gussie would drop everything.

Would Evaleen be like that, too? Would she drop everything to be with Hero any time he asked? Yes, she would, she decided. Any time at all.

Then she spotted Hero and Lark standing together talking. Hero had an intense look on his face. Lark looked angry. Evaleen wondered what it was about and if it had anything to do with her. She hoped not in a way and in a way she also hoped so.

She glanced at her watch. It was almost midnight. Time for the New Year's Eve kiss. She decided to leave before she saw Hero kiss Lark at midnight. Just the thought made her feel a little sick.

She went to look for Shu, found her standing with a new group of people, and interrupted her long enough to say goodbye.

"So glad you could come," Shu said. "It was so good to see you again." Her eyes darted nervously over to Sam, as though silently checking to see if talking to Evaleen met with his approval.

Evaleen thought that was strange. But what did she know? Maybe Shu was happier than she seemed. Evaleen hoped so.

Shu turned back to the group and Evaleen went to find Josh. She spotted him in the living room talking to two other people. She went over to say goodbye.

"You look like the cat that's just had some cream," he said.

"It's been a great party." She smiled.

"Oh, is that what it is?" he teased.

"Maybe," she teased him back. "Anyway, I'm going to leave now. I have a lot to do tomorrow and I need my beauty sleep."

"You don't need any beauty sleep," Josh said, "but I understand." He had a sad, disappointed look on his face. "Call me if you need me for anything."

"I will," Evaleen said.

She grabbed her coat from the pile in the bedroom and left only minutes before the clock struck midnight. As she drove home, she was thinking so intently about Hero that she ran a red light. Luckily, no cops were nearby.

#

Two days later Evaleen was still obsessing about Hero. Had she imagined the whole thing? If he was as interested as he said he was, why didn't he call? Their time in the pantry was probably just a joke to him. He probably told every girl he loved her.

She tried not to think about him. It helped that she was so busy all the time. But the moment she had a few minutes to relax, her thoughts always circled right back to him. Nights in bed were the worst. Luckily it hadn't yet affected her sales, but if she didn't get hold of her own thoughts, that could change fast.

Today was colder than usual as she left the house carrying her big pack, but that didn't stop her. The cold meant that most of the housewives would be at home, rather than off running errands. Business had fallen off after the holidays, but Evaleen wasn't too worried. In spite of the rotten economy, the month leading up to Christmas had been one of her best. It helped that more people had jobs, thanks to Roosevelt's alphabet soup of programs. Foreclosures were still rampant and people still lived in Hoovervilles, but conditions had begun to improve. And by going to better neighborhoods, where there weren't so many foreclosure signs, she was able to find women who had money to spend on their looks.

She was trudging along to the third house in a row when she heard a horn honk. She turned to look and was astonished to see Hero at the wheel of his Ford Coupe. She stared open mouthed as he parked, jumped out of the car, leaving the driver's side door open and the motor running. He dropped to his knees in front of her on the icy sidewalk.

What was that about? What was he thinking? He must be insane. Two women walking down the street stopped and stared. Another woman appeared at the door of her house.

"I know it's kind of fast," he said, "but I'm serious. I never felt like this before about anyone in my whole life. I want to marry you."

His words tumbled out in one long breathless stream. "Will you marry me, Evaleen? Come on, say yes. Please."

Evaleen was so stunned she couldn't speak at first, then her heart filled with excitement and delight.

"Yes," she said quietly.

"Was that a yes I heard?" Hero said, his eyes wide in amazement.

"Yes, you heard a yes," Evaleen said in a louder voice, before bursting into tears.

Hero stood up, brushed off his wet knees, took out his white linen handkerchief and handed it to her. When she could stop crying, he handed her a pale cream box from Johnson's Jewelry, one of the few jewelry stores in Emerson that were still open.

"It's real," he said. "The jeweler said you can cut glass with it."

Evaleen started crying all over again. Hero took the diamond ring and slipped it on her finger. She held her hand out unbelievingly to admire it. The half-carat diamond caught a beam of light and sparkled. What she had hoped for, dreamed of, was actually happening.

"Why didn't you call me after the party?" she asked, wiping her eyes.

"I wanted to find the perfect ring," he said. "And now I have."

It was all happening so fast she didn't have time to wonder why he was asking to marry her so quickly. The only thing that mattered right now was that her dream was about to become a reality and life was so wonderful it was almost unbearable.

Chapter Nine

Josh had taken two tests that morning – a spot quiz in Economics and a test in Accounting Practices and Procedures. That afternoon at his part-time job at the brokerage, a long-time client came in at the very end of the day, desperate and close to tears. He had lost his money in the stock market and was about to lose the family's home. Concerned for the man and his family, Josh stayed two extra hours after work helping him draft a proposal to the bank in an effort to help the man stave off foreclosure.

When he had done all he could, he wished the man well, left work and headed to the grocery store, where he cashed his paycheck and bought some cheese and bread for supper. Then he picked up a couple six-packs of beer at the liquor store for the monthly Saturday poker night with his college buddies. He was tired from his long day and looking forward to making himself a grilled cheese tonight and simply taking it easy.

At home in his tiny two-room apartment, he had barely taken off his coat when the phone rang. He picked it up, heard the tinkling of glasses in the background, and was surprised to hear Hero's voice.

"Hey, old man, I've got some big news," Hero said in a rush of words. "Evaleen and I are getting married tomorrow, and I want you to be my best man."

"Tell him we wouldn't consider getting married without him." Evaleen's excited voice spoke in the background.

Josh collapsed into a kitchen chair. Evaleen and Hero? Married? A car's lights chose that moment to shine through the window and flit across Josh's face, blinding him. He closed his eyes, but could still feel the brightness behind his eyelids. Other than helping Evaleen with her business plan, Josh hadn't spent much time with her in the last year. Either she was busy or he was. But would that have made any difference? Especially where Hero was concerned? As long as Josh could remember, Evaleen was attracted to Hero. Not Josh. Hero.

He always secretly hoped she would wake up one day and see Hero for what he really was – a playboy. When that happened, he planned to make his move. In the meantime, he didn't want to risk losing her friendship by declaring himself too soon, or before he could support a wife, so he kept quiet about his feelings. And now it was too late. She was marrying Hero. Tomorrow. Not Josh. Hero. Damn, damn, damn.

"Isn't this kind of fast?" Josh said, weakly. "I didn't know you two were dating."

"We've known each other all our lives," Hero said in a joking tone. "We just didn't know we were in love. Now that we do, we don't want to waste another minute. Come on, old man. Say you'll do it. It would mean a lot to us, especially to Evaleen, who considers you one of her best pals."

Josh took in a deep secret breath to calm himself.

"Of course I'll be there," he said. He was surprised at how normal he sounded, though he felt cold and strangely disconnected from reality. "Tell Evaleen I wouldn't miss it for the world."

He almost choked on the words.

"Great," Hero said. "It'll be at the Suffolk County Courthouse tomorrow. Two o'clock, Room Two-Twenty. See you then."

Josh hung up the phone. Evaleen and Hero. What an awful thought. A profound hate for Hero struck him like a cold wind. He despised the man. Hero would destroy Evaleen; destroy her for his own thoughtless, selfish, cruel reasons. He would ruin her life, cheat on her like he cheated on every other woman he'd ever been with, then drop her as if she didn't count for anything. It was too much, too much.

Josh sat at the table, staring into space. His thoughts sped from trying to understand, to accepting it, to fury, to self-pity, back to trying to understand, to not caring at all, to anguish and a feeling of being betrayed. Looking for relief, he opened a warm bottle of beer from one of the six-packs he had just purchased. He took a big swallow, then another, and another after that. It didn't help. Nothing helped. Just made him feel even worse.

He chastised himself for his unruly thoughts. It was wrong to hate Hero just because Evaleen had chosen him instead of Josh. Besides, it was his own fault. He hadn't been able to bring himself to tell her how he truly felt, out of fear that he would lose her completely. He regretted not expressing his feelings earlier, before they became close friends, so he wouldn't have to see her as a friend every day while endlessly longing for more. Evaleen held the key to his heart, he just wished he would have found a way to tell her without risking their friendship.

And now she was marrying someone else. Oh, dear God. True, even if Josh had spoken up and she agreed to be his girlfriend, he had nothing to offer her. Not yet, anyway. But what the hell did Hero have to offer? The guy didn't even have a job. That must not have mattered to Evaleen. What she wanted was Hero. Period. Not Josh. Hero!

He took another swig of his beer. Be a man, he chided himself, choking back tears. Tell her she's making a big mistake. Tell her you love her and want to marry her as soon as you can afford to support a wife. Tell her, you damn, weak-kneed fool. Tell her.

The drunker he got, the more positive he was that telling her was the right thing to do. After drinking more than he had ever drunk before at one sitting, he stumbled off to bed and passed out cold.

#

In spite of the clear sunshine, the day was cold and windy. Josh tightened his scarf around his neck as he stepped from his car and headed towards the courthouse. He was hung over with a pounding headache, and felt sick to his stomach. As he walked along, he saw a group of men and women singing union songs in loud raucous voices as they picketed Amerston's, a large department store. The sheer noise of it all made his head throb even more painfully. One of the strikers, a middle-aged man, whose young daughter stood next to him, handed Josh a leaflet which stated in bold letters,

UNDERPAID AND WORKING FOR FREE OFF THE CLOCK. Three policemen stood by, staring grimly straight ahead, hands on their night sticks, ready to pounce if the crowd became unruly.

Josh had a lot of sympathy for the strikers and wished he could join them, let a little of his misery out by chanting slogans. Instead, he gave them a thumbs-up and went plodding slowly along. He climbed the stone stairs of the courthouse slowly, like an old man. He found the right courtroom and plopped down on a bench in the hall to wait. He hoped Evaleen had changed her mind, but knew better when he saw her coming down the hall. Her face was alive with happiness. She was breathtaking, in a white wool suit with a corsage of pink roses pinned to one lapel, her coat over one arm.

Hero was right behind her. Alcohol fumes emanated from him like a cloud.

Apparently I wasn't the only one who needed some liquid courage, Josh thought, meanly. But why would Hero need to drink? He was the winner here.

"I'm so glad you could come," Evaleen said, smiling. "It wouldn't have been the same without you."

"I hope you'll be happy," he said, trying to sound normal, while breathing in the sweetness of her lilac perfume.

"Oh I will, we will," she said excitedly. "I woke up crying last night, I was so happy. I still can't believe we're actually getting married."

"Glad you could make it, old man," Hero said.

"Congratulations," Josh said, reaching out to shake hands and hating himself for congratulating the man who had bested him.

Shu arrived then like a blast of cold air, with her husband Sam close behind her. Her huge belly made it difficult to get too close but she managed to give everyone a big hug. Sam stood by, saying nothing, a sullen look on his dull, broad face. Josh was amazed to see how far along Shu was. She looked like a ripe melon about to burst. Her formerly voluptuous figure had turned to a kind of bloated, motherly fat. Her beautiful face was full of blotches, and her breasts looked like huge, soft pillows.

"You screw them and this is what happens," Sam said, and laughed at his own joke.

"I wasn't the one who wanted to screw in the first place," Shu shot back, a hurt look on her face.

"Hell, you could've fooled me."

Josh stood uncomfortably by. He wondered what the voluble, outgoing Shu saw in Sam, who never seemed to have much to say about anything. He had a reputation on the football field for being volatile and always aching for a fight. And here was Evaleen, his Evaleen, about to marry Hero, a man also totally unsuited for her. He shook his head. He would never understand women.

Seeing Hero and Evaleen together made him feel like crying. Before he broke down in front of everyone and made a complete fool out of himself, he excused himself and rushed off to the men's room. Standing at the sink, he wiped his eyes and chastised himself.

"Tell her she's making a big mistake. That she'll regret it her whole life. Tell her you love her. That you want to marry her. Tell her, you damn fool. Say something."

When he was able to calm down to the point where his grief wasn't written all over his face in the mirror, he summoned his courage and returned to the wedding party, determined to say something at the very first opportunity, at least ask her if she didn't think this was a little too fast.

He was about to step forward and ask Evaleen if he could speak to her privately when Gussie appeared, all bustling, practical energy and good cheer.

"Let's get this show on the road," Gussie said. "I haven't got all day, you know. I've got a job and I don't want to be late. Hey, Evaleen where's your Ma?"

"She hates to leave the house these days, and I didn't want to upset her by forcing her to come," Evaleen said. "I thought we'd tell her after it's all over."

"Makes sense," Gussie said. "Your poor Ma really hasn't been herself since your father died, has she?"

"No," Evaleen said, a momentary cloud of concern in her expression. "She really hasn't."

A rotund man in a suit appeared at the courtroom door, and indicated for them to come inside. The judge, a horse-faced man with droopy eyes and large ears, wearing a long black robe, was waiting for them.

Seeing the judge, Josh's desperation grew. Gussie and Shu both acted happy for her. What was wrong with everyone? Couldn't they see she was making a terrible mistake? Was he the only one who saw this? It was too late now to speak to Evaleen privately. It would have to be when the judge asked if any person could show just cause why this couple must not be joined together. God knew, he had just cause. Evaleen would be miserable married to Hero. He would make a lousy husband and a worse father. For Evaleen's sake if not for his own, Josh would have to speak up.

At the judge's behest, everyone took their place. Josh stood next to Hero, every muscle in his body tense, ready to speak the moment the judge spoke those words.

The judge began. "Dearly beloved, we are gathered here in the presence of these witnesses to join Herodotus Lyon the Third and Eva Doyle in holy matrimony, which is commended—"

Shu let out a huge squeal, like an animal caught in a trap, interrupting the judge and startling everyone.

"Oh my God, I think the baby's coming," Shu cried out. She had a frightened, vulnerable look on her face. "For God's sake, Sam, do something."

"What the hell do you expect me to do?" Sam asked, giving her a hard look. "I don't know nothin' about babies."

Shu let out another squeal of pain, and her eyes filled with panic.

Gussie rushed to her side and guided her to a bench at the back of the room. Evaleen followed.

"I'll be in my chambers," the judge said nervously, and headed for the door. His face was as white as chalk. "Let me know when you're ready to recommence the ceremony."

"I need a cigarette," Hero said and quickly left, followed by Sam close behind.

Josh stepped out to the hall, but hovered by the door in case he was needed. Sam and Hero stood together at the end of the hall, smoking. Instead of feeling sad or worried for Shu as he normally would have, he rejoiced. The whole wedding was collapsing. It was a sham. He felt a crazy, delirious relief. This marriage could not go forward. Not now. Not ever. Thank God. As for Shu, he wasn't too worried. Gussie was with her, and bringing babies into the world was something Gussie was eminently qualified for.

"Can I borrow your coat?" Gussie asked, appearing at the door.

"Gladly," Josh said. The fact that it was his good camel overcoat, the only coat he owned, occurred to him, but he handed it over anyway. His coat wasn't important at a time like this. From outside the door, Josh heard every grunt and every squeal. He worried for Shu some, but it didn't seem real or nearly as important as the fact that the marriage had been delayed, maybe even postponed. Hopefully, forever.

That thought was interrupted by Shu's long, loud scream, which seemed to echo down the hallway of the courthouse. Evaleen appeared shortly afterward at the door.

"I know it sounds bad," she said, "but Gussie says it's all perfectly normal and nothing to worry about."

"That's good," Josh said, then decided to take advantage of this moment. "Evaleen, there's something I need to say to you."

Before Josh could get out another word, Shu screamed again and Evaleen rushed off to be with her.

"We need newspapers," Evaleen said, the next time she appeared at the door.

Josh rushed down the hall, past Hero and Sam, and found a pile in a garbage bin in the janitor's closet. He ignored the two men and hurried the papers back to Evaleen, waiting at the door. Josh had barely sat down again when he heard what sounded like an animal grunting in pain. A baby started to cry. Josh breathed a huge sigh of relief.

Gussie appeared at the door this time. "Josh, do you have a pocket knife?"

Josh could smell the slightly metallic odor of blood from the room, and it made him feel a little sick as he handed over his pocket knife. Moments later, Evaleen appeared and, ignoring everyone, raced down the hall, returning shortly with a pile of rags from the janitor's closet. She disappeared inside the courtroom before Josh could ask her what was happening.

She reappeared a few minutes later, a big grin on her face, to inform Josh, Sam and Hero, all standing together now outside the courtroom door, that they could come in. The three men, all acting sheepish and tentative, approached Shu. Her face was bathed in sweat, and two wet spots showed on the bosom of her dress, as she held a tiny, red-faced infant in her arms, swaddled tightly in cleaning rags.

Sam looked scared and smaller than usual as he peered down at his child. Hero's face was unusually grey as he, too, looked down at the baby. Josh stared at this tiny, wriggling, red-faced human being, who only a short time earlier had resided in Shu's swollen stomach. He felt pure amazement at seeing this brand new human being for the first time.

"Her name is Adreanna, after my grandmother," Shu said. "If it was a boy, we planned to name him Sam, Junior."

"This kid came so fast, you should name her Bunny," Hero said with a grin.

"Bunny will be her nickname," Shu said, and laughed.

Even Sam had to smile.

Gussie and Evaleen accompanied Shu and Bunny, a name the baby would carry for the rest of her life, to the ladies' room to finish cleaning up. When Shu reappeared grinning tiredly, her baby in her arms, Gussie went to inform the judge he could now recommence the ceremony.

Everyone lined up again, including Josh. In the few harrowing moments while Shu gave birth, he had gained some perspective. His line of thinking changed: This was what Evaleen wanted, had always wanted. And now it was happening for her. It was Hero she wanted. Not Josh. Hero. It hurt terribly, but it was her choice to make. Not his. All he could do now was to wish her the best.

The judge began again, speaking the beautiful words quickly in his hurry to get it over.

"You may now kiss the bride," he said finally.

Josh looked away, unable to bear the sight.

Chapter Ten

The sky, the dark shadows, the moon with its hazy halo, even the snow seemed extraordinarily beautiful to Evaleen as the wedding party finished their celebratory dinner, said goodbye and went their separate ways. Evaleen was so happy she couldn't stop smiling.

"How about a kiss from the missus?" Hero said, jokingly when they were both in the car.

She was thrilled to oblige. One kiss led to another, and to another after that. But before it could get out of hand, Evaleen reminded Hero it was already well past seven and they needed to drive over to his parents' house to give them the news before it was too late. Hero gave in, but not happily. As Evaleen rearranged her clothing and reapplied her lipstick, she worried. She knew she didn't belong in Hero's parents' world. She wasn't sure how they would feel about their marriage, but they were his parents and as uncomfortable as it was, they needed to know.

On State Street, Hero made a right turn and parked in front of the first house on the block. Evaleen was surprised at how small and ordinary-looking the house was. She knew his family lost their mansion and lived in a warehouse for a time, but somehow she expected them to live in an upper-class neighborhood now, or at least in something larger than this.

"Beats the warehouse," Hero said with a shrug, when he saw the look on her face.

"I'm sure it does," Evaleen said quickly, as she stepped from the car. Hero offered her his arm and she happily accepted it, as they hurried up the icy, un-shoveled sidewalk.

At the front door, he turned the key in the lock and let himself in. Evaleen, feeling nervous and strangely unsure of herself, followed him into the living room.

The house was eerily silent and had a musty, dry smell. At first glance, the living room appeared to be overflowing with a mélange of mismatched armchairs, lamps and end tables. There was no actual clutter, but the room had an uncared-for air, as if everything were covered with a fine film of dust.

"Anybody home?" Hero called out as they headed towards the back of the house.

Hero's mother appeared at the doorway to the kitchen. Evaleen was taken aback at her appearance. She seemed dangerously thin, and the skin on her face looked like waxed paper. Her eyes were deep set and filmed over with cataracts, which gave her a blank, haunted air. In spite of that, she stood stiffly erect in her faded black dress, like a dowager queen. She wore a single strand of pearls around her neck, which Evaleen would later learn she rarely took off, even for bed. She moved into the room slowly, as though in great pain.

Hero's father came in behind her. He wore a tattered grey sweater filled with old food spots, and grey dress slacks, shiny from too much ironing. Evaleen felt a wave of sympathy for this fragile couple who had fallen so far.

That is, until Evaleen noticed a small, almost unnoticeable sneer cross his mother's face, as though she'd bitten into something sour. She had noticed Evaleen standing next to Hero. Evaleen recognized the look and felt a familiar twist in her stomach, the same feeling that she still got sometimes when she had a bad day, positive she was nothing at all, a nobody pretending to be a somebody.

But not even his mother's sour look could defeat her right now. This was her moment. She was happy, happier than she could ever remember and nothing and nobody could spoil it for her.

"I didn't hear you come in," his mother said. Her voice was thin and flat.

"Well, here we are, and I have some great news," Hero announced, almost shyly.

No one sat down. It was awkward and Evaleen felt self-conscious. More than anything, she wanted his parents to like her.

"You remember Eva Doyle. Although she's known as Evaleen these days."

His father glanced over at Evaleen. He pursed his lips in a frown. "Evaleen. Hmm. One of your little school chums, I presume."

Evaleen stiffened at the condescension in his voice, her joy quickly fading.

"Yes, Dad," Hero said evenly, as though holding himself back. "We went to the same school. She has her own business now. She makes beauty creams and sells them door-to-door."

"Oh, is that so," his father said, obviously not impressed.

Listening to them discuss her, as though she were not standing right there, made Evaleen feel a little sick. All the careful work on herself, the hair, the makeup, the clothing, was just an attempt to cover up her innate inferiority, and it wasn't working. They could see behind the mask. Sweat stains began to appear beneath her armpits.

"I have something important to tell you," Hero said, with a forced smile.

Both parents came to attention, an identical suspicious look on their pale faces.

"Evaleen and I were married today." Hero spit out the words as though he couldn't get them out fast enough.

His mother's face appeared to collapse. She sank down into the closest chair, put her head in her hands and sobbed, great wrenching sobs, as though someone she loved had just died. Hero's father, an angry, bewildered look on his face, patted his wife clumsily on the shoulder in an attempt to console her.

"Now look what you've done," he said. He had a phlegm rattle in his throat, as though he were choking out the words with great effort. "You've upset your mother by going off and marrying this, this nobody. We had bigger plans for you than that."

Evaleen was shocked at his words. She expected them to be upset at not being invited to their wedding, but calling her a nobody when they didn't even know her?

"I was hoping you'd be happy for us," Hero said, in a lost voice.

"Happy?" his father echoed, as if he couldn't quite believe his ears.

His face turned red and the veins popped out on his forehead. "You've eloped with this..." he nodded angrily at Evaleen, "...and you expect us to be happy? She's probably knocked up and you're the sucker."

Evaleen was devastated by his viciousness. Once again she was plain Eva Doyle with newspapers in her shoes, a dirty spot on her completely inappropriate dress that no amount of cleaning would ever get out, a third-rate girl that nobody would ever give a second glance. No amount of makeup, hair or clothing would ever change the fact that she was low-class and it showed. Tears of shame and despair choked her, then quickly changed to fury.

"How dare you say such a thing?" she said in an icy tone. "I am not pregnant. And for your information, I don't need Hero or anybody else to support me. I'm doing fine on my own."

She turned to Hero. "Please, Hero, take me home."

"Not quite yet," Hero said, then turned to his parents. He was so angry he was shaking. "You don't have the right to judge her or anybody else. This is my wife now. She would be acceptable to anyone in the world except you two. Shame on you both."

"Get out," his father shrieked his pale face distorted with rage, "and take your little whore with you. And don't come back."

"Don't worry, I won't," Hero shouted back at them. "Ever."

He grabbed Evaleen by the hand and pulled her towards the door.

"Come on, babe," he said. "Time to get the hell out of this dump."

Evaleen could hear Hero's mother sobbing as they fled out the door.

Outside in the brisk, cold air, away from the stifling atmosphere of those horrible people, that musty house, Evaleen broke down in tears.

"How can they say such things?" she said, choking out the words through her sobs.

Hero put his arm around her and held her close. "Don't take it personally. They look down on everybody. They always have. Want to hear something funny? My parents always looked down on everybody, and now everybody is looking down on them. Lucky for them, they're too numb to notice. Anyway, to hell with them. I love you and you love me. We don't need them or anybody else. We're a team, Babe."

"But they're your parents," Evaleen sobbed, wiping her tear-stained face with the back of her hand.

"Not when they act like that," Hero said.

#

It was well past nine when they arrived at Ma's apartment. The radio was blaring and Ma was watering the pots of red geraniums Evaleen had bought to grace the three large front windows. When the sun was shining, the flowers appeared to glow from within, a sight which always cheered her and made her feel like she was actually getting somewhere. Seeing Ma and the geraniums made Evaleen feel a little better.

"Ma. Guess what?" Evaleen blurted out. "Hero and I were married today."

"That's nice," Ma said, as if they had announced that it was time to eat.

Surprised, Evaleen decided she must not have heard her. Evaleen went over to the radio and turned it off.

"Ma, Hero and I were married today," Evaleen repeated. "Didn't you hear me?"

Ma put her watering can down on the kitchen table, then, to Evaleen's surprise, sat down and began to cry like a frightened child.

"Don't worry, Ma." Evaleen said, going to her mother and putting her arms around her shoulders. "I'm going to be right here. We'll all live together. I'll never leave you. I promise."

"We both promise," Hero said, patting her shoulder. His tone was tender and loving.

Evaleen was grateful to Hero for this kindness. She felt like the luckiest girl in the world to be such a wonderful man's wife.

"That's nice," Ma said, wiping her eyes and smiling a small, nervous smile. "This calls for a celebration. Come sit down and I'll make us some coffee and bring out some of those sugar cookies I made the other day."

As Hero and Evaleen sat down, Ma went over to the cupboard and reached into it for the cookie jar. All of a sudden, she grasped the edge of the counter and stood stock still for a long moment. Then she shakily sank down onto a chair at the table, as though to catch her breath.

"What happened, Ma?" Evaleen asked, worried.

"I don't know," Ma said, shaking her head as though to clear it. "I just had the strangest feeling – it was like I went cold all over, and the nerves in my legs felt like they were jumping out of my skin, and...oh, hello, Hero," she said. "What a surprise to see you here."

"Ma, don't you remember?" Evaleen asked, worried. "We told you we just got married."

"You did?" she said, obviously surprised. "When was that?"

"Today."

Ma stared at Evaleen, a puzzled look on her face.

"I think we should call the doctor," Evaleen said, her fears mushrooming.

"No, please don't," Ma said. "I just get a little light-headed sometimes. It's nothing, really. I'm fine, now. Honest. Now come on, I'll put on a pot of coffee and we'll celebrate. I've got some sugar cookies here somewhere."

Evaleen looked over at Hero. Neither quite knew what to do.

"I'm so happy," Ma said inanely, as they waited for the coffee to perk. "I'm just so darn happy for you both."

But she didn't look happy. She looked scared. And she forgot all about the cookies.

#

They made love that night, being careful not to disturb Ma. Hero took into consideration that this was her first time and was a gentle and affectionate lover. He said he loved her body, although she felt self-conscious about it and was careful to stay beneath the sheets so he wouldn't see her poochy stomach and thick thighs.

Afterwards, she felt like pinching herself to make sure it wasn't just one of her favorite fantasies, that they really were married. Not only had they just made love and were husband and wife now in every sense, but Hero Lyon was right here in her very own bed. He was hers forever, or at least until death do us part.

Chapter Eleven

In the days that followed, Evaleen floated around in a cloud of bliss. Hero, too, seemed always to be smiling. Even Ma seemed more alert and happy than usual.

The only sour note in their otherwise perfect life was Hero's parents. As far as she knew, Hero had not talked to his parents since the day they were married, nor had his parents called them. She felt sad for Hero, but he rarely mentioned his parents, so she was careful not to mention them either, not wishing to remind him of the evil things his father said about her.

In spite of this she was happier than she'd ever been. The first year of their marriage sped by in a glow. Just waking up next to Hero every morning was a huge thrill. He still had not found a job, but Evaleen did not blame him. For every job opening, there were still a thousand applicants, although the economy was beginning to improve.

The money Hero did make from playing cards or pool at O'Dooles was mostly sent to his parents, who still hadn't spoken to him a year later. Nor did he make an effort to call them. Evaleen felt that no matter what, they were still his parents, and they needed help. Sometimes, though, when she made barely enough to pay the bills and put food on the table, she resented his parents and their inability to care for themselves.

One morning in the middle of June, Evaleen was up and about, but moving slowly as she made her way to the kitchen for a cup of coffee. She had gone to bed early and woke up late, but she was still tired. Her breasts were tender, too. This was happening more and more lately. Hero was already dressed for the day, drinking his morning coffee and reading the newspaper.

"Good morning, sleepyhead," he said, putting his newspaper down and smiling at her in his easy way.

"Good morning," she said, barely getting out the words before a wave of nausea hit her. She turned quickly towards the front windows, not wishing Hero to see her distress. These last couple of weeks, she felt as if she had a constant case of the flu, and she was tired all the time. It took every bit of strength she had to go door-to-door, when all she really wanted was to go home and take a nap. If Hero noticed anything different, he didn't say.

Watching out the window, Evaleen saw a baby wren teetering on the edge of a nest in the old oak tree on the boulevard, which was just beginning to have a few buds. The mother perched nearby, watching. The baby bird hopped down a few branches, then flew back up to the nest, where it stood shakily for several moments before trying again. Evaleen felt the wonder of nature and her own situation as she watched the baby bird struggle. She had missed her period for the second time and was positive she was pregnant. She had not told Hero or Ma, as she was waiting for a special time to make her announcement.

When the nausea passed, she turned back, opened up the cupboard and took out a few Saltine crackers to settle her stomach. Still a little queasy, she poured herself a glass of milk rather than having the coffee, which had begun to give her heartburn. She sat down opposite Hero at the kitchen table.

The sight of Hero nonchalantly reading the sports section irritated her today. Why wasn't he reading the help-wanted section? And did he have to look so cool and elegant in his gray flannels and white dress shirt, when all he was doing was hanging out at O'Dooles?

"Wow," Hero exclaimed. "This kid Ted Williams is something. He's right at the top of the American League in RBIs."

Ignoring his outburst, Evaleen picked up the society pages. One of her favorite things was seeing what the society women were wearing, how they did their hair, what they were doing, who they were with, and to imagine herself as one of them. But today she had difficulty concentrating on anything, and everything got on her nerves, Hero most of all. She kept taking furious little glances at him as he continued to read the paper, oblivious to her or anything else except the sports section. Usually she didn't feel secure enough in his love to criticize him. But today she didn't give a damn.

"You look good," she said, unable to keep the sarcasm from her tone. "Ready for another big day at O'Dooles?"

"Unemployment is still really high, or haven't you heard?" Hero shot back, storm clouds in his eyes. "What the hell do you want me to do? Sit around here all day, listening to soap operas with your mother? At least at O'Dooles, I feel like a man. Nobody there knows my wife is supporting me."

His words cut into her like the sharp edge of a knife. Maybe she was being too harsh. It wasn't as if he didn't try. He'd applied for several jobs, but someone always seemed to be ahead of him in line, actually hundreds of somebodies. And he was too proud to take one of the WPA jobs, which he claimed derisively were nothing more than a way for the government to keep the bums off the street. Sorry she'd spoken so harshly, she decided to try another tack, something she'd been thinking about a lot lately.

"I need help," she said, forcing her voice to remain even. "Selling days, making creams at night, ordering and picking up supplies, it's just too much to do for one person." She sighed heavily. "And I'm not making enough money to hire help right now."

She had more to say, but stopped abruptly when Ma shuffled into the kitchen and poured herself a cup of coffee. Ma was dressed in a cotton house dress, but her grey hair was uncombed and still flattened from sleep.

"Have you heard?" she asked. "The Prince of Wales and that Simpson woman are now living in France. I heard they're not welcome in England at all."

"Oh, is that so?" Evaleen said, feigning interest.

"And what's worse, his brother George can't even say a sentence without stuttering and he's the king," Ma said, turning on the radio in the living room and settling down in Pa's old chair with her coffee. "What a mess."

"Beauty creams," Hero spat out, just loud enough for Evaleen to hear. "That's a woman's business."

"Pays your bar bills," she shot back.

"Couldn't help yourself, could you?" His face was contorted with rage.

"No matter what excuse you use, playing pool and poker are play," she said, feeling too queasy right now to cater to his manly ego.

"I win most of the time," he said, his voice low and menacing.

"Doesn't seem to make much difference around here. And what about all those women that hang out there? Think I don't know about them?" she said, blurting out her secret fears. "You're crazy, you know that? I'm not one of the guys, Hero, you can't fool me. I know what goes on down there."

She hadn't meant to say that. She'd heard the rumors and worried about them, often obsessively, but so far had managed to keep it to herself. The last thing she wanted was for him to know how insecure she was where he was concerned.

There was a brief hostile silence before Hero blurted out, "Bullshit. And who are you to talk? I see the way Josh Goldman looks at you. Don't tell me there's nothing there."

Evaleen was surprised that Hero noticed it, too. Last Sunday, Josh volunteered to teach her how to set up her books more efficiently for tax purposes. She had kept her receipts in a shoe box and he said that wasn't a good idea, that she needed a system.

They had sat together at the kitchen table. He explained that she needed to put her expenses into different categories in one folder and cash receivables in another. At one point, she looked over at him. She saw such love and tenderness in his eyes that for a moment she was taken aback.

Josh's face turned a bright red, obviously embarrassed at being caught. He immediately began to lecture her about the importance of keeping proper records, and the kind of tax trouble she could get into if she didn't.

Later that day, she told herself that what she saw was merely the concern of a dear friend for her and her business, and that she shouldn't take it personally. But in a way she couldn't explain, she enjoyed the way he looked at her. She felt strangely pleased. Still, she better find someone else to do her accounting from now on. She didn't need the trouble.

"Josh is far too much of a gentleman to even think of such a thing," she shot back. "He's not like you."

The moment the words were out, she was sorry, but it was too late.

He gave her an incredulous look.

"That does it," he said, slamming down his paper. He headed angrily for the door.

Shocked that things had escalated to this point, she stood up and rushed to the door to head him off. "I'm sorry, Hero. I didn't mean it. Please don't go."

He opened the door.

"I'm pregnant," she blurted out, to stop him from leaving.

Regret ripped through her the moment the words were out. Too late now. The deed was done. She waited, fearful to see how he would react.

He stopped in his tracks, shut the door slowly, then leaned up against it for support. He took in a deep breath, as if he needed to replace all the air that had suddenly slipped away. He had a scared look on his face.

"Is it mine?" he asked.

"What do you mean?" she asked, shocked and hurt that he would even think such a thing. "Of course it's yours. What a terrible thing to say."

Tears flashed in Hero's eyes, but he quickly recovered himself.

"I'm sorry," he said. "I didn't really mean that. Josh is such a straight shooter, he would never do anything to hurt you or me. It's, I, I… don't know if I'm ready to have a kid. Can we even afford one? What are we going to do?"

"Have the baby," she replied bluntly. "What else is there to do?"

"You're right." His tone and the look in his eyes changed to one of love and tenderness, which surprised her. Hero was a man of considerable charm, but tenderness was something new for him.

Then Hero did something that astounded her. He came to her, put his fingers to her lips to hush her, and gently took her into his arms. Gladdened by his reaction, she leaned into him, thankful to stop arguing, relieved to unburden herself of her big secret.

"I love you so much," he said, burying his face in her hair.

"I love you so much, too," she said.

"Hard to believe during one of those hot times, we made a baby, huh?"

"It is, isn't it?" she said, amazed herself.

Hero kissed her gently on the lips. As he did so, wave after wave of exciting little thrills burst through her body, like flashes of heat lightning. The fury she felt moments earlier changed into red hot need. He must have felt it too, because the kiss became more and more passionate. She could feel the growing evidence of his passion against her stomach.

"I hate it when we fight," she said, when they finally came up for air and she could think again.

"Oh, I don't know," he teased. "You turn me on when you're angry. You look so beautiful, your cheeks all flushed and sexy. Maybe we should fight more often."

"You're terrible," she said and laughed. "I don't know if I would have married you if I would have known in advance what a crazy man you are."

"Tell the truth. You love it."

"Okay, I love it, but I've to get going. I'm already late getting started."

A huge thunder clap suddenly boomed across the sky.

"It's gonna rain," Hero crowed, a triumphant look on his face. "You can't do a thing until it stops."

Evaleen had to laugh. "You're right."

"I always am," he said, raising an eyebrow for emphasis.

He took her hand and like two teenagers sneaking off to make out, they tiptoed past Ma, who had fallen asleep in her chair. In the bedroom, they shut the door gently behind them and sat next to each other on the edge of the bed.

He kissed her again, even more deeply this time. She felt a welling up of love for him as she kissed him back. At that moment she would have given anything, done anything to keep him with her forever. To hell with work. To hell with business. To hell with everything. He was the only thing that mattered, the only thing that had ever mattered. When he touched her breast, shivers of delight swept through her entire body. The spicy, masculine smell of him made her feel dizzy with desire. They fell on each other like two animals and made quick hot love. Afterwards, lying contentedly together in bed, they listened to the rain, cuddled and talked.

"Maybe I could wash dishes for a dollar a day," Hero said.

"Why not work with me?" she asked, choosing her words carefully, taking advantage of his obviously tender feelings for her right now. "I need help. Especially now."

A look of despair crossed Hero's face. "I'm sorry. I really am, but I just couldn't face myself in the mirror every day, knowing I was involved in women's beauty creams. I, I just couldn't."

"You won't have to make beauty creams or sell them," she persisted. "You'll take care of the money, do the books, order supplies, the kind of work men do at any company."

At the look of horror on his face, she decided to try another tack. "How about if I make you my business partner?"

"No."

"Come on, Hero," she wheedled. "There's lots of things you know that I don't."

"Like what?"

"For one thing, you're a lot more organized than I am. Look at your side of the closet. All your shirts are lined up just so, while my side is always a mess. You pay a lot more attention to detail, too. I've seen you go over our electricity bill like an accountant, looking to see if they overcharged us. Please, Hero. You could handle the business end, while I handle the making and selling end. We'd be great together."

"I don't know," Hero said slowly. He seemed to shudder inwardly. "Is this what you really want?"

"Yes, more than anything," she said, pressing her advantage. "It would mean a lot to me and our baby, too."

Hero let out a heavy, resigned sigh. "I guess I could give it a try."

"You won't be sorry," Evaleen said, ignoring the stricken look on his face. "Really, you won't."

Chapter Twelve

Hero's resentment at being in a business whose only purpose he saw as catering to women's egos, became more and more obvious over time. Still, he kept his word and worked hard. He paid the bills, searched for and found better quality and cheaper suppliers, wrote and printed up brochures, delivered phone orders, collected and handled the money, and made sure Evaleen always had everything she needed. He even mapped out a daily route system for her to cover, eight blocks in one direction and two in the other, in better neighborhoods that had more houses and fewer businesses.

By this time Evaleen was bringing in around twenty-five dollars a week going door-to-door. They were both extremely busy. She missed cuddling and talking with him in the morning like they used to, but mornings had become so hectic they had to get up extra early just to finish everything they needed to do. She promised herself they would have more time for each other when things let up a bit. Nights were also busy. And now that she was pregnant, going door-to-door was becoming more and more difficult.

Hero came up with the idea of expanding into department stores, where they could reach more people at one time. Evaleen thought it was a great idea, but wasn't sure she could pull it off. Hero reminded her that if it didn't work, she would just continue to go door-to-door. That helped to quell her fears. She set to work writing a pitch while Hero, working across from her at the kitchen table, worked on some statistics to prove this was a viable idea.

Evaleen loved seeing Hero across from her at the table, and she would look up from time to time just to enjoy the sight. She still counted it a miracle that they were together. She knew that Hero resented being in business with her, and it worried her. But she needed him. There were so many things he did better than she ever could, or had time for. She loved talking to people and making her creams and making sure the jars looked good, but hated all the little details, like keeping track of everything for tax purposes, making sure she had all the ingredients she needed, and dealing with various distributors, all of which Hero was extraordinarily good at.

So, thanks to her work and thanks to Hero's work, she was ready when, the day after a snowstorm hit Emerson, she, hugely pregnant, took in a big breath to calm her nerves, got in her car, a baby-blue Packard with V8 engine and blue velvet interior, and headed downtown. Hero had spotted the Packard one day when he was out buying supplies. The car had a big sign in a side window stating, "$100 Will Buy This Car. Lost Everything. Must Have Cash." Hero paid the man, drove the car home that day and handed the keys over to Evaleen.

"You need to look successful," he said, when he showed it to her. "Driving your father's old jalopy just makes people think you're desperate or crooked."

Evaleen loved driving such a beautiful car. It was so much better than her father's old car, with its bald tires and tendency to stop at the most awful times. But she loved Pa's old car too, and hated to give it up. She remembered going for rides with Ma and Pa in the car as a little girl, looking out the window, going to the drugstore for a chocolate soda in the days when Pa still had a job. This was followed by a wave of guilt whenever she thought about her father. He seemed always to be slipping in and out of her thoughts these days, especially whenever something upset her or scared her or made her feel anxious.

The worst times were when she recalled his death. In her mind's eye, she saw him lying on the sidewalk. She needed to be strong to do what she was planning to do, and she could not give in to these thoughts, especially now when she didn't have an appointment and wasn't sure if anyone would even talk to her. It was Hero's suggestion that she just show up and see if she could find someone to pitch her idea to.

"If nothing else, it will give you a chance to practice," he said.

"You're right," she said, positive as always that he knew more than she did about everything.

She was scared, but fear was like an old, bad friend that haunted her days and often her nights. So far she was able to continue on in spite of it, even when people slammed the door in her face. It helped to pretend she was someone else, but not always. To keep up her courage now as she maneuvered the big car through the unplowed streets of Emerson, she reminded herself what that guy on the radio, Napoleon Hill, said about rejection knocking out the weak.

To hide her growing pregnancy, underneath her oversized wool coat she wore a long white lamb's wool sweater over a pair of black, wide-legged, gabardine slacks, with an elastic waist stretched to capacity. Evaleen had purchased the slacks in a larger size. She had two other pairs in her regular size, also purchased new. She tried to return Shu's slacks several times but was never able to catch up with her, and Shu didn't return phone calls anymore. It wasn't until Evaleen stopped at the grocery store to pick up some milk that she actually ran into Shu and was able to finally give the slacks back. She remembered it well.

She wasn't sure at first if it was Shu, because her friend looked so haggard. Her normally lustrous hair was greasy and her face looked puffy. Her usually voluptuous body looked thin, even skeletal.

"Hey, Shu," Evaleen said, catching up with her. "Is that you?" she blurted out. "You're so skinny."

"Thank you," Shu said. "I was a little too heavy before. I needed to lose a few pounds."

"No, you didn't," Evaleen said, biting her tongue at the sharpness of her words.

Seeing the hurt look on Shu's face, Evaleen quickly changed the subject. "How's Bunny?"

"She's doing fine. Growing like a weed. Look I, I really don't have time to chat," Shu said, not quite looking Evaleen in the eye.

"Please don't go yet," Evaleen pleaded. "I've been trying to return your slacks for the longest time. They're in my car. It will just take a minute. I'll run and get them."

"Can't you give them to me some other time?" Shu asked.

"No," Evaleen protested. "This is the only time I've been able to see you."

"Well, could you make it quick?" Shu said. "Sam's waiting for me in the parking lot."

"I'll be back in a sec," Evaleen said. She left her shopping basket in the aisle, raced out to her car and grabbed the slacks. On the way back, she saw Sam sitting in his car smoking a cigarette, a scowl on his broad face. He didn't see her and Evaleen was glad. Back in the grocery store, she caught up with Shu as she was beginning to check out.

"Thanks so much, Shu," Evaleen said, handing her the slacks. "They made a real difference. If I can ever return the favor, let me know. And please call sometime. I really do miss you."

But Shu was not listening. All of her attention seemed focused on the cashier, as though mentally hurrying her along. The moment her groceries were paid for and bagged, she rushed out the door without a backward glance.

Evaleen didn't know what to think. Strangest of all, Shu didn't seem to notice that Evaleen was pregnant. The old Shu would have noticed immediately and kidded her about hiding a watermelon in her pants, or something like that.

Now in downtown Emerson, she forgot about Shu and everything else as she parked two blocks from Rosen's, in the only parking spot big enough for her car. She stepped out and hurried for the store. A fear headache started, and threatened to escalate into a full blown migraine. It was one thing to talk to housewives, quite another to talk to some big-deal person at a large department store.

But she had to do it before the baby arrived, because after that there would be no time.

As she passed a dry goods store, she reminded herself that the worst thing that could happen was that nothing would happen, and she would still be fine. Unlike the time she begged the banks for money, her livelihood did not depend on getting into a department store, because although she wasn't getting rich going door-to-door, she was able to pay their bills, put aside some money to pay the doctor for when the baby came, and continue to give a little money to the Salvation Army for unwed mothers in her father's name.

That thought gave her confidence, and she relaxed a little. Outside Daniel's Hardware, she saw three Pinkerton Detectives menacing two men handing out pro-union leaflets. Defiant at their thug-like tactics, Evaleen took a leaflet, thanked the man extravagantly, and gave the Pinkerton detectives a dirty look.

She wondered if this was the kind of work Hero had done in Chicago. She had asked him once, but he said he didn't want to talk about it.

Further on, a haggard looking woman sold apples from a small cart while a little girl clutched at her ragged skirt. Evaleen gave the woman all the cash she had, three dollar bills, and told her to keep the apples. The woman thanked her profusely. The Supreme Court recently reversed an earlier decision and upheld the minimum wage law for women, so if a woman could get a job, at least she could make the minimum wage. It disgusted Evaleen that women had to fight so hard for something men took for granted.

As she hurried along, her fashionable high heels began to pinch her swollen feet and her ribs began to ache from being kicked so much by the baby. Nearing Rosen's, she saw a long line of people, with several small children shivering in their thin jackets and coats, who waited in a long line for free coffee and soup. She felt sorry for them, and understood from her own experience how desperate they must feel. Seeing them was a reminder that she needed to keep going, no matter how tempting it was to simply get in the car and go home.

Outside Rosen's, a small contingent of the Salvation Army corps earnestly tooted "Oh, Little Town of Bethlehem," on their brass horns. The band members had such serious looks on their faces, and played so badly, it made her smile.

Seeing them, her fear changed to a crazy kind of hope. Maybe things would work out. Maybe the manager or buyer or whomever she could get to speak to her would be in a good mood because of

Christmas. Buoyed by this thought, she hurried through the swinging doors of Rosen's Department Store.

Inside it was as if the Depression had never happened. Bright lights revealed shelves filled to overflowing. Signs indicated a sale on crepe de chine pajamas today, and shoppers thronged the area.

"Excuse me," Evaleen said, as she tried to push past several well-dressed women hovering over a display of silk nightgowns.

One woman, irritated at having to move, gave her such an insolent look as though to say, what are you doing here? A wave of inferiority hit Evaleen and she stopped in the ladies room to compose herself and double and triple check her makeup. Thankfully, she was alone.

"It didn't kill you when the bankers said no," she said to herself in the mirror. "You didn't die then, and you're not going to die now."

She took a compact from her purse, re-powdered her nose and patted her hair. She knew she wasn't a beauty, but figured she didn't look half bad today, either.

With that bit of knowledge helping her along, she took in a big breath, let it out, then marched briskly to the corporate offices at the back of the store, where a little round woman clad all in black, with long thin bleached blond hair that made her look older than she already was, stood behind a counter.

"May I help you?" she spoke in a squeaky, child-like voice.

"I would like to speak to the manager," Evaleen said, in the voice she always used to approach a new customer.

"He's busy. Can I ask what you want to see him about?"

"I have a business proposition," Evaleen said quickly, looking the woman directly in the eye, something else she'd learned to do.

"He isn't seeing anybody that he isn't already doing business with these days."

"Thank you and good day, then," Evaleen said, and left.

Determined not to take it personally, she drove the three blocks to Mason's, the largest department store in downtown Emerson. It was Hero's idea to start at the top and work her way down, although right now starting at the bottom and working her way up sounded better.

She needn't have worried. She received the same quick response at Mason's as she had at Rosen's.

But being rejected did not scare her like it used to when she was just starting out, so she went back to her car and drove to Bomberg's, which had a reputation for low prices, but was located further away from the loop than Mason's or Rosen's.

At Bomberg's, near the front, a young woman with short, wavy blond hair, stood in front of Estee Lauder's counter with a spray bottle of perfume. Evaleen saw the woman look at her, size her up and decide not to give her a free sample. That hurt. If she looked too poor for even a free sample, how could she convince anyone of anything?

For a moment, she was tempted to give up and go home, then she spotted the empty counter at the back. There it stood, empty and waiting. For her. Buoyed by the sight, she hurried through the store and stepped into an elevator.

It was hot in the elevator and Evaleen unthinkingly unbuttoned her coat, then remembered her pregnancy and quickly buttoned up her coat again. It was close to noon.

You can do this, she said to herself. These people don't know you. You could be the queen of Siam for all they know. Evaleen smiled at the ridiculous thought.

She stepped out of the elevator, cleared her throat twice nervously, then, reminding herself she was Evaleen the Queen and just as important as anybody else, she marched down the hall and through the double doors marked "Corporate Office."

An older woman sat behind a desk going through a pile of papers. She had chalk-white skin and bright red lipstick that made her mouth look like a red slash in her pale face. Her hair, the color of shoe black, was pulled back so tightly into a bun that it gave her eyes an oriental look. Evaleen, assuming she was the receptionist, took a quick breath and approached her before she lost her nerve.

"I would like to speak to someone about an interesting business proposition," Evaleen said, forcing energy into her voice.

"Oh dear, you poor thing," the woman said sympathetically, recognizing the bulge beneath her coat. "You should be home sitting down."

"You're probably right," Evaleen said with a sigh. The simple friendliness of the woman felt good. "But first I need to talk to someone about my business proposition."

"It's customary to call and make an appointment first if you wish to talk to someone, my dear, but since you're here already, you might as well tell me what's on your mind. My husband's the owner, along with me, of course. I made sure of that. My name's Mrs. Henry Bomberg. You can call me Phyllis. So go ahead, honey, give me your pitch," she said, easing back into her chair.

Evaleen sat down and nervously began her prepared speech.

"I have been going door-to-door selling a lubricating skin care cream from a recipe I inherited from my grandmother. She was the envy of everyone for her beautiful skin, even into old age." Evaleen spoke quickly before her voice gave out from her dry mouth and shaky nerves. "I have discovered going door-to-door that even during these hard times, women can usually dredge up a few pennies when it comes to their looks. With your permission, of course, I was hoping that I might set up a counter in your store to sell my wonderful creams to the public."

"Hmm," was all Mrs. Bomberg said.

"Can I give you a free demonstration?" Evaleen continued in a rush. She had asked this same question to so many women previously that it was almost automatic.

"Why not?" Mrs. Bomberg said with a shrug.

Encouraged, Evaleen took out a jar from her bag, opened it up with shaking hands, and with Mrs. Bomberg's permission, proceeded to tissue off her heavy makeup, then massaged the Fresh-As-A-Daisy skin lubricating cream gently into her face and neck, while extolling the benefits of her cream. She was careful not to get grease spots on Mrs. Bomberg's silk blouse.

When Evaleen finished, she took a mirror from her large purse and held it up for Mrs. Bomberg to see. Without all her makeup, Mrs. Bomberg's olive complexion had a nice, healthy glow.

"Oh, that feels so good," Mrs. Bomberg said, touching her face. "My skin feels just like silk. But truthfully, my dear, we're all bought out for Christmas. And with the Depression, we can't afford to add one more line. I'm sorry, but we really can't."

"But this wouldn't cost you anything," Evaleen said speaking quickly. "I saw an empty counter in the cosmetic section. Right now that space is not making you a dime. In fact, I bet it's costing you money."

"You're right there," Mrs. Bomberg said, with a sigh. "The line we had in there went broke. Unfortunately for us, empty space in a store is worth money and that space has not been pulling its weight for a while, now. Maybe we could work out something."

Mrs. Bomberg wrinkled her mouth, as though thinking hard. "You could maybe set up the counter at your own expense. Of course, we'll have to charge you rent, based on your sales, although we could give you a bit of a break on your first month or two."

"That sounds wonderful," Evaleen said, almost disbelieving.

Before she could say more, a pain hit her so hard she winced.

"Is something wrong?" Mrs. Bomberg asked instantly.

"It's nothing," Evaleen said, letting out a breath as the pain subsided. "I'm fine, really."

"If you're sure, dear; although you look like you're about to pop to me. How about we meet again in thirty days? You can give me your projections for the space and tell me what you plan to do, and we can sign the contract then, purely on a contingency basis, you understand, since neither one of us can be sure this will make any money. That will give you a chance to think about what you want to do and obviously to have your baby."

She smiled an indulgent smile.

Evaleen sat stunned, her thoughts spinning madly. Oh, dear God. She said yes. Mrs. Bomberg said yes. Yes. Yes. Yes. She said yes. She really did.

Evaleen made an effort to appear cool and confident, but her heart was pounding so wildly it felt like it would fly out of her chest. She couldn't wait to go home and tell Hero and Ma.

"How about January 6th, say two o'clock," Mrs. Bomberg said, consulting a calendar on her desk. "Christmas and New Year's will be over and things will be a little slow, then. It will give you a chance to be up and running before spring, when business picks up again. Will that work for you?"

Evaleen was so thrilled she was tempted to jump up and throw her arms around Mrs. Bomberg, but restrained herself.

"January sixth sounds wonderful," she said, sounding a lot calmer than she felt. "Thank you so much, Mrs. Bomberg. You won't be sorry. You'll see."

"No need to thank me," Mrs. Bomberg said with a shrug of her shoulders. "Either you'll make money for us or you won't. Actually, I'm glad you stopped by. That counter has been empty since September, way too long. Now you go on and have a nice holiday and have a nice baby too, dear," she said, standing up.

"Thank you, I will," Evaleen said.

She left, eager to tell Hero and Ma.

On her way out of the store, she stopped for a long moment to admire the empty space that would soon be filled with her very own products, before rushing out through the swinging doors and home.

Chapter Thirteen

As Evaleen drove home, her elation turned to worry. The space was so small and dark. Would anybody even notice it so far in the back? They would need lamps to light it up, for sure. And what about packaging? The packaging she had now was fine for going door-to-door, but how would it look featured in a glass case in a department store?

And what about Hero? He would have to care for Ma and the baby while she worked at the store. How would he feel about that, especially when he hated being home all day, crowded by all of her equipment and supplies, which had begun to take over their apartment.

Was she even smart enough to pull a big deal like this off? How could she ever believe she could pull something like this off? Pa was right. Who did she think she was, anyway?

She began to feel a little better when she pulled up to a stop light and saw a large two-story empty brick building that used to be a factory. She fantasized seeing 'Evaleen' in huge neon letters at the top of the building and herself looking chic and professional in a big office with a window. Hero's office would be right next to hers, so they could talk to each other off and on all day and have lunch together in the executive dining room. That would be so fun. The center of the building would be her factory. In the back would be her laboratory, where she would spend her days developing more of her grandmother's recipes to expand her line.

It could happen, she told herself. If Mrs. Bomberg was willing to give her a chance, maybe others would, too. This was the biggest breakthrough of her career.

She would have to make it work. But she didn't know anything about traditional retail. And if she messed up, her one big chance might be gone forever. And...would Hero go along?

She needed him now more than ever, but more and more lately, he would just disappear. She assumed he was going to O'Dooles, but couldn't be sure. This upset her sometimes, but she didn't complain because she figured he needed some time by himself, to think or recover from their hectic days.

She smiled ruefully as she drove. She was probably worrying for nothing. They were doing fine together. She still thought he was the most exciting man she had ever known, and was thrilled to be his wife. He seemed happy too, and they still made love in spite of her growing tummy. And now, with Fresh-As-A-Daisy products about to be represented in a big department store and the baby coming, life could not be more perfect.

"We could become rich, kiddo," she said, patting to her tummy, "and possibly by the time you grow up, too. By then nobody will care that I didn't graduate from high school, or that I'm not the most gorgeous woman, or least likely to succeed. And who knows, maybe someday you'll join us in the business, and between all of us working together we could provide jobs for all those unwed mothers and their babies. What do you think about that, kiddo? Nice, huh?"

As if in answer, an excruciating cramp hit her. It stopped almost as quickly as it started, but if the pain meant anything, the baby would be arriving soon. She couldn't wait to become a mother. She was positive her baby would be an elegant, brilliant little boy, the very picture of his handsome father. Thanks to the latest child-raising techniques, which she had been reading at every opportunity, he would be perfectly behaved, all smiles and sweet charm, not like those little monsters she saw screaming in the grocery store.

She was still feeling excited at all the possibilities when she arrived at home, and only deflated a little when she saw the dirty dishes piled high in the sink. Hero was sitting at the kitchen table drinking coffee and poring over the daily sports news.

"So how'd it go?" he asked, looking up.

"Mrs. Bomberg said yes," Evaleen said, leaning down for his kiss.

"Yahoo," he cried, jumping up from his seat and punching the air.

"You did it," he said, giving her a hug. "We're gonna be rich, babe."

"Yes, we are," she said happily.

She felt cheerful and satisfied and extremely proud of herself, and him, too. Things were definitely going their way. With Hero by her side, anything was possible. She quickly filled him in on the details of the interview.

"So tell me about the space," he said grabbing a pencil and some paper and sitting down at the kitchen table. "How much of everything do you think we're gonna need?"

"The space is at the back of the cosmetic section, so we'll need at least two lamps and maybe three to light it up," she said, "also I want a big sign at the back. I also need to come up with a few more products, like maybe a shampoo and hair conditioner, which are in my grandmother's notebook. The shampoo recipe calls for Castile soap, which isn't difficult to find and..."

A cramp hit her again. Hard.

"Oh God, Hero, I think I'm in labor," she said, holding her stomach.

Hero continued his calculations as though she hadn't spoken. Evaleen was hurt by his lack of concern, but it was also understandable. The first time she had false labor pains, Hero had become flustered with fear and excitement. The second time, not as much. Now he barely noticed. She had tried to discuss her false labor pains with Ma, but Ma wasn't interested in anything unless it was happening to her soap opera characters.

Another cramp hit Evaleen, and another five minutes later. Hero didn't notice this time, either. Evaleen decided to call Gussie, who had helped her own mother give birth, to see what she had to say. When it came to such things, there was nothing Gussie didn't know.

"I think I'm in labor for real this time," Evaleen said, when Gussie picked up the phone.

"Are you sure? Have you had a blood show?"

"A blood show?"

"My ma could always tell she was in labor when a little show of blood appeared in her panties," Gussie said. "The other big symptom is when your water busts. That usually happens right before labor commences. According to my mother, labor can start with a cramp, like when you get your time of the month, or you could feel like you're about to have a bowel movement. It's different every time."

"Well I haven't had any blood show, nor has any water come out, nor do I feel like I have to go to the bathroom, so I'm probably good for now." Evaleen laughed.

Feeling better, she told Gussie what happened at Bomberg's.

"Congratulations for having the guts," Gussie said. "I never could have done it myself."

"You could if you had to," Evaleen said.

As they talked, Hero stood up and began to roam the apartment, picking things up and putting them down, opening the refrigerator, going to the window to stare out.

Evaleen ignored his restlessness, and asked how things were going for Gussie.

"Bill still hasn't left his wife," Gussie said, her voice purposefully low so her sister wouldn't hear. "I don't really blame him. What kind of a man would he be if he left his sick wife?"

Evaleen could hear the sadness in Gussie's voice.

"I feel guilty but I love him so much, I just can't seem to stay away. He must feel the same way, because he can't stay away from me, either. Believe me, we've both tried many times."

Evaleen worried that Gussie was in for a big letdown, and had warned her once. Gussie let her know in no uncertain terms it was Gussie's life and Evaleen should butt out. Not willing to lose her friendship, Evaleen kept her mouth shut after that, but she continued to worry about her friend.

After they hung up, she had a huge urge to call Shu. Shu was the only one she knew who'd actually had a baby, and would understand better than anybody what Evaleen was going through. Evaleen had tried several times after Bunny was born to talk to Shu, but Sam always answered the phone and said Shu was busy, or otherwise indisposed. One day Evaleen on a whim, wishing to try to connect with her friend one more time, picked up the phone and called. For once, Shu answered the phone.

"I can't talk now," Shu said in a whisper. "I'll call you back later."

She never did call and Evaleen finally gave up. She didn't want to force her friendship on someone who obviously wasn't interested. Still, she missed Shu and felt the loss deeply. She thought about calling Josh, but this was a woman's business and would probably just make him feel uncomfortable.

To keep her mind off her situation, she shredded some Castile soap, olive oil and lemon juice into a pan for her new type of shampoo, placed it on the stove and lit the burner. She was stirring it all together when she was stopped by a labor pain, then another one, and then nothing. Would this baby never arrive?

Hero had stopped pacing, and was now going through a pile of papers.

"I feel like I've been pregnant forever," she said.

Hero didn't respond, and she felt a stab of resentment. She was glad that he stayed home with her instead of going out, but wished he would be a little more concerned about her.

#

Christmas Eve morning. It was after nine. Looking at the clock, she realized she had overslept, which was unusual for her. The air in the apartment felt cool, like the super hadn't turned the heat up again, although their rent was up-to-date, and there were only three vacancies in the building these days. The other side of the bed was empty. She put on her bathrobe and went to the kitchen, expecting to see Hero at the kitchen table, drinking a cup of coffee and reading the paper. Ma was there, but Hero was nowhere to be seen.

Where could he possibly have gone so early? Especially now, when she was so close to giving birth. She went to the front windows and looked out. Snow blew in windy swirls, causing the windows to rattle.

His car, usually parked out front, was gone. He probably went out to get a newspaper like he did every morning or, hopeful thought, maybe he went to buy her Christmas present. But the stores didn't open until ten. He must have set up an early morning business meeting. That was probably it.

She was tempted to get dressed and head out herself. Housewives might be on the lookout for one more little present, in case they had forgotten someone. She made a face. No. She couldn't risk it. Not today. She was way too close to giving birth.

An hour later, Hero still had not shown up. She leaned against the front window, her head against the cold glass and looked out for the fifth time. So many men had left their families under the strain of the Depression, was he about to join their ranks? Would she be one of the abandoned women?

"It'll be alright, dear," her mother whispered, as she came shuffling into the kitchen.

Evaleen was surprised. Ma was trying to comfort her. Evaleen had to be the strong one here.

She smiled as brightly as she could manage. "Of course it will, Ma. It always is. Would you like some breakfast?"

"Yes. I would," Ma said, turning on the radio and settling down next to it. A dazed expression crossed her face, and Evaleen knew that she was back in her world of make-believe.

Evaleen made Ma eggs and some toast, and told herself she was worrying for nothing. Hero would be home any minute with some logical explanation as to why he had to go out so early.

But by noon he still had not come home. Christmas carols bleated depressingly on the radio. Evaleen fixed Ma a bowl of tomato soup, but was too distraught to eat herself. She tried to work but had trouble concentrating, ended up burning the wax for a lipstick she was developing and was forced to throw it out. She was furious with herself. She wasn't making the kind of money where she could afford to waste anything.

She shook her head. It wasn't fair beating herself up. She was doing the best she could, she would just have to buck up and try again later, when she could think clearly.

All the fears she had about Hero burst forth to plague her. Was he with somebody else? Somebody more suitable? Somebody prettier? Somebody who wouldn't force him to work in a business he hated?

The tense air must have rubbed off on Ma, because she stood up and sat down several times, as though confused. Evaleen forced herself to act calm so Ma would calm down. She longed to talk to her mother, tell her how she felt right now, and ask her what it was like when Ma gave birth, but it was hopeless. Evaleen would have given anything to join Ma in her fantasy world, everything would have been so much easier.

Four o'clock came and went, and still no Hero. Was he in a terrible accident? Was he dead? Oh dear God, where could he be?

Chapter Fourteen

Christmas morning. After spending a sleepless night having false labor pains off and on, and waiting, worrying, praying for Hero to come home, Evaleen was exhausted. Her ribs and back ached like a bad toothache, the skin on her stomach felt as tight as a drum and she felt horrible in general.

She forced herself to get up, dress and make some coffee. Ma appeared a short time later, sat down by the radio and turned it on, although all there was to listen to were Christmas carols and the news. For Ma's sake, Evaleen tried to act normal, but she was growing more and more anxious about Hero and the baby, especially the baby. The baby had stopped kicking an hour ago. Was that normal? Was the baby okay? Was Hero okay? Where was he? Her mind was a seething mess.

The Christmas tree, which seemed so beautiful once, now looked cheap and tawdry with its dime-store ornaments. Ma and Pa had never made much of a fuss about Christmas – "too much trouble," Ma always said. But Hero had extravagant Christmases growing up, and insisted that they have a tree.

He brought one home as a surprise a week ago. As her contribution, Evaleen purchased lights and ornaments on sale at Bomberg's, and made sure there were presents under the tree for Ma and Hero. After they had decorated the tree, Hero and Evaleen sat together on the davenport, drinking hot apple cider and admiring their handiwork. Even Ma joined in. They were so happy, then. At least she was.

Had something happened since then that she didn't know about? Would she ever see him again?

Desperate, she did something she promised herself she would never do. She picked up the phone and called O'Dooles, hoping against hope that he was there and safe.

The phone rang and rang. No one answered, and she gave up. Even the drunks stayed home on Christmas.

She was about to pick up the phone and call the hospitals again, when she felt a popping sensation. Warm water began to trickle down her legs and onto the floor. Gussie warned her this would happen, and to call the doctor when it did.

Evaleen picked up the phone and dialed.

The doctor's wife, who was his nurse, answered. It took the doctor a while to come to the phone, but when he did, he said he would be on his way shortly.

True to his word, she had barely dried herself off and changed into a clean nightgown when the front door buzzed. Grabbing a robe, she rushed downstairs to answer it.

The doctor, a man about 50, with skin so yellow it looked like wax, and his wife who was as round as a grape, waited there. They smelled strongly of medicinal soap.

"Thank God you're here," Evaleen said.

"Sounds like we're not a moment too soon," the nurse said with a smile.

She and the doctor followed Evaleen back up the steps. Ma looked up as the threesome entered the apartment.

To Evaleen's surprise, she rose up out of her chair and followed them all into the bedroom.

"Who are you?" she asked.

"I'm a nurse, and my husband's a doctor," the nurse said kindly. "We've come to help your daughter deliver her baby."

"That's nice," Ma said. Then she mumbled something unintelligible and returned to her spot by the radio.

Evaleen had another contraction, this one harder than the previous one, followed by another.

"Four minutes," the nurse said, checking her watch.

"Sounds like you're just about ready to go, little lady," the doctor said. He opened his little black bag and set out his equipment, while his wife busied herself covering the bed with a rubber sheet.

Evaleen felt chilled and anxious, but a little less frightened now that the doctor and nurse were here. As the doctor looked away, she took off her bathrobe and nightgown and slid beneath the cotton sheet the nurse placed over her to protect her modesty.

"The baby's head is in the proper position," the doctor pronounced, after he examined her.

In between her painful contractions, Evaleen obsessed about Hero. He knew she was about to give birth. Was he scared about her having a baby? Was it too much responsibility? Was he planning to leave her and never come back? That was probably it. How sad that she too would be one of those abandoned women, raising a child without a father.

Her mood switched sharply to anger. Maybe Hero would die, hopefully a slow, miserable death, so he would have plenty of time to regret being such a lousy husband and father. Then she could be a widow. People would feel sorry for her. Maybe she could use being a widow as a sales tool. Damn him. Before she could vilify Hero further, a contraction hit so hard her mind went completely blank.

Moving fast, the nurse shoved two rubber-coated pillows under her bottom, and advised her to bring her knees up to her chest, grab them, and the next time she had a contraction, to push as hard as she could.

Evaleen didn't have to be told. Her muscles felt like they were being twisted and wrung out, as each contraction became more and more brutal. She began to grunt like an animal trying to push its way out of a snare. The pain in her bowels was excruciating, but she was not in control of her body, or anything else.

"Push, dear," the nurse instructed. "You're not pushing hard enough. Push. Push. Push."

Evaleen did not hear her. She was no longer aware of anything except her body's massive urge to rid itself of its burden. After one long, especially hard push, a baby burst forth, with a full-throated scream.

"A perfect little boy," the doctor proclaimed, as he caught the baby on its way out.

A powerful thrill shot through Evaleen's entire body and literally took her breath away at the sight of her tiny, scrunched-up, wrinkled, crying son.

He stopped crying suddenly, as though in awe of himself for actually having made it into the world.

Moving quickly, the nurse suctioned his nasal passages, weighed and measured him, put some ointment in his eyes, dried him off and placed a blanket around him, then placed him in Evaleen's arms, who anxiously awaited her child.

"He's beautiful, and perfectly normal in every way," the nurse declared and smiled.

Looking over her son, Evaleen's feelings were complicated. She was already in love with this beautiful little being, but wasn't sure at all that she was equipped to keep this little fragile fellow alive until he grew up. In her inept care, he would surely die.

She was also sad at the idea that she would likely be raising him alone, since Ma wasn't much use. How she would do that, she did not know. And what were those white spots on her baby? Did he have some terrible disease?

The baby started to cry. With the doctor and nurse watching, Evaleen held the baby to her engorged breast and struggled to help him latch on. Instead of nursing, he just pursed his little lips, and refused.

"Maybe he just doesn't like breast feeding," Evaleen worried, after trying several times.

"Don't worry, dear," the nurse said. "Everything's normal. The spots will go away in a few days and as for nursing, he will get it and so will you. It just takes a little time."

She took the baby from Evaleen to bathe him, powder him, and dress him in the clothes Evaleen had prepared. She gave him back to Evaleen, who was anxiously waiting for his return.

In the meantime, the doctor took out a pen and filled out the birth certificate. He asked Evaleen for the baby's name.

"Courtland Herodotus Lyon," she said, spelling it out for him.

Evaleen and Hero had chosen the name Courtland from a baby name book they had consulted. They liked it for the sound, and because it meant brave.

Hero had rejected Herodotus as a first name. He said three people named Herodotus were plenty, and they didn't need another one. But Evaleen loved the name and insisted it be his middle name.

When the nurse finished her work, she handed Evaleen a pamphlet on nursing and child care, then she and the doctor left.

The moment they were gone, Court began to cry. Evaleen again tried to nurse him, and this time to her great relief, he latched on with no problem. Afterwards, she changed his diaper, burped him like the nurse showed her, kissed him on his soft little egg of a head, put him in the buggy and covered him with a flannel blanket, then wheeled him into the living room to meet his grandmother.

As usual, the radio was blaring away. Evaleen shut the radio off with a snap.

Ma looked up, irritated. "What'd you go and do that for?"

"Ma, I just had our baby, your new grandson," Evaleen said, patiently.

Ma looked over at the sleeping baby in the buggy, then at Evaleen.

"That's nice," she said, reaching over to turn the radio back on. Her eyes were flat, completely devoid of interest or emotion.

Evaleen was devastated. She didn't blame her mother, because she didn't think Ma could help being the way she was, but it hurt just the same. Something had gotten lost, and as far as she could tell it was never coming back. In the old days her mother would have loved having a grandchild, but those days were now gone.

Evaleen heard a car door slam out front. She ran to the window and anxiously looked out.

It was Hero. Finally. Every nerve in her body was tense as she watched him get out of the car and head toward their building. Court was now fast asleep. Not wishing to wake him, she pushed the buggy into the bedroom, then returned to the living room to wait.

The door opened and Hero appeared. Liquor fumes, cigarette smoke and some smell she couldn't identify proceeded him in a wave. His eyes were bloodshot and he was unshaven. The cuffs of his grey trousers were wet and filthy. It was obvious he had been having a high old time, while she had been at home, having a baby, and worrying about him!

"Did you have the baby, yet?" he asked, slurring his words.

"What do you think?" she hissed. "How could you leave me at a time like this? I hate you."

"I hate you, too," he said, sounding equally angry.

What? She couldn't believe her ears. She was the injured party here. What was wrong with him? Her pent up anger grew into a rage so great that, had she not been weakened from giving birth, she might have slugged him.

"What could I possibly have done to you?" she said, articulating each icy word.

"You got pregnant," he said, spitting out the words. "And now the kid needs a real man for a father, not some stupid joker working in women's face creams."

"Oh, Hero," she said, starting to weaken. "How can you even think that way? There are so many people out of work, and we're able to pay our bills and even have a little left over. And we just had a beautiful baby boy. I don't understand why…"

"A boy? We had a boy? Oh, my God. Where is he?" A look of awe crossed his unshaven face. "Can I see him?"

"He's in our bedroom," Evaleen said.

Hero raced to their bedroom and bumped the buggy in his rush to get a look. The bump woke up Court, who began to cry. Evaleen picked up her crying baby and held him close.

"Now look what you've done," she said, furious at him all over again. "You woke him up. Thanks a lot."

"You're welcome," Hero said, glaring back at her. Court continued to cry.

"Why don't you go back to wherever you came from," she said, jiggling Court in an effort to calm him, "and leave us alone."

"Good idea," he said in a cold, curt voice. He spun around and left, and this time she was glad to see him go.

He knew she was in labor. How could he leave? What did she ever see in such a man? Divorce was the only answer. Anything would be better than being married to that, that – she couldn't think of a bad enough word to describe him.

In truth, she was more hurt than angry. All she really wanted was for him to say he was sorry, and tell her he loved her, and give her a rational excuse for where he was and why he had stayed out all night, like he'd been involved in a bad accident, or he was helping out a sick friend, or something that made sense, anything...

Court began to cry, demanding to nurse. Seeing the dear, screwed-up little red face, she made herself calm down enough to nurse him.

#

While Court slept, Evaleen made herself and Ma some scrambled eggs, toast and coffee. She had no appetite, but forced herself to eat something to keep up her strength. She was exhausted from giving birth, and her mind was chaotic and abuzz with how she would support both Ma and Court by herself.

Christmas music was blaring so loud on the radio and her thoughts were so chaotic that Evaleen didn't hear the door open.

Hero reappeared. His clothes were even more disheveled than before and he looked shrunken, somehow. He carried a big box of chocolates and a dozen roses.

"I'm sorry," he said. He looked down at his shoes, like a little boy expecting to be spanked. "I was wrong. I know I let you down. Can you ever forgive me?"

Evaleen sat at the table in front of the now-cold food. She did not stand up, and made no move to accept the candy or flowers.

"I admit it," he said, setting the flowers and the candy beside her on the kitchen table. "I am an asshole. I was scared. It's such a lot of responsibility. I'm not sure I'm ready to be a father. And what happens if I don't like this kid? I mean, it's possible. I don't know anything about kids. I'm a rotten husband. I'll probably be a rotten father, too."

"I don't want to upset the baby or Ma any more than necessary," she said, speaking in a slow, deliberate way. "So please, just go away and leave us alone."

Even as she spoke, she knew what she was saying wasn't true. She loved him, and missed him, and was relieved he had come back, but she had her pride too, and didn't want him to think she was so desperate she would do anything, say anything, to keep him.

He made no move to leave. Instead, red-faced and mournful, he reached into his pocket and pulled out a crumpled cigar.

"I don't suppose you want one?" he said. "I bought these to celebrate."

"Oh, Hero, do you think you're the only one who is scared here? I'm scared, too. This baby is as much a stranger to me as he is to you. I don't know if I'll be a good mother, either. It's all brand new to me, too."

"Easy for you to say," he said. "You're a woman. It's normal for you to be a mother."

"Somebody told me once that children were the great love affair of our lives," she said. "I don't know about that, right now. He'll need a lot of things and I'll have to hire someone to help us take care of him and Ma, and I don't know how we're going to pay for it all, or manage it all. But you're right about being a bad father. What kind of a father would walk out when he knew his wife was about to give birth to his child?"

"You're right, you know," he said. "I wouldn't blame you if you never wanted to have anything to do with me again. I'm weak and disgusting. A snake's belly is too high for me."

He looked like a twelve-year-old who'd been caught shoplifting. Seeing him looking so pathetic and ridiculous and un-Hero-like, Evaleen began to soften towards him.

The hint of a smile appeared on her lips.

"Does this mean you forgive me?" he said, picking up on her smile.

"No," she said. "I will never forgive you."

But even as she spoke the words, she felt herself melting.

"Well, does this mean at least I can stay and spend the rest of my life trying to make it up to you and our son?"

"Our son needs you," she admitted, "and I need you, too, but that doesn't mean I like you right now, because I'm not sure I do."

She sighed heavily. "You should probably call your folks and let them know they're grandparents."

Although Hero's parents made it perfectly clear they wanted nothing to do with either one of them, they didn't seem to mind accepting Hero's money. Still, they were Court's grandparents, and for that reason alone she felt it was important to let them know.

"Think they'll be pleased?"

"I don't know," she said, "but I think they have a right to know they have a new grandson."

Court began to cry. Evaleen picked him up, changed his diapers, and kissed his head, then went to the kitchen.

She sat across from Ma, who was in Pa's old easy chair, staring into space listening mindlessly to Christmas music. Hero sat at the kitchen table and dialed his parents.

"Don't cry, Mother," Evaleen heard him say. "This is where I belong now – with my family. We just had a little boy, your first grandson. We named him Courtland Herodotus Lyon. You should see him, mother. He's perfect in every way. I can't tell who he looks like right now, but he's got red hair like Evaleen and…"

Hero hung up the phone without saying goodbye, and turned to Evaleen, a stricken look on his sallow face. It was obvious his mother had hung up on him.

"Guess they're not interested, huh?" she said.

"Guess not." He shrugged.

Evaleen also tried to shrug it off, but that they did not want to see their first and only grandchild felt like a knife through her heart.

To make herself feel better, she tried to remind herself that it was their loss, although that didn't help much. For some odd reason, at this very moment, she thought about Josh.

She was sure he wouldn't disappear when she needed him most. He would be a great father and his parents would probably be wonderful grandparents, too.

She thought about her own father, and wondered how he would have felt about being a grandfather. Would it have made any more difference to him than it did to Ma? She cleared her head – thinking about all this just made her feel bad. Best not to think at all.

"Let's open our presents," Evaleen said, in an effort to cheer everyone up. "Far as I know, it's still Christmas."

Hero turned the Christmas music up as he and Ma opened up the presents Evaleen had purchased at Bomberg's earlier – a dress shirt and tie for Hero and a new bathrobe for Ma. As for Hero's gifts to Evaleen, the flowers were already beginning to wilt, and the chocolates turned out to be stale.

Chapter Fifteen

Evaleen loved spending time with her new baby, but soon found the endless routine and drudgery of housework stultifying. Ma wasn't much company, either. She spent her days listening to soap operas, and didn't seem to be interested in her new grandson except when his cries interrupted her program, which obviously irritated her.

Evaleen was glad Ma had her soap operas to keep her company, but the constant blaring of the radio and her mother's growing helplessness sometimes got on her nerves. She missed going to work every day. Hero helped in his way, but he wasn't much good around the house and refused to change Court's diapers or bathe him.

"That's woman's work," was his explanation.

Evaleen used Court's nap time to work on her plan for the space at Bomberg's. At night, when Court was in bed, she worked at making and stockpiling her products, so she would be ready when it was time to return to work, either going door-to-door, or hopefully at her counter in Bomberg's. She still wasn't sure that was real.

Hero had no such problem. To Evaleen's surprise, he seemed almost as happy and excited about this as she was. He even went so far as to order a big sign to be hung on the wall behind her counter announcing the grand opening of Fresh-As-A-Daisy Skin Care. She was grateful for his help and thankful that he was interested and seemed to care almost as much as she did.

Finally, January sixth arrived. It began with winter sunshine flooding through the front windows, a hopeful sign. Evaleen was up and dressed and ready to go, hours before it was time. Hero, too, was up and ready early.

When it was finally time to leave, Evaleen kissed her mother goodbye, then handed Court over to Gussie, who was available to babysit because her boyfriend was out of town.

Seeing Evaleen leave, Court began to cry.

"He'll be fine the minute you're gone," Gussie said.

Sure enough, just as Gussie predicted, Evaleen heard Court stop crying the moment she shut the door behind her.

It had snowed the night before, and on the street the bright sun made the snow look filled with glitter. Evaleen held onto her hat to keep it from blowing away, as she stepped into the passenger side of the waiting car.

"Alone at last," Hero said, and grinned a wolfish grin as she settled in. "Too bad we have to go to Bomberg's. Too bad we can't just go somewhere like a motel and have a little party. Seems like forever since we've actually been alone."

He leaned over and gave her a lusty kiss.

She kissed him back with gusto, but worried about smearing her lipstick and wrinkling her new gray wool dress and making it to Bomberg's on time.

Since Court was born, Hero seemed eager to please her. She noticed and loved him for it, but something fundamental had changed between them. She no longer trusted him not to let her down in some disastrous way. Perhaps it was because Hero never did offer any explanation of where he went on Christmas Eve.

She didn't push it either, not wishing to find out what she didn't want to know.

As Hero drove, she redid her lipstick in the small compact mirror she carried in her purse. Looking at her face, she was hit by a fresh wave of inferiority. She was a big-boned, plain looking girl, unlike Hero, who was tall and slender and as handsome as a movie star. No amount of makeup could change that. Would Mrs. Bomberg wonder what he saw in her? And would Hero come through for her?

She couldn't be sure of anything where he was concerned. He seemed to like the idea of working with her, but then he would sabotage her efforts by not buying enough jars, or smearing the ink on the labels, or not getting the facts and figures together until the very last minute. Still, he always did come through in the end.

Hero parked in the street right in front of Bomberg's. As they hurried through the swinging doors, a blast of heat hit her in the face like a blessing. Inside, her heart pounding with a mix of fear and hopefulness, she took a deep breath to help her relax, and quietly reminded herself that like Napoleon Hill said, success comes to those who try. God knew she was trying.

"Hey, Evaleen," Hero said, as they approached the cosmetic section. "Is that the empty counter you were talking about?"

"Yes," Evaleen said happily. "That's it."

"It's so small and dark," Hero said. "Nobody's going to see you back here."

That fact didn't bother her. That it was empty meant it was still available, a good sign.

"It'll look a lot better and bigger when it's all lit up and the shelves are laden with my products."

She could almost see the space all lit up, stacks of jars in gleaming little pyramids on the counter, herself looking chic and professional as she rubbed cream into a customer's face, while several other women waited patiently in line for their free demonstration.

"We better get moving," Hero said, interrupting her daydream.

"Yes," she said, snapping to attention.

They hurried past shelves and shelves of sale items, greatly reduced now that Christmas was over, surprising since the Depression seemed to continue unabated.

At the executive office, Evaleen took a deep nervous breath, then entered along with Hero who didn't seem nervous at all. A striking young woman with bobbed hair and bright red lipstick greeted them.

"Mr. and Mrs. Lyon, I presume?" she said. "Mrs. Bomberg is waiting for you. Follow me, please."

They followed her to a large office with a window, where Mrs. Bomberg sat behind a large cream-colored desk. She greeted them with a smile and bade them sit on the upholstered chairs in front of her desk. Evaleen took note of her expensive black wool suit, white silk blouse and pearls, and tried not to be intimidated.

After talk about the new baby and the weather, Mrs. Bomberg got down to business.

"Tell me your plans for the space."

Sounding a lot calmer than she felt, Evaleen began by discussing how she planned to decorate the space, what products she would be selling and the specials she planned to offer for their grand opening. She and Hero had discussed all this.

When she finished she sat quietly by as Hero discussed what their projections were for the coming year, and what their plans were for promoting the space.

"We can open March First," Hero said, summing up. "That will give us enough time to get up and running, place a few ads and work out any bugs before the summer season hits."

He sounded optimistic and confident. Evaleen was proud of how handsome he looked, and how smooth and in control he seemed, even flirting with Mrs. Bomberg a little.

"Sounds good," Mrs. Bomberg said. "You'll need to sign our standard contract, which we ask of everyone who sets up a stall at our store."

She handed the contract to Hero. Hero took his time reading it, while Evaleen and Mrs. Bomberg talked about the new baby. When Hero was satisfied, they both signed the contract.

"I know you will be a wonderful addition to Bomberg's," Mrs. Bomberg said, standing up. "Congratulations and welcome aboard. We'll see you on March the First."

Evaleen felt a burst of joy, and didn't bother to hide it now that the deal was done. "Thank you so much for giving us this opportunity. You won't regret it."

"You don't need to thank me, my dear. This is purely a business proposition for us. You will either make money for us or not. I'm counting on the former."

She smiled. "Either way, the counter will no longer be vacant. And that's a good thing."

Afterwards, Hero acted strangely subdued, but Evaleen was too elated to care.

#

On opening day, Evaleen was ready. She had hired Mrs. Kelly, a widow with five grown children, to care for Court and Ma. Mrs. Kelly said she was glad for the money, as she was barely getting by. Evaleen felt lucky to have her. Everyone else she contacted refused to take on the care of a grown woman, in addition to a small child.

She might have left Ma alone, except that twice in the last two weeks Ma forgot to turn the stove off after she was heating up some coffee, and Evaleen worried that with no one around to check on her, she might burn down their building.

Mrs. Kelly's only condition was that she preferred to care for Ma and Court at her place, because she hated to leave her apartment so early in the morning. Since Mrs. Kelly lived only two doors down, Evaleen was happy to agree.

Thankfully Ma did not put up a fuss and agreed to go along.

Evaleen was now so anxious to get started, she spent the night wide awake, willing the time to pass. She and Hero had set up the counter the previous night, after the store closed, and were ready for business, complete with a big banner behind her counter proclaiming, "Grand Opening. Fresh-As-A-Daisy Skin Care by Evaleen." Seeing that banner for the first time gave her a huge shiver of excitement.

She wore her usual uniform of a white blouse with a silk daisy pinned to the lapel and black cotton slacks. She wore her long, red hair down and loose, just like Rita Hayworth.

She began the day by lighting the two new lamps, which gave her counter a soft, golden glow, the better to admire the carefully placed pyramids of her skin-care products. Sprinkled here and there were silk daisies like the one pinned to her blouse.

She took a moment to admire it all, then set out the sign Hero had ordered, stating, "Free Demonstration Today." She unlocked the cash register and stood behind her counter, and anxiously waited for the first customer to appear.

Two hours went by. Not one person stopped, although there seemed to be plenty of customers at the other counters.

Finally, an older woman came over, but said she was just looking and refused a free demonstration.

Two other women stopped by, but only to have a quick look. Evaleen knew from going door-to-door if she could get someone to sit for a free demonstration, there was a good chance they would buy her cream, but the few women that did approach were not interested in a free demonstration.

Around two o'clock, desperate, her back aching from standing in one place for so long and with no customers in sight, she decided to try something new. Before she could lose her nerve, she locked up the empty cash register, placed a bunch of her samples in a bag and went to the front door. She stood where people would see her, the moment they entered.

"'Try this," she said, trying to sound confident as she handed a sample to a woman in a fur coat, as she entered the store. "It'll do wonders for your skin. We're giving away free facials today at Fresh-As-A-Daisy. It only takes three minutes and could change your life."

The woman took the sample and kept on going. This went on for a while, until just about the time Evaleen was ready to believe this wasn't working either, when to her great relief, a well-dressed woman took her up on her offer.

"Sure, why not?" the woman said. "It's not like I'm doing anything else today, since my Morty died a month ago."

"I'm so sorry to hear that," Evaleen said with real sympathy, as she guided the woman back to her counter. She placed the stool from behind the counter out front for the woman to sit on.

"Hopefully, this will make you feel a little better," she said, as she cleaned the woman's face with cleansing cream.

As the woman went on and on about her Morty, and what a wonderful husband and father he had been, Evaleen removed her makeup and rubbed in her skin lubricating cream and enjoyed the silky feeling beneath her fingers.

"Oh, that felt so good," the woman said afterwards, admiring her face in the handheld mirror Evaleen passed to her.

She ended up buying two jars of the skin lubricating cream, one for herself and one for her daughter.

Energized by that one sale, Evaleen returned to her station at the front door. Smiling through the pain in her back and hips from standing so long in high heels, she continued to give away free samples and free demonstrations when she could get someone to agree to it.

She ended her first day by giving two more facials, although she only made one more sale. But to Evaleen, it was one of the most exciting days of her life. She would have gladly stayed until midnight, had she been able to sell even one more jar, but the store closed at six and she was forced to quit for the day.

She picked up Ma and Court, took them both home, enjoyed a cuddle with Court, got Ma situated next to the radio, then made their evening meal and cleaned up afterwards.

Around ten, after making her to-do list for the following day, she went to bed.

Hero showed up an hour later. He had alcohol on his breath and he was in a foul mood, as he barely said hello.

Not wishing to start an argument, she pretended to be asleep as she didn't want to know where he had been, or what was bothering him. Today was a good day, one of the best, and she wasn't about to let him ruin it for her.

The following morning, he was gone before she woke up. She noticed, but was too excited about her new business at Bomberg's to worry about it or him.

She sold five jars of her grandmother's skin care cream, and two jars of cleansing cream that day. She worried about Court, and hoped he didn't miss her too much and that Ma was able to listen to her soap operas, but refused to think about what Hero was or was not doing.

#

Six months later, the business was beginning to grow. It was painfully obvious to Evaleen and Hero that if they were to continue at this pace, they would need more space. Every available nook and cranny in the apartment was packed with baby paraphernalia, beauty supplies, or the simple clutter of everyday living. Even Ma had begun to complain about feeling crowded.

After discussing it at length, Hero found a restaurant near downtown Emerson they could use for both storage and production. The owner had gone broke, and simply walked away one day. They went to look it over.

Dirty dishes still sat in the sink, and a thick layer of grease covered everything.

Hero said the bank that owned the property was willing to rent it out dirt cheap. Evaleen was glad, as the kitchen had a nice deep sink, a big six-burner gas stove, a large farm table, a big refrigerator, and plenty of cupboards for storage space. Hero figured he could work out of one of the big booths in the front. They agreed to rent the place.

Then it took three Sundays to clean it up enough so they could actually work there.

One Sunday while Court slept and Ma listened to the small radio Evaleen purchased to keep Ma occupied while they were all at the restaurant, Hero and Evaleen sat together in one of the booths and talked.

This was something they hadn't done in a long, long time, since both were always so busy. Both were exhausted yet neither seemed able to relax.

Evaleen brought up the idea of giving a small gift with each purchase to introduce her customers to new products, something Helena Rubenstein was doing. Hero wasn't sure they could afford it, but was willing to test it out. Hero mentioned that Court seemed fussier than usual, lately. Evaleen reassured him that Court was teething and that his fussiness was normal. They also discussed Ma, and how distracted she seemed lately. Neither knew what, or if, they could do anything about it. They talked about everything except how they were feeling and what was happening between the two of them.

#

One day, a spring rain kept falling off and on. Business at Bomberg's was almost non-existent. Evaleen decided to take advantage of the bad weather and the lack of customers to ease the guilt she was feeling at not spending more time with Court and Ma.

She called Bitsy Junior Johnson and asked her to cover for her. Bitsy Junior often filled in at the other cosmetic counters when anyone needed a day off, or went on vacation. She was seventeen years old, tall and slender, with creamy skin, curly black hair worn in two ponytails, one on each side of her head, and always carried herself with a natural elegance. She told Evaleen she was named for her grandmother who had been named Bitsy by a younger sibling, who couldn't quite pronounce her real name, Betsy.

"My grandmother, a tiny little thing, became Big Bitsy and I, who am twice her size, became Little Bitsy. Anyway, somehow along the way I became known as Bitsy Junior, and don't ask me how that happened either, because I don't have a clue."

Evaleen liked Bitsy instantly. She wasn't surprised to find out that Bitsy Junior had excelled at everything she ever tried. She was a Girl's State Representative, editor of the yearbook at her high school and in the top ten in her class, although she had stopped attending school lately. Evaleen asked her why.

"I need a job more than I need school, right now."

"I didn't finish high school, either," Evaleen said, "although I wish every day that I would have. I often feel like I'm missing important information, somehow."

"I don't feel like I'm missing anything," Bitsy Junior responded. "School was a big fat bore. It's a lot more fun to be working and making money, especially now."

Realizing the futility of arguing further, Evaleen commenced to show Bitsy Junior what she needed to do, when and if she sold anything.

Then Evaleen left, happily looking forward to spending time with her son.

At Mrs. Kelly's building, Evaleen went up the steps and knocked on her door. No answer. She tried again. Still nothing.

Thinking Mrs. Kelly hadn't heard, she turned the knob, which was unlocked, and went inside. What she found stunned her.

Court sat in his swing. His diapers were soaked and dripping urine. A bottle of sour milk lay on the floor beside him.

Seeing her, he reached out his little arms and began to howl at the top of his lungs. She rushed over, picked him up and held him close.

Furious, she went to look for Mrs. Kelly and Ma. But neither Ma nor Mrs. Kelly were anywhere to be seen.

Fear and anxiety knotted inside her as she changed Court's diapers, made him a fresh bottle, fed him and waited impatiently for Mrs. Kelly to show up.

Where was Ma? Had she wandered off? Was she with Mrs. Kelly?

The more time ticked by, the more worried she became. A half hour later, which felt more like three hours, Mrs. Kelly showed up, her hands full of grocery bags. Ma was not with her.

"Where's my mother?" Evaleen demanded, her voice a deadly calm.

"She was here when I left," Mrs. Kelly said, not quite looking her in the eye.

"Here when you left?" Evaleen repeated, growing angrier by the minute.

In a cold fury, she picked up the phone and called the police to report her mother missing. Mrs. Kelly stood by, not saying a word, guilty tears streaming down her broad face.

"You're fired," Evaleen said coldly when she hung up the phone. "I never want you near my child or my mother again. You'll be lucky if you don't go to jail for neglect."

She pulled a ten dollar bill out of her purse, flung it at Mrs. Kelly, and left with her son.

Frantic with worry, with Court on the car seat next to her, she circled the neighborhood several times, but found nothing.

Desperate, not knowing what else to do or where else to look, she drove to the workshop to tell Hero and ask him to help her. Of course, he wasn't there. Thinking there was no way he could be at O'Dooles at this time of day, but having no idea where else to look, she took a chance, picked up the phone and dialed.

"I'll check," O'Doole said, in his gruff voice.

A few minutes later, Hero came to the phone.

"What's up?" Hero asked. He sounded annoyed.

Evaleen was tempted to ask him why he was at O'Dooles when he was supposed to be at work, but that would chase him off. Instead, she forced herself to remain calm as she told him what had transpired.

"I'll meet you at home," he said quickly, without further explanation.

He arrived shortly afterwards, reeking of alcohol and cigar smoke. Evaleen didn't say anything. She had learned that reprimanding Hero did absolutely no good. He did what he wanted to do and no amount of arguing changed anything, except to make matters worse. Besides, finding Ma was more important than arguing with him right now.

With Hero driving and Court on her lap, they looked everywhere they thought Ma could possibly be, even up and down alleys. They also stopped people on the street and asked if they had seen her.

When the daylight faded into evening, and still no Ma, they went home.

Evaleen wasn't ready to give up but Hero insisted saying they had looked everywhere it was possible to look. And what if she wandered back home? They would need to be there for her.

So they went home. Tense with worry, she fed Court and put him to bed. Thankfully, he fell asleep almost immediately.

She was just about to call the police again to ask if they had heard anything yet, when the doorbell buzzed.

Hoping, praying, Evaleen raced downstairs and opened the door.

To her great relief, two burly, red-faced policemen stood on either side of Ma, who looked exceedingly tiny next to them. She was wearing her coat, although it wasn't buttoned. She had a happy, excited look, as if she were on a date.

Seeing her mother safe and sound, Evaleen burst into tears of relief.

"We found her on Pennington Avenue," one cop said. "She was standing in the middle of the street, waving at the traffic. A good thing her address was in her purse, or we never would have known where she lived. She couldn't seem to remember where she lived."

Ma stood between the two big cops, smiling a goofy smile.

"Thank you so much for bringing her home," Evaleen said, when she could speak without breaking down. "We were so worried."

"Well, keep a better eye on her in the future," the taller of the two policemen said sharply. "You're lucky she had on a coat. It can get pretty cold at night. "

Back in their apartment, Evaleen felt completely at fault. She should have tried harder to find someone to care for Court and Ma. But how could she have known Mrs. Kelly would be so irresponsible? She assumed because the woman had already raised a family, she would do a good job. Next time, Evaleen would be sure to check references.

"I wouldn't worry too much," Hero said, noting Evaleen's obvious misery. "She seems to have had a pretty good time for herself."

Ma grinned at Hero's assessment as she plopped down in her favorite spot and turned on the radio, as though it were a day like any other.

Evaleen made a quick supper. Afterwards she and Hero sat down at the kitchen table, trying to figure out what to do next. The plan they came up with was strictly one of desperation. Hero would stay home with Ma and Court and do whatever work he could do at home while Evaleen worked at Bomberg's. Weekends, they would all go down to the workshop together so Evaleen and Hero could get their work done.

It seemed to work, at least for a little while. Hero did what business he could while Court napped. And if he could convince Ma to turn the radio off for an hour or so while Court was still sleeping, he would make phone calls.

But the minute Evaleen arrived home, he took off. He always had an excuse. It was the only time he was able to speak to a client, or visit a distributor, or sometimes he just needed a break. Evaleen was sympathetic and didn't protest, although she missed him and would have preferred he spend more time with her at home.

On Sunday mornings, they did try to make time for each other. Evaleen would give Court a bottle to quiet him, then she and Hero would spend time together in bed, talking about everything and making love.

In spite of this, something profound had changed between them permanently, although neither would have admitted that this was even a possibility.

Chapter Sixteen

From a young girl hungry for acknowledgment, desperate to have her life mean something, Evaleen was quickly becoming the success she had always dreamed. With Hero's help she was able to support her family decently, a practical result that gave her a feeling of worth and solidity when her fears of rejection and doubts threatened to overcome her. But with a child to raise, a mother who was becoming increasingly forgetful, a growing business and a husband who was also her business partner, life was becoming more and more complicated.

Added to this were her feelings of guilt at Pa's death and the pure loss of him, which popped in and out of her mind every single day and often haunted her dreams. She wondered if it would have made any difference had he known how well she would end up doing with her grandmother's creams. Probably not, because she felt sure that had she not stolen the money he would still be alive. Anyway, it was impossible to know that, or if he ever would have forgiven her.

That Friday, while doing the dishes after supper, her thoughts were not about Pa or finding a replacement for Mrs. Kelly, but about Gussie, Shu and Josh and how much she missed them. Josh likely had a girlfriend by now. He might even be married.

Did he ever think about her? Did he miss her? She sure missed him, but she was a married woman and calling him would be improper. Thankfully she did hear from Gussie once in a while, but that too was becoming more rare, since Gussie was so preoccupied with her married lover. As for Shu, Evaleen had given up ever hearing from her again.

Court began to fuss, snapping her back to reality. She picked him up and forgot everything as she tickled his little tummy, making them both laugh. Her little boy was already crawling and pulling himself up at every opportunity. Evaleen felt bad that she had to leave him and Ma so much.

She felt bad about her marriage, too. Hero never seemed to be home. The only day he didn't go to O'Dooles was Sunday, and that only because the bar was closed.

"What's so fascinating about O'Dooles that you would rather be there than at home with us?" she asked once.

"Maybe it's because I feel like a man there instead of some eunuch who works in his wife's beauty business," he said, his voice filled with disdain.

"At least you have a job," she shot back. "There are a lot of men who would love to be in your position."

"Maybe some fancy boys would like it. Not me."

"Hero, it's a business and a good one," she protested. "And we're partners."

"Yeah, right. No matter what you say, it's still your name on the business, not mine."

She gave up. Arguing with Hero was a waste of time. Besides, she didn't blame him for wanting to leave. She wanted to leave, too.

If it weren't for Court and wanting and needing to spend time with him, she'd be gone all the time. Truth was, she felt more alive, more aware, more excited when she was at Bomberg's or at the workshop producing and bottling her creams than she ever felt at home. When her first customer of the day appeared, she felt a rush like an alcoholic must feel when about to take that first drink of the day. And if a customer actually bought something, she was thrilled and couldn't wait to do it again. She felt the same way when a batch of her creams turned out perfectly and smelled delicious. That she preferred working to being at home added to her guilt, but it didn't change how she lived.

After cuddling with Court and putting him to bed, as always she went to work. Although tired, she laid out colored pencils on the kitchen table to sketch some new packaging ideas. She wanted a more professional look, more like Estee Lauder's elegant packaging. Hero had made an appointment for her to meet with a professional package designer next Tuesday, and she wanted to come up with a few ideas to show him.

She was still working at nine when Ma snapped off the radio and went to bed, not bothering to say good night. That wasn't unusual these days. Ma seemed to be growing quieter as each day passed. Evaleen would notice her mother staring off into space and wonder what she was thinking about. If she asked, Ma would say, "Nothing," and wouldn't elaborate.

She hadn't come up with anything worthwhile by ten o'clock, when the phone rang. She was tempted not to answer because she was so tired, but fearing it was important, she picked it up. To her surprise, it was Gussie.

"He's gone," Gussie blurted out in a tiny, flat voice.

She broke down crying.

Evaleen was more surprised to hear Gussie cry than shocked at what she said. She'd never heard Gussie cry before. Gussie was always the strong one.

"Gone?" she asked, confused. "Who? What?"

"Bill died," Gussie said, choking out the words between sobs. "I just found out. My sister showed me his obituary in today's newspaper. It said he died of a massive heart attack. I didn't know who to tell, so I called you."

She broke down in a fresh torrent of sobs.

"I'm coming right over," Evaleen said, thinking fast. "I just have to call Hero so he can come home and watch Ma and Court."

Before Gussie could protest, Evaleen hung up and dialed O'Dooles. Normally she hated the thought of calling there, but this was an emergency.

"O'Dooles," came the gruff voice of old man O'Doole himself.

"I need to talk to Hero," she said. "It's urgent."

"Let me see if he's here," O'Doole said.

She heard him call Hero's name above the noise of the jukebox and people talking in the background.

Moments later, Hero came to the phone. He sounded annoyed.

"I need you to come home right now," Evaleen said, not mincing any words. "Bill died and Gussie needs me."

"I'll be there as soon as I can," he said.

He knew that it was a point of pride for Evaleen not to call O'Dooles, so if she called it had to be important.

True to his word, he arrived a few minutes later. Evaleen thanked him and left in a hurry.

The night was still hot, although black and starless. As Evaleen drove, she felt bad that Gussie's life had come to this. Gussie had given up everything good in her life for a married man, who obviously had no intention of ever leaving his wife. In a way, Evaleen was glad he was gone. Maybe now Gussie could break free of the iron hold he seemed to have over her.

At Gussie's sister's house, Evaleen rang the doorbell. Her sister Sally answered the door. Sally was even rounder than Gussie, with permed curly bleached blond hair that had a strange orange tint. She looked irritated.

"She's downstairs in her bedroom and won't come out."

"Poor Gussie," Evaleen said.

She followed Sally down the steps to the basement.

"Brought it on herself," Sally griped in a self-righteous tone. "You mess with fire you're bound to get burned. What did she expect?"

Evaleen was tempted to ask Sally why she let Gussie do all the housework and care for the children while she played pinochle all day with her friends, but kept her mouth firmly shut. This was not the time or place to get into an argument with Gussie's sister.

"She's in there," Sally said, stopping at the only room in the basement with a door. "Maybe you can talk some sense into her. She won't listen to me or anybody else."

To Evaleen's relief, she spun around and went back upstairs.

Evaleen could hear muffled sobs coming from the other side of the door. She knocked lightly. No answer. Feeling uncertain but determined, she peeked inside.

Gussie lay on an unmade bed, curled up in a fetal position. Her face was swollen from weeping. There was no window in the room. Weak light came from a single bulb hanging by a wire attached to the ceiling.

Evaleen had assumed that Gussie was living in a spare bedroom, not in this dungeon. Even more shocking, the bed was unmade and the floor was covered with newspapers, completely out of character for Gussie, who was always so neat and organized.

Evaleen sat on the bed next to her friend. "I'm so sorry, Gussie."

"I wouldn't have even known if Sally hadn't seen it in the newspaper," Gussie said bitterly, raising her head. "And Bill's awful wife is still around. Can you believe it? She was always so sickly, but he's the one who died. Guess the joke's on me."

Tears of sympathy came to Evaleen's eyes.

"What are you going to do now?" she asked, wiping them away.

"I don't know," Gussie said, dabbing at her eyes with her soaked handkerchief. "And I don't really care."

Evaleen took a fresh handkerchief from her purse and handed it to Gussie, who wiped her dripping red face and blew her nose.

"He was such an amazing man. I always wondered what he saw in me."

Evaleen understood that feeling only too well. That's what she used to think about Hero.

Like Hero, Bill had been debonair and dashing. He always wore the most expensive suits and shirts, and looked like the railroad executive he was. Gussie was one of the nicest, kindest people Evaleen had ever known, but no one would call her a beauty.

When the attraction between them grew and became physical, Gussie, not wishing to be a home wrecker, quit and moved in with her sister, who said she could stay until she found another job. But Bill showed up at her sister's house and everywhere else she went, begging her to take him back. Gussie wasn't strong enough to fight her attraction for him, and was soon back in his arms.

As she admitted to Evaleen once, there was never a moment she didn't feel guilty about seeing a married man, but she couldn't seem to stay away from him no matter how hard she tried, so their sad love affair continued. To be available whenever he called, Gussie didn't even try to get another job. Instead she babysat, cleaned and did all the cooking for Sally and her family.

Her sister responded by letting Gussie know how much she disapproved and how lucky she was to have a roof over her head, while taking advantage of her willingness to help out. About all Gussie had left to show for her grand love affair were a few pieces of cheap jewelry, some sexy lingerie, and her memories.

"I have no excuse except I loved him," she said. "And he must have felt the same way too, because he called me every day no matter where he was, sometimes several times a day."

She stopped to blow her nose. "When I didn't hear from him, I was extremely upset, but what could I do? Call his wife? And I can't even go to his funeral because I don't belong there. If his family knew, they would hate me, and I don't blame them. I'd hate me too, if I were them."

A fresh wave of tears poured down her broad cheeks. "Oh God, I wish I were dead, too."

"Nonsense," Evaleen said, angry Gussie would even think such a thing. "Don't you even dare think like that. Oh, Gussie," she said, her anger changing to sadness at such a terrible thought. "I would miss you so much. I couldn't bear it if you did something like that."

As the two women sat together, Evaleen was hit by the most wonderful idea, which she immediately blurted out. "Why don't you come live with us until you get on your feet?"

The moment the words were out of her mouth it felt as though God Himself had spoken. This was the answer to both of their problems.

"I would just be in the way. Your apartment's too small for another person."

"You wouldn't be in the way," Evaleen said quickly, "and you could sleep on the davenport and keep your things in Ma's room. I'm sure she wouldn't mind."

"I don't know anything right now," Gussie said. "I don't know what to do. I don't know what to say. All I know is Bill is gone. I can't think straight, I—"

"We could help you and you could help us," Evaleen said, speaking quickly as she thought it out. "It would be mutual. Hero and I need someone to help us care for Court and Ma. To cook and keep up the place while we work. Everything's a mess all the time, it's driving me crazy. We need help so bad. Hero says he can't get anything done with the radio blatting all day and taking care of Court and Ma, too. I can't keep up, either. We're both falling behind. We'd pay you a decent wage. It would give us both such relief knowing that Court and Ma would be taken care of by someone as wonderful as you and—"

"No thanks," she interrupted. "I grew up in a family with way too many kids. That's the last thing I want to do."

Evaleen understood perfectly. Gussie's parents were loving, well-intentioned people, but they had both grown up as spoiled only children, where their wish was their parents' command. Practical skills seemed to allude them both. Evaleen remembered when Gussie was twelve and decided her parents needed some structure in their life and got them to go to church. Her goal was to make them strong enough so they could care for her and her siblings.

"You stand up, you sing, you pray, you sit down, then you stand up and everybody reads something together, then you pray, then you sit down," her mother said. "What's the point?"

"I don't get it, either," said her father. "You listen to some old fart who never lived a day in his life telling you how to live your life. What a waste. If I feel the need, which I don't, I can talk to God perfectly well at home."

They never went again, although Gussie continued to attend Sunday school anyway, because she enjoyed hearing the choir sing the old gospel hymns. Their basement, full to the ceiling of broken furniture her father planned to fix someday but never got around to, was a metaphor for their chaotic life.

In response to their childhood, Gussie's sister Sally had become fanatically clean, the kind of person who, according to Gussie, would throw a tantrum if you so much as wrinkled a seat cushion or set something down on a table without a coaster underneath. As for her other sisters, they just faded away after her parents died, her father of lung cancer and her mother of heart failure. They rarely kept in touch with each other.

"And Court is still a baby," Gussie said, as though talking to herself.

But Evaleen caught the tiniest bit of interest in her voice. She began to feel hopeful.

Gussie went on. "As far as I can tell, he cries a lot."

Evaleen jumped on the opening. "Oh, Gussie, he cries a lot because he doesn't get nearly enough attention. I bet you'd love him as much as we do, if you got to know him."

"And your mother's senile."

"She's not completely senile, but you're right in that she just mumbles and shuffles around, talking to herself and listening to her soap operas all day. She doesn't always make good sense sometimes and she can be forgetful, but she still uses the bathroom and can feed herself and she's not much trouble at all, really. Besides, you can't be any worse than Mrs. Kelly, who let Court drink sour milk and never changed his diapers and treated Ma like she was already dead."

"Oh, yes I can," Gussie protested.

She blew her nose with the soaked handkerchief. "Just ask Sally. I can be much worse. She'll be happy to tell you that nothing I do is good enough for her."

"I know you better than your sister does, Gussie, so save your breath. At least I'll pay you for your work. And I promise I will never give you a hard time like she does. And it'll be so wonderful having you nearby. Please Gussie."

Evaleen was beginning to enjoy this little battle. She had the distinct feeling she would win if she could just hang on long enough.

"Maybe I could get a job at Hallorhans," Gussie said. "I heard they were hiring."

"They probably are," Evaleen said, thinking fast. "There are more jobs now than there used to be. But unemployment is still really high, so I wouldn't be too sure. If you don't like working for us, you can quit. My feelings won't be hurt, I promise. I'll give you a good reference, too. I'll even put it in writing in advance and you can date it later. As for pay," Evaleen said, desperate to convince her. "We can start you out at five dollars a week, including room and board and Sundays off, Saturdays too if you need them. We'll raise you yearly as we make more money in the business. Since President Roosevelt signed the Social Security Act, Hero can fill out the papers and make sure you become entitled to an old-age pension when you retire. The only bad side is you'll have to share your room with Ma until we can find a bigger place. Please, Gussie. I'll do anything you ask. Anything."

There was a long silence. Evaleen held her breath.

"Anything?" Gussie said finally, in a tiny voice.

"Anything." Evaleen worked to keep the triumph out of her voice.

Gussie's swollen tear streaked face took on a new, serious look.

"Okay," she said, her voice shaky but determined, "here's the deal. One, you let me take care of Court my way. If he cries, don't get mad if I don't run to pick him up every single time, the way you and Hero do. And two, I can manage your mother for now, but if she gets to the point where she needs diapers or becomes more of a problem, I'll need help to manage her. As for sharing a room with your mother, it's got to be better than being in this dank, dark hell hole. Anything is."

In spite of Gussie's disclaimers, Evaleen knew she would be wonderful and loving with both Ma and Court. Gussie had the kindest heart of anyone she knew.

"You won't be sorry, Gussie." Evaleen said, glorying in her triumph. "I'll make sure of that. When can you start?"

"Soon as I get my things," Gussie said wiping her face with the back of her hands. "It'll be a relief to get the hell out of here. You can't even put your feet up. Sally expects me to scrub the damn floor every time someone walks on it, and she never passes up an opportunity to let me know what a bad influence I am on her and her family."

"Well then, pack up and let's go," Evaleen said.

She was anxious to leave before Gussie decided to change her mind.

"I don't know," Gussie said hesitating. "I should probably give my sister some kind of notice so she can find somebody else to take advantage of."

"Not necessary," her sister said, knocking perfunctorily before entering the room. She must have tiptoed back downstairs and been listening at the door the whole time. "I was just trying to help you out."

A superior, self-righteous look spread over her broad face. "You can leave any time you like."

"Great," Gussie said shooting her sister a dirty look. "I will. Doing your own housework will give you something to do besides gripe all the time."

"And that's the thanks I get," her sister said furiously.

She spun on her heel and left.

"That's settled, then," Evaleen said, pretending not to notice. "Come on. I'll help you pack your things."

It was two in the morning before Evaleen, with Gussie in tow, finally arrived back home. She made up the davenport for Gussie, then went to bed.

It had been a long night and she was exhausted. In spite of this, she remained wide awake. She could hear Gussie's muffled sobs and felt sorry for her friend, but was thrilled to have her so close by.

During the days that followed, Gussie managed to hold herself together as she cared for Ma and Court, but at night, she continued to cry herself to sleep. Days, Evaleen did not interrupt Gussie when she went on and on about Bill and what a good man he was and how amazing and brilliant and handsome, nor did Evaleen give advice. Mostly she just listened and did whatever else she could to help her friend get through this hard time.

Three months later, Evaleen knew that Gussie was beginning to recover when she came home earlier than usual and discovered Gussie and Court sitting on the floor banging pots and pans in time to Beethoven's Fifth on the radio.

They were both laughing hysterically. Ma too was smiling.

In the spirit of the moment Evaleen took her son from Gussie and danced him around. Instead of laughing, he began to cry and reached for Gussie. Thankfully, Gussie refused to rescue him and he finally relented, but it was obvious that he preferred Gussie.

Evaleen was hurt, but figured that was what she got for working.

In her defense, she tried to make it home in time at least to put Court to bed most nights, but something always seemed to come up at the last minute, making it impossible. So Court grew closer and closer to Gussie.

Seeing the results of so much absence, Evaleen vowed to try harder to spend time with him.

Chapter Seventeen

Sunday, December 7, 1941. It was late. Evaleen and Hero were at the workshop, busily gearing up for Christmas. Hero was working in the front on ordering and Evaleen was busy in the back, only half-listening to the radio as she screwed caps on jars of newly made face cream. Evaleen was hurrying, as she was anxious to get home in time to spend some time with Court before he went to bed. Suddenly the music stopped and a man began to shout.

"We interrupt this program to bring you an important announcement. The President just announced that the Japanese have attacked Pearl Harbor by air. The attack was on all US naval and military activities in the area."

Evaleen, not sure she had heard right, turned up the radio.

"Japan has launched a surprise attack on our naval base at Pearl Harbor," the man continued in an excited voice. "Six battleships have been sunk and another one hundred twelve vessels were destroyed or damaged and one hundred sixty-four aircraft have also been destroyed."

"Damn it, Evaleen, turn the radio down," Hero said, suddenly appearing in the back. "I can't concentrate on a damn thing with the radio blatting away like that and—"

Evaleen put her fingers to her mouth to shush him. Hero stopped in mid-sentence.

"Two thousand of our servicemen have been killed, one thousand on the battleship Arizona alone, which has been completely destroyed," the man continued. "Only chance saved three other US aircraft carriers and only because they were elsewhere. Over a thousand U.S. citizens have been injured. It's horrible, horrible."

Evaleen and Hero stood together, both speechless, staring at each other in disbelief. There had been a lot of talk of war on the radio and in the newspapers in the last few years, but somehow it never seemed real. She had no idea where Pearl Harbor even was. Moments later the sound of airplanes could be heard roaring overhead.

"I'm going to sign up tomorrow," Hero said, when they could hear each other again.

The thought shattered her.

"You can't," she said. "I need you here."

"My country needs me a hell of a lot more than you do," he said, speaking in a quiet but firm voice.

"I can't do it alone," she argued, determined to convince him. "There's too much. We'll go broke."

"Yes, you can," he argued back, equally vehement, "and anything you can't do, you can hire someone to do."

"No, I can't," she persisted.

She realized she was acting like a pathetic fool, but she didn't care. "You can't leave now. You can't. I need you, the business needs you."

"Yes I can," he argued, "and I will, and there isn't a damn thing you can do about it, either."

"Hero, you have a child. We have Ma to care for. Soldiers don't make enough to feed that many dependents. Your son will go hungry."

They argued back and forth heatedly for over an hour. Evaleen finally won the argument, saying the whole family was depending on him and that if he were gone, the business would go down and they would all be in dire financial trouble, including him.

But he wouldn't look her in the eye afterwards. And instead of going home after work, he went to O'Dooles. Or at least that was where she assumed he went.

Alone at home, Evaleen tried not to think about Hero, or the fact that whenever something bothered him, he used it as an excuse to leave, or their argument about his working in the business instead of going off to war. Instead, she distracted herself by playing with

Court, helping him build a Tinker Toy car, while listening to the radio with Ma and Gussie for further news of the upcoming war.

She went to bed right after putting Court to bed. Hero arrived home around midnight, waking her up. He smelled of booze and cheap cigars. Not wishing to spend the rest of the night arguing with him, she pretended to be asleep.

The following Thursday, Germany and Italy declared war on the U.S., just as it was predicted they would. Neither Hero nor Evaleen spoke of his signing up again, but the way they carefully avoided the subject spoke louder than any words. Hero continued to work in the business but he stayed away from home even more than before. Evaleen realized how unhappy he was but didn't say anything to him about it, not wishing to start yet another argument.

#

Five months later, Evaleen and Hero sat at the kitchen table, eating breakfast and reading different sections of the newspaper – Hero the sports and Evaleen the family section – when an article about the problems soldiers were having with camouflage caught her eye. According to the article, to camouflage their faces many soldiers were being forced to use burnt cork or mud, which often contained harmful bacteria and caused serious skin problems.

The thought flashed through her mind that here was an area that she and Hero could do something about, an area he could be proud of.

Last Sunday, Court had asked him why he wasn't a soldier like all the other daddies.

"Ask your mother," Hero replied, unable to look his son in the eye.

"Not all daddies go to war," she explained softly. "Some daddies are needed at home."

Court seemed satisfied with that explanation and went to play with his truck.

Hero had left the house shortly afterwards, saying he needed some fresh air. Evaleen noticed and it hurt, but she needed him too much to argue.

So now today, her heart filled with growing excitement.

"Hero, here's something we can do," she said.

"Do what?" Hero said, obviously annoyed at being interrupted from reading an article about baseball.

"Here." She handed the newspaper to him. "Read this and tell me what you think."

Hero skimmed the article and handed the newspaper back.

"So?" he said, anxious to get back to his article.

"Don't you see, Hero?" she said. "We could do this. We could make camouflage makeup that would be safe for our boys. Think of it. We could actually do something to help our soldiers fight this terrible war, and increase our business at the same time."

A look of interest appeared on Hero's face, and he put down his newspaper. Evaleen was thrilled she had gotten through to him. At that moment, the general uneasiness between them since Hero agreed not to sign up began to dissolve. Both became intrigued at all the possibilities.

That very same afternoon, Hero approached a metal manufacturer. He wanted to make a deal to produce a short run of small tin cans to replace the fragile glass jars they were using for their beauty creams. He also purchased a variety of tints from an art supply store for Evaleen to mix into her creams.

When he showed her his purchases, they both gloried in their new mutual interest.

The next day, Evaleen was so anxious to begin experimenting that she had trouble concentrating at Bomberg's. As a result, she didn't do nearly as well as usual. All she could think of was how to make and produce the camouflage cream.

The moment the clock hit six, she was out the door and off to the workshop, anxious to begin. Hero was waiting when she arrived, and helped her get started.

In the days that followed, because of their mutual excitement, they were like a couple in love, although it wasn't quite as exhilarating as before, more companionable and appreciative of each other. Hero, to Evaleen's delight, even stopped disappearing so much, and spent more time at home. Most nights in bed together, they spent hours talking and planning for the future. They even made love more often. Evaleen felt a bottomless satisfaction with her new life. Even her walk had a sunny cheerfulness. Hero too seemed more upbeat than he'd been in a long time. Ma, Court and Gussie also seemed happier than usual these days.

#

When they agreed the camouflage cream was as good as Evaleen could possibly make it, Hero began to make phone calls to the Army, Navy, and anyone else who might listen. After two weeks of getting nowhere, Hero finally thought to call their Congressman, whose campaign they'd previously given a few dollars. With his support, they got through to the commander in charge of requisitions and supplies for the United States Army at their local army base. Although he didn't act particularly excited by the idea, he agreed to meet with them for a demonstration.

So on a hot, steamy day in August, with Bitsy Junior manning the counter at Bomberg's, a seemingly calm Hero and a nervous and eager Evaleen arrived at the Army base near the Emerson airport. After passing muster, two soldiers escorted them to a Quonset hut. Shortly afterwards, several men in uniform came in and sat at a long table, where they looked straight ahead without speaking. Not a smile, not a word of greeting, just a cold nod from the base commander for them to begin.

Seeing those stone-faced men made Evaleen even more anxious than she already was. She sounded stiff and unnatural to her own ears as she spoke about the benefits of their camouflage cream, while she shakily applied it to Hero's face and hands. When she finished she sat down. Hero stood up in full camouflage to give his spiel. Evaleen admired how confident he was, how calm and how handsome he looked, even with his face covered in camouflage makeup.

Afterwards, to both of their surprise, there was no question and answer session. The base commander simply stood, thanked them for coming, shook their hands and left, followed quickly by the rest of the men at the table.

"We were obviously wasting their time," Hero said, sounding depressed in the car as they headed back to the workshop.

"Maybe that's their standard operating procedure," Evaleen said, but she didn't feel any more hopeful than he did.

At the workshop, Hero said he had errands to run and dropped her off. Evaleen was pretty sure one of those errands included O'Dooles, but she did not protest.

Alone in the workshop kitchen painting daisies on glass jars, something she normally enjoyed, she pictured the women at O'Dooles attracted by Hero's looks, his charm, wanting to please him. Not wishing to think about that, she thought about Shu instead. She missed her and wondered how she was doing. She knew it was useless to call and felt bad that was so.

She missed Josh too, even more than she missed Shu. How long had it been since they'd spoken? She felt a desperate longing just to hear his voice again. Thinking about Josh and Shu hurt almost as much as worrying what Hero was doing or how badly their presentation went today. Best to just keep busy and try not to think at all.

#

Off and on for months afterwards, Hero kept talking about signing up. Just his mentioning it could throw her into a panic but she kept quiet, not wishing to nag or cause another argument. Better to say nothing and hope it would all go away.

At the end of one day, Evaleen was at Bomberg's, adding up her receipts. To her surprise, Hero showed up, grinning wildly.

"You're not gonna believe this, darlin'," he said.

He took an envelope out of his pocket and handed it to her.

Evaleen was distracted from adding up her sales, but took what looked like an official envelope from him and opened it. She skimmed the sheet of paper inside.

Then, staring at it in disbelief, she read it again, more slowly. It was an order from the army for camouflage cream.

Dumfounded, she looked over at Hero who looked back at her, a huge smile on his face.

"That's right, Babe," he said. "They want 200 cases of your camouflage cream to start and they want it as soon as possible."

Evaleen couldn't help herself. She began to cry.

"It's true," he said, sweeping her into his arms. "We did it. We won."

Evaleen wiped her eyes with the back of her hand. She read the order twice over again, letting it all sink in.

"Let's celebrate," Hero said.

With a shiver of joy, she closed down her counter. Like two school kids playing hooky, they went off to the Chateau de Paris, one of Emerson's finest restaurants.

Since it was only a little after six, they were able to get a table right away. The restaurant was all dark wood, subdued lighting, and soft music. Every table was covered with snowy white linen with a small bouquet of flowers in the center. Lit candles gave off a romantic light.

Hero ordered a bottle of champagne and they toasted their future. They were both happily tipsy as they ate their Chateaubriand with béarnaise sauce, baked potatoes and a salad. Today was their day and they were happy together.

#

The very next day, it was a thrilled Evaleen who hired Bitsy once more to cover for her at Bomberg's so she could work full time at fulfilling the army contract. With the addition of camouflage makeup to her work load, Evaleen was working even more hours every day. She missed dealing with her customers and spending time with her family, but she was also excited about their future. As for Hero, she saw him off and on all day, but both were too busy for anything more than a quick kiss and a few minutes of conversation.

Thank God for Gussie, who waited up for her every night and kept her company and informed her of all the happenings at home or she wouldn't have had any idea what was going on there.

During these conversations Gussie seldom spoke about her married lover but Evaleen knew it still bothered her. The mere mention of his name could sometimes cause tears to well up.

In spite of her own busy schedule, Evaleen made it a point to stop at Bomberg's a couple of times a week to see if Bitsy needed anything. Bitsy was putting on a lot of weight, and her white lab coat was becoming extremely tight across the middle.

"What's happening, Bitsy?" Evaleen asked one night after work.

They were having dinner together at a local diner, a monthly practice Evaleen had begun so as to stay informed.

"You probably noticed that I've gained some weight lately," Bitsy blurted out.

"Can't buy a decent girdle anymore because they need the rubber for the war effort," she joked. "Can't even get a decent stick of gum lately, for that matter. I used to love that Double Bubble but you can't even find it anymore... Oh damn. I'm fat because I'm pregnant," she said, not quite looking Evaleen in the eye. "I'm too big to hide it anymore."

"Oh," Evaleen said, not quite sure how to respond. "You must be happy, right?"

"No," Bitsy said, "I'm not, I, yes, I don't know, I..."

Soon the whole story came out. Bitsy had fallen madly in love with Tom Banks, a boy at her school. She was positive he loved her back until she told him she was pregnant.

After that he began to avoid her. When she caught up with him one day outside their school and asked why, he admitted he wasn't ready to be a father. His parents must have agreed because he was sent to live with his aunt in Minnesota the very next week.

Bitsy hadn't heard from him since.

"He didn't even say goodbye," she said, wiping the tears carefully from her eyes so as not to smear her mascara. "When I told my parents, they both went nuts. My father didn't say a word when my mother called me a tramp and kicked me out."

Bitsy stopped for a long moment to compose herself.

Then she continued. "The Salvation Army took me in. I've been living there ever since. Want to hear something stupid? They give you a fake name. Mine is Madonna. Can you believe it?"

She laughed a bitter laugh. "We're supposed to wear fake wedding rings when we go anywhere. But it's been really tough. I've been trying real hard to save my money for after the baby comes, because I don't know how much longer I'll be able to work. I don't think Mrs. Bomberg or anyone else will believe that I have a basketball in my pants much longer. I probably should have told you sooner, but I need the money and I was afraid I would lose my job."

Instead of being upset at Bitsy's deception, Evaleen felt a quick pulse of excitement. Here was her chance to begin her lifelong dream of helping abandoned women, since Bitsy was now so obviously one of them. God was handing her a golden opportunity to do something important, something meaningful, a way to help resolve her guilt about her father's death and pay back for her own good fortune. Was she up to the challenge?

"Are you planning to keep your baby?" Evaleen asked, all brisk practicality now.

"Yes," Bitsy Junior said. "I'm getting a lot of pressure at the home to give my baby up for adoption, but I can't bear the idea. Some of the other girls can't make themselves do it either, so we came up with a plan. We pooled our money and rented the lower half of a four-bedroom duplex on River Street. We figured that we could help each other with the rent and babysitting until we get going again. We're all pretty excited about it. The other girls have had their babies and already moved in. I plan to join them as soon as my baby is born."

"I can help you all with jobs," Evaleen blurted out, barely able to contain her excitement. "We have more work than I can keep up with since we got the military contract, and we make enough money to hire help. I'm pretty sure we can pay you a decent wage, although I'll have to talk to my husband about it. He handles all the money. We'll let you keep your babies with you at the workshop. He'll figure it all out. He's good at that kind of stuff."

Bitsy Junior shut her eyes as though in prayer, then let out a deep breath.

"You don't really mean that," she said.

"Yes I do," Evaleen said. "I've never meant anything more in my whole life."

#

True to her word, the following Sunday, bubbling with excitement, Evaleen arrived at the duplex where the girls lived. Bitsy Junior met her at the door and invited her inside.

The apartment was plain and simply furnished with obvious castoffs, but it was clean and neat and organized in spite of the baby gear everywhere. Bitsy Junior told her to watch out for the middle spring on the couch as it had a tendency to break through. One of the girls brought her a cup of tea. Another girl brought a plate of ginger cookies.

"Enjoy it while you can," she said airily. "I heard on the radio that sugar is about to be rationed for the war effort."

As Evaleen drank her tea and enjoyed the delicious cookie, the girls told her their stories.

Renee began. She was slender with light brown hair worn in a page boy and blue eyes so pale they seemed almost colorless. As she spoke, she pushed the buggy containing her sleeping baby girl back and forth with her foot.

"I fell in love. Unfortunately it didn't last very long. By the time I figured that he wasn't Mr. Right, I was pregnant. When my parents found out, not wishing to deal with what would surely be a huge scandal, they told everyone I went to live with my aunt although I was here at the Salvation Army in Emerson the whole time. The day my baby was born, I called my mother to tell her she had a new grandchild and to come and meet her."

She stopped and stared at the floor for a long moment. "She said I had made my bed and I could now lie in it and not to bother calling her again." She spoke quickly, in almost a whisper.

"But you now have a beautiful, healthy daughter," Evaleen said reassuringly. "That has to feel good. And she looks just like the Gerber Baby with those big, blue eyes."

"You noticed it too," Renee said, obviously pleased. "I thought I was the only one."

Virgie, short for Virginia went next. She was a big-boned farm girl with short, wildly curly brunette hair and a clean, plain face. She said she had already born one child at age sixteen with her boyfriend Joe that she was forced to give up, so when she discovered she was pregnant again by him, she hated the thought of giving up another child and decided to keep the baby.

"I loved Joe and he loved me. He loved telling jokes and he could always make me laugh."

Her baby Henry suddenly giggled out loud, a mischievous look on his little round face. "He's a lot like his father," Virgie said and smiled.

"Anyway, Joe joined the Navy, hoping to save enough money to go to college and become a teacher. We were planning to be married when he came home on leave. Only he didn't come home. The ship he was on was torpedoed and everyone on board was killed. He didn't even know I was pregnant. He would have loved being a father."

Remembering brought tears flowing down her face. Embarrassed at being unable to control her emotions, she handed Henry over to Evaleen and rushed off to the bathroom to wipe away her tears in private.

As they waited for her return, Henry explored Evaleen's face with his chubby little fingers, finally settling on her nose. When she pried his little fingers loose, he began to explore her mouth, giggling the whole time. Of course, Evaleen fell totally, instantly and completely in love with him.

When Virgie returned and took Henry back, Mabel told her story.

"I hate to admit this," she said, "but I had too much to drink at a party and I must have started messing around with someone, although I don't remember who. There were a lot of boys there that night. Well, as you can imagine, I got pregnant. My mother didn't disown me but made it plain that she was through raising kids, her own or anybody else's and that's why I'm here."

As she spoke, her fat little baby, Lola May, sat quietly on her mother's lap, sucking contentedly on her own stubby little fingers.

Being around the girls and their babies made Evaleen's heart swell with love. They had so much pride in their babies and all seemed to be good mothers. She felt sorry for them, too. It must have been so hard to be pregnant when all of society looked down on you. At the same time she felt energized. She was positive this was her real destiny.

She proceeded to tell them her plans, which she made up as she went along. Bitsy Junior would work at Bomberg's until she gave birth. Then Mable, Virgie and Renee would take turns filling in for Bitsy until she had her baby and could return. Whoever was not working at Bomberg's would be trained at the workshop to do everybody else's job in case anyone got sick.

The only exception was making the actual beauty products, which Evaleen would do herself since the recipes and production techniques were proprietary. They could take turns babysitting, on a schedule to be worked out among themselves.

The girls all agreed immediately, obviously thrilled that they would have good jobs, stay together and be able to keep their babies nearby while they worked.

When Evaleen left, they walked her to her car, thanking her over and over again.

As Evaleen drove away, she felt a bottomless peace and satisfaction. Even though she wasn't that much older than them, she felt like they could all be her daughters. When she told Hero what she'd done, he agreed with her decision to hire them all and only teased her a little about not consulting him beforehand.

"You've been overwhelmed and needed help for months," he said. "I'm glad you found them."

Evaleen was pleased at his response and felt a whole new wave of love for him.

To expedite matters, Hero hired a carpenter to build a large penned-in area to keep the babies safe while their mothers worked. Evaleen brought in some of the many toys that Court no longer played with, and purchased a few others.

In the days that followed, Bitsy Junior trained the girls to fill in for her at Bomberg's and Evaleen trained them to help her at the workshop. In no time, or so it seemed, Evaleen and the girls were ready and waiting for the next big order from the army to come in. The only problem was, it didn't come.

A week after it was due, Hero made several calls to the military, but either they weren't willing to talk to him or they sent the call off to someone who sent it to someone else. Desperate, he finally called the War Department in Washington. It was even worse there. Nobody seemed to know anything about anything.

A month went by. They were becoming frustrated and desperate. Evaleen had long run out of things for the girls to do and with their only income coming from Bomberg's, Hero had to borrow money to make the payroll. Out of desperation, Evaleen had begun to train the girls to go door-to-door, when suddenly they received another blow.

On a Monday morning they were sitting around the workshop trying to come up with money-making schemes, one more outlandish than the next, when Mrs. Bomberg called and asked to speak to Evaleen. Evaleen was surprised to hear from her.

Mrs. Bomberg seldom talked to Evaleen. If there was anything important to discuss, she usually talked to Hero. She said she wanted to meet as soon as possible.

"Is tomorrow at two good for you?"

"Two is fine," Evaleen replied.

"Good, I'll see you tomorrow."

And that was it – no chit chat, nothing. Strange.

Something was obviously wrong, but Evaleen couldn't imagine what it could be. To her knowledge, they were doing fine. Hero had no idea, either.

On her way to Mrs. Bomberg's office the next day, she stopped to say hello to Bitsy, who seemed to be growing larger by the minute, before hurrying off to meet with Mrs. Bomberg.

The moment she stepped into her office, the atmosphere, which had always been warm and friendly before, felt strangely cold.

"I want to talk to you about Bitsy Danson Junior," Mrs. Bomberg said getting right to the point. Her voice sounded strange to Evaleen's ears like she was giving a speech, not bothering to make the usual small talk.

"She's a wonderful employee," Evaleen said. "Our customers love her. Both Hero and I think she's a real asset to our business."

"She's pregnant and unmarried," Mrs. Bomberg said impatiently. "Bomberg's does not wish to be associated with the kind of girls who go off and get themselves pregnant without a husband. This is not the kind of image that we at Bomberg's wish to convey to the public."

Evaleen was shocked at her words but reacted quickly.

"I would say we're doing quite well, wouldn't you?" she asked in full Evaleen the Queen mode.

"Yes, but that doesn't mean it's all right." Mrs. Bomberg's penciled eyebrows drew together in an angry frown. "What do you think that says about us?" She articulated each word.

"First of all, I'm sure most people are way too concerned about themselves to care about Bitsy's pregnancy," Evaleen said, equally icy in return. "Second, she doesn't wear a sign saying 'I am an unwed mother.' Third, she stands behind a counter so most people can't tell whether she's pregnant or not, and fourth, it's nobody's business. She's a good girl and she works hard and that's all you should care about."

Mrs. Bomberg turned red in the face. "Our name is on the business and that means something in this town," she said in an imperious tone, as she obviously struggled to control her temper. "My husband and I have worked hard to build a good reputation. I will not have you ruin it by hiring some cheap floozy."

"Bitsy is not a cheap floozy," Evaleen said, matching Mrs. Bomberg's angry tone of voice. "How dare you think so? She made a mistake. Haven't you ever made a mistake, Mrs. Bomberg?"

"Not that kind," Mrs. Bomberg said, coldly. "Now, I don't want to waste your time, so here's how it is. Either you fire her today or I will consider your contract rescinded immediately, for ethical reasons."

"Do what you want," Evaleen said, almost too furious to speak. "I'm not firing Bitsy or anybody else."

There was a moment of astonished silence. Evidently not many people stood up to Mrs. Bomberg, and she had fully expected Evaleen would kowtow as well. For a moment she looked indecisive: Fresh-As-A-Daisy was bringing in a lot of money for Bomberg's these days. She drew a shaky breath and changed tactics.

"I'm sorry about this, but Bomberg's has a position to maintain," Mrs. Bomberg said, taking on a wheedling tone. "Try to understand our position in this town."

"I don't understand," Evaleen said, "and I never will. Bitsy is a wonderful girl. She works hard and neither she nor we deserve to be treated like this."

She stood, anxious to escape Mrs. Bomberg and her self-righteousness.

"Good day," she said and left.

The moment she stepped into the hallway, panic set in. What had she done? What would they do now? How long could they keep paying everybody with no money coming in?

Evaleen found a pay phone and immediately called Hero. For once he was at the workshop where he was supposed to be. She told him everything.

"I wouldn't do business with someone that small minded if she were the last person on earth," Hero said, as furious as Evaleen was. "I don't give a damn if we go broke or not. The sooner we get away from that place, the better. I'll be there as soon as I can round up some boxes to help us pack."

Evaleen was grateful for Hero's support, glad that he was acting so quickly and loved him for it as she went to tell Bitsy they were leaving Bomberg's and would have to pack up immediately.

"This is because I'm pregnant and unmarried, isn't it?" Bitsy said in a miserable tone when Evaleen gave her the news. "I knew by how she wouldn't look at me or even say hello when she passed by the counter that she was mad. This is all my fault."

"Mrs. Bomberg is a narrow-minded shrew," Evaleen said. "I don't want to work for such a person and you shouldn't either. Good riddance to her and her husband."

Hero arrived with a pile of empty boxes. He angrily ripped the sign off the wall, then with Evaleen and Bitsy's help, loaded the boxes and hauled them out to his car. They left the counter as empty as the day they occupied it.

Back at the workshop, Bitsy told everyone what happened. Evaleen reassured them all that they still had a job, but Evaleen wasn't nearly as sure as she sounded. Nothing was working out for them lately and they had a lot of extra mouths to feed these days. Evaleen was scared but refused to let it show.

At home later, she told Gussie what happened. As always Gussie was a sympathetic listener and reminded her that what she had done before, she could do again. As for Hero, who knew where he was. He had disappeared again.

#

Word got around fast and by the following day it seemed as though everyone in the whole town of Emerson knew what happened. It was all anybody could talk about and very little work got done that day, not that there was much work to do. No one seemed able to concentrate. Evaleen felt their fear combined with her own.

But around three o'clock, Evaleen came up with a bright idea. She shared it with Hero, who was figuring out their bank balance to see how much longer they could last with no money coming in.

"Call the Army base after hours," she told him. "All the people intercepting our calls would have gone home except the bosses who usually work late in most offices."

Hero agreed to give it a try that very day. They waited until the girls had gone home for the day, then around six o clock, with Evaleen standing next to him encouraging him, he called the number of the officer in charge of acquisitions.

It worked! The officer answered the phone himself. Hero quickly explained their plight and gave him all the specifics.

The officer listened patiently, but then said, "Sorry, I can't help you. That's not my department."

Without another word, he hung up.

Hero also called their congressman. His secretary answered and promised to relay their message, but he didn't call back.

Discouraged, not knowing where else to turn, they gave up.

Evaleen worried that Hero would join up for sure now, and she couldn't blame him. Nor would she make any effort to stop him. Their business was going nowhere.

If there were an escape for her, she would have taken it too, but she had promised herself she would always provide work for the girls and take care of her mother. She wasn't about to renege on her word.

Then it all changed again.

A week later, around one o'clock in the afternoon Evaleen was in the back sharing her various spiels with the girls for going door-to-door, when Hero appeared at the door right in the middle of 'what to say when a customer seems interested but reluctant,' grabbed her, bent her way back and kissed her deeply right in front of the girls.

"Thirty thousand cases," he crowed, when they both came up for air. "We got an order for thirty thousand cases. How about that? Apparently that last phone call must have worked. Don't ask me how because I don't know. Maybe the congressman's secretary got to him or maybe the general got involved. It doesn't matter. We got the order."

Evaleen finally caught on to what he was saying and returned his kiss wholeheartedly.

The girls cheered. Hero called the liquor store and ordered a case of champagne. They all celebrated by getting a little tipsy and going out to eat at the Chicken Shack afterwards before going back to work.

"My biggest fear was always that the girls would leave us before we could get going again," Evaleen said to Gussie that night over cups of tea. "Especially now when anyone who wants a job can have one. That new factory down the street is churning out parts for B17's like crazy and they're hiring anyone who comes in off the street. I understand the money's good too, even better than we can pay."

"Maybe so but what about being able to take your kids to work and knowing they're properly cared for? Not too many places do that. And you pay a good wage, I know you do. Anyway, let's celebrate and have another cupcake. Enjoy it, because I won't be able to buy sugar again for another month."

As the two women enjoyed their cupcakes, the subject changed to Court, who attended a pre-school program five mornings a week, and how he had learned to spell his name and do his ABC's. They also discussed the girdles Gussie and her friends were giving up for the war effort.

"The government was asking for rubber donations," Gussie said. "I was thrilled to give mine up for the war effort. Feels good to be able to breathe without feeling like I'm encased in rubber."

"They can have mine, too," Evaleen said, glad to have an excuse to get rid of hers.

Ma appeared like a ghost, went to the kitchen and got a glass of water, then returned to her room without speaking to either Gussie or Evaleen.

Gussie shrugged. "She still acts like the soap opera characters are real. It's kind of sad but it makes her happy."

"Hard to believe she wasn't always this way," Evaleen said.

"Thankfully, she's no trouble," Gussie said. "That's a blessing."

The subject changed back to Evaleen's work and how Hero surprised them all with the news. And how elated and relieved everyone was to have work. They had all gone back to work in spite of being slightly woozy and full of chicken.

Then it was back to Gussie again. She and some of their neighbors had started a victory garden in a vacant lot and discussed in loving detail how well that was going.

"Court loves digging in the dirt," Gussie said. "I swear that child will grow up and be a dirt farmer someday."

"By the way, Don Johnson mentioned that he would like to get to know you better when he stopped by the other day." Evaleen said. "He seems like a really nice guy."

"What's that got to do with dirt and gardens?" Gussie asked.

"Nothing," Evaleen said and laughed. "I just remembered. You remember him, don't you? He delivers our mail at work. Anyway, we were talking about his victory garden and I told him about yours. That's when he asked me if I thought you might be interested in going out with him. You probably don't remember it, but you met him two weeks ago, when you brought Court and Ma to work to have lunch with us."

"I do remember him," Gussie said. "Nice looking guy. Seemed okay. But no thanks. I've had enough of men. You just can't trust them. All they care about is sex."

"Don't be so hard on men, Gussie. You just fell in love with the wrong guy."

"Marriage doesn't look like a good deal for anybody," Gussie said.

She poured herself another cup of tea and helped herself to another cupcake.

"Oh, come on, Gussie," Evaleen said, also helping herself to another cupcake, "it can't be that bad."

"I don't see anything better," Gussie said, giving her a pointed look.

Chapter Eighteen

One year later, on a hot and sticky night in August, the last of the light was filtering through the front windows of their home. Court was in bed, Gussie was fussing in the kitchen, Hero was at O'Dooles, or so he said, and Ma was in her bedroom listening to the radio – since there were no soap operas on, she had the radio tuned to news of the fighting at Guadalcanal and other news about a race riot in Harlem.

Evaleen was working at the kitchen table and visiting with Gussie off and on when the doorbell rang. Gussie went to answer it.

To Evaleen's surprise, she heard Josh Goldman's voice in the vestibule. Thrilled, she dropped what she was doing and rushed to the door to greet him.

He looked slightly rumpled, as though at the end of a long, hard day. Happiness radiated all through Evaleen at the sight of him. She grinned a loopy grin, embarrassed at herself for being so obviously, pathetically, ridiculously happy to see him again.

"Josh, what a lovely, lovely surprise," she said, unable to contain her joy. "I was sure you had gone off to war by now."

Instead of being as happy to see her as she was to see him, he seemed distraught.

"My number hasn't been called yet, although I'm expecting it any day now," he said, "but that's not why I came. I have some terrible news and I thought you should know."

Evaleen's happiness evaporated and changed to panic. Something must have happened to Hero. It had to be him, because Court and Gussie and Ma were in the house with her. Was he all right? Was he hurt? Was he dead? What happened?

Evaleen was tempted to shout her questions but held herself still, afraid almost to breathe.

"It's Shu," Josh said, in such a quiet voice that Evaleen had to strain to hear his words. "Sam beat her to death with a baseball bat and then shot himself."

He choked up momentarily then continued. "I heard it on the news an hour ago. A neighbor said she had called the police before on him when she heard him beating up his wife, but he always managed to run away before they showed up."

For a second Evaleen was relieved that it wasn't Hero, but then this new awful truth hit her.

"Shu?" she asked, whispering her name, afraid to say it out loud and make it real. "Are you sure?"

Josh nodded, a look of utter despair on his dear face.

"Oh, dear God," Gussie said and began to weep. "Not Shu. Please, God. No."

"Sam was always angry about something," Evaleen said, the horrible reality of it beginning to sink in, "but nobody could have predicted this."

"Poor Shu," Gussie said wiping her eyes.

"What about Bunny?" Evaleen asked, forcing back her own tears as an even more terrifying realization occurred to her. "Is she all right?"

"From what I understand," Josh said, "she's in police custody until they find a place for her. Unfortunately, Shu's folks are both gone and so are Sam's. I have no idea where her siblings are, except that they all left town after high school. Shu told me once that Sam had a sister in New York. I don't know if she's been notified or not. I'm worried about Bunny. That's why I came. I think we should do something. By the way where's Hero? He'll want to know, too."

"He might be at O'Dooles," Evaleen said. "He didn't say when he was coming home."

It embarrassed her to admit that he was hanging out at a beer joint, playing pool and drinking beer instead of being at home with her and the family, but this wasn't the time to cover up for him.

"I always thought Sam was crazy," Gussie said. She loudly blew her nose. "Remember how he acted at your wedding when Shu was about to have her baby? What a horrible man. And poor Shu for getting tangled up with such a monster."

She shivered. "It's just too much for a body to take in."

"I should have tried harder to get through to her," Evaleen said.

She forced back the tears that threatened to engulf her, something she'd become strangely good at during the previous years.

"Don't blame yourself," Josh said. "She was pretty obvious about not wanting to see any of us. But nobody could have predicted something as horrible as this. Nobody."

"It might be too late to help Shu, but it's not too late to help Bunny," Evaleen said.

"If they'll even let us," the always practical Gussie replied.

"Maybe they'll let us take her in until a relative shows up to claim her," Evaleen said.

She gathered her strength and began to take charge. "Otherwise she'll probably end up in a home with complete strangers, or an orphanage. Shu would hate that so much. Can you handle another little person in the house, Gussie?"

"You know I can," Gussie reassured her. "That poor child needs us."

"Thanks Gussie. It's so good to know I can always count on you. When Hero shows up," (if he ever shows up, she was tempted to say, but didn't), "tell him to meet us at the police station."

#

Outside on the street, Evaleen was hit by such a huge wave of grief that she broke down and began to sob uncontrollably in spite of her resolve not to cry. Josh put his arms around her and held her close. His arms felt good around her, comforting, solid, and something else she didn't want to think about right now.

Hero chose that moment to pull up in his car. He stopped abruptly in the middle of the street, leaped out of the car leaving the door wide open and the motor running. Josh and Evaleen flew apart as though they had been caught red-handed having an affair.

"Get away from my wife," Hero shouted. He gave Josh a hard shove with both hands.

"Relax, Hero," Josh said in a calm voice. "I'm not doing anything wrong."

"Don't try to fool me, you low-down cheating bastard," Hero snarled in a voice filled with hate.

Before Josh could respond, Hero slugged him in the forehead, opening a cut above Josh's eyebrow. Blood began to drip down his face.

"You're making a terrible mistake," Josh protested, wiping the blood from his forehead with the back of his hand.

"For God's sake, Hero, stop it," a furious Evaleen shouted. "Shu's dead. Sam killed her. Josh came to tell us. He was trying to comfort me. Shame on you for thinking anything else."

Hero stopped cold, his fists in mid-air.

"We're headed for the police station to see if Bunny's all right and has a place to stay," Evaleen said, speaking quickly. "You're being ridiculous."

Hero looked at her for a long moment. The mean look on his face melted into one of questioning, then shame. He put his hands back down where they hung like two limp things at his side.

"What are you saying?" he asked.

"Sam murdered Shu today," Josh said in a measured tone, obviously trying to control his rage. "I heard it on the radio an hour ago."

"Oh God, I'm so sorry," Hero said, all apologies.

He pulled out his handkerchief and dabbed frantically at the blood on Josh's face. "Can you ever forgive me?"

"We need to get to the police station," Josh said, not looking at him or answering him. "We'll take my car. I have plenty of gas at the moment."

Normally, Hero would have argued this point, insisting that he drive, but he had used up most of his gas ration that month, and so was forced to go along with Josh.

On the way to the police station Hero sat up front next to Josh while Evaleen sat in the back. Nobody spoke. Evaleen was still furious at Hero, but kept it to herself. Her feelings about him or Josh were not important right now, the only thing that mattered was trying to find out what happened to Shu's little girl.

At the police station, a sooty old brick building, Josh parked and they all went inside. The stench of cigarettes, sweat and urine hit Evaleen's nostrils as they approached the desk sergeant, a huge fat man sitting behind a tall podium.

"State your business," the cop said gruffly.

In a calm, sure voice, Josh uttered their request.

He must have been convincing because, after signing them all in and checking their identification, another cop appeared and indicated for them to follow him down a dingy grey hall with several small rooms opening off of it.

"She's in there," he said, stopping at the third room. Without another word he left them.

Through a two-way window they saw Bunny, an unusually beautiful child of six. She resembled her mother, with the same wide, mesmerizing green eyes, and dark, wildly curly hair. She appeared to be fussing over a doll with a porcelain head. A large motherly-looking policewoman sat at a table opposite her.

"She seems to be enjoying herself," Hero observed.

"She's probably in a state of shock," Evaleen protested.

"Poor kid," Josh said, shaking his head sadly as he knocked on the door.

"We're friends of her parents," he said, when the policewoman opened the door.

Before Evaleen could make the introductions further, a big, ruddy faced policeman came in and whispered something in the policewoman's ear.

She then relayed the news to Evaleen, Josh and Hero.

"The child's aunt has been called," the policewoman said. "She said she isn't able to care for her sister's child at this time. The girl will need to go into foster care."

"If it's possible, we'd like to take her home with us," Evaleen said quickly, annoyed at the policewoman for speaking so in front of Bunny.

"I don't like you, and I don't want to go home with any of you," Bunny said, her mouth turned up in an expression of disdain, her eyebrows slanted in an angry frown. "I want to live with my aunt in New York. She's got a big apartment there. I bet she has a much nicer place than you will ever have."

Evaleen could feel her face heat up, but reminded herself this child was deeply traumatized, and probably had no idea what she was saying.

"I'm so sorry, Bunny your aunt can't take you right now," she said, "but we were friends of your mother, we live here in town and you can come and live with us right now."

Bunny screwed up her mouth angrily. She had a hard, contemptuous expression on her little girl's face.

"I don't want to live with you," she said. "Mama told me about you. She said you still line your shoes with newspaper."

For a moment Evaleen was frozen with shame. It was true, she used to line her shoes with newspapers to make them last longer. Why would Shu tell her daughter something like that?

"We're not poor, Bunny," she said quietly. "We're not rich either, but I can promise you that I don't line my shoes with newspapers anymore, nor does anyone else in our family."

Bunny's beautiful face grew dark, and she seemed to swell up and grow taller.

"Yes, you do," she said pressing her lips together disdainfully. "People always lie to me and I hate it."

"Better be nice," Hero said sharply. "From the way you're behaving right now, no one will want you, rich or poor."

"I hate you, too," Bunny said.

She kicked Hero in the shin.

Hero shot her a look that said she had better not try that again.

Evaleen remembered how alone and frightened she felt after her father died. She put her arm around Bunny in sympathy.

"Get away from me," Bunny screamed, pushing her away. "I hate being touched by strangers."

Evaleen noticed the flat look in her eyes and shivered. She felt unsure of herself in front of this determined little girl, but also felt intensely sorry for her and the trauma she had just gone through.

"Bunny," Evaleen said, patiently. She got down on one knee and spoke to her face to face. "I'm so sorry about your mom and dad. This must be so horrible for you. And I understand your anger and pain, but you can't stay here at the police station. For some reason, your aunt is unable to care for you right now, and you have to go somewhere."

Bunny remained stone-faced.

"They're good people, Bunny," Josh reassured her. "You'll do fine. I promise you."

"Please, Bunny," Evaleen pleaded. "It won't be as bad as you think. We have a son, Court. I think the two of you will get along fine."

"I hate boys," Bunny replied. "They stink."

"To put it bluntly, kid," Hero said, impatiently, "it's either us or the orphanage."

The look on Hero's face said he'd just about had enough of Bunny's smart lip.

Bunny shut her eyes tightly, trembling a little as though she were thinking. You could almost see her brain working, calculating. When she opened her eyes, it was as though she had been transformed.

"I'd be happy to come and live with you," she said. She looked up at Evaleen with a sweet smile and stuck out her arms for a hug.

Evaleen was shocked at the transformation, but felt that after what Bunny had been through, anything was possible.

It was past midnight when Evaleen and Hero finally finished answering all the questions thrown at them and signing what seemed like a ton of papers asserting they were worthwhile, responsible adults, worthy enough to take Bunny home with them.

Josh drove them all home, then said goodbye, promising to call the next day.

"I need my own room," Bunny demanded when they finally arrived home and she discovered she would have to share a room with Gussie. "I don't like sleeping with anyone."

"It's the best we can do for now, honey," Gussie said.

"I hate you," Bunny said.

"No, you don't," Gussie said.

"Yes, I do." Bunny stuck out her tongue at Gussie.

Gussie gave her a look that said one more word out of her and...

Evaleen touched her on the arm to remind Gussie that this had been the most horrific night of Bunny's life and to be patient. Bunny remained stubbornly reluctant to comply but finally grew so tired, she gave in and went to bed.

#

Gussie woke up the following morning, and discovered Bunny was missing. Concerned, she threw on a robe and went hunting for her. She found her in Court's room and Court sound asleep on the davenport in the front parlor.

"What in heaven's name is going on here?" Gussie asked Bunny, who was just waking up.

"You snore," Bunny said.

Gussie didn't respond but went to look for Court.

"And what about you, young man," she asked Court. "What were you doing on the davenport?"

"Sleeping," Court said innocently.

"Was this your idea?" Gussie said, turning to Bunny who chose that moment to suddenly appear in the too-big nightgown Gussie found for her.

"Yes," Bunny said defiantly. "He doesn't need to have his own room, and I do."

"She needs her own room," Court said, parroting Bunny.

It was obvious already that Court worshiped Bunny. It was equally obvious that she felt nothing but disdain for him.

When Evaleen heard of this, she felt that since Bunny had been through so much, it was understandable that she would want some privacy, so she let it go.

#

In the days that followed, Bunny kept to herself, seldom interacting with anyone in the family if she could help it, going so far as to take her meals to her room. Nights were difficult for everyone as Bunny repeatedly woke up screaming.

Evaleen and Gussie both rushed to her side to comfort her, but Bunny refused to discuss her nightmares or be comforted. She also refused to discuss the murder/suicide with anyone, including the child psychologist Evaleen hired. If anyone said anything about it at all, she would immediately leave the room. The psychologist said that the only thing that could heal Bunny was time.

In the meantime, Gussie took the shelves out of the huge walk-in linen closet in the hall and turned it into a tiny bedroom for Court, complete with a new bunk bed and dresser. The room was crowded but Court didn't complain, unlike Bunny, who complained constantly that it wasn't fair that he got a new bed and dresser and she had to sleep on his "smelly old used bed."

As much as possible, they let her have her way, but nothing they could do seemed to penetrate the fury that hovered right beneath her surface at all times.

#

The day of Shu's funeral was windy and threatened rain. Josh and Evaleen and Hero arranged it all and shared the expense. The service was held at the same funeral home where Evaleen's father's service had been held. That caused her to remember in vivid detail the day her father died, which made a hard day even harder. Time had tempered her feelings somewhat, but whenever she thought about her father, terrible doubts, along with guilt, shame, sadness and a sense of loss, still assailed her.

Amongst the few mourners, Bunny stood out in a bright pink party dress. Unable to bring herself to go to Shu's apartment and pick up Bunny's clothes, Evaleen had taken Bunny shopping and bought her everything new. Bunny took advantage of the situation and demanded an entire new wardrobe for herself, her doll and a new pedal car.

When she saw a pink party dress, she insisted that Evaleen buy it for her to wear to the funeral. Evaleen protested that it was inappropriate but Bunny carried on so loudly that Evaleen gave in and bought her the dress.

Having gotten her way, Bunny now sat calmly beside Evaleen, dressed in the pink party dress, her hair a mass of dark curls. At Bunny's request, Gussie had put her hair up in pin curls the night before to make her look more like Shirley Temple.

Bunny spent the entire service staring straight ahead, fiddling with her hair. She showed no visible signs of emotion other than irritation at having to sit still for so long. Court sat on Evaleen's lap, happily playing with a toy truck. Josh sat next to Evaleen. He sat so close she could almost feel his body warmth. She was tempted to reach out and hold his hand, but fought the urge. Hero sat on her other side, a bored look on his face. Evaleen, sick with a grief that threatened to wash out of her in waves, forced her tears back, not wishing to upset Bunny any more than necessary.

Afterwards, one of the mourners, a man named George who had been a friend of both Shu and Sam, had car trouble. Hero and Josh gave the car a push and it finally started. Their antics were like watching a Marx Brothers' movie. Evaleen had to smile in spite of the sadness of the day.

After the brief ceremony at the grave, they all returned to Hero and Evaleen's home, where Gussie had prepared a luncheon of potato salad and assorted cold meats. She also made a yellow cake using only one egg and a half a cup of sugar she managed to borrow from a sympathetic neighbor who had a little left over from her ration. It turned out to be delicious, if a little less sweet than normal.

After everyone left, Evaleen called Bunny's aunt using the number the police matron gave her. She introduced herself and told her about the funeral and that Bunny was staying with them for now.

"That's good," the aunt said. "Actually, I wouldn't mind at all if you and your husband kept Bunny permanently. I'd be willing to sign something giving you custody, if that's necessary. I just don't have room in my life for a child right now."

She sounded so cold, so disinterested in Bunny or Shu's funeral, it seemed to Evaleen that Bunny would be better off with anybody other than this iceberg of a woman.

"That would be fine with us," Evaleen said. "We loved Shu and we would love to have Bunny stay with us. We all feel so bad this happened to Shu. She was always such a fun and loving girl."

"Yes, well, they deserved each other, didn't they?" the woman said in a harsh voice. "They were both a couple of boozers."

The monstrous comment jolted Evaleen, but for the sake of Bunny who was nearby, she did not respond.

"I'll have our lawyer draft something and send it to you," Evaleen said, forcing herself to sound a lot calmer than she really felt at that moment.

The woman hung up without saying goodbye. Evaleen shook her head. Hard to believe that she had so little interest in her sister or her niece.

"Sounds like anything's better than that horrible woman," Hero said, after she told him what happened.

"Yes," Evaleen said. The moment the words left her mouth, Evaleen became aware that Bunny was standing in the doorway, staring at her and listening. Her expression was coldly hostile.

#

The following Sunday threatened rain. Evaleen felt chilled and depressed as she and Hero drove over to Shu's duplex to clean it out. They spoke little on the way over. She dreaded this day and tried to steel herself to do what she had to do. She felt better when she saw Josh standing by his uncle's pickup truck, waiting for them. Evaleen was glad to see him again, even under these sad circumstances.

An older woman in a plain but clean housedress answered the door on the first floor of the duplex that Shu and her family had lived in. Hero explained to her why they had come.

"I'm so glad," she said. "I haven't been able to bring myself to even look at their apartment. It's terrible, terrible. They had that little girl, too. I would hear the parents fighting sometimes and I always felt so sorry for that child. I called the police more than once on him when he was beating her up, but he always ran off before they showed up and she refused to press charges. And now this. I need to rent their apartment, but I've just been too upset to deal with it. Maybe after you're done, I'll be able to go up there again."

She shook her head sadly, then handed Hero the key from a ring inside the door.

The moment Evaleen stepped into the apartment, she felt sick to her very core. Hero and Josh looked sick, too. There was a stench of old food and the metallic smell of blood. Chairs were overturned, papers scattered about, and cushions from the davenport lay on the floor. Everything seemed to be wrecked or ruined or upside down.

There were blood spatters all over the wall in the living room and kitchen. The thought of Shu fighting for her life, and of Bunny having to witness such horror, made Evaleen feel so sick she ran to the bathroom and vomited.

Then, determined to get through this day somehow, she washed her face with cold water and forced herself to return.

She scrubbed the blood from the wall and carpets in the living room as best she could, but had to stop from time to time to go to the bathroom and vomit. It seemed to her that no matter how much she scrubbed, the blood remained. This was Shu's blood. She must have been so scared. The last time Evaleen saw her, Shu seemed so nervous. This was probably why. Evaleen should have suspected something was terribly wrong. Now it was too late to do anything about anything. Oh, dear God. Poor Shu.

Josh, who was also visibly miserable, began to gather up dishes in the kitchen and put them in the empty boxes he had brought for this purpose. Hero, looking sick himself, piled up books and magazines in the living room, emptied ashtrays and other debris and placed it all in large grocery bags that he hauled down to the garbage can. By the end of the day, the only thing that remained was a miniature cedar chest filled with photographs and a few pieces of cheap costume jewelry that Evaleen had saved to give to Bunny as a remembrance of her mother.

Evaleen and Hero said goodbye to Josh, who was off to the dump to unload his pickup, then left themselves. Evaleen and Hero barely spoke in the car, each lost in their own thoughts.

Hero dropped Evaleen off at home then headed to O'Dooles, not bothering to explain or make up an excuse. She understood his need to get away and might have liked a drink herself, but the last place she wanted to go when she was this upset was a beer joint. What she wanted more than anything was to simply take a hot bath and try to wash off the horror and despair of this awful day.

At home, Evaleen told Gussie what happened. Hearing it all, Gussie broke down in tears all over again. The two women held each other and mourned together for their friend and how she must have suffered all that time.

"I need to talk to Bunny," Evaleen said finally, when she was able to control her emotions once more. "I brought her a few things to remember her mother by."

"She's in her bedroom, as usual," Gussie said.

Evaleen took a deep breath and went to Bunny's room. The door was open. Bunny was sitting on her bed, playing with a doll that was an exact replica of the doll she played with at the police station. Evaleen had purchased the doll hoping the toy would give Bunny some comfort. It was one of the rare times that Bunny had actually thanked her.

Evaleen hesitated at the door to calm herself. Bunny was busy with her doll and did not look up.

"I brought you some things from your mother," she said entering the room. "I know how much she loved you, and I'm sure she would want you to have this."

She handed the tiny cedar chest over.

"Thank you," Bunny said perfunctorily. She put the doll down, took the box from Evaleen's hand and dropped it on the bed, without bothering to look inside.

Evaleen was shocked at her reaction.

"Your mother received this as a gift from her mother when she graduated from the eighth grade," she explained. "It had a watch inside. I still remember how excited she was that day."

Bunny opened up the box, seeming only mildly curious, and looked inside. She brushed the family photographs aside, which Evaleen had made sure to include, and picked up a rhinestone necklace. Then she shut the box again and set it aside.

"Thank you," she said again, and smiled. Then, like someone snapping off a light, the smile disappeared and she returned to her doll, winding the rhinestone necklace around the doll's neck, then backing away a bit to admire her handiwork.

"Isn't she beautiful?" she said.

"Yes," Evaleen said, unsure of what else to say.

There were so many times lately that she wanted to simply take Bunny in her arms and just hold her, but the few times she tried, Bunny pushed her away, letting her know in no uncertain terms that she did not want to be touched. Ever.

Bunny returned to her doll, letting Evaleen know without words that she wasn't wanted.

#

In spite of the horror and sadness of Shu's death, their own good luck continued. Hero was just finishing up the day at the workshop when the chief buyer at Rosen's called, said he heard they had left Bomberg's and wondered if they would consider setting up a counter at Rosen's.

Two weeks later, Bitsy Junior was behind a new, larger, better-lit counter, situated near the front of the store instead of hidden at the back. Bitsy had her baby a week later, a perfect little girl she named Madeline for no reason except that she liked the name.

Her daughter had the same wild, curly hair, cupid bow lips and easy-going disposition her mother had. The other girls took turns covering for her while she was out on maternity leave.

A month later, Bitsy was back at work. Evaleen was thrilled to have her back doing what she did best, which was sales, something that came as naturally to her as breathing did to others.

With the war in full swing, they were busier than even before, so Evaleen was relieved when the girls could once more concentrate on producing camouflage cream at the workshop. They were so busy that Hero was forced to hire even more employees, sticking to their original plan to hire abandoned women and unmarried mothers. With over 20 employees, the workshop was seriously overcrowded. Hero began a frantic search for more space.

He soon found an unoccupied warehouse, had it cleaned and retrofitted with a huge steel vat and a mixer that would create large quantities of cream at a time. Six months later they all moved in. Evaleen loved the big mixer and the machine with a conveyor belt that sterilized and filled the jars, screwed on the covers, then stamped a label on them. The jars still had to be boxed by hand, but Hero was working on having that automated, too. Hero also had a state-of-the-art, glassed-in laboratory built for Evaleen to develop new products.

She loved having her own special space. She spent most of her time there with the new assistant she hired herself. His name was Nelson Geneson. He was a chemist who previously worked for Helena Rubenstein and wanted a change, which Evaleen was thrilled to give to him. Nelson was a fussy, feminine little man who put his sparse hair up in pin curls at night and still lived with his mother, whom he adored. He was a perfectionist, obsessed with skin care and beauty creams. He was fun and Evaleen enjoyed his company.

Evaleen loved her laboratory but her favorite feature of the warehouse was a gift from Hero. Hero surprised her one night when she was working late, when he stepped into the lab.

"I want to show you something," he said.

She had no idea what he was talking about, but dutifully followed him outside.

There she saw the new sign, glowing in the dark in tall letters at the top of their building, like a mighty beacon in the night, broadcasting to the world: EVALEEN, INC.

Its green neon letters could be seen a mile away. All she could do was stare and stare and stare at the sign that seemed to glow with an unearthly light.

"You did it, my love," Hero said putting his arms around her. "And here's the proof. Your name up in lights."

"We did it together," she corrected him, her eyes wide with wonderment.

"Yes," he said, "but it's your name on the sign, not mine."

Chapter Nineteen

At six years old, Bunny still acted like she didn't trust anybody, and refused to talk about what happened to her parents. Whenever the subject of her parents came up, she would turn away and retreat to her room. The psychologist Evaleen consulted said that all they could do right now was to love her and give her affection, but only when she sought it. But Bunny never sought affection, and still refused to let anyone touch her. The only thing that seemed to excite her was going shopping. Still, she did well in school and was exceedingly bright. She had few friends, but the friends she did have came from very rich families. Evaleen, Hero and Gussie did what they could for her, but had difficulty keeping up with her demands. Court continued to admire her and she continued to push him away. He never seemed to take the hint.

#

The war raged on and the orders for camouflage cream continued to flood in. They were so busy that Evaleen and Hero promoted Bitsy Junior and the other girls to supervisors over the newer hires, and gave them each a hefty raise, enough so they could each afford their own apartment. The girls managed to find an apartment building with enough vacancies so they could all have their own place while still being together in the same building. Virgie was now engaged and planned to get married to her soldier boyfriend when he came home on leave. Her boyfriend planned to pick up where he left off, working on the family farm. Virgie loved the city and the city life and even more her independence, so this was becoming a problem between them.

"I've had enough of farm life to last a lifetime," she said. "I hated being so far from everything, having to pump and heat water just to do the dishes, forget about taking a daily bath, using an outdoor biffy, and being chased by a crabby rooster. Worse was eating meat from animals that I knew personally, except when we ate that nasty rooster, which I must say I enjoyed."

Their letters flew back and forth, with each side stating their case. Virgie read the less intimate parts to the other girls, who all urged Virgie to take her time before actually going through with it. After much thought, Virgie decided that getting married before they had hashed out their differences was not a good idea.

"But I don't want him to be put in jeopardy because of me," she said. "I'll break it to him when he comes home. Give him time to think it over, too."

#

One day, after a particularly hectic week, Evaleen decided to go home early, have dinner with Gussie, Ma, Court and Bunny, and spend some time with them all. Bunny, now seven, was still distant, haughty and demanding, but she was also very bright. She excelled at all of her studies, although her teacher said she never could seem to look anyone in the eye. Court, at five, was not doing as well in kindergarten, probably because he was so preoccupied with baseball lately. He had trouble hitting the ball and dropped it more than he caught it, but it was what he lived for. As for Ma, she was a little more disoriented than before, but not unusually so. It helped that she was sweet-tempered. Thanks to Gussie, everything went smoothly at home, or as smoothly as any household with two young children could.

But Evaleen's other reason for coming home early tonight, other than spending time with her family, was to spend some special time with Hero. They were so busy they rarely spent any time together and an uncomfortable silence had grown up between them. It had been way too long since they made love and she missed being in his arms and simply talking together. She hoped tonight would change all that.

To her surprise, the moment she opened the front door at home, two tiny white puppies greeted her, barking squeakily and trying to bite her feet. Even more surprising, their tiny doggie butts were covered with diapers. Evaleen laughed at the ridiculous sight.

"Are you babysitting puppies, now?" she said to Gussie, who was busy setting the table for supper.

"I see you've met Myrt and Gert," Gussie said. "They're not potty trained yet."

She spoke in a nervous rush of words. "They're miniature poodles. The neighbor dog had puppies. The owner was going to take the last two to the dog pound. I just couldn't let her do it. Why, they might have been killed. Aren't they the most adorable things? Don't you just love them? Don't they look like a Gert and a Myrt with those big eyes and curly hair, like they've just had a perm?"

Evaleen agreed they were definitely adorable. She picked up Gert, who was jumping up and down on her. Gert's fur felt silky, like a new powder puff, and her little tail wagged madly as she tried to bite Evaleen's fingers. Myrt in the meantime tried to chew on her shoe.

"They're teething," Gussie explained, apologetically.

"Oh, is that it?" Evaleen replied, falling instantly in love with them both.

"I don't like them," Bunny announced.

"They probably don't like you, either," Court teased back.

Bunny reached out to swat him and Court ducked.

"Stop it, you two." Gussie said firmly. "Mind your manners and sit down. It's time to eat."

Evaleen gave Gert a kiss on the top of her little doggy head, and an extra squeeze. She placed her on the floor, then took her place at the table. It had been at least a month or possibly more since Evaleen sat down with her family for a meal. It felt good to do so. Gert tried to jump up on Bunny as Bunny sat down, but Bunny swatted her.

"Go away," she said. "I hate dogs. They're germy and disgusting."

Gussie ignored Bunny's outburst as she passed the canned ham casserole to Evaleen.

"So," Gussie said, "to what do we owe this unexpected pleasure?"

"Do I have to have a reason?" Evaleen said, dodging her question. "I just missed you all."

"I hate canned ham," Bunny said, before Gussie could reply. "That's all we ever eat around here. Why can't we have a decent piece of meat for a change?"

"Listen here, young lady," Gussie said sharply, "you're lucky to get any meat at all with the war going on."

"We can still get bubble gum down at the gas station once in a while," Court said. "It's really good, too. I can blow the biggest bubbles you ever saw."

Bunny continued to dawdle and frown over her food.

Unlike Bunny, Court ate every bit and asked for seconds.

"He's like a human vacuum cleaner," Gussie said to Evaleen.

"I can see that," Evaleen said, smiling indulgently at her red-headed son.

Court made noises like a vacuum cleaner, which made everyone laugh except Bunny.

"You are so annoying," she said to Court.

Court looked sheepish.

Ma sat quietly, shoveled in her food quickly as though to get it over as soon as possible, and paid no attention to anyone. Bunny gave Ma an evil look, but Gussie put up a finger warning her not to say what she was so obviously thinking.

"Bitsy Junior said a celebrity stopped by her counter the other day," Evaleen said, in an effort to get Bunny's attention. Bunny loved all things celebrity, especially anything having to do with Margaret O'Brien.

"Who?" Bunny said, suddenly interested.

"Venus Ramsey."

"What did she look like? Was she beautiful?"

"Bitsy said she was extremely tall and very pale. She ended up buying ten jars of skin lubricating cream. She told Bitsy she can't live without it."

"I'm tired," Ma said, and yawned.

"She's tired because she was awake all last night whistling," Gussie said as she passed around pieces of the sugarless apple pie she made that morning. "I'm surprised it didn't wake you up."

Evaleen had to laugh.

"I didn't hear a thing," she said. "I didn't even know that Ma knew how to whistle."

"She has other talents too," Gussie said. "One night, she got out of bed, made the bed, got back in, got out, then proceeded to make the bed again. The noise woke me up. When I asked her what she was doing, she said she was too busy working to talk."

Ma laughed a small laugh, as though someone had told a good joke.

"Can I be excused, now?" Bunny said, obviously annoyed.

"May I, please," Gussie corrected her.

"May I, please," Bunny echoed, her voice dripping with sarcasm.

"Yes, you may," Gussie said.

Bunny shot Gussie a mean look, then ran up to her room and slammed the door behind her.

Court also asked to be excused. When Gussie gave him permission, he, too, hurried upstairs. A moment later, he could be heard banging on Bunny's door, begging to be let in.

He returned to the kitchen a few minutes later looking dejected, but seemed to quickly forget all about it as he played with Myrt and Gert on the kitchen floor.

"He loves her so much," Gussie said, as she and Evaleen did the dishes together. "He will do anything to get her attention and she can't stand him. She spends most of her time in her room making faces at herself in the mirror and playing with her doll. I don't know what to think. I don't understand her at all. If I mention her parents, she just turns away as though she hasn't heard me."

"Poor kid," Evaleen said, picking up Myrt who, now that Court was off playing elsewhere, was jumping up on her. "I'm sure she's still traumatized."

"I realize that," Gussie said, picking up Gert and settling the puppy into her ample lap. "She's just a little girl, but she seems so angry. I don't know what to do."

"She can be sweet sometimes, too," Evaleen said, defensively.

"Only if she wants something. She's like a bottomless pit of need and yet 'thank you' is not part of her vocabulary. Nothing I do for her is ever enough, and nothing I say seems to make any difference. Thank goodness Court is no problem. The only time he gets into trouble is when Bunny sets him up."

The two women continued to talk until it was Court's bedtime. Evaleen put him to bed and read him a story. He seemed to enjoy it and she was glad to spend this time with him. He soon drifted off to sleep.

She watched him sleep for a while and felt sad that she was missing so much of his childhood, sad that her life had become so hectic lately, sad that she and Hero were more like two strangers than husband and wife. She hoped tonight would be different.

She poked her head into Bunny's room to say goodnight. Bunny was sitting up in bed, reading a book of fairy tales. She did not acknowledge Evaleen's presence.

"Good night, Bunny," Evaleen said softly. "Sleep tight."

Bunny kept looking at her book, as though Evaleen were not standing right there. Taking the hint, Evaleen left.

Evaleen tried not to feel rejected, but she did anyway. Bunny was a very closed little person and Evaleen felt sorry for her. She hoped that the psychologist was right, that Bunny would change over time, but was beginning to wonder if it would ever happen.

Around ten-thirty, Evaleen excused herself to go to bed. She ran a bubble bath and lay in the tub, bubbles up to her neck, enjoying the sensual feeling of the hot water on her bare skin. She thought about Hero and the kind of emptiness that seemed to have sprung up between them like weeds coming up through the crack of a sidewalk, ever since they had gone into business together. In spite of the camouflage work, she knew he still disliked being in what he called derisively the Evaleen business. But he was so good at what he did, and she was grateful for him.

At the same time, she longed to connect with him in a way that had nothing to do with business. She hoped that tonight they could at least talk, and maybe even make love, something that had not happened in months. When the water began to grow cool, she stepped out of the tub, toweled herself off and slipped into the new grey silk negligee she had purchased on her way home from work.

Standing in front of the full length mirror on the closet door in her bedroom, she examined herself closely and critically. In spite of the beautiful negligee, her belly was still too round, her ankles too thick, her breasts no longer perky. She sucked in her stomach and stood up straight to improve the view. It didn't help.

She was exhausted and it showed in the sallowness of her skin and the puffiness under her eyes. To combat this, she rubbed some skin lubricating cream into her face, then spread some blush lightly on her cheeks, chin, forehead and eyelids. She completed her makeup by patting on some powder to hide her freckles and penciling in her eyebrows.

She then combed out her long, red hair, which she had begun to dye to cover up the few grey strands that had begun to appear. She wasn't beautiful and she knew it, but with the help of cream and makeup and a beautiful nightgown, maybe the illusion of beauty would suffice. Now if she could just lose a few pounds…but that wasn't going to happen anytime soon either. The truth hurt, but it was the truth. She finished by spritzing her pulse points with Tempest, the new perfume she had developed, which came in its own pure crystal fluted bottle.

Gussie had changed the sheets that day and they smelled deliciously of air and sunshine from being outside on a clothes line that same morning.

As she waited in bed for Hero, she leafed through a copy of Life, which she'd been intending to read. On the cover was a picture of the American flag with "United We Stand." Inside were pictures of soldiers and articles about the war in Europe. She felt terrible for the young men who returned home from the war often maimed, confused and inconsolable. Not wishing to be in a bad mood when Hero arrived, she turned to a more upbeat article about a group of people who went around collecting fat for the war effort to be used to make weapons. How fat could become a weapon she did not know, but then sugar and everything else was rationed for the war effort these days and some of it made no sense, either.

In another upbeat article, a group of "Rosie the Riveters" working in an airplane factory were quoted about their pride in making sure that every plane was as safe as it could be for "our boys." She continued to thumb through the magazine in an attempt to distract herself.

At midnight the house seemed abnormally silent in spite of its usual creaks and groans. She was tempted to turn off the single reading light near her bed, which cast gloomy shadows around the room, give up waiting and go to sleep, for she was having more and more difficulty keeping her eyes open. Still she willed herself to stay awake and wait. She tried not to become irritated at Hero for being so late. He didn't know she was waiting for him. How could he?

She used to think it was her fault that Hero preferred being at O'Dooles to being at home, but justified his behavior by saying he was always restless and could never sit still. Going to O'Dooles was the only way he could relax, turn his mind off by having a few drinks and lose himself in a game of pool or a card game. Or at least that was what he said.

The thought of the women who also hung out at O'Dooles always bothered her, but she tried to put it out of her mind and sometimes she succeeded.

She became disgusted with herself for even thinking that way, especially since she couldn't do anything about it. She also began to feel a little ridiculous for thinking that she could put on a sexy nightgown and this would make up for all the times she and her husband barely spoke about anything other than business, much less made love. Still she waited, and hoped this night would be different.

At one A.M., she gave up waiting and cleaned off her makeup, took off her sexy negligee, put on her cotton pajamas, went to bed and turned out the light. But in spite of her exhaustion, sleep was impossible. Her mind buzzed with a million clattering thoughts about Hero, about the business, about Bunny and Court and Ma and all the things she needed to do the next day.

Thoughts of Josh crept into her mind, too. She hadn't seen him since Shu's funeral and she missed talking to him and just hearing from him in general. As always, she also thought about her father, and as usual when she thought about him, she felt a surge of guilt.

How she wished she would have waited until she had made some money on her own to begin her business instead of taking the little bit they had saved for emergencies. But it was too late and it would always be too late, a thought that made her feel terrible all over again.

She thought about Bitsy, too, and how grateful she was for her and the other girls. Bitsy especially was a godsend. She was smart, capable, and got along well with everybody. Evaleen was thinking of promoting her again, but hadn't quite decided where to put her next.

Her thoughts were interrupted when she suddenly heard Hero's footsteps on the stairs. She sat up in bed, snapped on the light and looked over at the clock. It was two o'clock in the morning.

When he appeared at the bedroom door, his dark eyes were bloodshot, his suit jacket was slung over his shoulder, and his shirt was open, half-in and half-out of his trousers. His tie hung limply out of one pocket. In one hand he held two empty champagne glasses by their stems and in the other a bottle of champagne. He had a loopy grin on his face.

"You're awake," he said, when he entered the room. "Good."

"It's late," Evaleen accused.

Hero laughed.

"It is, but I haven't been up to anything, Evaleen, my love," he said. "I've been in a poker game at O'Dooles. And guess what? I won."

"Good for you," she said, sorry for sounding so harsh.

"I didn't win any money," he said. "I won something even better."

He reached into his pocket, pulled out a crumpled piece of paper and with a little bow, handed it to her.

She straightened the paper out and looked it over. It was signed by George Goldstone, president of Goldstone Construction. The gist of the note said that he was turning over two adjoining lots on Mount Curve Boulevard worth eight thousand dollars apiece to Mr. and Mrs. Herodotus Lyon the Third.

Evaleen looked at Hero, then at the paper, then back at Hero, dumbfounded.

"I won it fair and square," he said, "and I'm going to build a big house for us on it."

Mount Curve Boulevard, one of the ritziest streets in Emerson? He was going to build a house on Mount Curve Boulevard? Was that even possible? Didn't you have to be wildly rich to live there? Wasn't that where the governor lived?

Hero must be kidding. Was this all just a big joke?

"You don't have to believe me," he said, reading her mind. "Why not wait and see for yourself? It'll be a surprise when you discover it's real. Oh, I can't wait to see your face when it's all done. But for now, well, if you want to thank me, why..." he said, stripping off his clothes.

Hero lied all the time about small stuff, like how much he had to drink or where he was going, but he never lied about anything really important. So it was real.

All the best, most important people lived on Mount Curve Boulevard. Of course, she would never fit in. But still it would be nice to live in a bigger house. They could use one lot for a garden for Gussie, who loved to garden, and the other lot for the house. The idea rose up like a wonderful shadow.

She smiled, matching the big grin on his face.

"That's exciting, Hero," she said all happiness now.

"Let's celebrate," he said. "What do you think? How long has it been?"

"Months and months," she said, catching his drift. "Oh Hero, what happened to us?"

"Life, I think," he said. "It just got between us somehow. Anyway, let's not think about that right now. Let's celebrate. Oh, you smell so delicious. Wait right here while I run and grab a quick shower," he said, with a leer.

"Hurry up," she said and smiled an inviting smile as he hurried away.

As he showered, she quickly slipped out of her pajamas and into her new negligee. She lit the candles again, combed her hair, put on a little makeup and returned to bed.

She sat up against the pillows, waiting and trying to take in what he'd just said. Eva Doyle and Hero Lyon on Mount Curve Boulevard. A shiver ran up her arm. Could it be?

Hero appeared, completely naked, smelling deliciously of soap and toothpaste and Old Spice. He popped the cork on the champagne, then poured them both a glass before joining her in bed.

"To us," he said, lifting his glass, "and to our new home. It's going to be a doozy, you'll see."

"Yes," Evaleen said. "To us."

She couldn't quite bring herself to say our new house, because a part of her still wasn't sure she believed it.

She'd seen the signed paper, so they owned the lots, but building a house? It seems so unreal, like one of Bunny's fairy tales, which she couldn't get enough of lately.

"It's true," he said seeing the questioning look in her eyes. "You'll see."

Seeing Hero next to her in the bed, deliciously naked in all his male glory, a series of thrills shot throughout her entire body. She forgot about the house and everything else as he reached over, held her close and kissed her deeply.

All her pent up feelings for him, feelings she had been too busy to acknowledge and wasn't even sure she had anymore, raced through her as she returned his kiss.

Chapter Twenty

One year later, with a rare hour to spend at lunch (her previous appointment having canceled at the last minute) on a day when the birds were back and singing wildly, a spring day filled with longing and promise, Evaleen's curiosity about her new home grew into huge proportions. The more she tried not to think about it, the more she thought about it and the more she thought about it, the more curious she became.

Whenever she asked Hero about the house, all he would say was, "Relax, you'll see it when it's done."

But what could possibly be taking so long? Not being able to see for herself what was going on with their house was becoming an unendurable agony.

Her actual intention today was to do a little shopping but instead, as though led by an unseen hand, she got in her car and drove to the new house. She had memorized the address from the slip of paper Hero gave her the night he won the property, and had been tempted many times to go have a look but so far had held off. Until today. She had become obsessed with seeing it in person and couldn't stay away another minute. She hoped Hero would forgive her for not keeping her word, but she had to see her new house. She simply could not wait one more day. Damn the consequences.

Her wildest dream was for a large kitchen, a sun-filled living room and enough bedrooms with good sized closets for everyone. Two bathrooms would be nice too, one being for Ma, as she was becoming somewhat incontinent these days. And as long as Evaleen was dreaming, a big victory garden for Gussie and a small book-lined study where Evaleen could work in the evenings, plus a nice play area in the basement for Bunny and Court. But she had to tamp down her expectations. They couldn't afford so much.

Driving along Mount Curve Boulevard, she admired the beautiful homes, each more impressive than the next. At the address where her new house was supposed to be, she expected to see a cottage. Instead she saw a black, wrought-iron fence surrounding a lot the size of a small park. The sound of hammer and saws rang out in the spring air as workmen swarmed over the huge building at the center. It looked to her more like a public library than an ordinary house. She stopped the car and stared out the window, shocked, sure she had made a mistake. She double checked the black wrought iron numbers on the front gate, but they were the same as the numbers on the slip of paper.

For a moment she felt dizzy. Her heart began to pound dangerously. This couldn't be right. The house was way too big. She rolled down the window to get a better look. Even if they could afford such a huge house, they could never afford to fill it with decent furniture or pay for the maintenance and taxes There was a war going on and building materials were needed for the war effort.

We'll be bankrupt, she thought. All of our hard work will be for nothing. We'll be ruined. The more she thought about it, the more upset and panicky she became.

She wrote down the builder's name and phone number from the sign out front, then sped back to work. She was shaking when she arrived.

"Call this number," she barked, handing the sheet of paper to her secretary, Georgia. "I need to talk to this guy right now."

Georgia looked at her boss strangely, as she wasn't used to being spoken to in such a harsh tone, but did as she was told.

Evaleen shut the door of her office and sat down at her desk. She took several deep breaths to quell the feeling that her heart was about to bounce out of her chest. It didn't help.

The intercom buzzed.

"Mr. Johnson on line one," Georgia said.

Evaleen took in another big breath and picked up the phone.

"I'm calling the house off," she said before he had a chance to speak. She tried to control herself, after all it wasn't his fault, but her words still came out sharper than she intended. "I'm really sorry but this is more expensive than we can possibly afford. I'm afraid you'll have to tell your men to stop work immediately."

The builder began to stutter.

"I've committed a crew for at least another eight months," he said, when he could finally speak.

"I'll make sure you're paid for what you've already finished," she replied. "Believe me when I say I'm sorry, but you need to stop now, while we figure out what to do next."

She said goodbye, hung up the phone before he could argue further, and let out a deep breath. Maybe they could salvage something out of this, and still avoid bankruptcy.

Moments later, an enraged Hero burst into her office.

"The builder just called me," he said. His voice was ice cold. "What did you do?"

"What do you mean, what did I do?" she spit back. "I saw the house. We'll be bankrupt. We'll lose everything we've worked so hard for."

"Are you out of your mind?" he said, glowering. "I was hoping to surprise you, but you've ruined that now."

"Maybe we can sell it to some rich people and they can finish it," she said, backing down. "Oh Hero, how could you?"

Tears began to drip from her eyes. "And with the war going on, too?"

"Like hell I'm calling it off," Hero said. His face was white with rage. "It's our house and we're going to live in it when it's done. We're not using anything needed for the war effort. We're using materials from other properties that have been torn down. I checked to make sure. This house is going to be finished, and that's that."

"Well, I refuse to live in a house that's going to bankrupt our family's entire future and cost our employees their livelihoods," Evaleen exploded, her rage matching his.

"Don't worry," Hero said bitingly. "Nobody's going to make you do anything."

He poked his head out of her office door.

"Get our accountant on the line," he said to Georgia. "Tell him to drop everything and get over here, pronto, and bring the books for the last two years."

"Yes sir, Mr. Lyon, right away."

While they waited, Hero paced and Evaleen nervously shuffled papers, both too filled with indignation to look at or speak to each other.

The accountant appeared ten minutes later. He was a man whose grey face bespoke the fact that he rarely saw the sun. With a discreet cough, he opened up the books, spread them out on the desk in front of Evaleen and explained in a monotone the company's bottom line for the past two years. Then, as he wasn't one to make small talk, he said a formal goodbye, and left as quietly and quickly as he'd come.

"We can afford two houses if we want them, maybe even three," Hero said, his tone softening. "We're doing great, Evaleen. We're not poor anymore. You don't have anything to worry about. We're rich."

For a long moment, Evaleen was speechless.

"I...I knew we were doing okay, but I had no idea we were so well off," she said, at last. "Are you sure?"

She was still not quite sure he was telling the truth. "I don't feel rich. Do you?"

"Well, you are. We both are. If you'd ever look up from your work once in a while, you might learn something."

His eyes widened in sudden tenderness and he burst into a huge gust of laughter. "My God, you should have seen the look on your face. Oh, Evaleen! You looked so scared. Nobody would believe the great Evaleen was afraid of anything. I wish I would have taken a picture."

A tentative smile reached her lips as her amazement turned into embarrassment.

"I...I'm sorry," she said, still in a state of shock. "I didn't know."

"I'm sorry, too," he said, smiling at her. "I should have insisted you see the books once in a while. You need to see them. But you never want to be bothered. We'll have a quarterly meeting from now on. You've always been so happy just roaring ahead with your own projects. You've made this business a huge success, you know. I'm just the supplies and money guy. But you. Whew. People believe in you, Evaleen. Those women you keep hiring work for you like beavers at a dam."

He put his arms around her and held her close. "I'm so proud of you."

Then, for the first and only time, when Evaleen looked up into his eyes, she saw tears. Tears for himself, tears for her, or tears for them both? She would never be sure.

#

One year later, on an unusually warm day for March, the whole family piled into Hero's car for the ride to the new house. All that is, except Ma. She became so agitated when Evaleen told her they would be moving that Evaleen decided it would be best to leave her at home for now. When Myrt and Gert also realized they were being left behind, they went to their crates and wouldn't come out.

"It must have been rough all those months dealing with the house and the business," she said to Hero.

"It was," he acknowledged, "but I think you'll agree it was worth it, when you see how it looks."

"I'm sure I will."

Now that she knew they could afford it, her excitement at living in such a beautiful place was almost unbearable.

Everyone had dressed up for this special occasion. Hero wore a grey suit with a white linen dress shirt and pale blue tie. Evaleen wore a pale green and white linen dress with a matching picture hat. Gussie's ample body was poured into a corset and looked almost slender in her flowered dress. Bunny looked adorable in a red dress with a strand of real pearls at her neck. Normally Bunny's amiability was something she put on and took off like a coat depending on what she wanted, but today, to everyone's relief, she appeared to be genuinely happy. Court's good linen shirt was already rumpled and coming untucked from his gabardine trousers.

When Hero pulled up to the black iron gates of their new home, Evaleen was awestruck as he slid in a key. The big gates opened as if by magic. Hero drove through and slowly up the majestic driveway past a row of fully grown oak trees. He parked in the circular driveway near the front entrance.

"We're not going to live here, are we?" Evaleen said meekly as Hero held the car door open for her. "It's so, so…big."

She hesitated, unsure. "Are you really sure this is ours?"

"See those lions guarding the entrance? That's us, my dear. We are the Lyon family and this is our new home. I've named our house Lyon's Lair. Do you like it?"

"I love it," Evaleen agreed, her eyes wide, taking it all in.

"Geeze," Gussie said, her voice filled with awe. "I've never seen anything like this in my whole life, especially not up so close."

Court just stared, his mouth hanging open, but Bunny seemed unfazed, as if she had always lived here and this was just an ordinary day. As they approached the massive front door, Evaleen had the surreal sensation that she was walking into someone else's life, someone much more important than she could ever hope to be.

Before Hero could ring the bell, a tall dignified looking man opened the door. He wore a grey morning coat, which seemed to be wearing him more than vice versa. Evaleen tried not to stare.

"I would like you each to meet Mortimer," Hero said. "He will be your chauffeur, butler and man of all work. Mortimer, this is your new mistress and my wife, Evaleen Lyon."

Mortimer bowed from the waist. "I'm very pleased to meet you, Mrs. Lyon."

"Good to meet you too, Mortimer," she said, feeling a little lightheaded.

Bunny swept past Mortimer and went inside. Her reaction seemed to amuse Hero as he grinned and waved everyone else into a foyer that was larger than their entire living room at home.

The scent of roses greeted Evaleen. It came from a huge bouquet of white roses in a silver vase on what looked like an antique table in the middle of the room. Evaleen felt disoriented and stood for a long moment to get her bearings. Gussie stared openmouthed, an uncertain look on her face. Hero stood, grinning, obviously enjoying Evaleen and Gussie's reaction.

Bunny hurried off to investigate the other rooms, with Court close behind her.

A wide, curving dark oak staircase led up to the second floor. Over the stairwell was a domed ceiling with a bas-relief of a Greek god, with a fig leaf in the right place.

"Remind you of anybody, Mrs. Lyon?" Hero teased.

"You," she said, then thought to herself, when you were young.

These days, Hero's face was puffy, his black hair had begun to thin on top, and he had developed a bit of a pot belly. He looked nothing like the dashing lad he'd been before they were married. Unrelenting hard work had worn them both down, and she knew it probably showed in her face, too.

"How did you ever do this with all the shortages?" Evaleen asked.

"I have my ways," he responded, with a sly grin. "Anyway does it really matter? We did it." He put his arms around her.

"Yes, you did," Evaleen said, enjoying his arms and this moment.

Gussie, oblivious to the two of them, walked into what appeared to be the formal living room and plopped down on a yellow linen sofa. "Oh, that feels so good."

"Goose down," Hero said, following her in. "That's what makes it so soft."

Then he turned back to Evaleen who stood at the doorway. "What do you think? Do you like it?"

"I love it," Evaleen said, although she was too befuddled by the gloriousness of it all to think clearly. "It's like something you'd see in a movie."

"We've both worked very hard and we deserve it."

"Oh, Hero. I never could have envisioned something this grand. Thank you so much."

"You're welcome. Now come on, I want you to see the rest of the house."

In the library Evaleen gazed in wonderment at the book shelves, already half-filled with the business and self-help books she devoured before going to sleep most nights. All were now bound in leather and in order by subject and author. But what stunned her most of all was the huge portrait of Hero, Evaleen, Court and Bunny, which hung over the fireplace.

"I had it painted from a photograph," Hero said, proudly.

"We look like such a happy family," Evaleen said wistfully.

"And so we are, my love."

Evaleen did not contradict him.

"Oh, my God, eight burners." Gussie exclaimed when they entered the kitchen and she saw the huge stove. "How will I ever cook on such a beast?"

"You'll figure it out." Hero laughed. "I saw you fix the bathroom drain. This stove will be a breeze."

As Gussie tried all the burners to make sure they worked, Evaleen admired the bright, sun-filled breakfast room attached to the kitchen. The large round table was set with fine china and silver as though for a meal.

"You've thought of everything," Evaleen said, overcome with love and gratitude for Hero.

"Don't thank me," Hero said, seeing the look of wonder on Evaleen's face as he led them upstairs. "Thank Missy Moore, the decorator. Didn't she do a fine job? She's the best in town."

"Yes, yes she is," Evaleen agreed. Missy Moore was always being written up for decorating the homes of the town's most celebrated citizens.

Evaleen was still in a state of shock as they checked out Ma's new bedroom, where a brand new console radio sat next to a comfortable rocking chair in a small sitting area. Through a side door was a large bathroom.

"Ma's gonna love this," Gussie said.

In Court's bedroom, they found him lying on the bed admiring the signed poster of Ted Williams on the wall.

"He's a fighter pilot now," Court informed them. "Bet I could be as good as him if I worked really hard."

"I'm sure you can," Evaleen said, going over to give him a big hug.

Bunny's room was pink and white. A new Margaret O'Brien doll sat against a huge pile of colorful pillows on the four-poster bed. Since Gussie had taken Bunny to see the movie, "Meet Me In St. Louis," Bunny was in love with all things Margaret O'Brien.

"I don't think it's big enough for all my things," she said, coming out of her walk-in closet, a look of consternation in her eyes.

"Anyone would think the girl was born rich," Hero quipped. "She seems to come by it so naturally."

"She does, doesn't she?" Gussie agreed and they all laughed, including Bunny.

They toured Gussie's two bedroom apartment over the garage next. It had a small sunny kitchen filled with new appliances, and a living room furnished in country French antiques slip covered in creamy linen with navy blue piping. Best of all, as far as Gussie was concerned, was the private stairway at the back with a small garden and patio at the base.

"So you won't be able to see who my sweeties are," Gussie said slyly.

"We'd find out anyway," Evaleen said and laughed. "It'd show in your face. You never could tell a lie. Besides, far as I can tell, you don't seem much interested."

"I can't believe it," Gussie said, ignoring the last remark. "My own little place."

She shivered deliciously. "It's nicer than I could have ever dreamed."

"I was hoping you'd like it." Hero gave her a tender smile.

Gussie hugged him, then looked embarrassed at doing so.

Outside behind the house were three small cottages and a greenhouse. Hero explained that one cottage was for the butler, one for the housekeeper, and one for the gardener, and that they all consisted of a living room, kitchen, bedroom and bath and since they were occupied and private, they would have to take his word for it. They also toured the greenhouse, already filled with burgeoning plants.

Evaleen was overwhelmed. Hero did this. For them. He must care more than she realized. It made her feel good just thinking about it.

Back at the house, all their new employees lined up in the reception hall waiting to be introduced. There was Belinda and John Latimer, a round, cherry-cheeked married couple who resembled each other. They were in charge of general housekeeping. Pearl, a slim grey-haired woman, would be coming in twice a week to do the laundry. Joseph Crane, a little man wizened from days in the sun, was the gardener, and of course Mortimer was the butler.

Hero spoke a few words to the staff, saying that he and Mrs. Lyon looked forward to getting to know them all better, and thanking them for being part of their new home. Then he gave them all the day off with pay. Everyone happily dispersed, and then it was just Hero, Evaleen and Gussie.

"Oh, and Gussie, I forgot to tell you," Hero said, taking her aside. "Your salary has doubled, as of today."

"What?" Gussie said, her eyes wide with shock. "You don't have to do that."

"Yes, I do," Hero said, smiling. "It was Evaleen's idea, and as everyone knows, she's the boss. Besides it's a bigger place, you'll have a lot more work to do so don't think we're not getting our money's worth."

"Oh Gussie, you've been so wonderful, you deserve this and so much more," Evaleen said, joining in.

"If you say so," Gussie said, looking a little confused. "I must say, though, that this whole hullabaloo has worn me out. All I can think about right now is that cheesecake I saw in the fridge. If it's still there, I'm going to take a big piece up to my new place and I'm gonna sit in my new easy chair and eat my cake, drink a cup of coffee and listen to a soap opera on my new radio until I calm down. Ma's got me hooked on soaps, too. You're welcome to join me."

"Maybe later," Evaleen said. "Right now, I want to spend a few moments with my husband."

"About time," Gussie muttered under her breath as she headed towards the kitchen.

"She's right, you know," Hero said.

"She always is." Evaleen smiled.

"Now for the grand finale," Hero said, as he guided her down a long, art-filled hallway to a separate wing of the house. "This is just for us."

At the end of the hallway was a small sitting room. Through a connecting archway was the large master bedroom. The bedroom had a fresh pleasant scent, which came from a large vase of flowers and from the linen sheets. The room was dominated by a huge canopy bed covered by a hand-made quilt, which she immediately recognized as one her grandmother had made.

"How did you find that?" Evaleen asked, delighted.

Hero raised one eyebrow. "I have my ways."

Evaleen sank down on the edge of the bed. "Oh, this is so soft."

"It should be, it's a feather bed," Hero said. "If you think this is great, wait till you see what I have next for you."

Evaleen not believing it could get any more wonderful, followed him through a large dressing room and walk-in closet into a bathroom with a huge sunken tub. A smaller room held the toilet and something Hero called a bidet.

"You'll figure it out," he said, looking a little sheepish at the questioning look in Evaleen's eyes.

A door in the back of the bedroom led to a small study. Floor-to-ceiling windows overlooked the front lawn. Oak bookcases with built in drawers at the bottom and file cabinets stood empty, waiting to be filled.

"I know how you like to get up in the middle of the night to work, so I had this built for you."

"I love it," Evaleen said, "but what about you? Where is your special place?"

"You don't really think I would go to all this trouble and not have a special place too, do you?" he said.

Evaleen followed him through a side door in the bedroom she now noticed for the first time and into a smaller room with a bed, dresser and a large closet. For a moment, she was speechless.

"Are you planning to sleep here?" she said finally.

"Sometimes," Hero said, not quite looking her in the eye. "Be thankful. That way you won't have to listen to me snore every night. But hey, I don't intend to spend the night there tonight." He gave her a wink.

Evaleen didn't know what to say. They had always slept together, no matter what. They were married. That's what married people did. Even if they didn't talk much, they still spent their nights together. Why would he have a separate bed in a separate room?

She felt herself shrink inside.

Before she could protest, he rushed her off to show her his adjoining office. She was even more stunned when she saw the door from the office leading to the outside, with steps going down to the ground. What was that about? Why did he feel the need for his own private entrance? Why?

#

A month later, the Emerson Globe ran a photograph of a faintly smiling Evaleen, at twenty-eight, dressed in a simple but elegant black linen dress, with white cuffs and collar, standing next to the fireplace in her new home. Her red hair was worn in a wild mass of upswept curls, her makeup was perfect, thanks to the man who came every morning to do her hair and makeup. What the photograph did not show was how thick the air was with tension. She and Hero had a huge fight the night before, about him spending so many nights in his own bedroom. She managed a smile for the camera, although it felt fake even to her.

Chapter Twenty-One

Tuesday afternoon, August 14, 1945, was extremely hot and sticky. Evaleen was in her laboratory finishing up for the day, when she suddenly heard the whoop of sirens and people shouting and laughing. Curious, she looked out the window of her lab and was shocked to see several employees racing for the door. She stopped a worker to ask what happened.

"The war's over," the woman said in an excited voice. "Can you believe it? Japan surrendered. We just heard it on the radio."

Excited, Evaleen hurried off to find Hero, but he was nowhere to be found. Keyed up by the news, she checked with the security guard, gave him permission to lock up as soon as everyone left, then left herself in a rapidly growing bubble of joy and relief.

Out on the street, sirens sounded, church bells rang, cars honked, and people shouted, danced, and sang their joy. Finally the war was over. The atmosphere was electric with excitement.

Before Evaleen could get her bearings, a dark-haired young man wearing an army uniform grabbed her, bent her back and kissed her deeply, then raced off. At that moment a stream of papers landed on her head and slithered down over her clothes. She looked up and saw people standing at the open windows of their offices, shouting and waving and throwing paper. Drivers abandoned their cars in the middle of the street and joined the teeming, screaming, happy crowds.

Evaleen, not sure what to do next or where to go, or whether it was even possible to go anywhere when to her amazement, she spotted Josh in the crowd. He was wearing an army uniform, which surprised her. For a moment, all she could do was stare, not sure she was actually seeing him or just imagining it was him.

He must have spotted her too, because a huge grin crossed his face. He began to weave his way through the teeming crowds headed in her direction. Elated, she watched as he closed the gap between them.

When he was finally able to reach her, she was surprised by the tenderness in his expression. She had the crazy urge to kiss him deeply on the mouth right in front of everybody, but restrained herself.

"Oh, my God. It's so good to see you again," she said, her heart actually skipping a beat. He looked so fine in his uniform, that she felt weak and shaky.

"It's wonderful to see you, too," he said, smiling down at her.

The crowd surged forward then, almost knocking them apart.

"There's a small diner a block away," he said. "I think it's still open, or it was when I passed it earlier. Maybe we can go there and catch up with each other. I think that's about as far as we're going to get in this mess."

An air raid siren went off, making further speech impossible. Evaleen nodded.

With Josh holding her hand, they struggled through the teeming crowds of people, all of whom seemed to be going in opposite directions. They were finally able to battle their way to the diner, with its daily specials listed in the window. They stepped inside.

The place was deserted. Spotting a coffee urn behind the counter, Josh found some cups, poured them each a cup of coffee, and brought them to a booth. As they sat opposite each other, the last light of day filtered through the big front windows of the diner, giving the restaurant a soft, unearthly glow. Evaleen took a sip of the thick, dark, burnt-tasting coffee. Sitting across from Josh, she felt strangely awkward. Josh too seemed nervous. For a long moment, they sat in silence, staring at each other as though waiting for the other to speak.

"Thank God, the war's over," Josh said, finally.

"I read somewhere that only one in four servicemen were in actual combat," Evaleen said. "I so hope you weren't one of them."

"I wasn't. I would have gladly gone, but the army chose to use my expertise in high finance to order supplies," he said this with a self-conscious laugh. "So tell me, how's Evaleen, Incorporated, doing these days?"

"Amazingly good," she said, feeling a bit more relaxed. "Hero foresaw that war industries would be given priority on things like oils and alcohol, and many of the essential ingredients for our products would become scarce, so his penchant, even before the war, was to buy, buy, buy."

Josh's expression seemed to freeze at the mention of Hero's name.

She was reminded, crazily, of that moment when Hero was so jealous of Josh, the night Shu died. So much had changed since then, and it occurred to her that maybe Hero did have something to be a little nervous about, after all. It was a wicked thought and she enjoyed it. Josh looked as good as ever, but he had a maturity, a sense of solidity, which she found extremely attractive.

"Sounds like Hero," Josh said. "He always did enjoy buying more than selling."

They both laughed.

"I worried at first that we were being unpatriotic," she said, chattering away to cover up the huge attraction she was feeling for him, "but Hero wouldn't be deterred. The only really serious problem we had was getting jars. But our loyal customers dutifully washed out their old ones and brought them back for refilling, which was wonderful of them. Probably the biggest thing that happened to the company was that Hero managed to get a contract with the army to produce camouflage makeup. He got a deferment to do it, but he was never happy about it. He would have much rather gone to war, but the army considered making camouflage more important than his joining up."

"So, how's everybody else?" Josh asked, obviously anxious to get off the subject of Hero.

"Everyone is doing fine. Gussie is doing fine. I love having her live with us. Bunny still refuses to talk about her parents' death, and we don't push her to do so. She's extremely smart and her teachers love her. Court is in the second grade. He prefers sports to studying, but seems to be buckling down a bit more lately. Except for the red hair, he looks more and more like his father. Acts like him too, sometimes."

Evaleen noticed the raw hurt that glittered in Josh's eyes when she spoke about her family. She wondered if that was an overflow from her own heart or if she were just imagining things.

With an effort, she went on with her chatter. But at the same time, strange depths were stirring inside her and she felt an inexplicable longing to have him hold her close.

"Ma hasn't changed much," she continued, trying not to babble on too much. "She listens to soap operas all day and seems to prefer that to reality, but other than that, she's doing fine. What about you?"

She put her hand on his, then quickly drew it back, embarrassed.

His cheeks blazed at her touch. It was such a beautiful blush. A reckless feeling was overwhelming the tiny nudge of guilt she felt. She wasn't doing anything wrong. They were out in public. Anyone could see them. Nothing to feel guilty about.

"Well, I managed to finish college, thanks to a full scholarship, and went to work for Gubner Financial full time as an analyst. I was drafted into the army right after I finished college and got married soon after that."

Married? Josh? His words hit her like a wave of ice cold water. All her excitement and pleasure suddenly withered to nothing. She felt embarrassed at herself for acting like such a fool. Josh was just a very dear friend and that's all he was and they were both married. Period.

"When did you get married?" she asked, trying not to let her alarm show.

"Right after I joined up," he said. He grinned a crazy lopsided grin, as though he were enjoying her discomfort. "We eloped after I found out I was going to be drafted."

Outside a horn began to honk loudly, interrupting them. Evaleen used the interruption to try to get her nerves back under control.

"So tell me about her," Evaleen said, when they could hear again. She worked to keep her voice even, not let him know how badly his news had upset her, or how curious she was to find out who he had married.

"Not much to tell. Patricia's a schoolteacher. She comes from a large family and she has red hair. In fact in some ways, she looks like you."

That hurt even worse, somehow.

"We have a little girl Laura, named after Patricia's mother. She's two."

"You must be very happy," Evaleen said in as casual a voice as she could manage. "Are you?"

"Are you?" he countered.

It was exactly the wrong question to ask, at exactly the wrong moment. Evaleen was utterly open and vulnerable to Josh and he seemed to know it. She couldn't lie to him, nor to herself, either, but she tried to deflect the question a little.

"Oh, Josh, I don't know. We both work a lot, and when we're together we're usually pretty tired."

"You didn't answer my question."

"Neither did you," she said, feeling reckless.

"Well, let's put it this way. I'm not unhappy. How's that for an answer?"

She didn't reply because she didn't know what to say. It was as though suddenly a wall had grown up between them. Josh had someone else and so did she. They stared at each other, the truth of their attraction between them, but honor keeping them apart.

Outside the restaurant, someone began to bang garbage covers together. The noise brought Evaleen back to herself. It was all so ridiculous and hopeless that strangely laughter bubbled out of her.

Her laugh must have been infectious, because Josh started to laugh, too. Then they were laughing together, roaring at how crazy and upside down the whole world was right now. But though both laughed hysterically, they also stared deeply into each other's eyes at the same time as though magnetized.

Then, as quickly as they began to laugh, they became silent, utterly serious, the two of them alone in this place while the world roared outside. Neither could seem to tear their gaze away from the other.

"I would be a lot happier if I didn't love you so much," Josh blurted out, when the noise lowered to a din once more. It came out of him sounding raw and filled with pain. "I've always loved you. I just never had the nerve to tell you before. I was always afraid it would ruin everything between us and you would never want to see me again, and I couldn't bear that. Now that I'm safely married, I finally have the nerve to say it out loud to you. Oh, God help me. I don't know what I'm saying. I'm sorry, so sorry."

"I love you too, Josh," Evaleen said. She felt as though the words were dragged out of her soul, trembling as she admitted her own heart. "I wish I would have known it sooner, before it was too late, but I know it now, even though it's way too late for us."

The moment the words were out, she regretted them. But she was unwilling to take them back, either. Everything was so topsy-turvy today. The whole world had gone crazy and so had she. Later she might be sorry but right now nothing mattered except they were together in this place at this time.

He came over to her side of the booth and sat down next to her. Without a word, he put his arms around her, held her close and kissed her deeply. She could feel her blood rise as she kissed him back with all the repressed feelings she had saved up for years.

It wasn't so much a sexual kiss as a kiss of two souls touching, with nothing between them but their love. When they finally came up for air, she looked into his face and was taken aback at the love and passion and tenderness she saw there. The woman in her was desperate to let him know she felt exactly the same about him.

She turned her lips up to his once more and, yielding the last of her reserves, kissed him again, this time with more passion than she knew existed.

What she didn't realize was how much these few moments together would mean to her in the days to come, or that she would look back at this time as the first moment she had ever been truly, authentically in love. It was not the burning excitement she had felt for Hero as a teenager, it was the love of a grown woman and much, much deeper.

After their kiss, Josh buried his face into her neck, as though he were taking in her very essence. His lip moved against her skin, and she shivered. Tears filled her eyes and intense grief hit her so hard for this lost chance at real love, that it was all she could do to keep from breaking down.

"I dreamed of this moment so many times," he said, and kissed her again, long and slow this time, as the world outside clamored wildly, adding to the excitement and danger in the air.

"I love you," he said, when they pulled away.

"I love you, too," she said.

She broke down in tears that began to rack her entire body. It was hopeless. He was married and so was she. What fools they had both been, and now it was too late for either one of them.

"Did I hurt you?" he said, using his handkerchief to wipe her eyes.

She shook her head, no.

"I'm glad," he said holding her close. "I couldn't bear it if I did anything to hurt you."

She put her head on his chest and let all of her pent up tears flow.

"I don't understand why you married Hero," Josh said, the words coming from his own obvious pain. "Hero's a good man in many ways but when it comes to women, he doesn't have a conscience. I don't know how you've stayed married to him this long."

Evaleen wiped her eyes, took a deep breath and moved away from him.

"He's my husband and your friend," she said choking out the words. "No matter how I feel about you, I still can't bear to hear you speak of him that way."

"Please, forgive me," Josh said quickly. "I, I couldn't help myself."

She felt a strong urge to leave, to run away from him, from herself, from everything.

"I really must go," she said, and stood up. "My family's going to be wondering what happened to me."

"I'm so sorry if I…" Josh said, a pained expression on his face.

"Oh, Josh." A new wave of tears streamed from her eyes. "Please, don't be sorry. I really do love you, I just, I—"

The manager of the restaurant walked in at that moment, jerking them both back to reality.

"Thanks for holding down the joint," he said, with a drunken smile. He plopped down on one of the stools and laid his head down on the counter.

"You're welcome," Josh said. He stood, shaking his head slowly as though trying to clear it, then dropped some bills on the table.

Evaleen wiped the tears from her eyes with her hands, rose, and fled. Her emotions were raw and confusing as she hastened away through the teeming crowds. She forced herself to not look back, although the temptation to do so was unbearable.

Chapter Twenty-Two

Since the day that Evaleen last saw Josh, ten hectic years fled by. She clocked hundreds of thousands of miles of air travel, promoting and demonstrating her original skin care products, developing new and better ones, and working on her foundation for unwed mothers and homeless women. Because of her willingness to fly all over the United States and talk to anybody even slightly interested in beauty creams, and in spite of the loss of the camouflage business after the war ended, Evaleen Incorporated had grown twenty-fold. She had little time to enjoy her success, but in truth she preferred it that way. Better that than thinking about Josh or what might have been, or worrying about things she couldn't change, like her marriage or her children.

Ma still spent hours listening to soap operas on the radio and lately watching them on the new television set that Evaleen bought for her. Gussie and Mortimer remained employed with the family and continued on as more friends than employees. Gussie's two dogs Gert and Myrt passed away, and were replaced by two adorable black teacup poodles named Humpty and Dumpty that Mortimer purchased to surprise Gussie on her last birthday. Court and Bunny were both in high school at their respective boarding schools, rarely checking in with the family. Their excuses were always the same – they were too busy to call.

On this winter day in February, after a particularly draining trip to New York, Evaleen, was relieved to see Mortimer waiting in the limousine at the airport as she exited the company plane.

"How're you and Gussie doing?" she asked as Mortimer opened the door for her and she stepped into the passenger seat, where she preferred to sit these days.

No matter how much Gussie denied it, Evaleen knew her friend was lonely, especially now that Bunny and Court were nearly grown and didn't really need her anymore. She assumed that Mortimer, a widower, was lonely, too. Evaleen often thought the two would be perfect for each other as they both enjoyed going to flea markets, playing Bingo, and going out to eat, but she kept it to herself, knowing how Gussie felt about getting set up. She needn't have worried. Mortimer was slowly wearing down Gussie on his own. Lately they had begun to go to lunch and a movie on Saturdays.

"He's strictly a friend," Gussie said when Evaleen mentioned anything hopeful about the two of them becoming a permanent couple. But in spite of Gussie's protests, Evaleen couldn't help but notice that Mortimer was being included more and more in Gussie's conversations lately. Gussie finally admitted one day that she had feelings for Mortimer, warm, fuzzy feelings, maybe even a few sexy feelings. Evaleen was thrilled for them both and jealous. She still loved her husband, but it was more a feeling of gratitude than the love of a woman for a man. When they were together, they were like business associates, rather than man and wife. The fact that she thought about Josh more than she thought about Hero just added to her confusion where her marriage was concerned.

Mortimer dropped Evaleen off at the front door before putting the car in the garage and bringing in her luggage. Inside, the house was dark except for the light in the front entrance hall Gussie always left on when Evaleen was returning late. Evaleen was looking forward to a good night's sleep in her own bed. She was startled when she encountered Gussie in her nightgown, followed closely by Humpty and Dumpty wagging their tails in greeting.

"Something weird is happening to your mother," Gussie said. Her plain, round face was filled with worry.

Gussie didn't get upset easily, so seeing that look on her face came as a shock.

"What is it?" Evaleen asked.

"I don't know. It started after Mortimer left for the airport."

Evaleen flung her coat and purse on a chair and raced up the steps to her mother's room, with Gussie close behind.

"Get these spiders off me," Ma cried as they entered her bedroom. "They're crawling all over me and I hate it."

She thrashed about in her bed, madly swatting at herself. Her skin looked shiny and waxy and seemed unusually tight on her skull. Like a death's head, Evaleen thought, and shivered.

"They're horrible. They bite," Ma screamed, kicking off her blankets. "Please, please make them stop."

"Ma, there aren't any spiders," Evaleen said, forcing herself to sound calmer than she felt. "You're seeing things."

"Help me," Ma moaned. "Help me, Jesus. Please. Help me."

She mumbled other words that made no sense.

At Evaleen's behest, Gussie hurried to call the doctor, and returned shortly to say he was on the way.

"Thank you, dear Gussie," Evaleen said. Then, to her mother, "It's going to be okay. Try to relax. A doctor will be here soon and make it all go away."

Evaleen felt helpless as Ma continued to thrash about, cry for help and swat at imaginary spiders. She was greatly relieved when the doctor and his wife, the nurse, finally arrived.

"She obviously has dementia," the doctor said, trying to examine Ma as she swatted madly at the bugs that were not there.

"I would certainly say so, dear," his wife agreed, exuding a reassuring calm.

The doctor pulled a syringe from his black bag and filled it with some liquid as his wife efficiently pulled away the quilt, and pulled up Ma's nightgown. Before she could protest, the doctor gave her a shot.

Ma calmed down almost instantly, and fell into a deep sleep. Evaleen was relieved to see her mother's lips go from purple to pink again, as she went from panting to breathing in a normal fashion. The doctor and his wife left soon afterwards, promising to come back if needed.

Evaleen stood next to her mother's bed, watching her sleep. She was worried for her mother and so exhausted from her long day she felt almost hollow inside. Gussie, standing nearby, also looked extremely tired.

"Think I'll stay with Ma for a while," Evaleen said to Gussie, "so she won't be alone in case she decides to wake up."

"You're almost never home," Gussie replied, apropos of nothing.

"Guilty as charged," Evaleen said, responding to the reproof in Gussie's voice. "I've got a lot of people depending on me right now," including you, she wanted to say, but didn't, "and I have to keep building on the momentum we've developed."

She sighed heavily. "Have you seen Hero? We should probably let him know about Ma."

"Nope. He comes and goes and doesn't tell me. He could be in Timbuktu or in bed sleeping for all I know."

It was the truth. Hero had stopped telling anyone where he was going or what he was doing long ago. She complained at first, but Hero did as he pleased and it did no good. After a while she stopped asking, because the fact that he preferred to be gone somewhere to being at home simply hurt too much. Mostly she was too busy herself to dwell on it, and in truth, mostly she didn't want to know.

"I'm pooped." Gussie yawned. "Your mother seems to be okay at the moment, so think I'll go to bed. Give a holler if you need me. You should try to get some rest, too."

"I'll be fine," Evaleen assured her. "See you in the morning."

#

Alone with Ma, Evaleen kicked off her pumps, pulled the rocking chair over to the bed and sat down. Looking at her mother, so tiny and vulnerable, Evaleen felt sad. Years had gone by in a complete haze. Somebody said once that days are long and years are short. How true that was.

Gussie was right, Evaleen was always gone. So was Hero. And truth to tell, he didn't know where she was any more than she knew where he was. The only time they seemed to actually have a conversation was when they had important business to discuss. At night, he used the back stairway and slept in his own room. They never made love anymore.

One night when she was feeling particularly lonely and could bear it no longer, she knocked on his door and called out his name. He refused to answer, though she was pretty sure she'd heard him moving about a few minutes earlier. He'd probably drunk too much and couldn't perform, she rationalized. She was too proud and too afraid of being rejected to simply open the door. She didn't try again after that. Nor did he ever try, either.

As for Court and Bunny, Evaleen saw them about as much as she saw Hero. When they were kids, she would often leave before they woke up and return home after they went to bed. Sometimes a week or even two could go by without seeing either one of them. These days they were off at their separate boarding schools. During the summer when they were actually home, they were usually off with their friends. The family rarely sat down for a meal together. Even when they were all home, the house was so large she never knew if anyone was around or not. If it weren't for Gussie and Mortimer, she would have felt completely alone.

Ma stirred then, breaking into Evaleen's thoughts, but she remained sound asleep.

Evaleen rearranged her blankets and tenderly tucked them under her chin.

Sitting with Ma and feeling distanced from everything else, Evaleen began to look at her own life – objectively, coldly.

Everything I ever dreamed has come true, she thought. I have more money than I could have ever dreamed, I'm respected, admired, and on every 'A' list in town. I've helped a lot of abandoned women and unwed mothers and I'm proud of that, but the only time I feel really alive is when I'm working. Hero and I barely speak and I have no idea who my children are. I couldn't even list their likes and dislikes. The few times they share anything, it's Gussie they tell. If it weren't for her, I wouldn't know anything about either one of them.

Ma moved and Evaleen snapped back to attention. To Evaleen's great surprise, Ma's eyelids fluttered open. She looked strangely young, like she must have looked when Evaleen was a little girl.

"Did you have a good trip, dear?" she asked, as though it were just a normal day.

Evaleen was stunned to hear her speak in such a coherent way, something she had not done in a long time.

"Yes, yes, I did. Are you alright, Ma?" she asked tentatively.

"I'm perfectly fine, dear, just a little tired. How are you doing?"

"Everything is going well at work, Ma," Evaleen said, thrilled to be able to talk to her mother. It was a miraculous moment, a gift. "The business is making money. Gussie is a godsend, and Court and Bunny seem to be doing fine."

"What about you? Are you alright?"

Evaleen hesitated. "I'm doing fine but I still feel terrible about dad. I don't think I'll ever get over his death. I still feel that if it weren't for me, he'd still be alive."

"Oh, dear," Ma said, shaking her head. "I'm so sorry you still feel that way. Your father was drinking that day and he was angry because of the snow, because he had to ask his brother for money again, because of everything. He was mad at me, too, said I didn't keep the house clean enough. He was just looking to take his anger out on somebody and you were it. And he had a bad heart. His death was inevitable. You were just trying to help us. I'm sure if he were sober, he would have thought so, too. Now tell me, how is Hero doing?"

"He's working hard," Evaleen said, the impact of Ma's words not quite sinking in yet, "but he's still not crazy about the idea of being involved in the beauty business. Even after all this time he considers it ridiculous, but he works hard anyway and does a great job."

"Sorry to hear that he still feels that way after all this time," she said.

Then a jolt, like a streak of lightning, shot up the left side of her mother's body. Her whole body began to spasm. Ma opened her eyes wide. They were blurred and out of focus. The blue seemed to take up one entire eye, as though there was no white at all. She tried to sit up, but she couldn't make it and flopped back down on the bed.

Evaleen panicked. "Gussie," she screamed into the intercom. "Call an ambulance!"

#

The ambulance arrived, and Gussie raced downstairs to open the front door for them. Two men rushed up the steps and into Ma's room shortly thereafter. Evaleen anxiously watched as they checked Ma over, and gave her a shot of something. Then they lifted her onto a stretcher like she was dead weight.

"We're taking her to the hospital," they said.

Evaleen insisted on riding with her mother in the ambulance and the driver did not protest. Evaleen sat in the back of the screeching ambulance, holding Ma's hand. A huge lump of sadness, like a big black cloud, filled her throat, overwhelming her. For just one moment, she'd had a miracle – her mother come back to her. But it had not lasted and now her mother was even worse off than before.

For the next week, Evaleen canceled all her appointments and stayed with her mother at the hospital. Ma did not speak again, and remained in a drugged stupor. Evaleen felt like she was wide awake in a dream too sorrowful to be a nightmare. For once she did not think of business. She slept in a camp bed in the corner of her mother's room, to be close by if she woke up and needed something. She was desperately hoping her mother would come back to herself once more, but it was not to be.

Gussie and Mortimer dropped by every day. Even Hero visited, although Evaleen knew how much he hated hospitals and being around sick people. Court and Bunny were away at school, but Evaleen kept them informed daily, usually through messages left with whomever answered the phone at their dorm, since they seldom picked up the phone themselves or called her back.

Evaleen had never felt so alone. She'd taken it for granted Ma would always be there, even when her mother had become completely senile.

"I'm so sorry that I didn't spend more time with you," Evaleen said to her sleeping form. "You must have felt so alone after Pa died, and I wasn't much help either, because I was always so busy trying to make a living."

Ma opened her eyes, but they were completely out of focus. Her mouth fell open and she mumbled something. Evaleen leaned closer but couldn't make out the words. Ma shut her eyes again, and soon was snoring softly. As Evaleen stared out the window at the black skeleton of the tress, ice dripping from the branches, she thought about her mother's life.

She had married Pa when she was barely out of high school. She must have been in a state of wild excitement when she eloped with him six weeks after they met, against her parents' wishes. As a young wife, every second with her new husband must have seemed so precious and amazing, like Evaleen felt when she and Hero were first married.

Was her mother excited when she had a daughter? And why did they only have one child, especially when everyone around them was having such large families? Did they stop making love? Was that it? Or wasn't Ma able to get pregnant again? Maybe they didn't want any more children.

She thought about her father and how beaten down he must have felt after he lost his job. He never did like to socialize, and he enjoyed a drink or two on Friday nights, but it was only after he lost his job and had to beg his younger brother for money that he seemed to become so bitter and angry all the time. Before that, he used to sing around the house once in a while, and even take Ma and her to the drugstore for a strawberry soda. But those were rare times. Mostly Pa was silent and often crabby. He always thought people were out to use him. Because of his own fanatically religious upbringing, he never trusted people.

That old guilty feeling crossed her heart as it usually did when she thought of her father, but this time she also thought about what her mother said. His death was inevitable – if not that day then the next. And as Ma said, he had been drinking and was angry about everything, her included. The inexpressible guilt that haunted her whenever she thought of her father began to lessen somewhat. Like everything new, it would take a while for what she had heard to sink in and she would always feel terrible about the circumstances of his death and taking the money to start her business, but the healing where her father was concerned had finally begun.

#

The next morning, exhausted from being wide awake all night with her roiling, boiling thoughts about her father, her mother, her children, Hero, and her work, Evaleen left the hospital and grabbed a cup of coffee at a local diner to help her stay awake. Afterwards, she made a quick call from a pay phone at the diner to let Georgia know she wouldn't be at work that day and to please advise the other secretaries to continue to refuse appointments for her until otherwise directed. She then called Gussie and told her the latest news about Ma, and also called Hero, Court and Bunny. They were all unavailable, so she left messages, then returned to the hospital and Ma's room.

As she entered the room, she heard Ma make a strange, hollow sound, like a deep sigh, the same noise she remembered Pa making when he died. Evaleen shivered and felt strangely cold as an eerie silence seemed to permeate the room.

Just like that her mother was gone. Evaleen read somewhere that dying was a private matter, best done alone. Ma must have waited for Evaleen to leave before giving herself permission to die.

Evaleen faltered, trying to understand what had just happened, but she knew deep inside that her mother was gone. She reached over and gently closed her mother's eyes. She was surprised at how soft and gel-like her eyelids felt.

She was still sitting next to her mother's body when a doctor arrived and leaned over to check her heart. He left without a word to Evaleen. Outside the room, nurses and doctors rushed back and forth, as though it were an ordinary day. Evaleen found that strangely disturbing.

In what seemed only like moments later, two men in black suits arrived with a gurney. The older man expressed his sympathy and told her to please step out of the room so he and his colleague could prepare her mother for transport to the funeral home. It was the same funeral home her father had been taken to. Evaleen wondered numbly how they knew. Had she told them and not known it? She must have.

Evaleen felt as though she were floating underwater as she went to a phone and called Gussie to give her the news. She also called Court and Bunny and Hero, but as usual all were unavailable. She was forced to leave an urgent message for them to call home.

Driving home, everything seemed so unreal, like being wide awake in a dream. When she arrived, Gussie was waiting for her with open arms. Only then did Evaleen break down and cry. Hero, to his great credit, arrived shortly afterwards. He also had tears in his eyes, which surprised Evaleen, as she had never seen Hero cry before.

Gussie made tea and they all sat down together in the breakfast room. Evaleen filled them in on the details. Hero left an hour later, saying he had some work he needed to finish up. Gussie and Mortimer also left, knowing instinctively that Evaleen needed to be alone with her grief.

Alone in her private rooms, Evaleen despaired. She wished she would have spent more time with her mother. She also wondered why she ever thought having a big house was so important. The house was beautiful but it wasn't very comfortable and everything was so stiff and formal. She had never been able to completely relax in the house. The respect from complete strangers, the huge neon sign with her name on it, having her name in the society pages, also meant far less than she ever would have dreamed when she was so busily pretending to be someone named Evaleen.

Right now, she was Eva Doyle, a scared little girl who needed her mother. But Ma was gone and the truth was she had been gone for a long time. The only difference was she wouldn't be physically at home any longer.

The truth of that statement hit her hard and she broke down in tears. She cried for her mother, and her father, and her children, and herself. She cried for the loss of Josh and what a fool she was not to have noticed what a good, kind and loving man he was. She cried for Hero and wished she would never have asked him to join the business. But there was no going back there either, just the steady movement of their lives going forward, like a slow-moving freight train.

#

Court and Bunny called the following morning. Both protested that it wasn't a good time to come home, but Evaleen told them they didn't have a choice. For once they didn't argue. The wake was held three days later at the same funeral home where they had Pa's funeral.

Wishing to spend some time alone with her mother, Evaleen arrived early and stood alone at the back of the long narrow room. Her mother's mahogany casket stood at the front, surrounded by huge vases of flowers.

Hero had not arrived yet, although she expected him shortly. Since Ma had become sick, Hero had been running the business alone and was working twice as hard as usual. So, as Evaleen rationalized, there was no reason for him to come early. Even though they had all lived together, he and Ma were never close. And it wasn't his mother after all.

Hero rarely spoke to either of his own parents these days. When he did, it was about something financial or something they needed rather than anything personal. In some ways she felt sorry for him, but she also realized it didn't seem to bother him as much as it bothered her.

Evaleen stood at the back of the long room, grief circling her like a huge dark bird. Unable to bring herself to approach her mother's casket directly, Evaleen walked up to the front and read the cards attached to the many bouquets, mostly from employees or people they did business with. She was grateful they had bothered and made a mental note to herself to send thank you cards to them all.

Finally, unable to avoid it any longer, she steeled her nerves, took a deep breath and approached the casket and was horrified at what she saw. Ma's face was a ghastly orange color, and she had a severe look around her mouth as though she were angry about something. Ma never looked like that in her whole life. Evaleen was convinced that the funeral home had made a terrible mistake, this wasn't her mother, but when she looked closer, she noticed the small dimple in Ma's cheek and the tiny scar near her eyebrow where she had fallen against a table as a girl.

It was Ma alright, but with her face smooth and resembling something dipped in orange paint, she looked like someone completely different.

"She's probably listening to Ma Perkins through all eternity," Hero said brightly, as he came up from behind to join her at the casket.

Evaleen chose to ignore the liquor fumes that emanated from his person. She smiled at him, grateful he had showed up at all. The idea of Ma listening to soap operas up in heaven was a comforting thought.

Bunny arrived and stood next to Evaleen at the casket. Now seventeen, she had a sullen, impatient look on her extraordinarily beautiful face. Evaleen let that go, too. Bunny really didn't know Ma at all. By the time she joined the family, Ma was already like a ghost living in another world.

"Grandma was the only grandparent I ever knew," Court said, joining them. "I never did meet Dad's parents."

At sixteen, he no longer looked like the exact duplicate of his father, but still moved and acted like him in so many ways.

"They're still alive," Hero said. "They're just not interested in anybody but themselves."

"Just the same, I wish I knew them," Court said.

"Who knows, maybe someday you will," Hero said quietly, "but I wouldn't count on it."

#

The funeral was the following day. The day was cold and dreary, the sun hidden by dark clouds, and snow from a previous storm was piled high at street corners covered over with soot and dirt. Hero and Evaleen sat in the front row of the Methodist church that Ma attended as a girl, with Court and Bunny sitting next to them. Evaleen was surprised to see Josh and his wife approaching to pay their respects. With her long blond hair, his wife resembled the movie star Veronica Lake. This made Evaleen feel jealous and even more insecure than usual about her own looks. His wife had an irritated look on her perfectly made-up face, as though she hated wasting her time at a funeral of someone she didn't know and couldn't care less about.

"Sorry about your mother," Josh said, when he approached.

"Thank you, Josh," Evaleen said. "I'm so glad you could come."

"I don't think you've met my wife, Patricia. Patricia, this is my old school chum, Evaleen and her husband, Hero Lyon. I knew them both before they hit the big time."

"Nice to meet you," Evaleen said.

"Sorry for your loss," Patricia said in a polite, cool tone.

"Thank you," Evaleen said.

"Can't believe that Josh found himself such a good-looking woman," Hero blurted out. "Where did he ever meet a high class dame like you?"

"We met at a Chamber of Commerce function," Josh answered for her. "I was attending a business conference and meeting a friend for dinner. While I was waiting outside for him to appear, I met Patricia, who was also waiting for someone."

"Well, aren't you the lucky one?" Hero said.

"I think so," Josh said diplomatically and smiled an uncomfortable smile.

Evaleen glanced at Josh, and to her surprise found him looking back at her. Their eyes met for an uncomfortably long moment. She looked away, embarrassed at the intensity of his glance and her own feelings.

"We should probably go sit down," Patricia said.

Before anyone could say anything more, she took his hand and pulled him away. Josh looked embarrassed but did not argue.

Evaleen felt slightly ill at seeing Josh again. She had told herself over and over that what happened the day the war ended hadn't really meant anything at all. It was just another crazy event on a day filled with crazy events. They were old friends and barely that, since she almost never saw him anymore. She was married and so was Josh. End of story. Still it hurt her to see him and his wife together, more than she liked to admit.

The organist began to play, interrupting her thoughts and a woman began to sing, "The Old Rugged Cross," Ma's favorite hymn, thus signaling the ceremony was about to begin.

The minister was a tall, extremely thin man who looked a little like an ungainly stork. Ma had not gone to church for years, and Evaleen had not attended since she went to Sunday school as a young girl, so Evaleen wrote up some facts about her mother that the minister could refer to in his brief sermon.

When he finished, he moved aside and indicated for Evaleen to come forward and give the eulogy. As she approached the lectern, she had the strangest feeling of being calm from the waist up and trembling almost out of control from the waist down.

At the lectern, still shaking, she spoke about Ma and her favorite things, cupcakes and soap operas, and what she was like when Evaleen was a little girl and how they would listen together to stories about Rin Tin Tin, the wonder dog, and how once in a great while, they'd go out for hamburgers and French fries at the dime store and how happy her mother was to have her own mother live with them for a time.

Afterwards, the woman sang, "Shall We Gather at the River," another one of Ma's favorite hymns. Then it was all over, and time to go to the cemetery.

Josh and his wife left without saying goodbye. Watching them leave out of the corner of her eye, Evaleen wondered again if he were happy, but knew that Josh was too much of a gentleman to ever say he wasn't.

Chapter Twenty-Three

Being rich and successful had been Evaleen's drug of choice, but since Ma died she faced the truth that it was a drug that couldn't sustain you on those long, lonely nights when it was just you and nobody else. True, people looked up to her, wanted her opinion and asked her to be on their boards, all heady stuff, but they were not true friends like Gussie. She began to wonder lately if the people she knew liked her for herself, or because of who she was, or what she could do for them.

Wishing to have more of a personal life, she began to hand off many of her duties to Bitsy Junior, who had moved into an apartment hotel that catered to the needs of unmarried executives. With Bitsy's daughter off at a boarding school and no domestic chores, she was free to spend all of her time at work, which she insisted on doing, even though Evaleen protested.

Evaleen decided to begin this new phase of her life by trying to improve her relationship with her children. To begin, she decided to take some time off and visit them in their private schools. Court was now a sophomore in high school and Bunny was a junior.

After talking it over with Gussie, Evaleen decided to surprise Court at school on a day she knew he had off. She had her assistant Georgia set up an appointment on the same day to speak to the principle about Court's progress, something she should have done long before, but was always too busy to do. To make up for lost time, she decided to meet with his advisor first, in case there was something she needed to discuss with Court.

His boarding school was in Montrose, a two hour drive away. The day was pleasant. The trees were beginning to bud out and spring was most definitely in the air.

When they arrived, Mortimer parked in front of the brick-covered administration building and Evaleen, somewhat apprehensive, went inside. The smell of chalk dust and sweat reminded her of her own school days. Her hope was that both Bunny and Court would not only finish high school but go on to college, unlike herself, who had never finished high school. That remained a thorn in her side even now. She was greeted in the advisor's office by a balding, grey-faced man who introduced himself as Jim Spaulding.

"Your son's a playboy," he said, after they had sat down and chatted a little about the weather. "He's a smart boy and could get straight A's if he were willing to work at all, which he isn't most of the time. His grades aren't horrible, but he does just enough to get by, and even that usually at the last possible minute. A good time always seems to come first with him, although I must say he's a charming boy and seems to have a lot of friends."

Evaleen knew that Court liked to goof off, but she had thought he was doing fine in school because whenever she asked him, his answer was always the same, "Great, no problem."

She had assumed he was telling the truth. Apparently not.

She promised the principal she would discuss this with him.

With that over, Mortimer drove her to Court's dormitory, a building made up of several small apartments, each housing five boys. It was after four when Evaleen, feeling a little nervous, climbed the steps to the second floor where he lived. In her hands was a bag of his favorite chocolate chip cookies that Gussie made for him. Evaleen was leery of popping in on him unannounced, but hoped he would be happy to see her.

The door was wide open when she arrived. Court was sitting on the davenport with two other young men, listening to the baseball game on the radio as she entered.

"Surprise," Evaleen sang out as she entered, a hopeful smile on her face. "Mommy's here with goodies from home."

Instead of being happy to see her, the expression on Court's face was one of sour outrage.

"What are you doing here?" he said. He flashed a nervous smile that didn't quite reach his eyes.

"Aren't you happy to see me?" she asked. "Gussie made your favorite cookies."

She handed him the bag. She sounded uptight and desperate and she knew it.

"Umm. Yeah, good," he said, taking the bag from her.

"This is my mother," he said to his buddies, who stood by, enjoying his obvious discomfort.

"Hello, everybody," Evaleen said in a voice that sounded fake even to her.

His buddies all stood politely, said hello, and introduced themselves.

Court, looking intensely uncomfortable, also stood up. He indicated for her to follow him so they could speak privately.

Evaleen feeling miserable and self-conscious, followed him into his room, which he shared with a schoolmate, who was thankfully not there. They sat down on his unmade bed in a room littered with dirty clothes, candy wrappers and empty soda bottles.

"You could have called and let me know," Court said, not bothering to hide his irritation.

"I wanted to surprise you," Evaleen said.

"Well, you surprised me all right," he said.

"I met with your advisor," she said, blurting out the truth.

"You what?" he said, instantly furious. "Going behind my back? That was a rotten thing to do, Mother."

"I wouldn't have to ask, if you would call once in a while and tell me what's going on."

"I've been busy," he said, not quite looking at her.

"I understand," she said, immediately sorry. "I know I've been busy, too. Look, it's almost dinner time." She checked her watch. "You have to eat somewhere, how about having dinner with me? You choose the place. We can talk, then."

She sounded pathetic and she knew it but couldn't stop herself.

"I already made plans," he said coolly. "Really, Mother, you can't expect me to stop everything just because you decide to show up without any warning."

"I know," Evaleen said defensively, "and I'm sorry."

"I'm sorry too, Mother," he said, his tone softening, "but I don't have time today. I planned to go with my buddies to a game. Next time you get a hare-brained scheme to show up unannounced, at least have the courtesy to call first."

"I will," she promised, duly chastised. It almost felt like she was talking with Hero.

Court kissed her goodbye. She left, feeling miserable and humiliated.

Out on the street, Evaleen remembered that she was supposed to talk to Court about being more serious about his schoolwork, but she had been so upset, she forget to mention it. She would have to call him later, but right now that was the last thing she wanted to do. All she had accomplished today was to irritate Court and make matters worse between them.

"Don't worry," Mortimer said, after she told him what happened. "The boy will get over it, and so will you. He's still a kid and kids that age are pretty self-centered. He's probably already forgotten about it."

This did not make Evaleen feel any better.

At home she told Gussie what happened. Gussie tried to reassure her that Court was at the age when his friends meant more to him than his family or anybody else. It was normal, and she shouldn't take it personally. But it still took her days to get over the meeting.

Later, when she told Hero what happened, he said he would talk to Court. She was grateful and glad to let him, but also knew he would probably forget, as usual.

#

She also planned to see Bunny at the earliest opportunity, but after her fiasco with Court, she decided to inform her first. Before she could do so, Bunny called her, late one afternoon. Evaleen was surprised to hear from her. Bunny rarely called home and usually only if she needed money.

"I want to come home," she said.

She sounded scared, which amazed Evaleen, as Bunny always sounded so sure of herself.

"It's only April. The school year isn't even up yet," Evaleen said.

As far as she knew, Bunny loved the school, but with Bunny you never knew for sure. She didn't share much of herself with anyone.

"I'm being expelled," she said, and began to cry. "Nobody likes me here."

"Why?" Evaleen asked, dumbfounded.

"Everybody's blaming me for something I didn't do."

Evaleen was immediately wary. "What happened?"

"A boy got drunk, drove into a tree and ended up in the hospital and they say it's my fault and it's not."

She broke down in a fresh wave of sobs.

"Oh, dear God," Evaleen said, concerned for the boy. "Who is he?"

"Somebody. I don't know his name."

Evaleen was shocked at Bunny's callousness. "How could you not know his name?"

"He's nobody to me," she said, in a sneering tone.

"Why are they blaming you?"

"Because they're jealous."

Evaleen knew from past experience that it was futile to talk further. Bunny was never forthcoming about anything, especially if she might be in the wrong.

"Wait there. I'll get back to you in a bit." Evaleen hung up the phone.

She took a deep breath to calm her nerves, looked up the number of Bunny's school and called the dean of students, who quickly filled her in.

"Bunny was at a party with some older students and apparently there was some drinking going on," she said in a soft-spoken but firm tone. "As I understand it, she taunted Jeff Neilson to chug-a-lug more beer than was good for him. Sad to say, he was attracted to her and did as she asked. He became hopelessly drunk, and ran his car into a tree on his way home. He's in the hospital with a fractured pelvis."

Evaleen felt as if someone were throwing ice cold water in her face. "I...I don't know what to say."

"There were witnesses," the dean continued. "She's a beautiful girl, Mrs. Lyon, with a good personality when it suits her, and she's very bright. It concerns us at the school that she refuses to take responsibility for her part in the incident. The Board of Regents have chosen to suspend her for a month until we sort this all out. We don't want our students thinking there are no consequences for this kind of behavior. I hope you understand our position. We called several times to talk about this with you, but no one ever got back to us."

A wave of shame and guilt washed over Evaleen. For a moment she felt physically ill. The message was probably in a pile of phone messages that she hadn't gotten around to returning since her mother died.

Her only excuse was that since Ma died, she hadn't been herself and didn't feel as motivated to take care of business as she had been before. But that wasn't much of an excuse and she knew it. She had let Bunny, the school, and herself down. And now a young man was in the hospital and Bunny was involved and oh, dear God, what next?

"I'll come by and pick her up tomorrow morning, if that's all right with you."

"The sooner the better," the principal said.

#

Evaleen had Georgia reschedule her appointments.

"Court and Bunny need to get a job," Mortimer said, as he drove her to pick Bunny up. "Kept me out of trouble when I was their age. Those two both act like the world owes them a living, like they're special and entitled to have everything. They don't have to lift a finger. Past time to introduce them to the real world."

"You're probably right," Evaleen agreed.

She was distraught at what was happening to her children and blamed herself completely for being such an absent mother.

Bunny was waiting at the curb in front of the dormitory with her bags packed when Evaleen and Mortimer arrived. It was still early and Bunny was not wearing any makeup, which was surprising. Without makeup she looked like what she was, a scared little girl.

"I wasn't the one drinking," she said, once she was settled in the back of the limousine. "Why is everyone blaming me?"

Her eyes glistened with tears of self-pity.

"The dean said you egged the young man on to keep drinking when it was obvious to everyone he should have stopped," Evaleen said, trying not to let Bunny's tears influence her.

"Nobody twisted his arm," Bunny shot back. "He could have said no."

"Don't you feel anything for that young man?" Evaleen asked, shocked that Bunny could be so cold.

"Why should I? I didn't do anything. He was the one who drank himself silly and then drove into a tree."

What could Evaleen do about her daughter's thinking? She didn't know what to do. But others might. That she had learned from her years in the business world.

Evaleen had consulted a psychiatrist right after they moved into their new home.

When she complained about Hero having his own room, the psychiatrist said, "If he wanted to change, he would. Since he doesn't, you will have to decide whether you want to stay in the marriage or not."

Evaleen decided to stay, because she loved Hero still and believed that someday, when they weren't so busy, it would all work out. But she also began to act more independently, and although she wasn't conscious of it, she gave up the idea that it would ever be any different. Still, seeing the psychiatrist had changed her life for the better.

She hoped it would change Bunny's life as well. As soon as she returned home, she made an appointment for Bunny to see the psychiatrist who had helped her so much.

Bunny resisted, but finally agreed to go after Evaleen threatened to cut off her allowance, the only real leverage she had with Bunny.

After three sessions, in three days, the psychiatrist called Evaleen.

"She doesn't trust anyone, and she seems to be shut down emotionally. I think she's deeply hurt and angry about something. I'm assuming it has to do with her parents' deaths. I also get the feeling that she thinks the only thing she has to offer is her beauty. Because she is so beautiful, she uses that to get what she wants. Sadly, she bends the rules to suit herself, and then blames everyone else for not caring when she doesn't get her own way. I don't know if I can help her, but I do have one idea. I want her to visit the young man in the hospital and meet his family. Maybe that will penetrate her denial. Let's hope so."

Evaleen thanked the doctor for her advice.

She went to Bunny's room and told her what the psychiatrist had said. Bunny slammed down the fashion magazine she was reading and looked up at Evaleen, a furious, sullen expression on her beautiful face.

"Look, I did not pour alcohol down that boy's throat. His decision to swallow it was his own. And what about me? If it weren't for him, I'd still be in school, and everybody knew I was a sure thing for the next Rose Queen."

Evaleen could only shake her head in disbelief. Where was this girl's heart? Did she even have one?

"Bunny, tell me," she said, not bothering to hide her irritation at Bunny's complete lack of remorse. "Did you ever find out the young man's name?"

Suddenly, Bunny's face was filled with evil. Her eyes became flat and lifeless and hard.

"I don't need this and I don't need you," Bunny said.

She raced out of her bedroom and down the steps towards the front door.

"Where are you going?" Evaleen asked, rushing after her. "When will you be back?"

"I'm leaving this dump," Bunny said and marched out, slamming the front door behind her.

Evaleen ran after her, shouting at her to come back, to at least talk about this, but Bunny ran so fast that Evaleen could not catch up.

She didn't come home for three days. Evaleen, Hero, Gussie and Mortimer were all beside themselves with worry.

Evaleen would have called Bunny's friends, but she hadn't the faintest idea who they were. Nor did Gussie or Hero or Court. As it turned out nobody really knew Bunny, the people who loved her least of all.

Evaleen called the police the first day, but they said they couldn't report her missing until she'd been gone for forty-eight hours. Hero, Evaleen, Gussie and Mortimer all drove around in separate cars, searching everywhere for her, although to be honest, they could only guess where she might possibly be, since they really didn't know much about her.

To everyone's surprise, Bunny showed up again late Sunday afternoon. She looked tired and her clothes were dirty and disheveled.

Evaleen was overcome with relief. Bunny seemed glad to be home but refused to say where she had been or what she had been doing.

When she appeared for dinner that night, clean and pressed again, she acted as if nothing had happened.

"Why do you worry so, Mommy?" she asked, all sweetness and light. "I'm fine. Look at me, don't I look wonderful? Have I ever looked better?"

Evaleen shivered at the empty look in her daughter's eyes. In spite of her fear that Bunny would leave again, Evaleen insisted that Bunny do as the psychiatrist said.

Bunny finally gave in, but only when Hero said he would cut off her allowance permanently and take away her car keys if she didn't comply.

Monday morning, still half asleep, a reluctant, sullen, non-speaking Bunny climbed into the back seat of the family limousine to visit the hospital and to meet the boy's parents.

Bunny insisted on going alone, with only Mortimer to drive her.

Evaleen didn't argue. She was just relieved Bunny was going at all. She hoped the psychiatrist was right and that Bunny would learn something from it.

They were gone all day. Evaleen went to work as usual but had trouble concentrating and returned home early.

Bunny arrived home around dinner time. Gussie and Evaleen were waiting at the entrance when Mortimer pulled up and dropped her off. A sobbing Bunny raced past Evaleen and Gussie without a word, went to her room and slammed the door.

Mortimer reported what he knew.

"After seeing the boy at the hospital, the moment she stepped into the limo she started to cry. She became even more hysterical after she visited his family. She cried all the way home. I asked what was wrong, but she wouldn't stop crying long enough to tell me, so I'm not sure exactly what happened, but whatever it was, it must have had a huge impact to upset her that much. Far as I know she's never cried about anything before, so this is something completely new for her."

Although Gussie was a bit put out, Evaleen insisted on going to see Bunny alone.

She went to her bedroom door and knocked. To her surprise, Bunny opened the door and let her in. Her eyes were red and her face looked sore from crying so much. Evaleen sat on the small settee while Bunny sat on the edge of her bed and continued to sob. Evaleen longed to take her in her arms and hold her close, but from past experience, knew better than to try.

"Do you want to tell me what happened?" Evaleen asked gently, handing Bunny a clean handkerchief.

Bunny nodded.

"Jeff was nice about everything," she said, wiping her eyes and nose and looking down at her hands. "That's his name, Jeff. He was all strung up in his hospital room and I could tell he was in a lot of pain. He said it was his own fault, and he should have known better. Seeing him lying there so helpless, it hit me that he probably wouldn't have drunk so much if I hadn't egged him on."

She burst into tears, her head in her hands.

"Did you see his parents?" Evaleen asked.

"Yes. They were wonderful. They forgave me, too. At first, I thought it was all just a big phony act to get money from you. But when I mentioned that my parents were prepared to pay them for their pain and suffering, his mother said it wasn't about the money, it was whether or not her son recovered and if we had both learned our lesson. Oh Mommy, there were pictures of him in his baseball uniform all over the place. If he never plays baseball again, I'll feel so terrible," she said, choking on the words, "and he loves playing baseball more than anything."

Evaleen took a chance, went to her daughter, and put her arms around her. For the first time ever, Bunny did not push her away.

Evaleen felt intensely sorry for Bunny. Evaleen's own father's death still haunted her dreams. Even now, after what Ma said, barely a day went by when she didn't think about him.

And now Bunny would suffer all her life, knowing that her actions had harmed someone. The sad truth was, that there was no going back ever to change anything. What had happened, had happened and it would always be that way.

"My father told me over and over that people were no good," Bunny said, wiping her eyes, "that you couldn't trust anybody. He said that everybody lied all the time and that you should never encourage them, because all they ever wanted to do was use you. And then he killed my mother. He said she was having an affair. She wasn't. I know because he never let her out of his sight."

Bunny choked back her sobs. "He lied all the time about everything and I thought that was normal and that's what everybody did. But today, when I saw how those people acted, how much they loved each other and their son and how I almost destroyed what was most precious to them, I felt like dying myself."

She wiped her eyes. "I realized then that my father was wrong about everything and that I was wrong, too. These were good, honest people and they forgave me, just like Jeff did. Can you believe that, Mommy? They forgave me."

She burst into a fresh wave of sobs. "When I said I didn't know how I could ever make it up to them, his mother said that I should just go on, learn from this and live a good life. I suddenly realized how lucky I was. You took me in and you gave me a home when my aunt couldn't be bothered. I was there, I heard. If it weren't for you and dad, I would have ended up in an orphanage. Oh, Mommy, I've been such a terrible brat. I'll never forgive myself."

"It's all right," Evaleen said, fighting back her own tears.

She held Bunny in her arms until at last her daughter cried herself to sleep.

Afterwards, Evaleen did what she always did when disturbed. She went to Gussie's apartment and knocked softly on her door. Gussie answered immediately.

"Can I come in?"

"Of course. You're always welcome, you know that."

"For the first time ever, I think Bunny's going to be all right," Evaleen said.

The two women sat at Gussie's kitchen table, drinking coffee. She went on to tell Gussie everything that happened. Gussie too shed a few tears when she heard it all.

In the days that followed, Bunny could still be demanding and difficult, but glimpses of a new softer, kinder, more approachable Bunny began to emerge.

#

That summer, Evaleen and Hero decided to take Mortimer's advice and put Bunny and Court to work in the family business. Both protested, but Hero and Evaleen stood firm and told them that from now on they would have to work for their spending money. Their allowances were being cut off, permanently.

Court's job at Evaleen Incorporated was to deliver the mail and run errands. Bunny worked in the lab. To everyone's surprise, Court loved delivering the mail, and especially loved all the attention from the young women who worked there. It didn't hurt that the secretaries thought him as good looking as a movie star.

Bunny wasn't quite as happy as Court about being forced to work, but found the making of beauty products interesting, if not terribly exciting. Once in a while, she would become high-handed and let everyone know she was the boss's daughter, but stopped when both Hero and Evaleen let her know that such behavior would not be tolerated.

Evaleen, made it a point to check on them at odd times during the day. She also insisted they all have dinner together at night. Thankfully, for once they did not argue. Hero joined them from time to time, not as regularly as she would have liked, but at least a couple of times a week.

By sheer persistence, slowly the day's activities were discussed. Neither Bunny nor Court nor Hero were as enthusiastic about this as Evaleen, but they endured it and were polite and forthcoming when pushed.

Court's zeal soon earned him a promotion to assist Jordan Thompson, a big, easy-going man who policed the business, making sure that unauthorized people were not selling their products for less, and protecting the company's reputation and patents. Although Court's job was mostly to run errands and get everyone coffee, he enjoyed the power associated with his new job and took it very seriously. It was hard for him to get up in time to go to work, but when he was late, Hero docked his pay, and soon he became better, though still not perfect about showing up on time.

As for Bunny, Dave Smith, head of marketing, a quiet, serious young man barely out of college himself and obviously infatuated with Bunny, suggested that she model the product for their print ads.

"With her dark hair and creamy complexion, she'd be a natural," he rhapsodized.

After talking it over, Evaleen and Hero agreed to give it a try. After a few training sessions with a top modeling agency on how to move, and a complete makeover by Adrienne of Angelique, Bunny was ready. To nobody's surprise, the camera loved Bunny as much as Bunny loved the camera.

When the summer was over, both Bunny and Court were reluctant to return to school, but Evaleen and Hero's wishes prevailed. Evaleen felt sad to see them go but also relieved.

Although tensions could still arise, things between them were better than they had been in years. And when they weren't, Mortimer was quick to remind her, "They're teenagers. What can you expect?"

Chapter Twenty-Four

Two years later Evaleen sat in the back of a taxi cab, headed home a day early. She had finished her business in New York and saw no reason to linger. Normally Mortimer would have picked her up from the airport, but he and Gussie were on their honeymoon in Cape Cod, a wedding gift from Evaleen and Hero, along with Humpty and Dumpty, whom Gussie could not bear to be parted from.

Gussie had finally agreed to marry Mortimer when he took a course in CPR in case she had a heart attack so he would be able to save her. She had a mild heart murmur. Only then did Gussie finally believe he sincerely loved her.

"I couldn't imagine a life without him," Gussie admitted to Evaleen, right after their small wedding in June. "It just wouldn't be the same."

The wedding had been held outside in what was originally Gussie's victory garden and was now a formal garden, with a variety of flowers planned specifically by their gardener and her. They aimed to have something constantly in bloom from early spring to late fall, as well as several herbs sprinkled here and there to appease Gussie's practical side.

Evaleen was thrilled for them both.

At home, exhausted, looking forward to a good night's sleep in her own bed, Evaleen was climbing the stairs to her rooms when to her surprise, she heard a woman's high voice shriek with laughter. What was a woman doing here at this time of night? Evaleen heard Hero's voice too, although she couldn't make out the actual words. Her alarm turned to confusion. Hero and the woman were together? She felt strangely intimidated as, half in anticipation, half in dread, she quietly opened the door to Hero's room.

The only light came from two candles burning on tables on either side of the room, giving the place a strangely unsettling aspect, as though the bed that occupied the center of the room were some sort of grotesque altar.

Two naked people were on the bed, one atop the other, pumping away. It was animalistic, crude, disgusting, like watching a ceremony being performed by two primitive beings. At first she refused to grasp the truth of what she was seeing. Her emotions were tamped down by the scene – the linen sheets, the rich draperies covering the windows, the perfume mixed with perspiration that lingered in the air.

But, somewhere far away, she felt the horror, the doom of this moment.

She stood at the open door, confused, unable to move or breathe. She had the strange, dizzying sensation that she was standing in water over her head, that nothing was real.

The woman under Hero was blond and wore her hair in waves that had begun to unravel. She was completely naked, her large breasts spread out and quivering at each thrust. Her mouth was smeared with lipstick. Her eyes were completely devoid of emotion – a prostitute, Evaleen thought at first, before she realized with a start that she knew this woman.

It was Lark, the woman who she mistakenly thought was engaged to Hero so many years ago. The woman who was with him at Shu's party.

The woman glanced over Hero's shoulder and met Evaleen's eyes.

The woman slashed her long red nails down Hero's back.

"Get off," she said sharply. "Your wife's home."

Hero arched in agony, froze for an instant, then slowly rolled off the woman. His face was a mask of irritation.

Seeing them together, Evaleen felt helpless at first, then her mood changed to fury. Her rage exploded at him, not for the act of sex with Lark, not because she was jealous, but for the invasion of her home.

Hero flopped around like a clumsy fool, got off the bed and began hopping on one foot as he tried to pull on his pants. Lark remained in bed, the covers pulled up to her chin staring calmly at Evaleen. Did she think she was going to be allowed to remain there? Evaleen wondered, her wrath almost choking her.

"Get out of my house," Evaleen said in an icy and deliberate tone.

"You think you're such a big deal," Lark said, not moving. Her face was a glowering, sneering mask of rage. "Well, I got news for you, lady. Where do you think Hero was all those nights when he wasn't with you? He was with me. And guess what? He asked me to marry him and when I refused, he married you to get back at me. He loved me, not you. When he finally made enough money so we could be together, it was too late, because he was stuck with you and two kids and trapped in a business he hated and couldn't get out of. He never would have married you, if he could have had me. So you're the fool. Not me."

Evaleen marched over to the bed and slapped Lark's face.

"I said get out, and I meant it."

Lark spit at her like an angry hissing cat but got out of bed and began to dress.

Evaleen turned to Hero who was zipping up his pants.

"What could you possibly have to say for yourself, Hero Lyon?" she asked in a matter-of-fact voice.

"What is there to say, my love?" Hero said, clumsily buckling his belt. A look of hostility crossed his face. "I've been caught red-handed and I know it. You women work it out, like you always do. Let me know when it's over."

He brushed past her on his way out the door. Lark, a defiant look on her face, continued to get dressed.

"Hero and I have been together way longer than you've been married to him," she said. "Bet you didn't know that either."

"No, I didn't know it, nor do I really care anymore," Evaleen replied in a flat and deadly voice. "But if I ever see your face again anywhere on our property, I'll have you arrested as a trespasser."

The woman stepped back in involuntary alarm.

"I wouldn't do that if I were you," she blustered. "Hero wouldn't like it."

"Oh, you think so?" Evaleen said, her voice dripping with sarcasm. "An intruder? In my home? Who do you think the police will believe? You or me?"

Something Lark saw in Evaleen's face made her eyes widen with fear. She scooped up the rest of her clothes and inched towards the back stairs.

"I…I…" she squeaked.

She dove for the door, yanked it open, and ran down the outside steps.

Evaleen heard her scream something incoherent. Then came a thump and a series of bangs as she slipped and tumbled down the stair. A shriek of pain could be heard as she hit the bottom stair, then a burst of loud wailing as she fled off into the night.

Evaleen felt the tiniest sense of satisfaction at the woman's fear and flight. But her real fury was aimed directly at Hero. Lark could have him and his alcoholism and his gambling problems and his womanizing, Evaleen thought.

She stalked through the house, hunting him down. But he had obviously left, too. Good. Right now she hoped he would never come back.

She was still seething as she undressed and went to bed. She spent the night folded up into a tight little ball, trembling inside and out, her mind chattering frantically, going over and over everything all night long.

Was Lark telling the truth? Was it true that Hero did not love her when he married her? Did he only marry her to get back at Lark for marrying someone else? Was he with her when Court was born? Was that where he was?

When her anger finally dissipated, she broke down and cried. Not because of Lark or Hero, but because she had held the hope, ridiculous as it was, that someday, when they both had more time, they would find their way back to each other and be a happy family.

But the dream of a happy family was just a hopeless pipe dream, a lie, something to keep her going when things became rough at Evaleen, Incorporated. The truth, although it hurt to admit it, was that Hero had not been a priority of hers for some time and she was definitely not a priority of his. He was her business partner and not much more. Surprising they had lasted this long.

It occurred to her that her attraction to Hero was the same feeling she had about her father right before he died – wanting a love and concern he could not give her. The realization washed over her with surprising clarity. She also knew deep down, that tonight was the beginning of a whole new chapter in her life. She could no longer ignore the fact that the marriage was over, irretrievably broken, and had been for a long time.

She was learning, albeit slowly, as she wasn't very good at self-reflection. Everything she had cast her whole being into winning had become hers, but none of it had any meaning right now. Maybe if she would have married Josh, it would have been different, but it was too late for that, too. She had made her choices, now she was stuck with them. Sad but true.

On the good side, she was no longer that same frightened, guilty young girl making her grandmother's skin care cream to sell door-to-door, nor the desperate saleswoman weighing everything on the scales against whether it would improve sales or her status in the community, nor the mother who had hired others to do her mothering so she could be busy doing… what? Impressing complete strangers?

Suddenly, it was as though the most massive weight – of responsibility, of the need to matter – turned into a liquid and washed away. If Hero wasn't worth impressing, who was?

Her parents were gone, her children had their own lives, and her marriage was over. She was free, completely free to just be herself. Who knew? Maybe she would even discover that she liked herself, although she wasn't too sure of that or anything else right now.

She began to shiver, feeling strangely cold. Did such tremendous insights always happen as the result of such painful moments, she wondered. Maybe. But if everything she had strived for suddenly meant nothing to her anymore, then what did matter?

Tomorrow, she was going to start to find out. Inside she was still that little, stubborn Eva Doyle, hopeful, anxious, eager to try something new.

As the grey of dawn filtered into her bedroom, she realized she would have to tell Bunny and Court that their parents were separating. That would be hard. Court and Bunny worked in the business each summer now, when they weren't attending college. Bunny had become the face of Evaleen, and Court worked in marketing and sales. She rarely saw either of them.

Even when they were home they always seemed to be just leaving, in a hurry to go somewhere else. The only time she saw them, or so it seemed to her lately, was when they needed money.

Court always sounded happy to see her, but if she asked him to do something specific, like have dinner with her, he always seemed to be busy doing something else. It was the same with Bunny, who was heavily involved in a charity she had begun her first year of college to raise money for victims of spousal abuse. She had also begun to date Mark Watson, the son of Ansel Watson, who owned the large construction company responsible for most of Emerson's major buildings.

Evaleen thought Bunny at nineteen was a little young to be so serious, but Mark, who was 23, adored Bunny and was good to her, so she kept her feelings to herself.

What sustained her these days was the young unmarried mothers she had met so long ago. They were all department heads now, in charge of hiring others who like themselves in the beginning desperately needed a job to support their families. It pleased her and gave her a feeling of deep satisfaction. She still loved spending time with them. They seemed to enjoy it too, as they often invited her to their monthly get-togethers.

Gussie remained her dearest friend, but she had Mortimer now and the two of them were often busy with each other.

Evaleen was often lonely. She wished she could call Josh and talk to him, but it was inappropriate to call a married man. Anyway, what could they possibly have to say?

The day the war ended still haunted her dreams, but as she reminded herself, it happened a long time ago. Josh had probably forgot all about it. She wished she could.

Finally, after one of the longest nights of her life, she got up and faced the unavoidable day. Feeling a strange, fugue-like déjà vu, she showered and dressed. Maybe this wrung-out, drained feeling would go on for some time, but right now she needed to get ready for work.

The fact that Hero had the nerve to bring that woman into their home disgusted her, but much of what he did disgusted her these days, so nothing new there. He drank too much, gambled too much, stayed out too late, yet was able to go to work every day and do a good job, for which she was grateful. Even now.

But gratitude was not love. She did not love him, had not loved him for a long time, and obviously he didn't love her either, had never really loved her. Truth was, right now she was more tired at the loss of a night's sleep than angry at him. After all, Hero was just being himself, a playboy at heart.

In the breakfast room where she went to get a cup of coffee from the silver decanter that Gussie always had waiting and ready, she was surprised to see Hero sitting at the table, drinking coffee and reading the morning newspaper, just like nothing happened. He must have come back sometime in the middle of the night.

Seeing Evaleen approach, he put the paper down and looked up at her. By the looks of his pale and pinched face and bloodshot eyes, he hadn't slept, either. His hair, which was just beginning to turn gray, was greasy, uncombed and sticking up all over the place. He needed a shave.

Evaleen poured herself a cup of coffee, then sat down opposite him.

"Sorry about what happened," he said, not quite looking her in the eye. "I didn't expect you home so early."

"Most cheaters would have had the decency to take their bimbos to a hotel," she said, sounding angrier and more tired than she really felt.

"She wanted to see the house," he replied in a calm voice, as though they were speaking of the weather.

"Was that it? Well, I hope she enjoyed the tour."

Why was she bothering to talk to him, when she didn't give a damn? But somewhere at the bottom of it all, she was still a woman, with a woman's irrational fears, a woman's sense of betrayal. Hadn't she ever been worth anything to him, that he wouldn't fight at least a little bit to keep her?

"Look," he said, "I know it was wrong."

"Oh, let's quit the charade, Hero," she said. "I think we can both agree this marriage is over. A divorce would probably be best for us both."

"I loved you in the beginning," he said. A look of tenderness sparked momentarily in his eyes.

Evaleen was touched, but wasn't sure she believed him.

"I loved you too," she said, "but that doesn't really matter right now, does it? Our marriage has been over for a long time, and we both know it. As for the business…"

She shook her head sadly. "I'm sure we'll figure it out."

His eyes narrowed and became hard and cold. "Nothing to figure out. It's really quite simple. I want out."

She was furious to hear him speak so. The business they had both put years of their lives into meant nothing to him? Their marriage meant nothing to him?

"Well, you're just full of surprises, aren't you?" she said acidly.

"It's humiliating to spend my whole life worrying about something as ridiculous as face creams," he said, almost spitting out the words. "I always feel like I'm hanging onto my wife's coattails. Well, I'm not going to do it anymore. You don't really need me. You've got a lot of good people working for you. Bitsy Junior could take my place in a second."

His tone had begun to soften again. "She's smart and efficient and does a great job. She can't wait to go to work in the morning, whereas I hate every minute."

What a weak man he is, Evaleen thought, to have thrown his whole life away on things he didn't value. Her, the business, even his floozy who, if he had any guts, he would have left Evaleen for long ago. Who knew, they might have all been happier.

Funny enough, by holding everything in his life valueless, he devalued himself most of all.

That she would not do. Her actions did have value. What she had done had been worthwhile, no matter what he thought. Their business had provided people with good livelihoods, including single mothers and other abandoned women, and gave her own family a good life.

She was proud of that. Her work was not for nothing. Her life had value, as did his. She had seen to that. The fact that he did not was his loss.

"Let me think about what you've said," Evaleen said, not wishing to discuss any further what was now so patently obvious.

She was all business now as she stood up. "I'll get back to you later."

"You do that," he said, taking a sip of his coffee and returning to the sports section of his newspaper.

For a moment, she had to restrain herself to keep from laughing. He looked so pathetic, like a sad circus clown with his unshaved face, bed-head hair and puffy face. What had she ever seen in him?

In the next instant, she nearly burst into tears. In some ways she didn't blame him. She knew how much he hated working in the business, he had made that clear years ago.

She always hoped he would change his mind. It never happened. Even if their marriage had stood a chance, they lost it the day Hero agreed to join her in the business.

These days, she was referred to regularly in the society pages and the business section of the local newspaper, while Hero was rarely mentioned, if at all. She had gone along all these years making her creams and traveling to different cities to promote her grandmother's skin care products to any woman who would listen, oblivious to everything else, while Hero took care of his end of the business and did it extremely well.

She felt sorry for him, but the business had made him rich. Wasn't that worth something?

How would she manage without him? This last question spun through her mind like dust on a whirlwind as she drove to work. All she knew for sure was that what she felt for him was neither love nor hate. Somebody said the opposite of love was not hate but indifference, and now she knew the truth of that statement.

When Evaleen arrived at work, she calmly buzzed Georgia and told her to set up a meeting with Dave, her lawyer.

Dave showed up shortly afterwards asking what that was all about, since Georgia wouldn't say.

"I want a divorce," she said.

Dave hesitated for a long instant. Regret, sadness, shock: she saw all those emotions flash across his face, but not surprise. He sat down opposite her.

"It's pretty obvious to everyone that there's not much of a connection there," he said.

That shocked her. If he knew, probably everyone else did, too.

"Hero wants out," she said. "That must have been obvious, too."

"Yes," Dave said quietly. "It was."

It hurt Evaleen to know that everybody probably knew their private business, yet no one ever said anything to her. One of the problems with her life now was that people didn't share things with her anymore. They talked among themselves, but because she was the boss and owner, they were always careful when they spoke to her.

"So what do we do next?"

"Well, you're a tremendously rich woman," Dave said, "so you're not going to have any problems there."

He seemed relieved at being able to attack this as just one more situation to analyze and handle. "No matter what happens, the business will be fine. It's too big not to go on. Filing for divorce will be the easy part. Buying Hero out will be a little more complicated, if that's what you want to do."

"That's what I want to do," Evaleen said, her voice firm. "I don't know what Hero wants to do, you'll have to ask him."

"Splitting up a company this size has huge implications for a lot of people," he said carefully. "First, we have to get an accurate appraisal. We'll need to get Hero to agree on which outside firm to choose for the appraisal, and then go from there. In the meantime, I'll file the divorce papers."

He hesitated one more time and said in a tentative, lost voice, "Are you really sure this is what you want?"

"Yes," Evaleen said sadly. "Unfortunately, we were more successful at building a business than we ever were at building a marriage."

Chapter Twenty-Five

On a beautiful spring morning in April of the following year, Evaleen decided to take a walk to Saint Mark's Church. She stopped for a moment outside her house to admire the profusion of red tulips that her gardener had planted in a huge circle and the robin's-egg blue sky, filled with puffs of white clouds that looked so much larger and closer than usual.

She reminded herself to praise his work at the next gathering of the household staff, and have her accountant add a bonus to his latest paycheck. She knew from past experience that public acknowledgement of good work was a wonderful and powerful motivator. Anyway, he deserved it. He worked hard and the results were spectacular.

As she strolled along, the warm spring sun felt good on her bare arms. With time to spare for a change, she allowed her subconscious thoughts to surface.

Ever since she filed for divorce, Evaleen felt an emptiness she couldn't explain. Going to work no longer sustained her. With Bitsy Junior running the company, she was no longer in such a hurry and began to take whole afternoons off for no reason at all.

Maybe in that way, more than anything else, she had changed. Court and Bunny, as usual, were always busy. As for Hero, having him gone wasn't much different than when he lived at home. Thankfully Gussie and Mortimer, who were more like family than her own family, were still with her.

She felt restless lately, and although that was at least in part because of the divorce, her emotions went even deeper. She felt cast adrift, without meaning or purpose.

All that had fulfilled her, building a business that served others, provided people with a decent living, and gave women hope, still seemed worthy and right when she thought about it intellectually, but somehow in her bones, it was as though the business itself had left her behind. She had achieved her dreams, built a business she was proud of, and people still deferred to her, but in the past year she had set it up so they made their day-to-day decisions without her. They didn't need to consult her most of the time. The business, like Court and Bunny, was becoming more and more independent.

She was in that betwixt and between period where she knew she wanted to do something else with her life but wasn't quite sure exactly what that was. It was a lonesome, lost, even a bit scary sort of feeling. She tried to assuage it by visiting Saint Mark's Church a few times a week to spend some time alone with her thoughts.

At Saint Mark's, she stopped to admire a tree with golden flecks down one side where the sun hit it. She watched a red cardinal dance from branch to branch and realized it was carrying on for its mud-colored mate. She opened the big oak door to the church and stepped inside.

Sunlight shone through the stained glass windows, leaving a rainbow of colors on the stone floor. Evaleen stood in the center of that circle of light, enjoying the warmth and the feeling of peace. She felt blessed by the light. She strode over to the black iron rack filled with candles. She dropped several bills in the coin box, lit a few candles then knelt down before the statue of Mary. She prayed for her children, for Gussie and Mortimer, for her employees, and for peace between Hero and herself.

Finally, sitting down in a pew near the front, she stretched her legs, took a deep breath and began to relax. She thought about Court and Bunny.

When she told Court that she and Hero were getting a divorce, his only reply was, "What took you so long?" Bunny had sympathized briefly, but then went on to talk excitedly about her latest project to raise money to build a safe house for abused women.

Evaleen was proud of them both, but had little in common with them. Not only were they strangers to her, she realized, but she was also a stranger to them. And she was beginning to understand that would never change.

The truth was the truth and she accepted it, but it hurt just the same.

It occurred to her that everyone, including her, lived their lives like ships in a flotilla, seemingly going in the same direction, with signals and messages constantly being passed back and forth between the boats, but often missed or misinterpreted. Everyone was a separate entity, jostling at times, losing sight of each other even at the most critical moments, frightened they might crash, or lose each other forever, but almost never in charge of what actually happened.

From what Evaleen had heard, Hero and Lark were now living together. This bothered her a lot less than she would have ever dreamed. If she felt anything at all, it was guilt for urging Hero to go into business with her in the first place.

Maybe they would have had a better marriage had he found something else to do, something he could have been proud of. Or maybe it wouldn't have made any difference at all, since apparently there were always three of them in the marriage, right from the beginning.

She felt a shot of bitterness, but she could not go back or change anything. All she could do was go forward and do what needed to be done next.

The business was still in flux. At their last meeting, Dave had handed her the official appraisal and a complete financial statement. He tried to explain all the legal ramifications, but she left the meeting feeling too confused to make a decision.

In this alone, she still missed Hero, fiercely. Finance was the one aspect of her life she had always left to him. She was a fool for never asking him to explain all the intricate details of decisions he made and why he made them the way he did. But whenever she asked, he was always so impatient because she didn't understand as easily as he did. It had been easier to let it go, and focus on the sales and development of new products.

Now, she needed that expertise – their employees needed that expertise – and she couldn't deliver. But she wasn't entirely helpless, not in this, not in anything, anymore.

One thing she had learned after all these years in business – if she did not have the expertise herself, she could always hire it done. But finding people she could trust with something that had so many consequences for so many people was difficult. She had gone over her list of contacts several times but had not come up with anyone she trusted enough to keep the information confidential, or explain it to her in a way that she could understand.

A tall man entered the church and sat down in an adjoining pew, disturbing her solitude. The man's hair was filled with cowlicks, which reminded her of Josh.

How long had it been since she had seen him? It seemed like forever. She missed him terribly and wondered how he was doing these days and if he was okay. She hoped so.

He was a good, kind, loving man and deserved to be happy. He was also someone you could actually talk to, so unlike Hero, who seldom wanted to talk about anything, especially if it didn't pertain to business.

The tall man stood up to leave. Seeing him go, something clicked in her mind like a flash of light. She finally had a good excuse to call Josh. She could ask him for his perspective on the business. He would know what to do or who to call and she trusted him explicitly.

She said another prayer, this time thanking God for giving her such a brilliant idea and a good excuse to call Josh.

#

The house was quieter than usual when she arrived home. Gussie and Mortimer must be off somewhere, she thought, then remembered that the help worked on Saturdays and were off on Sundays and Mondays. No wonder it was so quiet.

Anxious to get started, Evaleen climbed the steps to her private rooms and entered her study. The heavy velvet drapes were pulled back and light poured in, making bright patterns on the blood red Persian rug.

She sat at her desk and looked up Josh's number. There were two listed – one at home, another at work. She chose his work number since this was a work issue, or so she reassured herself.

With trembling hands, she picked up the phone and dialed. When a woman answered, Evaleen, her heart pounding, gave her name in a voice that didn't sound normal to her own ears and asked to speak to Josh.

"My God, Evaleen, is that really you?" he said, when he picked up the phone.

To her great relief, he sounded thrilled to hear from her. "It's been forever. How the hell are you?"

Hearing his voice made her feel all tingly inside, like being a teenager again.

"I'm doing fine, but I need some advice about selling the business," she said quickly, before she lost her nerve. "I'm wondering if you can find the time to discuss it with me. I know your time is valuable, and I would be happy to pay you."

"What?" He sounded offended. "Don't you dare even think about it. If I can't help out an old friend, then I'm not worth much."

They both checked their calendars and set up an appointment for Friday the following week. He gave her the address and they said goodbye. She hung up the phone. She was so relieved that he was glad to hear from her that tears came to her eyes.

This is strictly a business meeting, she chided herself, wiping her eyes. He's a happily married man, so don't go getting any stupid ideas or make a fool out of yourself. He's just an old friend, that's all. Period.

But her heart didn't believe her and kept swooping and sailing like a drunken bird the whole rest of the day. It made her especially happy to know there was at least one other person out there besides Gussie and Hero who knew her from the old days. And he said he was glad to hear from her. That thought alone made her feel happy for the rest of the day.

#

Evaleen was so keyed up all week that she had trouble concentrating on business or anything else. Finally, after what seemed like a month, Friday morning arrived. She took more time and care getting ready than she had for years. She tried on several outfits, finally settling on a simple lime green jersey wrap dress and white open-toed wedgies. Gussie said the whole outfit made her look younger. She had creamed her face the night before, and creamed it again this morning, but kept her makeup purposefully light, adding only a little rouge to give her cheeks some color, an eyebrow pencil to highlight her eyebrows and some natural-looking lipstick.

She didn't want to look too overdone, like she'd spent all morning getting ready, which she had. A few years ago she had a little plastic surgery done on her chin to get rid of her jowls, and she was glad, especially now at fifty, when she wanted to look her very best.

She tried wearing her hair down, loose and flowing, then worried that she didn't look serious enough, and so tried it up in a French roll.

"Looks more dignified up," Gussie said, when Evaleen asked for her opinion, "if that's the look you're going for, but more fun and relaxed when you wear it down."

Evaleen ended wearing it up. She didn't want Josh to think she was seeing him for anything but business. She reminded herself several times that he was a married man and completely off limits.

This didn't keep her from being excited to see him. Nothing could.

The day turned out to be gorgeous, filled with fluffy clouds. Trees along the boulevard had that golden look they took on before turning into their full summer green. A perfect spring day. Mortimer drove because Evaleen was too nervous to drive herself. She was so filled with anticipation that she felt nauseous. She reminded herself again and again that this was strictly business and not to get any ridiculous ideas.

She looked out the darkened window of the limousine and thought about the times she had pushed Josh away, in so many subtle, small ways, because of her obsession with Hero. What a silly girl she was not to see that Josh was so obviously the better man.

Realizing she was letting her thoughts get away from her again, she reminded herself that she needed business advice and Josh was the best man for the job. It's just business. Don't go getting any crazy ideas. He's married, damn it. MARRIED.

Her treacherous heart continued to ignore all these stern admonitions, fluttering like a butterfly in her chest, sneaking in all the little hopes it could. Before she could shame herself any further, Mortimer pulled up in front of a large office building and stopped.

"This is the address you gave me," Mortimer said, when Evaleen asked him why he was stopping here. He pointed to a sign out front: "Goldman Enterprises."

Evaleen was awestruck as she stepped out onto the sidewalk and looked up at the tall glass and steel building. She'd read in the papers about the Goldman building and the architect who designed it, but for some reason hadn't connected it to Josh. Obviously, he had also done very well these past years.

She took a deep breath to calm herself then hurried through the revolving glass doors. Inside there was a feeling of almost Zen-like calm. Nervous, she crossed the marble floors to a security guard who stood behind a tall desk. She informed him that she had an appointment with Mr. Goldman. He checked his sheet for her name. Finding it, he indicated for her to follow him to a bank of elevators. He unlocked a private elevator that was off to one side, and said it would take her directly to Mr. Goldman's office in the penthouse.

As the elevator car moved upwards, Evaleen examined her reflection in the mirror that covered three sides of the elevator. Her hair looked as good as possible. She had tinted it auburn to hide the grey stands that had begun to creep in at an alarming rate. Her skin looked good because of daily cleaning and moisturizing, using her own products, and regular facials. Although the creams helped, nothing could hide the deep lines around her eyes and mouth, which she knew made her look tired. Would he notice and if he did, would it matter to him? She turned around to inspect herself from all sides.

She had put on a few pounds over the years and it showed, in spite of the good girdle. Before she could obsess about her weight and her legs, which she thought looked swollen, the bell dinged and the door opened, letting her out into a reception area.

Like the first floor, it was all marble, steel and glass – austere, clean, and modern, with the same air of serenity and calmness that the first floor had. A pleasant-faced young woman dressed in a gray suit with a peach silk blouse, looking as slick as her surroundings, sat behind a curved steel and black marble desk.

"May I help you?" she asked politely.

"I'm here to see Mr. Goldman," Evaleen said.

The woman's face lit up.

"Oh my God, it's really you?" she said. "You're Evaleen. I see your name in the society pages all the time. I love your moisturizer. My skin would simply dry up like a piece of tissue paper without it."

Surprisingly, this reaction calmed Evaleen – she was used to such a reaction from women who used her products. Almost unconsciously, she switched into what she secretly called her Evaleen the Queen mode. She studied the girl's face.

"You have lovely skin to begin with," she said, "but it is a little dry."

She pulled out a sample of her combination moisturizer and cleansing cream from her large purse. She always carried a few samples of their newer products for moments like this. Her philosophy was that you never know when you will run into a future customer.

"Give this a try," she said. "It won't dry out your skin and will give you a nice glow in the morning."

The young woman beamed as she accepted the gift.

"I can't tell you how much I appreciate that," she said, "especially coming from you. I'll let Mr. Goldman know you're here. I don't think he'd like it if I kept someone waiting who is as important as you."

"Thank you, dear. That's very sweet of you."

Josh must have been listening, because he appeared to greet her even as the girl was buzzing him on the intercom. Her knees grew weak and heat rose to her face at the sight of him. His hair was starting to show a little grey, but it didn't look quite as untamed as it had before. He was still as slim and straight as a general.

Suddenly she didn't know what to do with her hands, whether to stick them out to shake hands with him, or put them up for a hug, or keep them stuck to her sides. She did manage to notice that he wasn't wearing a wedding ring.

"Evaleen," he said, a big grin on his broad face. "How are you? How very wonderful to see you, again."

"You, too," she said, grinning back at him.

He kissed her cheek. The simplicity of the gesture warmed her heart, and its obvious sincerity gladdened her.

"It's been far too long," he said as he guided her to his office.

His office was large and spacious and stocked with leather-bound books. On the wall behind his desk were photographs of him with various people, including the governor and the mayor. One photograph was larger than the others – a picture of him and his daughter, who looked like she was in her early teens. There was no wife in the picture nor anywhere else. None.

Another piece of evidence to drive Evaleen wild. Instead of sitting down, she went over to the huge glass window, so she could squeeze in a moment to calm herself. She didn't want him to see how nervous she felt.

"The sky looks even bluer than normal up here," she said, calming down a bit.

"Glad you noticed," he said, joining her at the window. "I think so too. I had this building designed with that view in mind."

He hesitated, and something seemed to catch in his voice. "Evaleen," he said in a suddenly husky voice, "you look fantastic. It's hard to believe, but you don't look a day older than when I last saw you."

"I missed you, Josh," she blurted out.

She raised her eyes and met his gaze plainly. She felt the heat rush to her face, but she said no more than that – if by chance he was still married, in spite of the fact that he was not wearing a ring, she did not intend to wreck their friendly relations forever by doing something stupid like admitting her interest in him.

"I missed you too." His words came out in a tumbling rush. "I've thought about you a lot over the years. I'd drive by that big building with your name plastered out front in huge neon letters, or I'd read about you in the society pages and see pictures of you looking so gorgeous, or read about your foundation for unwed mothers and I'd wonder how you were. I even called you a couple of times, but I didn't want to upset Hero so I never left a message."

To her amazement she realized that he was as excited about seeing her as she was about seeing him. And he was just as uncertain as she was.

The realization calmed her and made her feel happy and more relaxed. Obviously, they still intended the best for each other and wanted the other to be okay, no matter what happened today.

"I think your building is bigger than mine," she teased. "I read about you in the business section when you joined Crump-Johnson Investment Advisers. I also remember the announcement in the newspaper when you became an investment banker, and later there was a spread about your getting into the real estate business. What I didn't do was put two and two together and realize that The Goldman Building was you. I must say, I'm extremely impressed."

"Thank you," he said simply. "I admit, I'm always a little amazed myself when I step into the building every morning and realize it's mine, well, actually mine along with a few hundred investors."

"I know exactly what you mean," Evaleen said and they both laughed.

This little back and forth gave them both a chance to reorient themselves, get back to reality a little bit. He waved her to a sitting area, where they sat down across from each other.

"So, how can I help you today?" he asked.

"Hero and I are getting a divorce," she said simply. "He has someone else."

"Oh, my God," he said, in a stricken voice. "That bastard."

His face showed the pain he felt for her.

"It's not as bad as you might think," she said. Speaking about it now, the pain hit her afresh. "I was always working and so was he. Neither one of us had much time for each other. And it always bothered him to be in the skin care business, so now he's out and I assume he and his girlfriend are happy about it. Fortunately, one of our long time employees, Bitsy Junior, was able to step right in and take over his place, so it worked out."

"Hero was always so charming and handsome," Josh said. "He always knew the right moves. Maybe it was all just a little too easy for him. But at the same time, he's lost so much being that way. He had a chance for it all, a chance for the kind of happiness any of us would feel was an utter miracle. The most wonderful and accomplished wife in the world, teamed with him in a brilliant business, the skills and talents to make that business prosper and two lovely children. And he threw it all away. To leave you, to not cherish you every moment he breathed..."

Josh shook his head sadly. "What a fool."

The fact that their marriage had been over for a long time did not keep Evaleen from feeling defensive about Hero. Even now.

"I actually hope the two of them are happy," Evaleen said. "You wouldn't think so if you read the gossip column in the newspaper lately, but I really do still want the best for him in spite of everything."

"A strange paradox is Hero," Josh said.

"Anyway, he wants out of the business, and I'm trying to figure out whether to buy him out and keep the business going alone, or sell it outright and spend more time on my foundation," she said in a more businesslike tone. "And that's what this meeting is about."

She handed over the file with the appraisal and a financial report of the business. "It's all gobbledygook to me. I don't understand a word. I was hoping you'd read it over and give me your opinion on what I should do. You're the only one I trust completely to tell me the truth."

"I'll be happy to go over this," he said, taking the file from her, "and I'll talk to my people about it and see what we can come up with. We can meet again in a few days if you like, and I'll tell you what I think."

"That would be great," she said, relieved.

Suddenly his serious demeanor changed to a mischievous look. "Hey, how about we forget about business and catch up with each other at high tea at the Café Monarch. What do you think?"

"High tea?" she said, suddenly excited and feeling a bit like a teenager. "Oh gosh, I've never been to a high tea before."

"Then we'll have to do it right now," he said.

Smiling wickedly at Evaleen, he buzzed his secretary and told her to make reservations half an hour from now at the Café Monarch.

"Just long enough," he said as he hung up the phone, "for a nice leisurely stroll to the restaurant."

They both stood up and, like two grinning kids playing hooky, they left. Out on the street, Evaleen spotted Mortimer waiting for her in the company limousine. He rolled down his window when he saw her approach.

"Josh and I are going to have high tea," she said, smiling goofily. "I'm going to be gone a while. Why don't you call Gussie and meet her somewhere for lunch. It's too beautiful a day to stay home. Charge it to the household account."

"Thank you. I'll do that very thing. Gussie's been wanting to go to Chi Chi's for a while, probably because she's so full of beans," he said and laughed at his own bad joke. "We should be back in an hour and a half. If you're not here, I'll wait for you."

"Great," she said, smiling.

She then returned to Josh. Mortimer could be heard whistling a happy tune as he drove off, the car windows wide open.

As Josh and Evaleen strolled by, a street musician played "O Solo Mio" on his violin. To Evaleen's delight, Josh dropped a twenty dollar bill into the man's violin case. The musician stopped playing, bowed his head and thanked them both.

Evaleen was so happy she felt giddy. Even her walk had a light spring of cheerfulness. Josh too seemed to have a bounce to his step. They took their time, enjoying the day and each other. They spotted a small flower stand. Josh stopped and purchased a bouquet of red tulips.

"For you, my dear," he said, "to celebrate your new life."

"Why, thank you, kind sir," she said, thrilled.

She carried the flowers the way a bride carries her wedding bouquet as they walked along. A man dressed in an Uncle Sam's suit passed by on stilts and waved to them. Laughing, they waved back. Evaleen felt as though she would burst from so much happiness.

They entered the restaurant, which had dark wood, linen covered tables and a muted atmosphere. Classical music played in the background.

"I've always wanted to do something like this," she said, after they were both seated. "But how could you know that?"

"I'm like an elephant," he said and grinned. "I never forget anything."

A young waiter, obviously an actor between gigs, appeared and in a theatrical voice announced the various kinds of tea available. They both chose black currant with clotted cream, which he said was the most popular.

"Don't touch your tea until the sand has sifted to the bottom of the timekeeper," the waiter warned them both, when he returned with two little ceramic pots of tea and a tiny hourglass. "Not a moment sooner or you won't have good luck."

"Yes sir. Scout's honor," Josh joked, placing his hand over his heart.

"I'll be watching to make sure he doesn't cheat," Evaleen quipped.

The waiter raised one eyebrow as though he didn't believe either one of them.

"So how are you and Patricia and your daughter doing?" she blurted out when they were alone once more.

"Our daughter is doing fine. She's staying with her mother right now."

"Why isn't she with you?" Evaleen asked, unable to stop herself.

"Patricia and I are divorced," he said in a matter-of-fact tone. "We have shared custody and this is our daughter's time to be with her mother."

All the little clues suddenly fell into place, the lack of a wedding ring, the picture of just him and his daughter. Her first reaction was a wave of sympathy for him followed by feeling secretly thrilled, followed by guilt for being so thrilled.

"Oh, Josh, I'm so sorry," she said, not quite as sincerely as she would have liked.

"Yeah, me too. I still beat myself up over it sometimes. I didn't do enough, I should have tried harder, not worked so hard, all that stuff. But the truth is we were simply too different to make it work. She was very social and always on the go. But I have a business and people depend on me for their livelihoods. I loved our vacations when we had them, but she wanted to be on vacation all the time. It seemed like we were always going to parties. I was always exhausted the next day, so after a couple of years of this, I gave up and quit going. As you can imagine, that did not sit well with Patricia. The upshot is, she found someone at one of those parties and she left me for him."

Evaleen could see the pain in his eyes and felt bad for him.

"At first I was devastated, and I guess in some ways I still am, but in some other ways, I'm glad it's over with. We probably shouldn't have been together in the first place."

He smiled wryly and shook his head. "Anyway, I'm glad you're here. Let's not ever go so long without staying in touch again. Promise?"

"I promise," she said, and meant it.

"I'm going to hold you to that," he said, leaning back in his chair. "Now tell me about you. How are the kids?"

"Both Court and Bunny are busy all the time. Bunny's very social. She has a boyfriend and spends most of her free time with him. She still represents the face of Fresh-As-A-Daisy and also does fashion shoots from time to time. An incident at school, where she felt responsible for a young man being hurt, changed her. It made her realize that people are basically good, something of which her own father had apparently convinced her otherwise. She seems to be a lot happier and a lot less angry these days. She still loves the finer things in life, maybe too much, but she's doing well in college and has become very involved with helping abused women find safe places to stay. I'm very proud of her. Court works in our business, but can't wait to leave at night and doesn't take anything very seriously, including work."

"Sounds a bit like his father," Josh said.

"He's a lot like his father," Evaleen said, "without the drinking and the gambling problems. As for Gussie, she's still with me and is now married to Mortimer, who also works for me. They have a lot in common and they seem very happy together. They're always going somewhere or doing something. When they're not working, I hardly see either one of them these days."

Evaleen had not expected how much it comforted her to talk about her family with an old friend. That she could feel the sexual frisson between them just made the whole experience even more exciting and wonderful.

The waiter reappeared, pushing a dessert cart.

"Goodies," he announced cheerily.

Evaleen studied the offering. There were honey pecan scones with lemon curd and Devonshire cream, tiny crustless egg salad sandwiches, little heart shaped chocolates, sugar cookies and little chocolate cupcakes with pink frosting piled in a swirl on top.

"We'll take two of everything," Josh said, when he saw how much trouble she had deciding.

The waiter had arranged the chosen desserts prettily on a white paper doily that covered a silver tray. He placed the tray on their table, along with two China plates with gold edging. As soon as he left, Evaleen took a small bite out of one of the finger sandwiches and pronounced it delicious.

Josh did the same and agreed with her.

"It's your turn, now," Evaleen said. She took a sip of her tea. "Other than the divorce, what's been happening with you?"

"Well, let's see. After the war was over, it seemed like everyone was looking for a house, so I began to buy real estate, fix it up and sell it at a profit. One thing led to another and I ended up buying office and apartment buildings. Then one day, I decided I wanted to have my own building, so I hired an architect, had the building built, and named it after myself. I've been living in an apartment in one of my buildings, but lately I have the urge to be able to walk out my front door and see some grass. Although when I will ever get a chance to mow it, I have no idea. Do you think that's a ridiculous idea for someone like me?"

"Not at all. But I can't see you mowing the grass, somehow."

"Me, either." He laughed. "But it's a nice little fantasy, don't you agree?"

"Yes. Fantasies are good sometimes, if they don't get you into trouble."

At that moment their eyes met and neither could look away. Suddenly Evaleen had the strangest feeling, like a string went out from her diaphragm and wrapped itself around Josh. The feeling was so real, so physical that Eva was stunned by it. Josh must have felt something too, as he seemed speechless for a long moment. Finally, they were able to look away, but the smoldering attraction between them remained.

"Is there somebody special in your life?" she asked, desperate to know and not willing to hold back anymore.

He was already shaking his head no.

"Nobody at the moment." He hesitated. "You?"

He went to take a bite out of his palmier, but his hands were shaking so bad crumbs scattered down the front of his shirt.

Why, he cared as much as she did, she realized with a start. A happy feeling of relief swept over her. "Nope, I haven't got anybody, either."

Their eyes met once more, but this time, although the heat between them remained, something else was there as well – a trust they had between them, allowing them both to relax, be themselves. Whatever was going on between them would take its own pace.

When it became obvious they had lingered way too long and the waiter needed their table, Josh left an extra generous tip and they left. They walked back in companionable silence to where Mortimer waited. Josh leaned down to give her a brief kiss goodbye before helping her into the limo.

"I'll be in touch," he said.

"Yes," she said, suddenly remembering that they still had business to discuss, the original excuse for them to meet. "Give me a call when you're ready."

And that was it.

All the way home, Evaleen felt nervous and giddy, like a high school girl with a crush. Mortimer, seeing her so light and happy, grinned, obviously anxious to get home and give Gussie the news.

#

The next day, Josh called her on her private phone at work.

"I've looked over the numbers," he said, "and we need to talk. Would you have some time next week to meet me at my office?"

She felt a little giggly as she checked her calendar.

"How about two o'clock on Monday?" she asked, smiling and thrilled.

After his call, she couldn't stop grinning. She felt light-hearted and excited.

Gussie noticed and teased her unmercifully.

#

The following Monday, she sat down in front of Josh's desk and tried to act businesslike, although inside she had difficulty sitting still. Josh too seemed nervous, but managed to get straight to the point.

"To buy out Hero, you're either going to have to borrow so much against the assets of the company, that in my opinion, it would endanger your whole business, or you can go public, or you can sell the business and divvy up the proceeds between you."

Evaleen was shocked. But she also felt a huge relief. There it was. All the choices laid out for her. The one that appealed to her the most was to sell the business outright, let someone else take over, who cared as much as she used to. Someone younger and stronger and hungrier, like Bitsy Junior. Bitsy loved working so much that Evaleen had to insist that she take a vacation every year, and even then it was a struggle. Evaleen reasoned that if she sold the business, she could concentrate on growing her foundation for unwed mothers and their children from a local charity to a national charity, something she'd been wanting to do for some time now.

"If I do this, Josh," she said, trying to think things through, "I want to hand over the controls completely. I think we have a good team in place that can run the business. Bitsy Junior can help it continue to grow, whether Hero or I are at the helm or not. I want to make her the C.E.O. and I don't know if I can do that if I sell the business."

"You can," Josh said. "Just add that as a contingency of the sale. Since your company is doing so well financially, I'm sure any buyer would be happy to agree."

"And it's important to me that the company still make hiring single mothers a priority if at all possible."

"That's the advantage of hand-picking your successor. With Bitsy in charge, she can make sure that policy will continue."

Evaleen nodded, feeling more and more hopeful.

"I'm sure Bitsy knows as well as I do how well that policy has worked for us. It's actually given us an edge in the marketplace with our customers. Bitsy is as committed to it as I ever was."

She hesitated, took a deep breath. "Okay, I think I'm ready to sell now. I'm sure that Hero will also be relieved to have it over with."

"I wouldn't mind taking things a little easier myself," Josh said. "Maybe travel, see the great cities of the world. I've never had much time off before, either."

She smiled at him, feeling just a little wicked and wild. "Sounds like you need to sell your business, too."

"Maybe," he said. "I'll have to think about it long and hard before I do."

He rose and came around the desk. She stood as well. She started to say goodbye, when he reached down and kissed her. It started as a peck and quickly turned into something more, something so fierce and passionate it frightened them both.

#

Three months later, the board of Evaleen, Inc. accepted an offer from Adamore Corporation for all shares of the company. Hero agreed to everything without protest. Once all the papers were signed, Evaleen and Josh took a vacation together to Santa Fe, New Mexico. It was a joyous time for them both, as they explored the City Different, with its unique cuisine and three separate cultures.

They found a place called Maria's that served coffee and little delicious pillows of fried pastry called sopapillas. Josh leaned closer.

"If we can travel together, spend hours alone together and still love spending time together, I think we have a future together, don't you?" Josh said.

"I do think so," she said, kissing him. She could never remember feeling happier.

Later, they sat on one of the white benches depicting the seasons on the plaza and watched some kids play hacky sack. She loved that moment, being with him, needing nothing.

Then, to her surprise, Josh took a small box from his pocket and held out a diamond ring.

"I love you, Evaleen," he said. "Will you marry me?"

"Yes! Oh my God yes, yes, yes," she said as he slipped the ring on her finger.

He wrapped her in his arms. They held each other close, to the delight of the young hacky sack players, who had seen the whole thing and were now grinning and cheering them on, to their surprise. It felt as though the whole world thought this should happen.

They were married in a simple ceremony in the garden of the home they purchased together. At Evaleen's insistence, it was half the size of the mansion she and Hero lived in.

Mortimer and Gussie stood up for them, and for once Bunny and Court were home at the same time. Josh's daughter also attended.

When the cottage next door came up for sale, they purchased it for Mortimer and Gussie, who continued to work for them. A reporter from Vanity Fair covering the story of their marriage asked Evaleen why she had chosen such a small house when they could obviously afford something much larger.

"I like living in a smaller home," Evaleen admitted. "I love knowing where everyone is. In my old house, I never knew who was home or not. And truthfully, we just don't need or want all that space or all that stuff. Thankfully, Josh feels the same way I do."

"She likes to keep an eye on me," Josh said, kiddingly. "I like to keep an eye on her, too."

Evaleen's eyes met his and she smiled indulgently at his little joke.

Epilogue

On a Saturday in September, Mortimer was driving Evaleen home after she'd given a speech at Emerson University to students receiving their master's degree in business. She happened to look out the side window and was astonished to see Hillel Brand, one of Hero's old drinking buddies. He was moving slowly, as though every step pained him. She instructed Mortimer to pull over.

"Hillel," she called out the window. "You old dog. How are you?"

A big smiled appeared on his deeply wrinkled face. He limped over to the car and stopped to talk, leaning on his cane for support.

"Old Arthur Ritis has got me in his clutches, but otherwise I'm fine," he quipped. "Yourself?"

"Doing fine," Evaleen said.

After the usual exchange, he asked, "Have you heard from Hero lately?"

"No," she said, surprised that he would ask. "I haven't seen him or heard from him in years."

"I don't know whether I should tell you this or not," Hillel said. "But Hero's very sick lately. I don't know if he's going to make it or not."

"What's wrong with him?" Evaleen asked, taken aback. She had taken it completely for granted that Hero would always be exactly the same, ridiculous as that thought was.

"What you'd expect from the kind of life he's led?" Hillel said with a shrug. "I quit drinking and gambling when my wife left me. Thank God she took me back when I started going to AA and Gamblers Anonymous. I tried to get Hero started too, but he said he enjoyed drinking and gambling way too much to give either one up. To him it was all just a big joke. He still smokes three packs a day and drinks as much as he ever did. He looks terrible. It's like he's trying to kill himself."

She was surprised to hear this. In spite of his various addictions, Hero had never been sick a day in his life.

"He's been living alone for a while now," Hillel said. "Why don't you give him a call? He could use some company, I'm sure."

"Maybe I will," Evaleen said "Maybe I just will."

At home, Evaleen went to the den where Josh was stretched out on the davenport watching a baseball game on television.

When she came in, he snapped off the television, kissed her hello and asked her how the speech went.

"It went as well as usual," she said, then told him about running into Hillel and what he had to say about Hero.

"It doesn't sound good," she concluded.

"Why don't you give him a call?" Josh said, kindly. "Put your mind at ease."

"Good idea," she said, glad that Josh was not the jealous type.

Evaleen tried several times to reach Hero that day and also the next. No answer. So Josh suggested she show up in person.

"The worst thing that can happen," he said, "is nothing will happen. And then at least you will have tried."

Evaleen agreed.

The following afternoon, she dressed more carefully than usual and did her hair up in its usual pony tail tied with a black velvet ribbon. She had stopped coloring her hair in the last year and it was now almost completely grey.

At sixty, there was something cleanly attractive and elegant about her. The years had been kind, the freckles had faded, and although she would have liked to be slimmer, she had come to accept her body as it was. A few years after she married Josh, she had her eyelids done. They had become a little droopy. But other than a previous plastic surgery on her jowls, that was all. Her skin, thanks to the constant moisturizing over the years, still looked exceedingly good.

Josh said that with her strong profile, she now had the look of an Egyptian queen. She liked the thought of being a queen. She was a queen, she reminded herself. Evaleen the Queen. Thinking of herself as a queen had been what gave her the courage to go door-to-door in spite of having the door slammed in her face. Being Evaleen the Queen made her walk straight and tall instead of round shouldered.

But these days, she no longer felt the need to pretend to be someone else. She had come to appreciate her real self, a woman who had started a business that turned out to be more successful than she would ever have dreamed. Someone who had managed, with Gussie's help, to raise two children she was proud of, someone who had the courage to go on after her father's death when she felt so guilty and unworthy, someone who kept going even after being told no so many times. In fact that was the theme of her speech today, the idea that to get to yes, you had to expect a lot of no's. That was how life worked.

Still, pretending to be Evaleen rather than plain old Eva Doyle had attracted Hero, and he had helped her succeed in business. Too bad they couldn't make it as a married couple, but she was happy now, and she hoped the same for him. She felt sad to think he might be sick.

Mortimer had the day off. She was glad, as she preferred to drive herself today. It had begun to mist lightly.

As she drove, Evaleen thought about Hero. She remembered being so in love that she would literally tremble at the sight of him. She also remembered hating him equally as much. All the little choices that had gone wrong over the years. All the chances at reconciliation they both had missed. What a mess they had made of their personal lives, and yet they had accomplished so much together.

What she felt for him now was more complex. It was like they were two old soldiers who had been in a series of wars, sometimes fighting against each other, sometimes on each other's side, but always with a certain respect and affection for each other.

After all these years, she now knew Hero to be a charming, but a weak man, a man who was bewildered and confused when he no longer felt himself the center of the universe, no longer the rich son of rich and successful parents. He seemed to need to lose for reasons she could never understand.

When his parents died, they were so estranged that Hero did not even attend their funerals, although he paid for everything. He never spoke about them. If they ever came up, he found a way to change the subject, but the estrangement must have hurt him. How could it not?

She turned onto Brownwood Street, the address listed in the phone book. She was surprised to see not mansions but a block of homes, almost identical, probably thrown together in a hurry right after the war. She parked in front of a white house with two arborvitae that had grown so tall they almost dwarfed the entrance. She wondered if Hero, like she, had grown tired of living in such a large home with its complicated maintenance, and had wanted something smaller.

As she stepped from the car, the mist stopped. The sun came out, turning everything into a beautiful mix of light and shadow. She paused to get her bearings, took a deep breath, then walked up to the front porch and pressed the doorbell. She heard the bell ring inside.

No answer.

She waited for a minute, then rang the doorbell again.

He had to be there, because a late model Ford was in the driveway, although Hero had always preferred Cadillacs.

Concerned now, refusing to give up, she rang the doorbell again. Finally she heard footsteps.

"Go away," the raspy voice said. "I don't want any."

"Hero, it's me, Evaleen," she said. "Don't you remember?"

There came a long pause.

"'Course, I remember." His voice sounded thin and feeble.

"Hero, let me in."

"No," he said. "Go away."

"Hero, I'm not mad at you," she said.

Hesitation. Then she heard a hand slowly turning the door knob, the door opening a fraction. It paused there.

"Please, Hero, let me in. I just want to see if you're okay. I ran into Hillel Brand. He said you're not well."

The door opened wider. Finally, he stood back to let her in. He looked nothing like the old Hero. He appeared shrunken and bent over and somewhat feeble. He had lost a lot of his hair and was now mostly bald, his previously handsome face now deeply wrinkled.

She tried not to let her pity show as she followed him into the cluttered living room, where the drapes were drawn even though it was the middle of the day. The look on his face reminded her of Ma, who had that same look on her face before she died, a look that seemed to say she'd had enough and was done with life.

Newspapers were strewn everywhere. Empty glasses, half-eaten food, overfilled ashtrays, and clutter covered every surface. The house smelled like an ash tray mixed with old booze. Was he so poor that he couldn't even afford a housekeeper, she wondered. He should have had plenty of money to hire help. How did this happen? Or maybe he just didn't care.

She removed some newspapers and other detritus from a chair and sat down.

"Care for a drink?" he asked.

She would have liked a cup of tea to calm her nerves, but figured it was beyond Hero's ability to make, and so politely declined.

"So, have you come to see me in my demise?" he asked, his voice filled with sarcasm. "Well, here I am, a wreck of a man."

As though to rub it in, he poured himself a straight shot from the bottle of whiskey that stood on the table next to him and drank it down in one gulp.

"I ran into Hillel," she said.

She watched him light up a cigarette, cough, put it out, and then immediately light up another one. He coughed, and put that one out, too.

"He said you weren't feeling well."

She hesitated, self-conscious, unable to come up with anything more to say.

"Well, now you've seen me. You can leave."

"Nope – not this time," she said firmly.

"You always were too stubborn for your own good," he said, with a weak smile.

"Well, you were always just the opposite. Everything was always fine with you."

"But we loved each other," he said wistfully, "didn't we?"

Evaleen remembered loving him so much it was all she could think of.

"Yes we did for a time, and maybe we still do, a little," she said. "I don't think it's possible to not care after we spent so many years together. Do you?"

"I still care," he said. "That never stopped."

"Only everything else seemed to."

"I'm sorry," he said. "I really am. I don't know why I'm like this. I just am."

"I forgave you a long time ago," she said. "It wasn't easy. I spent a lot of time in the beginning blaming you. For a while, it was all I could think about. Then one day, I realized I wasn't so free of blame, either. I insisted that you help me in a business that you hated and I kept you from joining up and going off to war like everyone else. I hope you can forgive me."

"Nothing to forgive," he said.

His hands shook as he lit up a cigarette and took a long drag, then let it out in a stream of smoke.

"Truth was, I was scared shitless to go to war, and was relieved when I didn't have to go. It just hurt my manly pride to admit it. As for working in the business, I admit I hated it in the beginning, but we accomplished a hell of a lot together in spite of my rotten attitude. I doubt if I ever would have admitted that before, but I don't care anymore. It's just easier to tell the truth than to pretend otherwise. Besides, the past keeps coming back like bad stomach acid, a problem I seem to be having more and more lately."

Evaleen had to laugh in spite of herself.

"It was always so important for you to be somebody," he said. "And now you are. That has to feel good."

"I am now Evaleen the Queen," she said, "at least that's how I am referred to by the media. Ridiculous, isn't it?"

They both laughed. His laughing triggered a bout of coughing, a dry, hacking, and worrisome sound.

"Are you all right?" she asked, concerned. "Is there anyone I should call?"

"I'm fine," he said, finally. "Anyway, there's no one to call. Speaking of people to call, how are the kids?"

"Bunny is fine, as far as I know. She calls once or twice a month, but I seldom see her in person. She's married now, and as far as I can tell she is happy. No grandchildren yet. She's very involved in her husband's family's education foundation and in her own charity for abused women. She's still the model and spokeswoman for Evaleen. I'm proud of her. She does a lot of good. I see her in the society pages more than I see her in person."

He nodded at that small scrap of information. "And Court?"

"I see him even less than I see Bunny. Do you?"

"He stopped a while ago for something. Can't remember what he wanted. He had a girlfriend with him."

"He always has a girlfriend with him," she said. "A different one every time."

"Probably got it from me," Hero said in a curiously unaffected tone, as though any relationship with his children had ceased to matter.

"Neither one of them ever really had much interest in the business," she said sadly. "But they both seem to be doing fine in spite of us, or maybe because of us. Who can tell? The business seems to be doing fine, too. They've expanded into Europe, according to Bitsy, and are thinking of moving into the Middle East. We left quite a legacy, Hero."

"That was your legacy, not mine," he said with a shrug of his shoulders. "Your name's on the company and everything else, including that foundation for unwed mothers and homeless women you started. It was all you."

He sounded bitter.

"You could have had your name on a few things, too," she said kindly. "You just never wanted your name attached to the beauty business. By the way, where's Lark?" she asked, desperate to change the subject.

"Who knows?"

He put out his cigarette and poured himself another drink, which he proceeded to drink down in one long gulp.

"She took off one day with most of the bonds I had in the safe, which I was dumb enough to leave open. I probably should have tracked her down and had her prosecuted, but I figured it was worth the money to get rid of her. That's what she really wanted all along. Money. Well, now she's got it. I hope she's happy."

Evaleen could see the pain in his eyes. She felt sorry for him and wished she'd never asked.

"What about you?" he asked, not quite looking at her.

"Just as you always suspected, I ended up with Josh."

She felt guilty admitting this to him. He was obviously already miserable, so why rub it in?

"What happened to his wife?"

"She met someone else."

"How convenient for you both," he said, a tinge of sarcasm in his voice.

"Gussie and Mortimer are happy," she said, ignoring his jab. "They're doing great."

"Too bad we didn't work out as well as a couple, but we were one hell of a business team while it lasted," he said, almost tenderly.

"Yes, we were," she agreed. "We did a lot of good, too. Think of all the girls we helped."

"That was your idea," he said. "Not mine."

"Maybe it was in the beginning," she said, feeling a surge of impatience with him and his inability to ever let himself care too much about anything. "But you did a lot of work with them, too.

You helped them to learn their jobs and gave them promotions and raises, even paying for their schooling and advising them when they wanted to start their own businesses. Don't forget, you were the one who actually taught Bitsy Junior what she needed to know to succeed in her position with the company in the first place. Now she's running the company and doing a great job. We funded quite a few start-ups for them during those years, too, and we provided a decent living for a lot of people. So I wouldn't feel too bad about myself, if I were you."

"Yes, yes, I guess you're right," he said, a look of wonderment in his bleary eyes. "Maybe I wasn't so bad after all."

"You were just as important in the business as I ever was," she said. "Stop selling yourself short."

He chuckled at her concern. "Even now, even with your ex-husband, you always put so much effort into worrying about others. That's my little Eva Doyle. Sweet, even when you are competing like a boxer in a prize fight."

"Well, I'm not competing anymore," she said.

She fought to keep the tone of her voice normal, not let him know that he was beginning to irritate her with his self-pity.

A brief, cynical smile crossed his face. "You're looking good. Obviously Josh is doing something right."

He hesitated, then spoke almost sourly. "Well, he's probably better for you than I ever was."

"We had our good times, Hero," she said, softening towards him. "We were just too different to make it work."

"I think that's true," he said. "You wanted to become somebody and change the world and I just wanted to be rich and have a good time. Not exactly a union made in heaven."

"I don't have any regrets," she said. "When it was good it was very, very good, and I'm never going to deny that."

"And when it was bad…"

"And when it was bad, it was bad. But I personally refuse to get upset about things I can't do anything about, anymore."

"You're right," he said, "although I haven't been able to convince myself of that truth quite yet. But then, you always were ahead of me when it came to simple common sense."

"And you were always ahead of me when it came to figuring out the big picture. When we were a team, we were a good team. By the way, our foundation is having a benefit at the Samoa ballroom next Saturday to raise money for college scholarships for single working mothers. Want to come?"

"No, but thanks anyway. I prefer sitting here wallowing in my own juices," he said, pouring himself another drink.

"Well, give me a call if you change your mind," she said.

There was nothing left to say after that. Evaleen stood up, leaned over and kissed him on the top of his head. He made no response, and she left, closing the door quietly behind her.

Outside, she let out a big breath as though she had been holding it in the whole time. She stepped into her car and put the key in the ignition, in a hurry now to go back home to Josh.

THE END

About the author: *Evaleen From Rags To Riches* comes from hearing stories about how, during the Great Depression, my painfully shy mother was able to make herself go door-to-door and sell furniture polish that my father made at home. As for me, I live with my husband, the writer P M F Johnson, in Minnesota.

If you enjoyed this novel, please try *Charlotte Parker Forty-Niner*, about a woman making her way during the California Gold Rush.

My other books:

Running Away To Santa Fe
Chez Tulips - Stories and Recipes
Crazy Little Liar

Made in the USA
Columbia, SC
21 October 2024